Revisioning Red Riding Hood around the World

Series in Fairy-Tale Studies

General Editor
Donald Haase, Wayne State University

Advisory Editors
Cristina Bacchilega, University of Hawai`i, Mānoa
Stephen Benson, University of East Anglia
Nancy L. Canepa, Dartmouth College
Anne E. Duggan, Wayne State University
Pauline Greenhill, University of Winnipeg
Christine A. Jones, University of Utah
Janet Langlois, Wayne State University
Ulrich Marzolph, University of Göttingen
Carolina Fernández Rodríguez, University of Oviedo
Maria Tatar, Harvard University
Jack Zipes, University of Minnesota

*A complete listing of the books in this series
can be found online at wsupress.wayne.edu*

Revisioning Red Riding Hood around the World

An Anthology of International Retellings

SANDRA L. BECKETT

Wayne State University Press Detroit

18 17 16 15 14   5 4 3 2 1

Library of Congress Control Number: 2013942573

ISBN: 978-0-8143-3479-9 (pbk.: alk. paper)—ISBN: 978-0-8143-3973-2 (ebook)

Published with the assistance of a fund established by Thelma Gray James
of Wayne State University for the publication of folklore and English studies.

Designed by Maya Rhodes Whelan

Typeset by Keata Brewer, E.T. Lowe Publishing Company

Composed in Minion Pro

828487123

To the globetrotting little girl in red who has
inspired so many revisions around the world . . .

And to Hailey, to whom I hope to read many of them

A GIRL WALKS INTO THE WOODS.

LITTLE RED RIDING HOOD.

NOTHING IN HER LIFE HAS PREPARED HER.

—Cornelia Hoogland, *Woods Wolf Girl*

Contents

Acknowledgments

A project of this international scope would not have been possible without the assistance of countless international colleagues, publishers, authors, and illustrators. The collection of works from so many countries was a challenge in itself. The majority of the texts are no longer in print, and I was often dealing with languages that were completely foreign to me. The translation of texts from such a range of different languages (as varied as Greek and Arabic) as well as the collection of permissions for texts and images were daunting tasks. I am deeply indebted to the many authors, illustrators, and publishers who generously granted permission for texts and illustrations to be reproduced in this anthology. Very special thanks go to the following friends, colleagues, students, and acquaintances, some of whom I have met only virtually, for their generous assistance with the translation of texts: Layal Aboukors, Evelyn Arizpe, Amina Ashi, Diane Bielicki, Irene Blayer, Nancy Brady, Sonomi Consul, Jennifer Dill, Anna Filipek, Sofia Georgiadou, Angela Yannicopoulou, Giorgia Grilli, Ewa Gruda, Luděk Janda, Linda Kristiansen, Sungyup Lee, Signe Mari, Claudia Mendes, André Muniz de Moura, Smiljana Narančić Kovač, Marita Papparousi, Eugenia Psaromatis, Gail Ramsay, Manuel Resende, Sigrid Rodríguez, Rolf Romøren, Ricardo Scucuglia, Sara Reis da Silva, Emma Wakim, Katarzyna Wasylak, and Sara Pankenier Weld. In some cases they were entirely responsible for the translation; in others cases they assisted me or, occasionally, another translator. Several authors were also kind enough to read or assist with the translation of their texts and offer their advice, notably Huda al-Naimi, Anne Bertier, Chico Buarque, Bohdan Butenko, Carles Cano, Claude Clément, Fam Ekman, Pierrette Fleutiaux, Wim Hofman, Anne Ikhlef, Ioulita Iliopoulou, Gérard Moncomble, Fabian Negrin, Manuel António Pina, Annie Riis, and Hara Yiannakopoulou.

Many other authors and illustrators graciously discussed their work with me. Numerous other colleagues from around the world have assisted in various ways by adding to my Little Red Riding Hood collection, introducing me to authors and illustrators, or inviting me to speak about my passion. I would like to mention in particular Cornelia Hoogland, who has written her own fascinating version, *Woods Wolf Girl*.

My sincere gratitude goes to the staff at the International Youth Library in Munich and the International Institute for Children's Literature, Osaka, notably Jochen Weber and Yasuko Doi. I wish to acknowledge the generous financial support of the Social Sciences and Humanities Research Council of Canada, the Humanities Research Institute at Brock University, and Brock University Experience Works Program. Several student assistants have shared my passion for the little girl in red over the years, and my heartfelt thanks goes to all of them, but especially to Darcy Berry, Jessica McQuiggin, and Jonathan Nelson, who assisted with this particular book.

1. *Les Contes de Perrault*, by Charles Perrault. Illustrated by Gustave Doré. Paris: Pierre-Jules Hetzel, 1861.

Introduction
A Global Fairy-Tale Icon

> . . . there once was a little village girl, the prettiest who was ever seen,
> and the most famous in children's stories . . .
>
> *Antoniorrobles, "Caperucita Encarnada pasó un susto . . . y luego ¡nada!"*

Little Red Riding Hood is a universal icon whose story has been recast count-less times by authors and illustrators around the world. Considered by many to be the most popular fairy tale of all time, "Little Red Riding Hood" has been revisioned and retold for readers of all ages in virtually every genre and mode imaginable. In the course of preparing two critical studies, *Recycling Red Riding Hood* (2002), which is devoted to contemporary retellings for chil-dren, and *Red Riding Hood for All Ages: A Fairy-Tale Icon in Cross-Cultural Contexts* (2008),[1] which examines reversions for diverse age groups, I have collected several hundred retellings of the tale in more than twenty languages from Europe, North America, South America, Africa, Asia, and Australia. As the majority of the works discussed in these two books are inaccessible to English-speaking readers, it seemed indispensable to translate a selection of these and other retellings and make them available in English. Originally the intention was to incorporate a number of translations in *Red Riding Hood for All Ages*, but a separate anthology allows the inclusion of a much larger selec-tion of the remarkably diverse international reworkings of the world's most retold fairy tale.

Despite the tale's immense popularity and the fact that many of the innovative international retellings are by major award-winning authors and illustrators, surprisingly few of these works in other languages have been translated into English. Versions for adults seem to have a better chance of appearing in translation than those for young readers, although even they are relatively rare. There are a number of short stories, ranging from the rather risqué remake from the Quebecois author Jacques Ferron's 1968 collection *Contes*, which was published in English in *Tales from the Uncertain Country* (1972), to the sensuous version by the Argentine author Luisa Valenzuela, "Si esto es la vida, yo soy Caperucita Roja" ("If This Is life, I'm Red Riding Hood"), from her 1993 collection *Simetrías* (*Symmetries*), translated the same year. Sometimes years may go by before an English version of even a prize-winning work is made available. It was more than twenty years before Manlio Argueta's novel *Caperucita en la zona roja*, written in exile during the civil war in El Salvador and published in Cuba in 1977, finally appeared in English, in 1998, under the title *Little Red Riding Hood in the Red Light District*. Often translations are available only thanks to scholars such as Jack Zipes, whose groundbreaking 1983 book, *The Trials and Tribulations of Little Red Riding Hood*, includes a Chinese and an Italian version, as well as several German and French retellings.

In light of the much larger number of retellings of "Little Red Riding Hood" published for children and young adults, appallingly few are translated into English. The tale "Le loup" (The Wolf), by the French author Marcel Aymé, is the first story in his classic *Les contes du chat perché* (Tales of the Perched Cat), published in 1934. It is one of the best-selling children's books of all time in France, yet it was not until 1951 that an English translation finally appeared under the title *The Wonderful Farm*. Although it was the very first children's book illustrated by Maurice Sendak, *The Wonderful Farm* is not well known, and it was not reprinted until the mid-1990s. Moreover, although "Le loup" is one of Aymé's most popular tales, the charming story—of two young girls who allow the "reformed" wolf into their house despite the fact that he admits having eaten Little Red Riding Hood in his youth—was not even included in the original volume. When the tale finally appeared in a subsequent volume, *The Magic Pictures: More about the Wonderful Farm* (1954; also published under the title *Return to the Wonderful Farm*), the translation presented a watered-down version that diverged radically from the original. The translator, Norman Denny, replaces the dramatic scene in which the reformed wolf swallows the two heroines while exuberantly playing the popular French children's game "Loup y es-tu?" (Wolf, Are You There?) with a very innocuous and highly anticlimactic scene that substitutes a flat iron for the girls. Thus even when a retelling manages to appear in English, it may be far from the same story. Since Aymé's tale is available in an English edition, albeit a disappointing one, it has not been included in this volume.

Even when the author is a laureate of the prestigious Hans Christian Andersen Award—sometimes called the Nobel Prize for children's literature—the retelling, as well as its author, often remains virtually unknown in the English-speaking world. Such is the case for Gianni Rodari, widely considered Italy's most important children's author, and his fractured fairy tale "A sbagliare le storie," from his very popular collection *Favole al telefono* (1962). Although it was published in Britain under the title "Telling Stories Wrong," in the 1965 collection *Telephone Tales*, the book has long been out of print and was never issued in North America. Fortunately, Rodari's tale is available as "Little Green Riding Hood" in Zipes's *Trials and Tribulations of Little Red Riding Hood.*[2] A number of retellings for children see the light in English only in the anthologies of scholars and are therefore unlikely to reach their intended audience. Such is the case for Philippe Dumas and Boris Moissard's witty, parodic remake "Le Petit Chaperon Bleu Marine" (Little Navy Blue Riding Hood), from their 1977 collection *Contes à l'envers* (Upside-Down Tales), which Zipes includes under the modified title "Little Aqua Riding Hood." In the second edition of *The Trials and Tribulations of Little Red Riding Hood*, Zipes adds another very original French recasting for children, Pierre Cami's *Le Petit Chaperon Vert* ("Little Green Riding Hood"), originally published in 1917 and reissued in picturebook format with illustrations by Chantal Cazin in 1996. Other children's texts in Zipes's volume include two 1970s works by German children's authors: Rudolf Otto Wiemer's poem "Der alte Wolf" ("The Old Wolf," 1976) and O. F. Gmelin's tale "Rotkäppchen" ("Little Red Cap," 1978). Occasionally, revisions by much lesser-known authors manage to get translated for children but still fail to reach English markets. The unusual retelling *O Lobo Mau reencarnado* (1974), by the Brazilian author Roque Jacintho, was published in English under the title *The Big Bad Wolf Reincarnate* by the Brazilian Spiritual Federation for the purposes of proselytism. Although it is already in at least its third edition in English, the story is not familiar to North American or British readers.

Revisioning Red Riding Hood around the World includes fifty-two retellings of "Little Red Riding Hood" which, with two exceptions, have never before been published in English. Vladimir Mayakovsky's "The Tale of a Red Cap" (1917) appeared in the English translation of *For the Voice*, which was published by the British Library Board in 2000, but it has been included to offer a Russian retelling. In the final stages of the anthology, I learned that the French publisher of Anne Bertier's *Mon Loup* (My Wolf), Grandir, had included in their 2009 catalogue an English translation by Eric Greenwald, which is available only to libraries and bookstores in France as a tool for primary-school teachers. As I had translated the text several years earlier, in consultation with the author, with the intention of including it in my book *Red Riding Hood for All Ages*, and because their English edition is not distributed outside France, it has also been retained in the anthology. A wide range of countries and cultures are represented, either by the author's or illustrator's origins or by the country in which the retelling was published, including Belgium, Croatia, Czech Republic (former Czechoslovakia), France, Germany, Greece, Italy, Mexico, Netherlands, Norway, Pakistan, Poland, Portugal, Spain (including Catalonia), Switzerland, Russia (Soviet Union), Egypt, Lebanon, Qatar, Japan, Korea, Argentina, Brazil, Chile, Colombia, Ecuador, Peru, Uruguay, Cuba, Mexico, and Canada. The stories were published in twenty-four countries and fifteen languages. Many of these works reflect the perspectives and experiences of writers and illustrators who belong to more than one culture or nation, or whose books are published across national borders. The texts span more than a century, from the early twentieth century to the present day, but the majority were published after 1970 and more than half since 1990. The earliest work is a poem published in 1908 by the Spanish poet Francisco Villaespesa, and the most recent is a picturebook that Sana Tayara and Talar Kizirian brought out in Lebanon in 2011. Many of the retellings are from the Western world, but it has also been possible to include several works from Africa, the Middle East, and Asia. All of these retellings are nonetheless inspired by the traditional and classic European versions of "Little Red Riding Hood" and remain in the Western tradition of the tale, although they may be transposed to other regional or cultural settings.

The present volume includes texts published for children, adolescents, and adults, as well as crossover works intended for an audience of all ages in the tradition of the early oral tales. A variety of genres are represented, including fairy tale, short story, novella, novel, poetry, illustrated book, and picturebook. If the texts were illustrated, an attempt has been made to include at least one illustration from each work, as the visual retellings obviously add further narrative layers and levels of meaning. Although it is unfortunate that picturebook texts had to be isolated from the images, at least one illustration from each picturebook has been reproduced. Book covers have also been reproduced in some cases. *Revisioning Red Riding Hood around the World* contains almost a hundred illustrations, both color plates and embedded black-and-white images. The anthology has not been structured in an arbitrary chronological order but has adopted the thematic approach of *Red Riding Hood for All Ages*, a structure that was very well received by readers and critics, who felt that it effectively highlighted both the essence of the classic story and the continuum between various thematic approaches.[3] The retellings in the present volume have been organized according to the same five chapter headings, to which have been added two further categories that reflect prevalent approaches adopted in recastings for young readers. Generally, there is a progression from works that recast the story of Little Red Riding Hood from more traditional perspectives through more playful versions to more innovative approaches that focus on the wolf or "wolfhood." Nor is it chronology that prescribes the order of the texts within the sections but rather the connections that are set up among them by common narrative strategies and thematic and formal approaches. Each text is preceded by an introduction to the author/illustrator and his or her work. The introductions are generally slightly longer for the retellings that were not analyzed in either of my earlier critical studies. Although they are not referenced in the introductions, much more complete analyses of many of the works can be found in *Recycling Red Riding Hood* and *Red Riding Hood for All Ages*.

The retellings in the first section, "Cautionary Tales for Modern Riding Hoods," all draw on the story's tradition as a cautionary tale or *Warnmärchen*. Charles Perrault penned the first literary version of the tale to warn girls and women against predatory males. Today "Little Red Riding Hood" can be seen as the archetypal tale of child abuse and rape. In the second edition of *The Trials and Tribulations of Little Red Riding Hood*, Jack Zipes claims that "it is because rape and violence are at the core of the history of *Little Red Riding Hood* that it is the most widespread and notorious fairy tale in the Western world, if not in the entire world."[4] There are undoubtedly other reasons for its popularity, but this controversial and topical theme certainly attracts a large number of authors and illustrators, especially, but not exclusively, women. Authors and artists who retell "Little Red Riding Hood" as a story of rape or child abuse generally adopt a very serious, even tragic tone, and their reversions seek to warn both children and adults of the ever-present danger of predatory males. Both the Chilean poet Gabriela Mistral and the Spanish poet Francisco Villaespesa interpret the tale, in the first half of the twentieth-century, as a story of male violence against a young, innocent child. Villaespesa places the blame squarely with men, absolving both little girls and wolves. In his first poem, as in Claude Clément and Isabelle Forestier's *Un petit chaperon rouge* (A Little Riding Hood), concerned friends and neighbors search unsuccessfully for the little girl when she does not return at nightfall. In the poem she never returns, while in the picturebook the little girl eventually comes home, but her escape from the wolf is not synonymous with a happy ending.

Nor do the more contemporary "Little Red Cap" poems by the Dutch poet Wim Hofman offer a happy ending, even when the little girl survives her ordeal. The Little Red Cap in Hofman's striking 1996 visual retelling, painted on a long, wooden board, suffers the same trauma after the terrifying events as does the heroine of *Un petit chaperon rouge*, a formerly outgoing little girl who withdraws into a mute, listless silence. Clément and Forestier offer a universal cautionary tale that addresses the topical subject of pedophilia in a story accessible to very young readers. According to the narrator of Kyoko Iwasaki's Japanese revision, "Little Red Riding Hood" is still being told precisely because its cautionary message is needed today; modern forests are no less "deep and dark" than those of Europe centuries ago. Before beginning her tragic story, the author explicitly warns readers against "wolves in human skin" and asks girls to beware of kidnappers. In her picturebook published in 2010, the Korean author and illustrator Mia Sim also tells the story of "a" Little Red Riding Hood who escapes not one but several would-be abductors. Despite its serious message or moral, which is explicitly stated in a paratextual note addressed to young readers on the back cover, this story for young children adopts a humorous approach and has a happy ending—the only happy ending to be found in this section. Even authors who work from the Grimms' more reassuring version of the tale generally create a retelling in a minor mode. Administrative duty prevents the woodcutter from saving the obedient and well-behaved heroine of Joanna Olech and Grażka Lange's subversive Polish picturebook. Manuel António Pina acknowledges the influence of the Grimms' version, but the hypotext from which the Portuguese author works most closely is Perrault's more tragic version, in keeping with the pastels of Paula Rego that directly inspired his complex, multilayered revisioning for all ages. Much more explicitly than in Clément and Forestier's picturebook, the wolf's behavior in Pina's crossover tale is that of a human predator, a pedophile who preys on young girls. With the exception of Vladimir Mayakovsky's political tale, the retellings in this section all present Little Red Riding Hood as an innocent child who is victimized by a predatory wolf.

The protagonists in the recastings of the first section—except perhaps Mia Sim's heroine—were not yet ready for an encounter with the wolf. The second section, "Contemporary Riding Hoods Come of Age," focuses on retellings that interpret the story in the light of feminine initiation and rites of passage. The protagonist may at first resemble the naïve, innocent heroine of the classic tale, but she proves herself to be clever and courageous, saving herself and often her grandmother as well. No longer a passive victim, the active, enterprising protagonist demonstrates her resourcefulness and outsmarts the wolf in his role of seducer. In the Norwegian picturebook by Fam Ekman, Little Red Hat is a naïve little country boy who nonetheless outwits and ultimately tames a seductive urban she-wolf and rescues his granny. The seemingly less naïve picturebook protagonist Red Red Red Riding Hood, created by Edward van de Vendel and Isabelle Vandenabeele, is visibly unperturbed by her bloody slaughter of the wolf with an axe and appears not to give any thought to the fate of her demanding, dreary, gray grandmother. The resourcefulness of many modern Riding Hoods is in keeping with the oral tradition from which a number of these retellings draw their inspiration, because most oral versions present an active protagonist who escapes without the aid of a male figure. The French storyteller Bruno de La Salle embeds a rendition of the traditional tale in a modern yet timeless story about a little girl who outwits a man-wolf with an updated variant of the trick used by her early predecessor. Although she set out to rewrite Perrault's version, the Spanish author Carmen Martín Gaite also presents a contemporary initiatory story in her fairy-tale novel about Little Red Riding Hood in Manhattan, in which the heroine overcomes her fear and introduces the wolf to her grandmother.

It is often said that the characters of children's stories never age. A number of innovative revisionings portray older Riding Hoods who have grown into young women or, in some cases, are already very mature, even elderly women. The French picturebook artist Anne Bertier turns the classic tale into a love story, in which the elegant wolf is seduced by a cautious, not-so-little Red Riding Hood. In her film and subsequent picturebook, the Pakistani-Norwegian author Iram Haq recounts the initiatory journey of a young woman caught between two cultures and stalked by a wolf who is her own uncle. The epilogue of Hernán Rodríguez Castelo's novel informs readers that Little Blue Riding Hood has been sent to Europe to pursue the studies that will best prepare him for his calling as a writer of tales. Ioulita Iliopoulou's Greek retelling is a continuation of the classic story in which Little Red Cap has grown up, found a job, and lives in her grandmother's renovated house near the woods, which she undertakes to protect from developers. Many women authors, including Carmen Martín Gaite and Pierrette Fleutiaux, present the grandmother as a wise woman whose knowledge is transmitted to her granddaughter, but in the case of Matilde Rosa Araújo's Portuguese recasting about Little Gray Riding Hood, it is the little girl in red herself who becomes the wise woman.

The section titled "Playing with the Story of Red Riding Hood and the Wolf" is devoted to versions that adopt an essentially playful approach to the tale. They may deal with themes that are considered in other sections, but they do so in a lighthearted, humorous mode. A number of witty renditions adopt a postmodern, metafictional discourse to question the classic tale and its codes and conventions, or even a single motif. After advancing a series of absurd hypotheses about the possible symbolism of the red color associated with the classic heroine, the French humorist Pef turns his nonsensical remake into a cautionary tale for writers and their readers. In "Little Red Cap Another Way," the Croatian author Zoran Pongrašić skeptically questions almost every element of the Grimms' version before pronouncing it "a silly fairy tale" and conspiratorially inviting the reader's concurrence. Another Croatian story also questions the way the classic tale is told and seeks to reestablish the "true" original in a short story embedded in the 1980s picturebook *Snježni kralj* (The Snow King), by the author Damir Miloš and the talented cartoonists Radovan Devlić and Krešimir Skozret. The Polish author Bohdan Butenko also sets out to tell the "true" story of the fairy-tale heroine in a very subversive, self-reflexive work. Many retellings that present the classic tale "another way" do so by portraying the protagonist in a different manner. Alois Mikulka's retelling, written in the former Czechoslovakia in 1974, could have been considered in the previous section, as his resourceful heroine, not unlike Anne Sharpe's 1985 "Not So Little Red Riding Hood," is trained in the martial arts (judo rather than karate in this case) and easily subdues and tames the werewolf. Despite his subversion of the heroine's role, Mikulka retains the classic Czech title of the tale.

Often authors prepare readers for a parody of the classic tale by changing the name of the eponymous protagonist in the title. In Janosch's nonsensical yet satirical tale about the electric Little Red Cap, published more than forty years ago, the heroine becomes a kind of automated doll, which can be interpreted as a critical and prophetic comment on the technological sophistication and commercialization of fairy tales and children's culture. In the case of Sana Tayara and Talar Kizirian's Lebanese picturebook, the name of the eponymous heroine does not signal a radical change, as Western readers might think, because "Layla" is the Arabic name of Little Red Riding Hood. However, this Riding Hood is a presentday heroine who uses her mobile phone to save herself and her grandmother. Many authors use the strategy of color substitution as the starting point for a parody of the classic tale, in which the title establishes clearly that their heroine is not to be confused with either Perrault's or the Grimms' protagonist. There is an accumulation of colored hoods in Grégoire Solotareff and Nadja's French picturebook about Little Green Riding Hood, in which the protagonist's older sister wears a yellow hood, her best friend a blue hood, and her worst enemy, an incorrigible little liar, a red hood. Dedicated to riding hoods of various shades of green, the story is presented as a cautionary tale with a tongue-in-cheek moral about the dangers of lying. Bruno Munari has offered a rainbow of Little Riding Hoods—including Green, Yellow, Blue, and White Riding Hoods—which had been translated for this volume but could not be included due to copyright issues. At the other end of the spectrum, Carles Cano presents one of the few Little Black Riding Hoods in a Catalan retelling set in Africa. More recently, the same author published a Castilian retelling about multiple riding hoods of various colors. Unlike the other retellings in this section, Cano's 2007 remake gives the wolf top billing in its title. Even in his retellings where a Riding Hood is the sole eponymous protagonist, Cano focuses equally if not more on the wolf, as is the case in *La Caputxeta Negra* (Little Black Riding Hood), where the wolf's role is played by an elephant.

The retellings in the section "Rehabilitating the Wolf" are also, for the most part, written in a lighthearted tone even when their authors wish to convey a very serious message. Over the past few decades, the marked attempt to rehabilitate the wolf in public opinion has had a profound influence on the wolf's literary image, especially in contemporary recastings of "Little Red Riding Hood." As early as 1964 the Spanish author Antoniorrobles published a playful version in which the wolf is pardoned and becomes the friend of Little Red Riding Hood, who had interceded in his favor during his trial. The wolf's rehabilitation takes place, however, only after he has committed the crime and been suitably punished with a year's imprisonment on a vegetarian diet. In a similar manner Jean Claverie's wolf gives up eating little girls and converts to a diet of pizza only after having been threatened with an axe by Little Red Riding Hood's mother.

Contemporary retellings are full of reformed, vegetarian wolves. Many wolves have already been rehabilitated prior to the start of the story, while others never constituted a threat in the first place. Since the early 1970s the rehabilitation of the wolf has served not solely to demystify children's fears and to reestablish the truth about wolves but more often to address ecological concerns and to present the wolf as an endangered species that must be protected. The story of Little Red Riding Hood, which, in the words of Jane Yolen's Wolfgang, had generated so much "bad press" for the wolf,[5] seems to have become a vehicle for promoting animal rights and, in particular, for rehabilitating the endangered *Canis lupus* after an alarming 1970s census reported their dwindling numbers. In the Spanish picturebook published in 1975 by José Luis García Sánchez and Miguel Ángel Pacheco, Little Red Riding Hood is heartbroken at the death of her friend, "the last wolf," at the hands of a callous, irresponsible hunter. The picturebook includes an afterword that contrasts the presentation of the wolf in popular folklore and children's tales with the reality of scientific research on wolves. The myth of the wolf as a predator of young girls is incorporated, through metafictional play, into the narrative of some retellings. Like García Sánchez and Pacheco, Meike and Susann Stoebe give the wolf equal billing with Little Red Riding Hood in a picturebook that seeks to demythologize the erroneous beliefs that have been associated with wolves for centuries. When a wolf that is very conscious of his literary reputation attacks a clever, modern protagonist, Waldtraut deconstructs the classic tale and gives him a lecture on "real wolves." In keeping with Antoniorrobles's recommendations of three decades earlier, the Swiss picturebook demystifies children's fears and ends with the friendship of the girl and the wolf. Some authors present a wolf that has never been guilty of any crime. In Gérard Moncomble's detective novel, Leloup, the accused killer of little Red-Ridinghood and her grandmother, is a vegetarian butcher who is the victim of an incompetent policeman by the name of Charles Perrault.

Many authors choose to focus on the wolf's story, which had long gone untold. The recastings in section 5, "The Wolf's Story," all put the spotlight on the wolf, telling his story from various points of view. In the Egyptian version by Abdelwahab M. Elmessiri and Safaa Nabaa, the wolf is the sole eponymous protagonist, although Riding Hood still plays a very important role. This Red Riding Hood only temporarily becomes a Green Riding Hood when she dons the beautiful new dress she has just received as a gift, causing such trauma for the wolf that he retreats from the real world into a picturebook, where he can be sure the right-colored Riding Hood will arrive. In the two chapters from Pierre Gripari's novel *Patrouille du conte* (Tale Patrol), the first of which is titled "Le loup" (The Wolf), an official government attempt to rehabilitate the wolf—to alter what is considered a politically incorrect fairy tale—backfires, and the wolf is eaten by the three pigs after only narrowly avoiding grandmother's pot, thanks to the intervention of Little Red Riding Hood. While the wolf's story is told by a third-person, extradiegetic narrator in his 1983 novel, Gripari adopts first-person narration in his poem "Le loup," published five years later. This strategy allows authors to lay bare the wolf's soul, to reveal his motives, thoughts, emotions, and dreams. Even when the wolf tells his own story in the first person, he is cast in a wide variety of roles, not all of them flattering. In a rather disturbing monologue, Gripari's wolf passionately and gleefully embraces the conventional image of the seducer and sexual predator.

More often the wolf tries to portray himself in a positive light and justify his behavior. The story of their relationship may be presented as a love story, in which the wolf plays the role of admirer, suitor, or consensual lover. In the Italian picturebook retelling by Fabian Negrin, the wolf, named Adolf, falls in love with the strange, beautiful animal in red whom he meets one day in the forest, and she, in turn, falls in love with him. Despite their mutual love, destiny keeps them apart in this world. Two Latin American poets tell rather erotic versions of the tale in verse for adults. In the poem by the Peruvian poet José Santos Chocano, the aging wolf portrays himself as the lovesick victim of the lovely Riding Hood, while the poems by the Cuban poet Raúl Rivero are narrated by a dead wolf who has been betrayed by his lover in red. The wolves of both Latin American poets are very conscious of their destiny as the tragic ending of the story of Little Red Riding Hood.

In sections 6 and 7, the wolf element is an integral part of Little Red Riding Hood's own story. The retellings in the section titled "The Wolf Within" present the wolf as a symbol of that which is hidden deep in the human psyche. For a number of Riding Hoods and other characters of the story as well, the wolf embodies the fear of death. In the challenging retelling by the Brazilian author João Guimarães Rosa, Green Ribbon's encounter with an inner wolf is synonymous with the experience of solitude and metaphysical angst that accompanies the existentialist *prise de conscience* and the discovery of our mortality. In the playful tale published two years later by the Brazilian author Chico Buarque, Little Yellow Hat, who is as yellow as her cap, withdraws from life due to unfounded fears and a wolf that does not exist. When she finally confronts the wolf, however, all her fears disappear. Some authors focus on the initiatory nature of the sojourn of Little Red Riding Hood in the belly of the wolf, a ritual death that is followed by a rebirth. Izumi Yamada's illustrated tale—about a protagonist who, not without fear, resolutely makes her way through the hell of the wolf's belly to rescue her grandmother—can be read from a psychoanalytical perspective. In the illustrated story "I Kokkinoskoufitsa apo mesa" (Little Red Riding Hood from the Inside), Hara Yiannakopoulou adopts a more sophisticated psychoanalytical approach. The wolf is once again a symbol of the fear of the unknown, but this retelling focuses on the protagonist's negative feelings toward a mother who would put her in danger and her own desire to face her fear. This Riding Hood overcomes her fear and chooses to be devoured, so that the girl, the grandmother, and the wolf are united and become one.

The final section, "Running with the Wolves," contains retellings in which the protagonist joins the wolf in some way. A number of Riding Hoods display wolf instincts. Others decide to live by wolf rules. Or they may set out to tame the wolf. Little Red Riding Hood has become a match for the wolf, since she now has a wolfish essence of her own. The first four texts in this section are all short stories intended for adults in which Little Red Riding Hood and the wolf become consensual lovers. In Pierrette Fleutiaux's feminist retelling from 1984, Little Red Pants tames the wolf before abandoning him to set out on her own. Pierre Léon's politically correct reversion presents an elderly Riding Hood who had seduced the wolf in her youth and who now tricks her former lover into eating her up again in an act of euthanasia. In the Qatari retelling by Huda al-Naimi, the protagonist and her cousin Layla both reject tradition to follow a modern, urban wolf. Some Riding Hoods are not content just to run with wolves but have darker animal instincts that, in some cases, are quite carnal. Annie Riis's protagonist offers herself to the wolf but ends up eating him and living happily ever after with the hunter.

Such latent, violently sexual content is not limited only to versions for adults. The final two retellings are picturebook texts which, despite the youthful target audience, are sensual, sophisticated, multilayered works that present disturbingly ambiguous heroines. In the picturebook by Patricia Joiret and Xavier Bruyère, Carmina Wolf embodies the roles of both Little Red Riding Hood and the wolf. This Riding Hood wolf not only displays wolf instincts and physical traits but also has wolf blood running in her veins. Although the tale is a version for young readers, this troubling young heroine is more disturbing and predatory than Riis's, perhaps the most dangerous Riding Hood of all. Anne Ikhlef and Alain Gauthier's picturebook is a provocative, nocturnal version that portrays a complex Riding Hood who plays multiple roles, including that of the wolf. Despite the different audiences and genres, many of the retellings in this section have a profound sensuality that sometimes borders on the erotic, and which is heightened in the picturebooks by the illustrations of Xavier Bruyère and Alain Gauthier. While these contemporary readings of the tale may retain the traditional sexual stereotype of the wolf, they also portray an empowered heroine in full control of her sexuality.

This thematic structure shows how various threads of the traditional tale have been woven together differently to reflect changing times, audiences, aesthetics, and cultural landscapes. The number and diversity of these retellings from the four corners of the globe demonstrate the tale's remarkable versatility and its unique status in the collective unconscious and in literary culture, even beyond the confines of the Western world. These reworkings find their place in the enduring, centuries-old Little Red Riding Hood tradition. The year 1997 marked the tercentenary of Perrault's version and 2012 the bicentenary of the Grimms' version, yet authors and illustrators around the world continue to offer new readings and to explore new issues and dimensions of this tale that patterns our unconscious. Likewise, critics remain fascinated by the story of Little Red Riding and the wolf and its seemingly endless variants. In the introduction to *Recycling Red Riding Hood*, published in 2002, I wrote: "When you wander into the woods with Little Red Riding

Hood, there is no telling when, or if, you will come back out again!"[6] More than a decade later, I am still following the little girl in red through the woods. While I was preparing my second book, the French author and illustrator Philippe Dumas commented humorously on my obsession in a letter that began, "Dear Little Red Riding Hood," and ended with a drawing portraying me as a mature Riding Hood wandering into the woods, lost in a Riding Hood book of some kind and leading on a leash a wolf that is visibly bewildered or exasperated by my fixation.

Elsewhere I have called the little girl in red an inveterate globetrotter,[7] but I have had to do a great deal of my own globetrotting to unearth all these Riding Hood stories. It is unfortunate that many retellings of "Little Red Riding Hood" never travel beyond national or even regional borders. Speaking of the Grimms' tales in general in *Sticks and Stones*, Jack Zipes writes: "Though not all contaminated reversions of the Grimms' tales are successful artistic endeavors of retelling and may have major flaws, they are all important because they collude in transforming the Grimms' pretexts to engender a different notion or conception of what a fairy tale should be in the twenty-first century."[8] *Revisioning Red Riding Hood around the World* offers English-speaking readers an opportunity to discover a wide selection of international retellings, which are all important in their own right. It is my hope that this anthology will contribute to cross-cultural exchange and facilitate comparative study of the tale from a global perspective. Perhaps it will even encourage publishers in the English-language markets to translate more of the diverse and innovative retellings that exist in so many countries, attesting to the eternal and universal appeal of Little Red Riding Hood.

2. "Cher Petit Chaperon Rouge," by Philippe Dumas, 2006. Used by permission of Philippe Dumas.

ONE

Cautionary Tales for Modern Riding Hoods

It's all in the story: the adults'
need to give (and have children receive) protection.
But there's always a wolf; the girl
is always eaten.

Cornelia Hoogland, *Woods Wolf Girl*

Little Red Riding Hood (Caperucita Roja)

Gabriela Mistral

The poet, educator, and diplomat Gabriela Mistral (1889–1957) was born Lucila Godoy Alcayaga in Chile and died in the United States. Known affectionately throughout Latin America simply as "Gabriela," she was a famous poet in her time and led a cosmopolitan life, traveling extensively in Europe and the Americas. Yet most North Americans have never heard of Mistral, even though she had the distinction of being the first Latin American to win the Nobel Prize in Literature in 1945. Sadly, Mistral's work has not received the attention it deserves even in her own country. This is due in part to the itinerant life of the poet, who left Chile at the age of twenty-four. The four books of poetry published during her lifetime were issued in four different countries, and much of her prodigious work remains unpublished. Ursula K. Le Guin discovered Mistral's poetry in the early 1990s and published a selection in English in 2003. Mistral was a compassionate author and fierce advocate for the marginalized and voiceless, especially children and women of all ages, as is demonstrated by her concern for the fate not only of Little Red Riding Hood but also of her poor grandmother. Her emotional style, with its unique rhythm, music, imagery, and vocabulary, brought a distinctive new voice to Latin American poetry, a voice that was at once regional and universal.

Some of Mistral's profoundest and purest lyrics are found in her second book, *Ternura* (Tenderness), a popular and influential collection that demonstrated her poetic genius and her innovative use of traditional forms to convey unconventional ideas. Written primarily for children by a young schoolteacher, the poems inspired young people, and to this day generations of Latin American schoolchildren of all races not only recite but also sing and dance to the simple songs and rounds that composers set to music. When Mistral published *Ternura* children's literature in Latin America was in its infancy or, as the poet herself put it, "still in swaddling clothes." She hoped with this book "to encourage its development," according to Doris Dana. The poet evoked the long and difficult effort necessary "to create such a literature out of folklore," which she considered to be "its proper source."[1] The poems of *Ternura* were nonetheless enjoyed all over the Hispanic world by adults as well as children. The cautionary tale of "Caperucita Roja," inspired by Perrault's version of the tale, is the final poem of the second edition, published in Buenos Aires in 1945 (it did not appear in the first edition). The poem was first published in 1923 in a Uruguayan school reader edited by José H. Figueira. Between 1925 and 1928, the poet would write two other verse retellings of Perrault's tales, "La Ceniciento" (Cinderella) and "La Bella Durmiente del Bosque" (Sleeping Beauty of the Woods), as well as a fourth poem, titled "Blanca Nieves en la casa de los enanos" (Snow White in the Dwarfs' Home), based on the

Grimms' "Snow White." The poems continue to have appeal and relevance for young readers today. In 2012 the Chilean publisher Editorial Amanuta published all four fairy-tale poems in picturebook format with illustrations by different Chilean illustrators. *Caperucita Roja* has bold, modern illustrations by Paloma Valdivia, who learned to read with Mistral's poems, and a critical commentary by Manuel Peña Muñoz. Amanuta will make it available in 2013 as their first online app, which will allow readers to change the ending.

Ternura was published in Madrid in 1924, but her homeland would continue to inspire the poet throughout her entire life. The universal story of Little Red Riding Hood is transposed to a rural Andean setting similar to the valley in the mountains of northern Chile where the poet had spent her childhood. The *pucherito* she takes to her sick grandmother is a stew made of meat and vegetables that is very popular in Chile and several South American countries. Children's innocence is a common theme in the volume, and in this particular poem the poet highlights the innocence, purity, tenderness, vulnerability, and littleness of the fairy-tale heroine, who is completely outmatched by the diabolical, cunning, cruel, and very large "Maese Lobo." Mistral's rendition of the formulaic dialogue is charged with the wolf's sexual arousal and the little girl's abject terror. The wolf's use of the Spanish diminutive *Corazoncito*, a term of endearment, casts him clearly in the role of seducer. Nor does the poet mince words in the final stanza, which describes the horrific aftermath of the dialogue that is usually avoided by authors. Le Guin did not attempt to translate "Caperucita Roja" or the other two long "tales" of *Tenderness*, relegating them to the "untranslatable" poems that she "abandoned." The American author does, however, end her introduction to the *Tenderness* poems by offering a translation of the final verse of Mistral's "straightforward rendition of 'Little Red Riding Hood,' with no heroic woodsman to provide a happy ending . . . , as a warning to those who may still cherish the notion of a sentimental Mommy-Mistral."[2] Mistral's tragic version of the popular fairy tale announces some of the dark, difficult poems of the poet's later volumes.

LITTLE RED RIDING HOOD (1923)

Little Red Riding Hood will visit her grandmother
who suffers from a strange illness in the next village.
Little Red Riding Hood, the one with the blond curls,
has a little heart, tender as a honeycomb.

At first light she has already set out
and is going through the woods with a bold little step.
She is accosted by Master Wolf, with diabolical eyes.
"Little Red Riding Hood, tell me where you're going."

Little Riding Hood is pure as white lilies.
"Grandma has become ill. I am taking her a cake
and a tender stew dripping in gravy.
Do you know the next village? She lives at the entrance to it."

And now, running enchanted through the forest,
she collects red berries, short branches in bloom,
and falls in love with painted butterflies
that make her forget the journey of the Betrayer . . .

The fabled Wolf with the whitened teeth,
has already passed the forest, the mill, the hill,
and he knocks on the Grandma's placid door,
and it opens. (The Betrayer has announced the girl.)

It's been three days since the beast had a bite.
Poor, invalid Grandma, who is going to protect her!
. . . Laughing, he ate her wholly and slowly
and immediately put on her women's clothes.

Tiny fingers knock on the door ajar.
From the crumpled bed, the Wolf says: "Who goes there?"
The voice is hoarse. "But Grandma is sick,"
the naïve girl explains. "From Mom."

Little Riding Hood has entered, smelling of berries.
Branches of sage in bloom tremble in her hand.
"Leave the little cakes; come to warm the bed."
Little Riding Hood succumbs to the claim of love.

Out from the bonnet emerge the monstrous ears.
"Why so long?" says the little girl with candor.
And the hairy deceiver, embracing the girl:
"Why are they so long? To hear you better."

The tender little body dilates his eyes.
The little girl's terror dilates them too.
"Grandma, tell me: why those big eyes?"
"My sweetie, to see you better . . ."

And the old Wolf laughs, and in the black mouth
his white teeth have a terrible brilliance.
"Grandma, tell me: why those big teeth?"
"Sweetie, to devour you better . . ."

The beast has crushed, under his coarse hair,
the little, trembling body, soft as a fleece;
and has ground the meat, and has ground the bones,
and has squeezed the heart like a cherry . . .

Little Riding Hood (Caperucita, 1908)
Little Riding Hood (Caperucita, 1954)

Francisco Villaespesa

The Spanish poet and novelist Francisco Villaespesa (1877–1936) enjoyed tremendous popularity during his lifetime. The prolific poet wrote more than fifty books of poetry. His home province of Almería in Andalucia marked his work throughout his life. It is there that he set his "Caperucita" poems. However, he traveled extensively in Latin America, and his poetry, like Gabriela Mistral's, was often read there in schools. Considered one of Spain's great modernists, Villaespesa also wrote poems that are romantic and sensual. Numerous poems are about children, whom he portrays as innocent, loving, defenseless, and the essence of life itself. Although his poems date mainly from the early part of the twentieth century, his concern about children's rights has a contemporary sensibility. He devotes poems to lonely, abandoned children whose parents have no time for them, starving children, and "Children of War"—"Young and innocent, fragile and helpless"—whom he compares to "little flowers trampled." Of particular interest in this context are his verses dealing with children who are the victims of abuse. "The Love of Children," a poem written "in memory of all the abused and molested children who were afraid to tell," asks quite pointedly who will tell children that it is all right for them to cry and that they do not need to hide their fears "when someone tries to hurt them." This poem could be a followup to his Little Red Riding Hood poems. The final stanza asks:

> Who will see their innocence, is that
> of a dove,
> Who will ask the question, who can
> take advantage of a sweet child's love?[3]

In Villaespesa's poems about Little Red Riding Hood—which both bear the same title, "Caperucita," a truncated version of the usual Spanish title of the classic tale, "Caperucita Roja"—her story is interpreted as one of male violence against a young, innocent child. The longer poem was first published in the poetry collection *El Patio de los Arrayanes* in 1908. It was the third poem in a section titled "Canciones de niños" (Children's Songs) and dedicated to the Peruvian poet José Santos Chocano, who would write his own poem based on this fairy tale in the 1930s. Using the form of a sonnet, the poet-narrator engages in a dialogue with several unidentified children from Little Riding Hood's village in an attempt to understand the circumstances of his little friend's disappearance. Seeing her demise through the eyes and in the words of her young playmates heightens the poignancy and tragedy of her fate, while at the same time making it more real. Villaespesa's original approach to the story demonstrates the collective grief of the villagers, the victim's family, and her friends, both young and old.

The other poem is the first of a series of six quatrains in a section titled "Canciones infantiles" (Nursery Rhymes) in the collection *La música del ángelus*, which was written in 1928 but remained unpublished during his lifetime. The first five poems are devoted to popular fairy tales, while the last is a commentary on the enduring mark fairy tales leave on our lives. The quatrain that follows "Little Riding Hood" evokes real-life Cinderellas who freeze to death while dreaming they are princesses in golden slippers. Villaespesa's second Little Red Riding Hood poem seems to constitute a postscript or epilogue to the first work, bringing readers up to date on the subsequent investigation of the little girl's murder. In his retelling Villaespesa not only restores the innocence of the fairy-tale heroine but also exonerates the wolf. In four short lines, the Spanish poet evokes and shatters cruelly the serene, idyllic image of a young girl sleeping in the woods. Contrary to widespread popular belief, Riding Hood's killer was human. The harsh reality of the final lines surpasses the cruelty and violence of Perrault's version. It is not a nursery rhyme for the fainthearted.

❧

Little Riding Hood (1908)

"Little Riding Hood, the smallest
of my friends, where is she?"
"To the old wood she went for firewood,
to gather dry firewood."

"Little Riding Hood, say, has she not come?
Why, so late, hasn't she returned?"
"Everyone went to the wood after her,
but no one found her."

"Tell me, children: what is going on?
What bad news arrived at the house?
Why those tears? Why those screams?

Little Riding Hood didn't return?"
"They only brought back her little shoes . . .
They say that a wolf ate her!"

❧

Little Riding Hood (1954)

The girl lay asleep,
Lay asleep in the wood . . .
Wolves didn't eat her,
men ate her!

Little Red Cap (Roodkapje, 1982)
Little Red Cap (Roodkapje, 1993)

WIM HOFMAN

Wim Hofman (1941–) is a highly original Dutch author, illustrator, and artist whose work was influenced by the CoBrA movement. Best known for his children's books, although he also publishes poetry for adults, he has won many awards for his writing as well as his drawings, including the 1991 Theo Thijssen Award for his oeuvre. His only book published in English is *A Good Hiding and Other Stories*, a 1991 translation of his story collection *Straf en andere verhalen* (1985). The world of folk and fairy tales plays a significant role in his writing and art. He won both the Gouden Griffel (Golden Pencil) and the prestigious Woutertje Pieterse Prize in 1998 for the dark fairy-tale novel *Zwart als inkt is het verhaal van Sneeuwwitje en de zeven dwergen* (Black As Ink Is the Story of Snow White and the Seven Dwarfs, 1997), which is read by both children and adults. In the poetic text and accompanying drawings, Hofman adopts a psychological approach to the tale of Snow White to examine the nightmare side of childhood experience. A common theme in Hofman's work is the powerlessness and vulnerability of children, who are often depicted as the helpless victims of adults. It is therefore not surprising that he has been repeatedly drawn to the story of Little Red Riding Hood in his writing and his art. He has reworked the tale several times in a variety of formats and mediums to explore the dark side of childhood.

Two of Hofman's poems have been included here, both titled "Roodkapje," the Dutch name for "Little Red Cap." The first poem was initially published in a collection of poetry and prose for children, *Van A tot Z* (From A to Z), in 1982. The menace of lurking evil pervades even this short poem, which isolates and develops a single, tranquil moment of the tale: the flower-picking scene that, in the classic tale, follows the encounter of Little Red Riding Hood and the wolf. The little girl in the red cap is described by a third-person narrator, but the final lines are focalized through the heroine, who thinks that the noise she hears in the bushes is the wind. Readers, of course, know differently, and their knowledge creates the menace that hangs over the otherwise idyllic scene.

The second poem, published more than a decade later in 1993, is one of four tales Hofman retold in text and image in a sequential form resembling comic strips. His intention was to publish the fairy-tale series together on a single poster, but the poster was never printed. The tales were published individually, beginning with "Roodkapje" in October 1993, in the children's magazine *Mikmak* (Mishmash). All four tales were reprinted in *Van Aap tot Zip* (From Ape to Zip), a beautiful anthology of his work published by Querido in 2006, but it is "Roodkapje" that has the place of honor as the opening text in the book. Each tale consists of four rhyming stanzas and four small, framed

21

illustrations. The work has been reproduced, as in the original, with the Dutch text under the four illustrations that are an integral part of the work. The prototype of the poster clearly reveals the striking structural resemblance of "Little Red Riding Hood," "Snow White," "Hansel and Gretel," and "Little Thumbling." In each case a child or children are sent or taken into the woods and end up at a house, where they confront "Evil (Death)" in the form of a wolf, ogre, or witch. The appeal of "Little Red Riding Hood" and other fairy tales for Hofman is precisely this omnipresence of menace, evil, and death. It was the belief that evil is the necessary "motor" for story that led the artist to do the series of retellings.[4]

Despite the comic style, the simple black-and-white drawings are not without menace: in the first frame the wolf lurks in a somber forest of tall trees that tower over the small child; later the little girl's feet, sticking pathetically out of the wolf's massive jaws, emphasize her vulnerability. Although Hofman retains the Grimms' more optimistic ending, and the little girl smiles in the final drawing as she is released from the wolf's belly by the hunter, the ending is not necessarily a happy one. The wolf's ultimate fate is foretold in the future tense in the final line, but readers familiar with Hofman's work will sense that not all has been said about Little Red Cap's own fate. In the visual retelling of "Roodkapje" that Hofman painted on a wooden board in 1996, he depicts the effects of the horrific events on the little girl, who, in the final scene, lies alone and traumatized in her bed, unable to sleep. The author's explanation makes it clear that he considers the fairy tale to be a story of sexual abuse: "The most terrible thing possible has happened to her. She's a little girl who's been in the clutches of a big man who could do whatever he pleased with her." Even in the Grimms' version, which the poem retells, Hofman feels that "things never really work out for Little Red Riding Hood" because you never fully recover from such an experience.[5]

Little Red Cap (1982)

A girl with a red cap sits in the grass.
She is making a wreath of flowers.
There are many growing.
She hears something in the bushes.
It is the wind, she thinks,
it is the wind
blowing through the bushes.

❧

Little Red Cap (1993)

Mother says: I'm a little tired,
So you take this to Grandma.
Stay on the path and walk steadily on,
Do not listen to wolves!

A voice calls: come in, quickly!
On the door hangs a cord.[6]
Little Red Cap pulls, the door opens . . .
The wolf has crawled into the bed.

In the bed lies, to her distress,
The wolf. And Grandma? Where is Grandma?
His mouth is wide and large and there
Goes Little Red Cap, she is swallowed whole[7] . . .

The hunter cuts open the wolf.
Little Red Cap jumps out,
The belly is closed, filled with stones.
The wolf goes away and will drown in the well.

3. "Roodkapje," by Wim Hofman. Copyright © 1993 Wim Hofman. Used by permission of Wim Hofman.

Little Red Riding Hood (Akazukin-chan)

Kyoko Iwasaki

Kyoko Iwasaki (1922–) is a Japanese author who has received numerous awards for her writing over her long career. Most notably she won the important Kodansha Children's Literature Award for *Shirasagi Monogatari* (White Egret Story) in 1963. She is considered an important figure in the field of Japanese children's literature. Her tragic version of "Little Red Riding Hood," which sets the tale in Japan during World War II, is a typical example of the wartime literature that is particularly prevalent in that country. It appeared in a twenty-book series for children titled "Senso to Heiwa" (War and Peace), whose purpose was to tell wartime stories to young readers to promote world peace. Although the titles of the individual stories seem unrelated to the general theme of war, each volume is a collection of short stories (ranging from two to eight) that all recount painful experiences during World War II. Iwasaki's retelling is one of six stories by different authors published in the twelfth book of the series in 1995, the fiftieth anniversary of the end of the war. The simple black-and-white illustrations by the Japanese illustrator Toshio Kajiyama (1935–) use the ancient Japanese art form of *sumi-e* or ink-brush painting, which seeks to distill the essence of a scene in the fewest possible brush strokes.

The narrator of "Akazukin-chan" addresses readers directly on several occasions to clearly establish the hypertextual relationship between her story and the classic tale. She obviously refers to the Grimms' version in the first lines, as red velvet is mentioned specifically. However, the subsequent reference to wolves in human skin and the tragic ending are in keeping with Perrault's version. Although the tale has become a painfully realistic short story, the traditional motifs are retained. The father's absence is explained in this story by the war. Many of the motifs receive Japanese touches. The protagonist's distinctive red headgear is a disaster hood to protect her from air raids. The velvet fabric of the Grimms' version has been replaced by meisen silk, a Japanese silk that became popular in Japan between 1920 and 1950 for casual kimonos, as it was more affordable and the colorful designs were seen as modern. Japanese schoolchildren still have padded disaster hoods as protection against fire and earthquakes, and they wear them during disaster drills. The disaster hood cannot save this little girl from the kind of danger she encounters, but it does protect her face, which seems to be the only part of her body left intact by the killer. The small illustration on the title page is a closeup of the heroine wearing her disaster hood. The little girl also wears a pair of *monpe*, which are Japanese work pants gathered at the ankles. Although their color is not specified, at the end they are red with the blood of the little girl. Despite the simplicity of Kajiyama's single full-page illustration, the Japanese dress of this Riding Hood is clearly recognizable.

4. "Akazukin-chan," by Kyoko Iwasaki. Illustrations by Toshio Kajiyama. Copyright ©
1995 Toshio Kajiyama. Used by permission of Toshio Kajiyama.

The little girl takes a box of red rice rather than a basket to her grandmother. Although it is impolite to eat in public in Japan, her mother finally agrees to let the little girl eat rice balls on her way to her grandmother's in order to add a carefree moment to her child's wartime life, an indulgence that proves to be fatal.

Like the other authors in this section, Iwasaki presents a very young heroine, emphasizing her vulnerability. Real wolves are eliminated very quickly by the detective investigating the killing. The little girl is the victim of a human killer who is never caught. The crime is rendered still more distressing by the possibility that the killer may even have been another child. The true wolf in this story is war, which turns humans into animals willing to kill for a little food. This retelling is unique in that it describes the pain and grief of the mother, who must identify the mutilated body of her daughter at the crime scene. Although she had cautioned her young daughter, she had not voiced her misgivings about the dark woods and no doubt reproaches herself bitterly. The narrator, on the other hand, makes her warning to young female readers very explicit. In her tragic cautionary tale, Iwasaki attempts to bring some consolation to young readers by describing the almost magical way in which the girl's pain gives way to serenity. The war will no longer touch her.

❧

LITTLE RED RIDING HOOD (1995)

You have heard of the story of "Little Red Riding Hood," haven't you? A grandma made a red velvet hood for her granddaughter. It is about a girl who was called Little Red Riding Hood by everybody, since she looked very pretty in it.

Once upon a time, the forests in Europe were very deep and dark, although it seems to be the same even now. Once children wandered off into the forest, they never returned alive. I've heard that there are real wolves as well as wolves in human skin, who are kidnappers. That's why the story of Little Red Riding Hood is being retold still. Please be careful, girls, not to be kidnapped.

However, when the darkness became deeper and darker in this country, a similar incident happened, as follows . . .

Mr. Tajima the tailor lived at the entrance of an alley in town. He was always working busily in the house.

From the street we saw Mr. Tajima and his wife tailoring clothes, facing each other across a big cutting board.

They had a girl about five years old, and she wore a disaster hood that protected her head during air raids. Her mother made it from red meisen silk, which she had worn when she was young. The girl really loved the hood, and she was always wearing or putting it over her shoulder. It really suited her.

Now, Mr. Tajima had to go to war, and the night before he left, he told his wife and child this:

"Tokyo is getting very dangerous. If the air raids increase, it may be very difficult for a female like you to run away with a child from a cul-de-sac like this. Moreover, the food shortage may get worse. Listen . . . Why don't you evacuate to my parents' country home? There are many relatives and enough food."

Thus the mother and the girl decided to go to Mr. Tajima's parents' country home. However, they did not have enough food there either, although it was not as bad as in Tokyo. Moreover, there was no relative who would feed someone who had no job. The mother made their living by stitching clothes in a farmer's storage shed.

One day, the mother got a small amount of sticky rice from the farmer's wife in return for stitching a pair of *monpe*.

The mother broke one of the girl's beanbags in order to make some red bean rice. "Hey, dear, could you please go to your father's parents' house and share a box of red bean rice with your grandmother? She loves red bean rice. Take care! You have to walk very fast."

See? It's the same story as "Little Red Riding Hood," isn't it?

The girl was not listening to what her mother said, since she was paying all her attention to the red bean rice.

"Hey, you, do you understand? Don't trip over a stone while you are looking around."

The girl looked up at her mother reproachfully as if she were a dog ordered to "wait." The mother cautioned the girl further. The biggest concern for the mother was the woods on the village border . . . But nothing could happen during the day . . . so she didn't mention it.

"Mom, could you make rice balls with the red bean rice? Can I walk and eat them on the way?"

"No, that's bad manners. Eat it before you go out."

"Because . . ."

The girl explained how she envied the farmer's children, who always showed off by eating rice balls and steamed sweet potatoes. The girl wanted to eat rice balls while walking and saying,

"Very delicious!" in the village dialect.

"Okay, my dear. It may be fun, like a picnic."

The mother understood what the girl was thinking.

In the story of Little Red Riding Hood, the girl is eaten by a wolf that arrived at the grandmother's house ahead of her, but in this story the girl was killed in the woods on the way to her grandmother's house.

They said that she had quietly lain down under an oak tree only five meters from the entrance to the woods.

She had scratches on her legs and hands. Some of them were very deep.

"Was she attacked by a Japanese wolf?"

The police inspector from the police headquarters looked back at the station constable who guided him.

"No, I haven't heard any rumors of a wolf near this village recently."

The constable thought that it might be cuts from a pocket knife, but he did not say it. Both her *monpe* and blouse were torn to pieces, and her *monpe* in particular was soaked with her blood.

It looks like she was killed by an amateur who did not know how to kill a person. For instance, a crime by a child?

The constable shook his head to rid himself of his ominous association.

Fortunately, her face had no damage. Her disaster hood must have protected it. The police inspector had the constable bring a sheet from a car and cover the girl's body.

Then, a pale and gaunt young woman appeared at the entrance to the woods. She walked with unsteady steps and looked like a ghost.

"Ah, she is her mother," the constable told the police inspector. The inspector nodded, and pulled off the sheet that covered the girl's face to show her mother. And he was puzzled. When he had covered the girl's body with the sheet, her face had been warped with pain, but now her face was completely serene. He thought, she has now gone and will never be back.

When the mother looked into her daughter's face, she did not seem to see anything. She did not seem to understand what had happened.

As soon as the constable tried to reach out his hands to pat her on the shoulder, she screamed "Aieee!" The constable was surprised and pulled his hands back. The police inspector should have gotten used to seeing this sort of scene, but he looked away.

The mother pulled the sheet off the girl's body and clung to her, and then started to cry as if she was howling. The police inspector wanted to ask her many things, but he waited for her to stop crying.

After a while, the police inspector got his ear closer to the mother, saying, "What? What happened?"

As he listened, the mother whispered something.

"What did you say, Mother?"[8]

"Where is the box?"

"The box?"

The police inspector turned back to the constable.

"The girl must have been carrying a box. Did you move it?"

"No."

The box was found deeper in the woods. Of course, nothing was left inside the box, not one grain of red bean rice.

The police inspector speculated that someone had watched the girl walking while eating a rice ball. When the person tried to steal it from her, she made a lot of noise. That's why she was killed.

"Such an easy case."

However, it was not easy at all. The criminal was never found. Strangers were always passing by, for example, a small number of village people who came to shop, and evacuated children who were always hungry and broke into farms. There were also malicious children who always bullied the girl, so the police were unable to successfully investigate the crime.

It happened at a time when people were killed for food. Oh, what a cruel story! A girl lost her life for a rice ball . . .

A Little Red Riding Hood (Un petit chaperon rouge)

Claude Clément and Isabelle Forestier

In the true storytelling tradition, the Moroccan-born French author Claude Clément (1946–), who writes poems, short stories, novels, and songs, insists that she does not address a particular audience. The majority of her works are put out by children's publishers, but many of her picturebooks and novels are read as often, if not more so, by adults. Children's book publishing allowed Clément to enhance her texts with high-quality illustrations and explore her passion for the interplay between text and image.[9] A year before the picturebook *Un petit chaperon rouge* (A Little Red Riding Hood), Clément had written the novel *La frontière de sable* (The Border of Sand, 1999), which tackles the difficult subject of sexual abuse in a sensitive and thoughtful manner appropriate for young readers. The same themes of overcoming the silence and shame experienced by the victim and of helping her deal with the trauma became the subject of the picturebook *Un petit chaperon rouge*, issued by the children's publisher Grasset-Jeunesse in 2000 for readers four years of age and older. Clément has collaborated several times with the French illustrator Isabelle Forestier (1954–), who has illustrated picturebooks for both children and adults. The illustrator was familiar with Clément's *La frontière de sable* prior to their collaboration on the picturebook, and she had already done three pastel illustrations based on the tale of Little Red Riding Hood. Forestier's longstanding interest in the tale dates back to childhood nightmares that were haunted by wolves. In fact, she admits that her "first book" was a Little Red Riding Hood story she wrote and illustrated at about eight years of age.

In Perrault's time the tale may have been a story about rape addressed largely to young, aristocratic girls at the court of Louis XIV, but in the context of the twenty-first century, when fairy tales most often are addressed to children, Forestier sees it more as "a story about pedophilia."[10] The heroine of this retelling, as the indefinite article suggests, is representative of every child who has been the victim of sexual abuse. To develop her characters Clément often refers to psychological works. Through this Riding Hood's story, the author and illustrator explore the psychological consequences of sexual abuse, as well as its judicial implications. (Clément holds a law degree.) Clément and Forestier have serious reservations about the moral of Perrault's tale, which they feel inappropriately assigns guilt to the victim. Their retelling absolves the little girl in red of the blame placed on her by the male authors of the classic versions. The moral of this story is that crimes of sexual assault and male violence must be brought into the open so that the perpetrators can be brought to justice and their victims given the assistance they need to recover.

While the cautionary nature of the tale predominates, "A Little Red Riding Hood" is also an initiatory story, as the unusual crimson bonnet the young girl

5. *Un petit chaperon rouge*, by Claude Clément and Isabelle Forestier. Copyright © 2000 Éditions Grasset & Fasquelle. Used by permission of Éditions Grasset & Fasquelle.

receives from her grandmother clearly symbolizes a ritual passage from child to young woman. This is particularly evident in a striking illustration of the reflection of the three generations of women in a large mirror. Later the same mirror reflects only the image of the limp bonnet, which seems to haunt the little girl huddled in the corner of her room (plate 1). She may be a "resourceful" Riding Hood who manages to escape from the wolf, but the once-outgoing little girl is seriously traumatized by the horrific events. Forestier's vivid, sensual illustrations, dominated by a rich, crimson color, often bleed into the blocks of text. The poetic quality of Clément's text, with its rhythms, rhymes, repetitions, and refrains, was emphasized in the picturebook by the verses' centering on the page. By blending the old and the new, the author and illustrator create a universal cautionary tale for children, adults, and society in general.

❧

A Little Red Riding Hood (2000)

Once upon a time there was
a charming, carefree, and happy little girl
who lived in an isolated quarter called the Cité des Bergeries.[11]

She was so nice,
she was so gay:
all her neighbors, all her friends loved her!
Her mother adored her!
But since she worked a lot and often,
she asked her own mother,
—whom they both called Grandmama—
to accompany the little girl to school.
So the delighted granny came,
each morning
and each afternoon,
from her old cottage with the roof of wood tiles,
to look after the little girl,
crossing the forest which separated her from the Cité des Bergeries.
Wednesdays
the mother took the child
to Grandmama's house.

All three got along well together.
And life went on slowly
with its joys and its cares,
in the Cité des Bergeries.

One fine morning,
Grandmama gave her surprised granddaughter
a crimson velvet bonnet
that had belonged to her in bygone days
and that she had worn when it was cold.

Trying it on, the little girl found it so beautiful
that she cried gaily:

"Look how tall it is, how it moves . . .
It will be my red ridinghood!"

And she didn't want to take it off,
not to play during the day,
nor to do her homework,
nor to eat,
nor even to sleep in the evening.

Henceforth, in the Cité, because of the long, tall bonnet
that she wore in all seasons,
they forgot her real name
and called her only:
Little Red Riding Hood.

Life went on,
slowly,
with its joys and its sorrows, in the Cité des Bergeries . . .

One Wednesday, the mother received vexing news:
the granny was in bed with a disturbing cough.
Her condition did not require too much care,
but she needed
to see her granddaughter
and have some good cuddles.

So before going to work, the mother said to the little girl:

"I made some croissants,
some cookies and some cakes.
Our Grandmama is fond of them . . .
Since Wednesday isn't a school day,
take our caddy with wheels,
put in the croissants, cookies, and cakes,
and go, all alone, because I am in a hurry,
and take them to her for your snack.
You are going to have a feast!
You will be careful, my darling Little Riding Hood,

for the path is a little long
to the old cottage
on the other side of the wood.
However, I have confidence in you:
you are a resourceful Riding Hood!"

And so it was that a little while later
Little Red Riding Hood tore down the stairs . . .

She crossed the Cité
greeting her friends in a joyful manner:

"I'm going to have a snack at my granny's!
She's sick, she's in bed . . .
Mom asked me to take her an appetizing snack
all by myself.
And I am sure that Grandmama will be well very soon."

Her friends answered all at once:

"Kiss her for us . . ."
"Wrap your scarf around your neck!"
"And once you are in the woods, take care . . ."
"Be careful . . ."

"Don't worry about me!"

Soon Little Red Riding Hood reached the forest
that she had already gone through,
very often,
in the company of her mother.

This time she was alone,
but didn't worry about anything, because she knew the way.
She trotted along merrily, stopping from time to time
to pick wildflowers.

Suddenly,
on the path,
she saw a shadow pass.
Raising her head, she saw a thick fur coat.
A wolf was coming to meet her, smiling with all his teeth.
On one of his paws, he wore a watch.

"Where are you going, sweet Little Red Riding Hood,
with your well-filled caddy?"

"I am going to my Grandmama's,
to take her cakes, cookies, and croissants."

"And where does your granny live,
Dear Little Riding Hood?"

"On the other side of this wood."

Looking at his watch, the wolf proposed:
"If you want, I'll come with you!
I'll take this path,
You'll take the second.
And we'll see which one of us arrives first.
Then we'll be able to have a snack."

Without waiting for the answer, the wolf dashed away . . .

But Little Red Riding Hood had no desire
to race or to hurry.
She found the wolf ill-mannered
to want to take advantage of her snack
without being invited.
So she continued to pick wildflowers,
to contemplate the clouds,
to skip after butterflies on the longest path . . .

Meanwhile the wolf arrived at the house.

He knocked on the little wooden door while disguising his voice:

"Rat! Tat! Tat! Grandmama, let me in!"

"I'm happy to, but . . . Who is it?"

"It's your cute Riding Hood who brings you a good snack."

"You know what to do to enter:
pull the bobbin toward you
and the latch will fall . . ."

In one go, the wolf pulled.
In one bound, the wolf entered.
In one mouthful, he swallowed Grandmama
and slipped under the sheets.

After a time,
Little Riding Hood arrived at Grandmama's.

Rat! Tat! Tat!

The child knocked on the little wooden door:
"Grandmama! Open . . . It's me!"

The wolf answered, disguising his voice:
"Pull the bobbin
and the latch will fall."

Amused, the little girl pulled on the bobbin.
And the door opened wide.

The wolf invited the child
to put away the caddy with the snack
and to undress
to join him under the sheets.

But Little Red Riding Hood refused.

Standing near the bed, the child wondered:
"Grandmama! What big ears you have . . ."
"The better to watch over your sleep."

Little Red Riding Hood insisted:
"Grandmama! What big black eyes you have . . ."
"My child, the better to see you."

Little Red Riding Hood worried:
"Grandmama! What big arms you have . . ."
"The better to embrace you, my child."

Little Red Riding Hood panicked:
"Grandmama! What big teeth you have . . ."

This time the wolf did not answer.
He leaped on the little girl and wanted to devour her.
But Little Red Riding Hood managed to escape.
While the wolf got tangled up in the blankets,
the child fled posthaste.

Evening fell on the Cité des Bergeries,
where life went on with its joys and its sorrows.
Everyone worried on not seeing the return of
Little Red Riding Hood.

The mother telephoned, but the granny didn't answer.
So the neighbors and friends searched the woods in vain
before reaching the little house and pulling the bobbin.

There, horrified, they saw
the wolf, snoring under the covers.
They pounced on him
and dragged him to the Cité des Bergeries.

He was thrown in prison.

For her part, Little Red Riding Hood
ended up returning home.
She was questioned.
But the little girl had lost the power of speech
and didn't even want to return to school.

For some time, she kept her secret.
Then her mother pointed out to her
that they could find Grandmama
if she related what had happened.
So Little Red Riding Hood told the truth.

The wolf stood trial.
He was condemned to be hung
head and legs upside down.

After a few hours,
the wolf retched . . .
Grandmama came out, in a sorry state.
But, by dint of tenderness, care, and cuddles,
they eventually consoled her.

Instead of keeping the incident secret,
everyone decided to talk about it,
so that it would never happen again.

That's why, since that time,
in the Cité des Bergeries,
life has resumed with its joys and its sorrows.

Pooh! How Did She Know?
The Story of a Little Red Riding Hood
Who Escaped from Her Abductors
(Ches! Eotteohge alassji?
Honjaseo gileul gadaga yugoebeomeul
mulrichin bbalganmoja iyagi)

MIA SIM

Mia Sim (1966–) is a Korean children's author and illustrator who began publishing for children after winning a "special mention" in a competition for new talent in illustration in South Korea. She is both the author and illustrator of this picturebook retelling of "Little Red Riding Hood," published for young children by Nurimbo in 2010. The lengthy, descriptive subtitle clearly establishes that this retelling is a tale of abduction. The author deliberately used the story of Little Red Riding Hood to create "a warning tale" about "a crime against children."[12] Before writing the story she consulted books on the topic, but they all seemed to be "rather heavy and too moralizing." Determined to avoid such heavy didacticism, she wanted her Little Red Riding Hood to be somewhat serious but above all joyful. With a light step, the little girl goes from danger to danger, managing to sidestep one threat after the other. Despite its serious moral, Sim's story of "a" Little Red Riding Hood adopts a humorous and playful approach. The lively, cartoonlike illustrations include a large map that plays an important part in the narrative. Young readers can trace the path taken by Little Red Riding Hood, as the important sites in the story are marked on it: Little Red Riding Hood's house, the fork, the shortcut, the pond, the big tree, and the grandmother's house. In the text, the three locations where the girl is accosted are indicated in boxes.

In this very simple story, Sim retains the traditional ternary narrative structure of folktales: her Little Red Riding Hood meets three would-be abductors. The repetition of certain phrases is also reminiscent of the oral tradition, a notable example being the words of the title, which each abductor, in turn, utters when the little girl discerns the danger. The mother's brief warning, which the girl seems to dismiss, echoes in her head later, saving her repeatedly. In a much more sophisticated manner, the cautionary voice of the mother also reverberates in the head of the protagonist of Luisa Valenzuela's "Si esto es la vida, yo soy Caperucita Roja" ("If This Is life, I'm Red Riding Hood") as she makes her way to grandmother's in the Argentine retelling for adults. In Sim's story the daughter seems to consider the unexplained presence of her mother's voice almost magical, and the grandmother later attributes it to love. The moral of the story is expressed explicitly and in

6. *Ches! Eotteohge alassji? Honjaseo gileul gadaga yugoebeomeul mulrichin bbalganmoja iyagi*, by Mia Sim. Copyright © 2010 Nurimbo. Used by permission of Mia Sim and Nurimbo.

much more realistic terms in a blurb on the back cover of the book that is reminiscent of the moral at the end of Perrault's tales. It is Little Red Riding Hood herself who addresses the moral to young readers, whom she calls "My dear friends":

> He who is ugly is bad?
> No, there are wicked among those who are beautiful.
> It is not wise to judge someone by appearance.
>
> If a boy or a man who lives in your neighborhood requests something
>   nicely?
> You must refuse if the request seems odd.

When you are in danger,
shout fearlessly: "Help!"
Everyone will quickly come to your aid.

In the narrative itself the author makes her point in a playful, less threatening manner by using well-known characters from other fairy tales. Stereotypes are inverted so that the evildoer is not the traditional Big Bad Wolf but the three macho pigs, a cunning-looking Frog Prince, and a Puss in Boots in a sports car. Among those who come to Little Red Riding Hood's rescue, it is the wolf that attacks the cat, giving him a powerful kick. Sim encourages her young readers to rely on their common sense and heed their instincts, but also not to be afraid to call for help. Korean children, like many Asian

7. *Ches! Eotteohge alassji? Honjaseo gileul gadaga yugoebeomeul mulrichin bbalganmoja iyagi*, by Mia Sim. Copyright © 2010 Nurimbo. Used by permission of Mia Sim and Nurimbo.

children, are taught to be quiet and well-behaved, so shouting is not customary behavior. The author expresses her intention in the following manner: "This book seeks to show the evolution of a child: becoming courageous and managing to think in order to (re)act. And I also wanted to say that familial love is necessary for a child to have a strong spirit and emotional, physical, and mental security." At the first encounter, Little Red Riding Hood merely remembers what her mother told her, whereas at the second, she is also able to perceive the danger, to reflect, and to react. She seems to sense instinctively that the Frog Prince's intentions are malicious. The final encounter represents a danger or an evil that Little Red Riding Hood seems unable to cope with alone, but her presence of mind allows her to escape with the help of others (plate 2). Unlike the other stories in this section, this cautionary tale for very young children ends happily, with an empowering and reassuring message. The Korean author was determined "to create a Little Red Riding Hood who is able to take the initiative and to reason rather than the one to whom moral values are taught."

Pooh! How Did She Know?
The Story of a Little Red Riding Hood
Who Escaped from Her Abductors (2010)

It is I who made all the cookies.
The chocolate cookies, the strawberry cookies . . .
I'm going to take the peanut cookies to my grandmother.
"Little Red Riding Hood, be careful!"
Don't worry! I can go to my grandmother's by myself!
It's very difficult for a child to visit her grandmother alone.
For me, everything is easy!
I walk without fear.
Suddenly, someone called me.
"Little Red Riding Hood!"
Ooooh! It's a wolf!
"She ran off without realizing that her cookies fell."

Whew, wolves are bad.
They look scary.

> When she passes the fork . . .

"Little Red Riding Hood, this path is a shortcut," said the three little pigs.
"But it's not lit well enough."
"You're afraid."

"I am not!"

"Take this shortcut then."

"Okay!"

"Little Red Riding Hood, wait!"

Huh? It's Mom's voice!

Then I stopped to think.

Mom told me a poorly lit road is dangerous.

I told the three little pigs:

"I'm not afraid. But I will take the other lit road!"

"Pooh! How did she know?"

But where does Mom's voice come from?

When she passes by the pond . . .

"Little Red Riding Hood, help me!" said the Frog Prince.

"My ball has fallen in the water."

"A golden ball?"

"Yes. Can you get it? You are strong, eh?"

"Okay!"

"Little Red Riding Hood, wait!"

It's Mom's voice again!

Okay, okay. I'm going to think!

I noticed then that it was a little odd.

In fact, the Frog Prince is stronger than me.

But why did he ask me to help him?

"Sorry. I can't help you!" I told him.

"Pooh! How did she know?"

But where does Mom's voice come from?

When she passes under the big tree . . .

"Little Red Riding Hood! Where is the fork?" a cat in a car asked me.

"I know where it is!"

Suddenly, a horrible hand grabbed me.

I was paralyzed with fear.

"Little Red Riding Hood, wait! You are a courageous girl!"

Yes! I am courageous!

Then I screamed with all my might.

"Help! Help! Help!"

Everyone came running.

The cat ran away crying.

He deserved it!

"Pooh! How did she know?"

BAM!

"Little Red Riding Hood, here are your cookies that fell."

"Thank you."

I felt sorry for the wolf.

"Do you want a cookie? They are very good; it is I who made them!"

When I see my grandmother at her house, I have a tear in my eye.

"Grandma, a cat who was in a car . . . tried to kidnap me . . . So I gave him a kick and he fled in tears . . . Grandma, I'm courageous, you know it, don't you?"

"Of course!"

"But Mom's voice followed me everywhere."

"It's because she loves you, Little Red Riding Hood."

"I knew it!"

Little Red Riding Hood (Czerwony Kapturek)

JOANNA OLECH AND GRAŻKA LANGE

Joanna Olech (1955–) is a Polish author, graphic artist, and illustrator of books for children and teenagers. Her numerous awards include winning the distinction of the Most Beautiful Book of the Year (2005) from the Polish Association of Book Publishers (PTWK) for the picturebook *Czerwony Kapturek*, a contemporary retelling of "Little Red Riding Hood" that was illustrated by Grażka Lange (1961–). Although "beautiful" is certainly not the first adjective that comes to mind, the graphic design, layout, and illustrations work together to create a striking and highly original picturebook, which also received an award for production and presentation excellence at the EDYCJA publishers' competition in 2005. The judges appreciated the unconventional interpretation of the story as well as the graphic design. Lange, who lectures at the Warsaw Academy of Fine Arts, is one of the most acclaimed contemporary Polish illustrators. The innovative artist has received many awards for graphic design and book illustration, including the PTWK award for lifetime achievement in 2008.

Olech and Lange's subversive retelling of "Little Red Riding Hood" was the first book in their series "Niebaśnie" (Un-Fairy Tales), an innovative collection they created to retell classic tales in a new light. All the books in the series address very current, controversial topics. Leszek K. Talko and Anna Niemierko's *Jaś i Małgosia* (Hansel and Gretel, 2005) deals with the exploitation of children in a story about a gang of organ traffickers, while Michał Rusinek and Małgorzata Bieńkowska's *Kopciuszek* (Cinderella, 2006), for which Lange also did the graphic design, is about the hegemony of the media and its reinforcement of gender stereotypes. According to Olech, the purpose of her retelling of "Little Red Riding Hood" was "to encourage children to be assertive and to warn them against pedophiles."[13]

Olech's story is inspired by the classic versions of both Charles Perrault and the Brothers Grimm. Although it includes a woodsman, the story retains the tragic ending of Perrault, as the male rescuer cannot save the little girl or her grandmother. The intextual play is emphasized by varying the font size. The irony in the parodic text will have particular appeal for older readers. Adults will appreciate, for example, the quirk of fate in the fact that Little Red Riding Hood's would-be savior is detained by official duties, which undoubtedly involve fruitless paperwork or pointless red tape. Olech retains the traditional Polish title "Czerwony Kapturek," which translates literally into English as "Little Red Hood" (*kapturek* meaning "little hood"), even though Polish versions of the tale are inspired by the Grimms' "Little Red Cap." The cap/hood slip is particularly appropriate in this retelling, as it was inspired by both classic versions. Rather than the "hood" implied in the Polish title, the protagonist is paradoxically wearing a *pink* cap, no doubt freighted with all its stereotypical gender nuances. On the dark penultimate spread that depicts the gloomy, empty interior of the grandmother's house, the eye is immediately drawn to the little cap lying forlornly in the bottom right corner (plate 3). Despite Olech's precise word choice of "pink" in the text, Lange deliberately chose an ambiguous color that has a decidedly reddish tinge and actually bears the technical name of "cold red" in the Pantone color system, although she says it could also be termed "cold pink."[14] This pink-red or red-pink is the only color in the otherwise gray, black, and white illustrations. Lange's bold mixed-media pictures, which combine painting, drawing in black ink, and collage, are deceptively childlike, but the result is a very sophisticated book in which every element has been carefully chosen to contribute to the overall effect, much like the work of Sara Fanelli. Lange stresses that she is a designer, rather than an illustrator, and compares herself to a film director, as she considers the whole conception before concerning herself with individual pictures.[15]

Olech portrays a polite and obedient Little Red Riding Hood who has been properly socialized and behaves exactly as a model child should in the presence of her elders. Lange's portrayal of Little Red Riding Hood as a simple, childlike figure is a surprisingly powerful, iconic representation of the classic heroine. Little Red Riding Hood's body language, especially in the portrait that accompanies the first page of text, suggests a demure, prim and proper, well-behaved girl. Despite the caricatural simplicity of her portrayal, Lange is able to show subtle emotions through expression and body language. In the first spread, she manages to suggest the child's submissiveness, insecurity, and lack of self-confidence. Although Little Red Riding Hood is less naïve than her predecessor, recognizing, for example, that the wolf's question about her destination is "none of [his] business," she nonetheless obligingly and courteously provides the expected response. The climactic dialogue is one of the few parts that adheres strictly to the classic version. The rather subtle changes to the classic text suffice to turn the moral completely upside down. Contrary to the Grimms' version, where Little Red Cap is eaten because she disobeyed her mother, Olech's subversive retelling presents a little girl whose demise is the result of her absolute obedience. Olech's last line about the parents' memory of the little girl is a highly satirical allusion to the classic version.

While Little Red Riding Hood herself is drawn in soft brush lines of diluted reddish paint, her cap is a solid, reddish-pink, triangular shape that is added by collage, highlighting the distinctive headgear that the heroine herself describes as "strange" and "terribly old-fashioned" (plate 4). As Little Red Riding Hood goes to Granny's, Lange continues to express a wide range of subtle emotions in the simple lines of her face, including discomfort, brief joy, and disquiet when she meets the wolf. Paradoxically, however, once she arrives at Granny's, where she will experience the strongest emotions, her face is no longer visible. The last depiction of the little girl is a striking, solid-black silhouette outlined against the red light of the doorway, where she is seen, or rather not seen, by the viewer from the same perspective as the wolf in the grandmother's bed.

The two sets of very different dark eyes that appear on the cover are multiplied on the black endpapers, where nine sets of eyes peer threateningly out of the darkness, suggesting ominously that Little Red Riding Hood is surrounded by predatory wolves. Some of the eyes clearly belong to the five male heads on the title page, heads that encircle somewhat menacingly the uncomfortable-looking eponymous heroine. The caricatural heads, drawn or painted entirely in black, are perhaps more disturbing than the solid black jaws of the wolf, which have already grasped one of her braids. A subsequent illustration depicts the heroine surrounded by similar female heads, also entirely in black. Both the male and female heads appear to be those of adults, as the illustrator is playing on the similarities between the children and the adults. She wanted to underscore the difference between Little Red Riding Hood, who is a "real child," and her school peers, who resemble adults.[16] The picture of a girl picking her nose—which is inset into the page of text describing the well-behaved Little Red Riding Hood, who never picks hers—indicates that they are indeed children despite their mature-looking faces. The multiple sets of male legs that bleed off the top of the first illustration continue the threatening male presence introduced by the heads on the title page. The wolf is represented throughout as a very rough black shape protruding onto the page from one side or the other, sometimes little more than a black shadow. The fact that only part of him, generally only his jaws, is visible emphasizes his huge size in relationship to the little girl, but also gives him a more symbolic status that is heightened by the shadowy, vague shape. From the moment of the first encounter, that dark figure is an ominous, threatening presence on almost every spread.

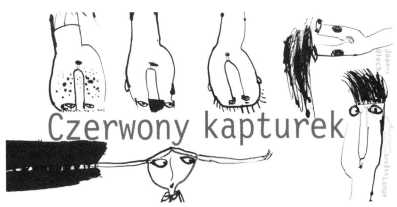

8. *Czerwony Kapturek*, by Joanna Olech and Grażka Lange. Text copyright © 2005 Jacek Santorski & Co., Agencja Wydawnicza, and Joanna Olech; illustrations copyright © 2005 Jacek Santorski & Co., Agencja Wydawnicza, and Grażka Lange. Used by permission of Grażka Lange and Joanna Olech.

9. *Czerwony Kapturek*, by Joanna Olech and Grażka Lange. Illustrations copyright © 2005 Jacek Santorski & Co., Agencja Wydawnicza, and Grażka Lange. Used by permission of Grażka Lange.

Olech's choice of roses—flowers unlikely to be growing deep in the forest—emphasizes the symbolic importance of the flowers, which become a recurring motif in the illustrations. The disquiet that can be read on Little Red Riding Hood's face during her encounter with the wolf is underscored by the fact that she drops the rose she was holding, a foreshadowing perhaps of her deflowering. During the ritualistic dialogue, Little Red Riding Hood herself is visibly absent from the illustrations, but she is represented by the pink-red roselike pattern against which the dark figure of the wolf is outlined, a pattern that is magnified in the climactic devouring scene. The large, regular rose pattern on the final spread resembles old-fashioned wallpaper, a perfect backdrop for the traditional black-and-white drawing of the encounter of Little Red Riding Hood and the wolf that accompanies the final ironic words: "Good morning!" Lange points out that we do not even know who is pronouncing the greeting—Little Red Riding Hood or the wolf. (The wolf's open mouth suggests it is him.) While the scene could be taken from an early edition of the tale for children, it actually constitutes an example of the traditional form of Polish needlework known as *makatka*, which appears to hang against the pink wallpaper. Hand stitching is visible on the red border that frames the encounter scene, while the words "Good morning" appear on the white, linen-like background in an ornamental red font that makes them look like they were embroidered in red yarn. Lange plays with conventions by linking the classic tale to the widespread traditional folk art of *makatka*. The illustrator believes that *makatka*, with their conventional images and texts, continue to have a profound influence, even if only subconsciously, on the rather traditional world view of the Polish people.

The subversive illustrations are a perfect foil for Olech's unconventional use of language. The author plays with words and expressions, often passing over common words for unexpected and odd-sounding ones to render the images more vivid, as in the case of "hair flocks." Olech and Lange's picture-book stands in stark contrast to the sickly sweet fairy-tale books that can still be found in the Polish children's book market. The tongue-in-cheek biography of the illustrator at the back of the book parodies the tale's ritualistic dialogue to criticize such books: "Why does she have such big teeth? In order to sharpen them for the producers of kitsch." Although the picturebook is targeted at young children, as a way to open their eyes to the ramifications of the Grimms' version in today's world, the subversive message and innovative graphics also have strong adult appeal.

❧

LITTLE RED RIDING HOOD (2005)

Over the hills and far away,[17] in a small cottage on the edge of the forest, an obedient girl lived with her parents. She ate spinach and liver without complaining, she never picked her nose, or splashed around in puddles, like her peers. She had clean ears and nails and two braids tied with big bows. Even when older girls called her a nerd and pinched her, she did not complain, only cried silently.

On her birthday, her mom gave her a pink cap she made herself. Mom worked on it very hard, so, although the girl found it rather strange and terribly old-fashioned, she put it on and thanked her politely. When she went to school wearing the cap, her classmates teased her mercilessly, and since then no one has called her anything but "Little Red Riding Hood." Soon, everybody forgot her real name.

Sometimes, she would dream that she played and climbed trees together with other kids, or even (oh!) ate chocolate bars before dinner. Yet when she woke up, everything was the same again—"Yes, Mommy!" "Of course, Daddy!"

One day, her mother gave her a basket with delicacies and a bottle of cough syrup for her ill grandmother, who lived beyond the forest.

"Don't stray from the path, daughter dear, and run straight to Granny's. The forest is very dangerous!" said Mom.

"Yes, Mommy," replied the little girl.

And she thought: "The forest is dangerous indeed ... mosquitoes and ticks ... is there anything else? No, I don't think so." So, she put on the cap she hated so much and set off.

She walked, and she walked, but since the basket was quite heavy, she stopped once in a while and gazed at butterflies and flowers. She picked a flower, then another ..." I'll make a bouquet for Granny." The prettiest roses grew deep in the forest. Picking flower after flower, she was going farther and farther from the path.

Suddenly, from behind the bushes, Mr. Wolf appeared. He bared his teeth in a big grin and combed out his whiskers with his claw.

"Welcome, Red Riding Hood!" he said.

"Good day to you, sir," said the girl, curtsying to him.

"Where are you going, little one?" asked Mr. Wolf, leaning slightly toward her. He had bad breath.

"None of your business!" thought the girl.

Instantly, she became ashamed of her boldness and answered politely: "To sick Granny."

"And where does your granny live?" asked Mr. Wolf.

The girl was crushing the bouquet nervously. She didn't like this nosy guy, but she was not brave enough to lie to him.

"Beyond the forest ... on Boletus Hill," she whispered.

"Speak up, I can't hear you," said the wolf, and pricked his ear. There were gray hair flocks sticking out of it.

"On Boletus Hill," repeated the child.

Mr. Wolf drew himself up. His face twisted in a sly grimace.

"Well, then give my regards to your granny and wish her best of health."

"Thank you, sir," answered the girl, and ran to the path.

Meanwhile, the wolf, who knew every path and every bush in the forest, took a shortcut to the house on Boletus Hill.

Within a quarter of an hour, the wolf was at the door. He knocked.

"Who's there?" asked Granny from under her duvet.

"It's me, your granddaughter!" lied Mr. Wolf.

"Just pull the latch and the door will open," said sick Granny.

The wolf dashed into the room and without further ado, gobbled up Granny together with her glasses and a hot-water bottle. Then he clambered into the bed, and, putting on one of Granny's caps, he waited. A moment later, Little Red Riding Hood stood at the door. You could barely see her from behind the bouquet of fading flowers. The girl knocked at the door.

"Who's there?" asked a muffled voice.

"It's me, Little Red Riding Hood," she said.

"Just pull the latch and the door will open," the wolf croaked in a thin voice.

"Come closer, Granddaughter," he told her, when he saw her standing on the threshold.

"Poor Granny has become hoarse," thought the girl, and approached the bed. She could see only a cap and bushy eyebrows sticking out from under the duvet.

"Granny, Granny, why do you have such large ears?" asked Little Red Riding Hood.

"The better to hear you, my child," mumbled the wolf.

"Granny, Granny, why do you have such big eyes?" asked the astonished girl.

"The better to see you," replied the wolf, and smiled falsely.

"Granny, Granny why do you have such big teeth?" squeaked the terrified girl.

"The better to eat you!" roared the wolf, threw the cap off his head, and gobbled Little Red Riding Hood up.

As luck would have it, the gamekeeper, who would normally pass Boletus Hill at that time, or even go up to Grandma's house for a cup of tea, was too busy in the office of the forest inspectorate and didn't have time to make his rounds that day. So, when the girl's parents, concerned by her long absence, arrived at Grandma's house at dusk, there was not a soul! The only thing they found there was a crumpled pink cap on the floor.

GOOD MORNING!

Then, whenever they remembered their lost daughter, they would always say:

"She was an obedient child!"

The Story of Little Red Riding Hood
Told to Children and Perhaps Not
(A História do Capuchinho Vermelho
contada a crianças e nem por isso)

MANUEL ANTÓNIO PINA

The Portuguese poet, author, and journalist Manuel António Pina (1943–2012) received Portugal's most prestigious literary award, the Prémio Camões, in 2011. Sadly, he passed away before this book went to press. In addition to poetry, plays, and fiction for adults, his extensive body of work includes approximately twenty children's books. This retelling of "Little Red Riding Hood" has a particularly interesting back story. It was the result of a challenge presented by the Museu de Arte Contemporânea de Serralves in Porto and the internationally acclaimed artist Paula Rego (1935–), whose important retrospective exhibition at the museum in 2004–2005 included her series of paintings *Little Red Riding Hood Suite* (2003). The author admits that it was only after much hesitation that he decided to undertake this "translation" or "game," which he describes in the following terms: "translate a translation; restore to the literary language (to [his] own literary language) the pictorial 'text,' while simultaneously remaining faithful to the ironic, visceral language of Paula Rego's painting, to the story of Little Red Riding Hood, and to [his] own processes."[18] Rego's six drawings are therefore an integral part of Pina's story and were incorporated in the book, which appeared in 2005 following her exhibition. Rego's name actually gets more prominent billing than the author's on the book's cover. The attractive volume was distributed with the daily national newspaper *Publico* and therefore reached a very broad audience.[19] It was also issued in Denmark in 2005, by a small publishing house led by Jorge Braga, following an exhibition of Paula Rego's work at the Corner Udstilling in Copenhagen.

Pina's text must constantly be read in relationship to Rego's pastels, which provide a very personal interpretation of the story of Little Red Riding Hood. Since the artist's visual retelling deviates significantly from the classic story, to which the author was also to remain faithful, his ingenuity was truly tested. According to Pina, his retelling goes beyond the nature of either a "rewriting" or a "pastiche." With a parenthetical comment that seems to allude to the ambiguous title of his own story, the author describes his project in the following terms: "It was more (or perhaps less, I don't know) than an interpretation, it was rather a reconstruction or a 'translation,' that is, a betrayal." For him, it was a "literary exercise" not unlike others he had undertaken in the past, an exercise that involved "a re-writing of a re-writing."[20] "The Story of Little Red Riding Hood Told to Children and Perhaps Not" is a complex dialogue that layers the plural voices of Pina, Rego, and the classic text. This retelling illustrates clearly the notion that, as Sara Reis da Silva puts it, "a text interacts with the tradition, with a kind of 'collective library.'"[21] The play with this tradition is highlighted in the striking typography, as the text is alternately printed in red and black, the two iconic colors of the tale. The third-person voice of the narrator, who pretends to use the traditional discourse of a children's tale, is in red (rendered in gray in the translation below), while the dialogue of the characters, who speak a contemporary colloquial Portuguese, is in black. The complexity of the language, with its different registers—the set phrases of the traditional tale; the parenthetical, conspiratorial comments of the narrator; and the everday speech of the characters—is skillfully rendered by means of a deceptively simple syntax and vocabulary. Pina's sophisticated recasting superposes on the traditional, moralistic tale a modern, immoral tale. The author has successfully captured the subversiveness and irony of Rego's visual interpretation and brought it to the classic tale, which, as penned by Perrault, is not devoid of its own irony.

The subtlety, complexity, and multilayered nature of this story give it appeal for readers of all ages. The original edition and the Danish translation were both published for an audience of young and old alike. In the title itself the author suggests that his retelling, like Perrault's hypotext, is not only, nor even perhaps primarily, intended for children. The idiomatical Portuguese expression "e nem por isso" was difficult to translate, because it can mean "perhaps not," "more than that," or "less than that," and, as the author explained, can modify either the verb *contada* (told) or the noun *crianças* (children), providing six different meanings. The title reflects Pina's skepticism with regard to distinctions between "children" and "adults." As a child he preferred books "not for children," and he thinks it is possible to write in a register capable of engaging simultaneously both audiences. In his mind "all books (or almost all . . .) 'are' for everyone, that is to say, for each reader, adult or child, who, in one way or another, can read him- or herself—according to his or her personal experience, culture, sensibility, reason and unreason—in reading it." Some people say that children do not understand Pina's so-called children's books, but the author feels such people believe that a literary work has "only a single reading ('their' reading)" that is beyond a child's understanding, when, in fact, they "cannot 'understand' children's readings of these texts."

Readers are put on familiar ground by the opening sentence, with its formulaic incipit "Once upon a time." Rego's initial drawing of a pretty little girl wearing a coat with a red hood against an indeterminate plain, white background does not undermine the familiar image unless readers know the title of the drawing. Her titles are not given as captions but appear only at the end of the book. The title of the first drawing, "Little Red Riding Hood on the Edge," instills the tranquil scene with a strong sense of foreboding.[22] Although the text is updated in keeping with Rego's artwork, the general plot line seems to adhere fairly faithfully to the classic tale. In a note at the back of the book, the author claims, in his characteristically elusive and sly manner, that the story "follows closely (although perhaps not always with the advisable fidelity)" either Perrault's "Le Petit Chaperon Rouge" or the later Grimms' version. There are as many ways of being faithful to the classic tale as there are authors retelling it. Pina retains the tragic demise of Little Red Riding Hood and her grandmother from Perrault's version, but he also appropriates the wolf's death from the Grimms' version, although it is now at the hand of the mother. The first lines evoke Perrault's opening, and there are numerous explicit references to the classic hypotext throughout—notably the last two lines of the moral, which Pina embeds in italics.

This is not, however, a story about the "original" Little Red Riding Hood. The classic tale is a *mise en abyme* in the story of "another" Riding Hood, for whom it remains a favorite, even though, at eleven years of age, she questions significant elements: the absence of the father and the perceived passivity of the mother. The questions she puts to her grandmother seem to foreshadow the tragic ending of her own story. However, readers unfamiliar with Rego's series may initially anticipate that this modern heroine will be rescued by a mother recast in an active role. Ironically, her working mother's violent intervention at the end does not save her daughter but merely serves her own vanity. In the face of the traumatic loss of both her daughter and her mother, the angry avenger has the presence of mind to carefully skin the wolf so that she will have a new fur stole. It is her new wardrobe and not the grief of a mother at the loss of both her daughter and her mother that is the subject of conversations in the days following the tragedy. If she experiences pain at the brutal annihilation of the "Happy Family" evoked in the title of Rego's second drawing, it is deliberately hidden by both artist and author. Furthermore, the mother's striking red dress and hat suggest that she has appropriated the role of her daughter, thus cleverly subverting the tale's initiatory meaning. The protagonist receives the ritual gift, the red coat with the hood, from her grandmother when she turns eleven and is on the threshold of becoming a woman, but it is the mother who wears the symbolic color at the end of Pina's tale.

The classic tale retains its cautionary role in the life of this Riding Hood, as the grandmother uses it to warn the young protagonist, who wants to prematurely spread her wings (suggested subtly by her red nail polish in Rego's first drawing). True to the versions of both Perrault and the Grimms, the protagonist dawdles to pick flowers for her grandmother, but she does not disobey the mother's injunction not to speak to strangers, which is often added in later versions. The wolf is a neighbor and friend of the family, someone she trusts, as well as a respectable "engineer" whose name happens to be Mr. Wolf. The wolf thus takes the human form that Perrault attributes to him in his moral, although the title and the capital are dropped very quickly as he reveals his bestiality. Pina's rendition of the famous dialogue illustrates his subtle reworking and layering of the hypotexts: the wolf's replies always follow the traditional Portuguese formula, whereas Little Red Riding Hood's remarks change in a manner that conveys a sense of growing intensity and urgency. Much more explicitly than in Clément and Forestier's version, the wolf's behavior is that of a predator, a pedophile who preys on young girls (plate 5).

The Story of Little Red Riding Hood
Told to Children and Perhaps Not (2005)

Once upon a time there was a very, very pretty girl who was, it can rightly be said, the darling[23] of her mother and her grandmother.

When she was eleven years old, the grandmother had offered her a red wool coat with a hood that suited her so well, so well that everyone started calling her Little Red Riding Hood, which was also the name of another very, very pretty girl in a tale that her grandmother had told her when she was a little girl and that she was so fond of, so fond of that, at night, before falling asleep, she still sometimes asked her grandmother to tell it to her again.

The tale told the story of a girl who was eaten by a wolf, and Little Red Riding Hood used to ask her grandmother why the girl's mother did not rush to help her and kill the wolf and how come the father did not even enter into the story.

"I do not know," replied her grandmother. "That was how I learned it. Perhaps her parents, like yours, were separated, or perhaps her father had died . . ."

"But the mother, why did the mother not kill the wolf?" insisted Little Riding Hood.

"How should I know, my dear," her grandmother said, shrugging her shoulders very patiently. "Nobody remembers these details; it is a very old story that teaches girls that they should not talk to wolves . . ."

And her grandmother recited some verses that ended thus:

"Girls, beware, well-mannered wolves
are the most dangerous of all!"

"Wolves?" marveled Little Riding Hood. "Where on earth do you see wolves walking around nowadays?"

"They used to, then . . . ," said the grandmother, tucking her in. "Go to sleep now, my dear, because tomorrow you have to get up early to go to school."

She gave her a kiss, turned off the light, and Red Riding Hood fell asleep full of fear and dreamed of fierce wolves with huge teeth that ate disobedient girls.

The mother, the grandmother, and Riding Hood lived very happily in a house with a large yard full of fruit trees, a quiet, clean neighborhood where everyone knew each other and people greeted each other amicably in the street.

One morning, when it was time to go to school, Little Red Riding Hood said to her mother:

"I'm already eleven years old, I don't need to be taken to school, I can very well go by myself . . ."

"Better not, my dear," the mother answered. "The streets are very dangerous, and the school is far away . . ."

"Now, Mom, it's around the corner! The other girls already go by themselves . . ."

"Remember the story of Little Red Riding Hood," intervened her grandmother, worried. "Remember the wolf . . ."

Red Riding Hood turned to her:

"Oh, Grandma, nonsense! In children's stories there are wolves . . . This is real life, Grandma, wake up. In real life there are no wolves in the wild attacking girls who go to school . . ." And mocking the grandmother's fears: "Unless the school is at the zoo . . ."

And Red Riding Hood insisted so much, begged so much, that the mother finally gave in:

"All right, all right, I'll let you go by yourself. But promise me that you will be very careful, that you will cross the streets at the crosswalk, and that you will not talk to strangers . . ."

The mother gave her a kiss, accompanied her to the gate, and bade her farewell saying:

"Today I have a lot of work at the office, but Grandma will prepare lunch for you. Don't delay on the way back after class, but eat everything cold . . ."

"I'll make that almond cake you like so much," said the grandmother, also giving her a kiss.

"Thank you, Grandma," said Little Red Riding Hood, and, taking the bag, went running to school, overjoyed.

After class Little Riding Hood returned home right away, as promised. She was very hungry and could think only about the almond cake. But on the way back, she decided to go through the public garden to pick flowers and make a bouquet to take to her grandmother.

In the garden she met a neighbor jogging, who, when he saw her, stopped, panting, by her side:

"Hello, Little Red Riding Hood. So today your mother did not go to pick you up at school?"

"Hello, Mr. Wolf" (the neighbor's name was Wolf; he was very nice and sometimes called in on them to have tea with her grandmother). "No, today I came by myself. I'm already a big girl."

"So you are, so you are . . . ," the neighbor said, looking her up and down. "Have you had lunch?"

"No, Grandma stayed home to make lunch. I came to pick flowers to take to her."

"That's a good girl," answered the neighbor. "Your grandmother will certainly be very pleased."

"But I cannot linger," continued Little Red Riding Hood, "or she will worry."

The neighbor (who, unbeknownst to anyone, was a disguised wolf) said to her, stroking her head:

"Look, pick the flowers and make a beautiful bouquet; I'm going to tell your grandmother that you are on your way, so she won't be worried. That way, when you get home, the table will already be set."

"Thank you, very kind of you . . ."

And so it went. The wolf began to run again and went to the grandmother's house, while Little Red Riding Hood was picking daisies in the garden and chasing squirrels and butterflies. It was the first time she was alone in the garden, and she had never felt so happy.

Once at the grandmother's house, the wolf knocked on the door.

"Who is it?" asked the grandmother.

"It's me," replied the wolf.

"Oh, it's the Engineer Wolf, come in, come in, dear sir,"[24] said the grandmother, recognizing the voice of the neighbor and opening the door for him. "I'm finishing up lunch; would you have some?"

But the wolf was barely inside the house when he fell on the grandmother and ate her. Then he disguised himself with her clothes and waited for Little Red Riding Hood to return.

In the garden, Little Red Riding Hood had a bunch of daisies so large that she could scarcely carry it. As it was starting to get late, and the grandmother might be worried, even though the neighbor had gone to warn her, she took the bouquet, put on her backpack, and went home. "How happy grandmother will be with such beautiful flowers," she thought, and quickened her pace, eager to arrive.

The backyard gate was open, but Red Riding Hood was not surprised. It was customary for people to enter and leave and forget to close the gate. Running across the yard, she knocked on the door.

"Who is it?" asked the wolf from inside, imitating her grandmother's voice.

"It's me," answered Little Red Riding Hood. "How hoarse grandmother is," she thought. "She must have a cold . . ."

"Come in, darling," said the wolf in the sweetest voice he could manage. "The door is open."

Little Red Riding Hood entered the house. The wolf had put down the blinds so the room was in semi-darkness, and he sat in a chair in front of the door with the grandmother's shawl over his head, so well disguised that Little Red Riding Hood did not suspect anything.

"Look at the flowers I have for you, Grandma. They are your favorite, daisies from the field . . ."

"How beautiful, how beautiful!" said the wolf, always imitating the voice of the grandmother. "Thank you, my darling. Put them in the vase and come sit down next to me . . ."

Little Red Riding Hood put the flowers carefully in the vase, took off her coat, and sat down beside the wolf. It seemed to her that her grandmother, who had soft white skin, was scary looking, but she thought it was the shadows of the room. The grandmother always smelled very good, of lavender, and now you would say she smelled of sweat, but Riding Hood thought it was from spending the whole morning doing household chores.

"Are you feeling all right, Grandma?" she asked.

"Oh, yes, very well . . . ," replied the wolf. "I just need to rest a little."

"Have you already had lunch?"

"Not yet," said the wolf. "I was waiting for you . . ." And he moved his chair closer to Little Red Riding Hood's chair, putting an arm around her shoulders.

"What a big arm you have, Grandma," said Little Red Riding Hood.

"All the better to hug you . . . ," answered the wolf, pressing her to him.

"What big eyes those are!"

"All the better to see you, my dear . . ."

"And what big ears!"

"All the better to hear you . . ."

"And the mouth, what a big mouth!"

"All the better to eat you!" said the wolf, rising to his feet suddenly, jumping on Little Red Riding Hood, and eating her.

When he had finished eating Little Red Riding Hood, the wolf, licking his chops, exhausted and satisfied, thought it was better to stay there and get some sleep while digesting. He had eaten the grandmother and Little Red Riding Hood one after the other and was stuffed, so he quickly fell asleep.

The mother came home from work and saw the wolf sleeping in the room and Little Red Riding Hood's clothing on the floor. In great distress, she realized right away what had happened. Very angry, she ran to the shed in the yard, brought a pitchfork, and stabbed the wolf with all her might, killing him. Then she got a big knife and carefully removed his skin.

"Anyway," said the mother, "I might as well get myself a stole . . ."

In the following days, the mother's *toilette* was the subject of much admiration among office colleagues: a crimson red dress that was very, very nice and a wolf skin around the neck.

The Tale of a Red Cap (Skazka o krasnoi shapochke)

Vladimir Mayakovsky

Vladimir Mayakovsky (1893–1930) was a Russian and Soviet poet, playwright, painter, and actor. He is one of the foremost representatives of the Russian Futurist movement. The poet would eventually define his work as "Communist Futurism." With his Futurist collaborators Mayakovsky produced propaganda posters for the Russian State Telegraph Agency. In the 1920s Mayakovsky became increasingly disillusioned with the path the Soviet Union was taking under Joseph Stalin, a regime that no longer appreciated the experimental art of the avant-garde. In 1930 the poet allegedly shot himself. After his death Stalin ensured Mayakovsky's canonization by proclaiming him "the best and most talented poet of our Soviet epoch."[25] Mayakovsky had a major impact on Russian and Soviet literature both before and after the Russian Revolution. Despite his short career, he is widely considered to be one of the pioneers of modern poetry.

"The Tale of a Red Cap" was the first of Mayakovsky's political *skazki* (fairy tales). Published for the first time in 1917, it probably dates from the period between the February and October revolutions. The poem begins with the traditional fairy-tale incipit "Zhil da byl" (Once upon a time). The tale contains the type of language—for example, hyperbole and diminutives[26]—that characterizes children's stories, and it addresses "kids" directly in the final line. Like many texts written for children in Russia in the early twentieth century, however, this story was also targeted at adults. Mayakovsky makes this clear in the original publication by ironically dedicating the poem "to the flower of the intelligentsia."

"The Tale of a Red Cap" is one of thirteen poems included in *Dlia golosa* (translated in an English edition as *For the Voice*), published in Berlin in 1923 by the Russian State Publishing House, for propagandist purposes. As the title of the volume suggests, Mayakovsky hoped the poems would be read aloud, thus spreading the revolutionary content. In describing the various rhythms used in the poems of *For the Voice*, the translator Peter France refers to the rhythm of "The Tale of a Red Cap" as a "pseudo-naïve popular jingle."[27] *For the Voice* is widely recognized as one of the finest examples of Russian avant-garde bookmaking, a tradition of collaboration between poet and artist, in this case between two of the most important figures of Russian modernism. El Lissitzky (1890–1941) was a Russian artist, designer, and typographer with an avant-garde vision of book design and typography. He had published his own *skaz* (tale), *About 2 Squares*, in Russian in Berlin the preceding year. In the 1920s Soviet Union, very prominent avant-garde artists enthusiastically turned to children's book illustration. Mayakovsky and Lissitzky were among those who believed that creating works for children was an important part of their role as artists of the revolution. Art was put to the service of molding young people into the adults of the new revolutionary age.

Lissitzky is the "book constructor" of *For the Voice*, providing the book design, typographic images, and text arrangements for Mayakovsky's poems. Speaking of this book in his essay "Typographical Facts," Lissitzky compared the relationship between his work and the poems to that of a piano accompanying a violin.[28] The graphic designs Lissitzky conceived for each of the poems are ideograms that integrate the verbal and visual forms. He even attempts to find visual equivalents of Mayakovsky's verbal puns. The innovative format of the book includes a distinctive thumb index that displays visual symbols and shortened titles. *For the Voice* is printed in two colors, black and red, lending itself well to the classic tale.

"The Tale of a Red Cap" is presented on two facing pages (plate 6). On the verso, the protagonist is portrayed by an image of typecase elements (rules, furniture, and geometric shapes) that has a simplified representational form. Martha Scotford refers to the construction as a "scarecrow figure,"[29] which evokes Kurt Schwitters's innovative book *Die Scheuche*, published in Germany in 1925, a children's book that also experiments with typography. Although Mayakovsky's poem is generally published entirely in rhymed doublets, in *For the Voice* the first eight lines are grouped into a stanza, a format has been retained here. This format echoes the shift in the poem from the image of the intact hat to that of a hat in shreds. This is merely one element of the Cubist interplay between visual and verbal in the poem of this Cubo-Futurist. Juliette Stapanian-Apkarian has demonstrated how much of the tale seems to be spun from a Cubist propensity for visual puns and realized metaphors, including the vivid realization of the epithet "volki revoliutsii" (wolves of the revolution), the political meaning of the color red, and the poet's literal exposure of those who attempt to disguise their true colors. Mayakovksy's interest in sound, rhythm, wordplay, association, and the meaning of individual letterforms in the Cyrillic obviously makes him a difficult poet to translate, as Martha Scotford points out in her essay in MIT Press's three-volume work on *For the Voice*.[30] Mayakovsky's tragic take on the classic tale turns it into a political fable for a dual audience. Unlike the other Little Red Riding Hoods in this section, this one is presented as deserving of his fate.

The Tale of a Red Cap (1917)

Once upon a time there lived a Cadet,
this Cadet he wore a red cap on his head.
Apart from this cap, his inherited headdress,
The Cadet was completely untouched by redness.
If he heard revolution, the sound that he dreaded,

Straight away on his head his cap would be ready.
So they lived in clover, Cadet after Cadet,
from father to son, taking all they could get.

Then a big wind rose up and blew that Cadet,
and blew the red cap into shreds on his head.

And then he looked black, and the wolves they saw red,
The wolves of revolution, they grabbed the Cadet.

As everyone knows, those wolves don't eat bread:
they ate up the Cadet and his gaiters instead.

So if you play politics, kids, don't forget
this sad little story about the Cadet.

Contemporary Riding Hoods
Come of Age

I have to go to the woods, and I have to meet the wolf,
or else my life will never begin.

Clarissa Pinkola Estés, *Women Who Run with the Wolves*

I am Red Riding Hood.
I am my own mother, I am walking toward my grandmother.

Luisa Valenzuela, "Si esto es la vida, yo soy Caperucita Roja"

Red Hat and the Wolf (Rødhatten og Ulven)

FAM EKMAN

Fam Ekman (1946–) is one of Norway's best-known picturebook artists. It is widely felt that her picturebooks are for adults rather than children, but only one of her books has actually been published specifically for adults. All her books have wide adult appeal and have often been described as *allalderslitteratur* (all-ages literature) since the term (referring to crossover literature) was coined in Norway in the 1980s. In Norway her books have also become collectors' items for adult connoisseurs. Fairy-tale themes and motifs play an important role in her work. Her retelling of "Little Red Riding Hood" was published in 1985, relatively early in her career. In 2001 she offered a highly original recasting of "Cinderella" titled *Skoen* (Shoe).

The title of *Rødhatten og Ulven* (Red Hat and the Wolf) reveals Ekman's intention to subvert the classic tale, as Little Red Riding Hood is traditionally called "Rødhette" in Norwegian. The shift from a hood to a hat signals the gender reversal in her reversion. The author casts a male protagonist in the role of Little Red Riding Hood, and he wears a distinctive cone-shaped, bright red hat that has been interpreted by some as having sexual connotations.[1] The red hat contrasts with the white Pierrot-like costume that highlights his innocence. The gender change allowed the author to achieve both "distance" and "difference" from the familiar story, but she admits that there were probably also unknown subconscious reasons.[2] Although Ekman includes the more typically absent father, his diminutive stature—he is about one-third the size of the imposing, buxom mother—reflects his minimal role in the story. Rather than cautioning her naïve young son before he goes to the city to visit his grandmother, the mother is responsible for his straying from the path. In fact, his sexy, full-figured mother in the low-cut dress seems to prefigure the seductive she-wolf salesclerk in a red dress and heels who accosts the little boy in the ladies' dress store when he goes there at his mother's request. This modern retelling makes a playfully satiric comment on consumer society and the unrealistic demands some parents put on their children.

Ekman uses a variety of styles, layouts, and palettes in the book's innovative illustrations. The full-page illustrations on the recto of each spread, which range from black and white to monochromatic with touches of color to full color, are complemented by small black-and-white vignettes under the text on the verso. The full-page illustrations include single, framed full-color pictures as well as pages divided into two, three, or four frames. Modern elements are woven into a story that retains the atmosphere of the traditional tale. The setting receives some subtle Scandinavian touches: the bustling city center is modeled after Gothenburg, whereas the fancy restaurant where the wolf takes Red Hat for hot chocolate is inspired by the Teaterkafeen or Theatre Café in

10. *Rødhatten og Ulven*, by Fam Ekman. Copyright © 1985 J. W. Cappelens Forlag. Used by permission of Fam Ekman and Cappelen Damm.

Oslo. The illustrations fill the gaps in the text with a multitude of humorous details. In the ladies' dress shop, the tiny figure of Red Hat is incongruously out of place, surrounded by ladies' wear and large, half-dressed ladies, and conversing with a sexy salesclerk she-wolf in a red dress and heels. Ekman focuses on the seductive sexuality of the wolf in the red dress during their tête-à-tête later in the restaurant, where viewer's eyes, as well as those of Red Hat (who sits with his back to the reader, with only his red hat visible) are aimed at her provocative décolleté. In several full-color illustrations, Ekman plays with the motif of the seductive gaze, but it is particularly powerful in this scene, where Red Hat's eyes are not even visible and the wolf's eyes are closed in a kind of ecstatic reverie (plate 7). Although the she-wolf's cleavage did not seem to be problematic when the picturebook was published in Norway in 1985, it was this scene that prevented the airing of a television film based on the book.

The gender reversal of the main characters in Ekman's playful retelling is a reminder that little girls are not the only ones at risk from wolves, and that wolves come in both sexes. Despite his naïveté and small size, Red Hat succeeds in overcoming and even domesticating the wolf. The final illustration depicts him leading a transformed and reformed little wolf home on a leash like a well-behaved dog.

❦

RED HAT AND THE WOLF (1985)

Once upon a time there was a lovely day in the countryside. The birds sang and the wind made wonderful sounds in the trees, the smell of autumn and expectation filled the air.

In an old house lived a little boy.

This little boy always wore a red hat, and for that reason everybody called him Red Hat.

One day Red Hat said to his father and mother: "I think I'll go and see Grandma in town."

"Do that," the father and mother said. "And please buy me a dress while you're there," the mother added.

They gave him a basket filled with apples and cakes for the grandmother, and money to buy a dress.

Then Red Hat got on his way.

He walked and walked; he had to walk day and night for the town was very far away, and he walked day and night.

"I'm glad I didn't meet a wolf on my way," thought Red Hat.

It was fabulous to get to town. So much to see everywhere: cars and shops, dogs and children and flashing signs. And finally Red Hat found the dress shop in Grand Shopping Boulevard.

There were a tremendous number of dresses in that shop, but Red Hat got the assistance of a nice saleswoman, who even wanted to escort him to point out the road to the grandmother's house.

"This may become a delicious steak," thought the saleswoman.

"May I offer you a cup of hot chocolate with whipped cream?" she asked, after they had walked for a while. She pointed at an elegant restaurant.

This Red Hat couldn't resist.

They were eating and drinking and having such a great time that Red Hat almost forgot the time.

"Nice having a drink before the meal," the saleswoman-wolf[3] thought. She stood up and said: "Excuse me for a moment."

Red Hat waited and waited. But she never returned. At last the waiter came to present the bill.

And since Red Hat had no money left to pay, he had to do the dishes in the kitchen instead. Because that's the way it is when you can't pay your bills in restaurants. And it took many, many hours, as there were many, many plates to be washed.

In the meantime the wolf had run to the grandmother's, where she found her lying in her bathtub. It smelled of pine and lavender, and the sloshing of the water was pleasant. The wolf stared at the old lady washing her soft arms with a sponge.

Suddenly, the wolf threw itself on the grandmother, and in a few seconds it had eaten her all up. Afterward it put on her nightcap, lay down on her bed, and waited for Red Hat for dessert.

Late in the night Red Hat finished doing the dishes. He hung his apron on a hook, put on his hat, and was finally on his way to the grandmother's.

He crept up the stairs and carefully opened the door, which made a long, drawn-out creak.

"Hello, Grandma!" Red Hat whispered, and sank down on a chair near the grandmother's bed.

And when he saw that the grandmother was awake, he started telling her about all that had happened.

All of a sudden he stopped. "But Grandma, what big ears you have?" he said.

"All the better to hear you with," said the wolf.

"But what a big mouth you have?" said Red Hat.

"All the better to eat you with," said the wolf, and pushed the blanket aside.

Red Hat jumped up, and the wolf followed. Round and round the room they ran, into the dining room and out again, into the kitchen and back through the hall, until the wolf suddenly tripped and fell. When Red Hat saw how fat the wolf was and realized he had eaten the grandmother, he grasped a fruit knife and cut open its belly in a single incision!

And out came the grandmother!

Red Hat was terribly happy, and they hugged each other again and again!

Later they held a feast on everything that Red Hat had brought with him, in addition to various other things they found in the wolf's belly: Champagne, fine cheeses, and a shrimp salad.

And the next morning they sewed the wolf together again, and he came back to life, but much, much scrawnier because of all that got lost in the seams. Grandma made him a nice ribbon, and waved farewell to Red Hat, and they started on their way home. And the little good wolf carried the dress box all the way.

Red Red Red Riding Hood (Rood Rood Roodkapje)

EDWARD VAN DE VENDEL AND ISABELLE VANDENABEELE

The Dutch author Edward van de Vendel (1964–) gave up teaching in 2001 to devote himself full time to writing. His works, which have received many awards, include novels, poetry for both children and adults, picturebook texts, and song lyrics. In 2004 the picturebook *Rood Rood Roodkapje* (Red Red Red Riding Hood), which was published in 2003 by the publisher De Eenhoorn in Belgium, was awarded a Vlag & Wimpel (Flag and Pennant) from the Griffeljury (Pencil Jury) for its text and a Zilveren Penseel (Silver Brush) for its illustrations by the Flemish illustrator Isabelle Vandenabeele (1972–). Vandenabeele completed all the artwork before the publishing house asked Van de Vendel to write the text. Three years later the author collaborated again in the same manner with Vandenabeele on the picturebook *Een griezelmeisje* (A Creepy Little Girl), also published by De Eenhoorn. Vandenabeele combines traditional lithography and woodcuts with digital techniques in her distinctive illustrations. *Rood Rood Roodkapje* is a story told in three colors—red gray, and black—with all their symbolic meanings (plate 8). This Riding Hood loves the color red, and all her wishes are red, but her days are gray, as she takes a gray path through a gray forest to a gray grandmother, until the day she encounters a big, black danger. The story begins with the traditional fairy-tale incipit, but immediately deviates from the classic tale.

Vandenabeele's visual recasting of "Little Red Riding Hood" is somewhat reminiscent of *Ulvehunger* (Wolfhunger), published by the Norwegian picturebook artist Elise Fagerli in 1995. The two books use strikingly dramatic woodcuts in black and white with eye-catching touches of red. Fagerli's tale, too, opens in a conventional manner but deviates radically, portraying a Riding Hood who eats the wolf as well as her grandmother. Both books present very determined little girls whose surprising actions are all the more powerful for being depicted in simple, rather rough woodcuts that suggest a horror-like atmosphere. The woodcuts of these contemporary female illustrators seem to converse with Gustave Doré's powerful nineteenth-century engravings, which had such a profound and lasting influence on later illustrators of the tale. Their rather homely, willful heroines can certainly not be accused of having any seductive charm or beauty. In the climactic spread of the slaying, the little girl appears exactly as she does on the cover, in an impassive, pensive stance, with her hands behind her back and her head tilted, but she now holds a bloody axe, as blood fills her grandmother's doorway and flows out into a pool on the ground beside her. The brief text in small letters beside the axe—a conjunction and an onomatopoeia ("but: chop.")—contrasts with the enormous type of the terrifying wolf sounds on the preceding pages and suggests the calm, quiet, but deadly efficiency of the little girl. The final,

11. *Rood Rood Roodkapje*, by Edward van de Vendel and Isabelle Vandenabeele. Copyright © 2003 by Uitgeverij De Eenhoorn. Used by permission of Uitgeverij De Eenhoorn.

rather ambiguous spread depicts the little girl standing in a blood-red room littered with toys, including a small black stuffed wolf, and staring at the enormous black wolf skin that covers most of the floor, as she dreams of doing red things.

RED RED RED RIDING HOOD (2003)

Once upon a time there was a little girl with small wishes. She didn't want much. She wanted nice red clothes to wear. She wanted to play marbles with little red marbles. She wanted red cabbage and beets—no, she didn't, but she did want tomato sauce and berry juice. She wanted a red carpet, she wanted red cushions on her bed. That was all she wanted, because red made her happy. Red made her laugh. With an open red mouth, with a red tongue and red lips.

When she was allowed to choose her own name, she took the most beautiful one that she could think of. She shouted it through the house, in the garden, on the path, across the whole forest: "Red!" she shouted, "Red Red Red Riding Hood!"

Her small wishes were red. But the long hours of the day were gray. In those hours there was no place for little marbles or redcurrants, mushrooms, or red gaiety. Instead, she had to walk through the forest, along gray, muddy paths. Instead, she had to visit her gray grandmother. Alone.

Grandma was lying in her bed, waiting for a visit, and she always thought that Red Riding Hood was late, far too late. That Red Riding Hood's little basket of goodies should have been fuller. That the goodies in her full little basket should have been more delicious. That the little basket full of delicious snacks should not have been a little but a big basket. Full.

At times, this made Red Riding Hood sigh. "Don't sigh," Grandma then said. "The only one who is allowed to sigh here is me. I am ill." And when Grandma said that, Red Riding Hood saw how everything about Grandma was grayer. Not only Grandma's hair, but also her skin, her cheeks, the things she said, the things she thought. The lint on the blanket, the flowers on the wallpaper, the boards on the floor.

But:

"Just get going," her mother said every day. "Grandma is ill and she loves you, and I don't have time and you never know when it will be the last time. Hup."

The last time? thought Red Riding Hood. So far, it had never been the last time. She set off once more. Alone, as always. Mom here, Grandma there, and the forest in between. She was thinking such things as she walked through the woods. Full little baskets are also heavy little baskets. She had thought of all these things before. She couldn't help it. If you often do the same things, you also start to think the same things. Red are the berries that pop. Red is your hood free in the air. But she shouldn't think about these things now. She shouldn't do that.

Suddenly she stopped. Listen—did she hear breaking branches? Sniffing? Trampling paws?

Yes, she heard strange noises, she smelled a different odor. Silence again, it came closer. What would she see, what would it be? Something new? Something for the first time?

A big beast. And black! Not gray, not red, but black. A wolf.

A wolf, with his jaws forward, with his black nose, his pitch-black nostrils close to Red Riding Hood's red cheeks. She saw his open black jaws, his black tongue, his curled black lips . . .

No! thought Red Riding Hood, and no! she shook her head. No, no, no, no, no, no, no, no, no, no, no, no, no, no, no, no. Louder and louder, wilder and wilder. Her cap almost fell to the ground. No, no, no, no, no, no, no. Red Riding Hood said it out loud now: "No! No! No! No! No!"

The wolf was startled and stepped back. Red is saying no, thought Red Riding Hood. And then she said something else. She said: "Now I have to go. On my own. As always. My grandma is waiting for a visit."

The wolf cocked his black wolf's head. Red Red Red Riding Hood stepped aside. She pointed to where she had to go. She was startled—did she show the wolf the way?

The wolf knew the way himself. His nose knew the way. Down the path, straight ahead, straight ahead, up to the little house, the door smashed open, then through the kitchen and the room, up to the bed and grrrowlsnarrrlrrroarrrgrrrowwwwwwww.

Red Riding Hood began to run. Her full little basket was still as heavy, but she did not feel it. She ran down the path, straight ahead, straight ahead, up to the little house, the door . . .

she panted, with an open red mouth, and a red tongue and red cheeks . . .

inside there was also panting. She opened the door, very softly. She put her little basket in the kitchen, the heavy basket, full, with all kinds of heavy things. She walked through the kitchen, into the room, up to the bed and . . .

no,
no
grrrowl
snarrrl
rrroarrr
grrrowwwwwwww,

but: chop.

Today, thought Red Riding Hood, it had been the last time after all. Now she would never again have to go alone along the gray, muddy paths through the forest. Could she go and do red things? Just like that? Red is all kinds of things, she thought, red are new wishes, new toys, a new carpet. And what did she really think of black?

The Little Girl Who Knew How to Fly
(La petite fille qui savait voler)

Bruno de La Salle

The author and storyteller Bruno de La Salle (1943–) is responsible for initiating a revival of the tale and oral literature in France. He is the director of CLiO, the Contemporary Conservatory of Oral Literature, which he founded to promote such works. In his eyes oral literature meets the cultural needs of our society, and is the poetic art of the future. For more than thirty years, the storyteller has been exploring new forms of narration and initiating a new generation of storytellers. "Little Red Riding Hood" was the first tale La Salle recalled when he decided to become a storyteller. It has been part of his repertoire since 1969, when he began experimenting with a form of contemporary oral literature called "narration musicalisée" (musicalized narration). He produced two such works, which are transposed versions of the famous fairy tale. In 1986 he also published a picturebook, illustrated by Laurence Batigne, which draws from various oral versions of the tale. A rendition of "Le Petit Chaperon Rouge" figures among the favorite tales La Salle included in *Le Conteur amoureux* (The Enamored Storyteller), a reflection on the art of the tale and storytelling published in 1994. It bears a striking resemblance to "La petite fille qui savait voler" (The Little Girl Who Knew How to Fly), which appeared two years later in the collection *La pêche de vigne et autres contes* (Bush Peach and Other Tales). For La Salle, the retelling of a tale, especially this particular tale, is a never-ending process.

Drawing from the wealth of documents and versions now available, including those of Paul Delarue, La Salle set out to reconstruct personal versions of the most famous tales. While he felt it was necessary to transpose these tales into the contemporary world, he also recognized the danger of destroying their fragile symbolic meanings. La Salle brings to this highly original retelling of "Little Red Riding Hood" fragments from literary versions— both Perrault's and the Grimms'—and diverse oral versions, of which the best-known is "The Story of Grandmother." These are blended with ancient mythologies and cosmic rites symbolizing natural cycles as well as elements from contemporary culture to create a multilayered, timeless tale. He introduces the highly unexpected notion of a flying girl and a form of magic more in keeping with tales of the Orient, where much of this story is situated. The author even manages to turn the familiar fairy tale into an etiological tale or origin story in the closing lines. There is no direct reference to the classic tale until the meeting of the little girl and the wolf, when they assume the roles of the fairy-tale characters in a rather postmodern metafictive scene. Archaic expressions, ritualistic formulas, and traditional structures are retained, although they are often given an unusual twist or treated playfully. Traditional

12. "La petite fille qui savait voler," from *La pêche de vigne et autres contes,* by Bruno de la Salle. Illustrations by Catherine Rebeyrol. Copyright © 1996 L'École des loisirs. Used by permission of L'École des loisirs.

motifs, themes, characters, and events are humorously updated. While drawing from ancient sources, La Salle brings to his retelling the techniques of postmodernism and contemporary issues of war, oppression, and greed.

La Salle's innovative retelling is strongly marked by his experimentation as a storyteller in the contemporary tradition of the art. In retelling well-known tales such as "Little Red Riding Hood," he seeks particularly to restore by means of the written word the "oral music" they had often lost.[4] Readers are immediately struck by the musical, poetic, and theatrical language of his retellings. This results in a unique, written "oral" style. La Salle's story is illustrated by Catherine Rebeyrol (1939–), a French illustrator, painter, and costume designer. The ten small, simple, black-and-white illustrations punctuate the text without disrupting the storyteller's voice. With the exception of only one full-page illustration at the beginning— which portrays the heroine happily flying over a beautiful landscape on her way to her grandmother's faraway land—the small illustrations are embedded in the text. Like the author, the illustrator draws from various sources. The man-wolf is depicted initially as a well-dressed man in a suit, later as an anthropomorphic animal, and finally as a realistic animal. La Salle's retelling is at once a cautionary tale in the tradition of Perrault, presenting a wolf whose behavior is disturbingly like that of a pedophile, and an initiatory tale that is strongly influenced by the oral tradition. In this initiatory tale La Salle portrays a clever, enterprising heroine who, as in most oral versions, escapes thanks to her resourcefulness.

The Little Girl Who Knew How to Fly (1996)

Once upon a time there was a little girl who knew how to fly . . .

She had a grandmother who lived very far away, in Asia, in a wonderful garden so peaceful that neither you nor I know where it is.

As her parents both worked and could not look after her, they decided to send her to her grandmother's.

As it was a very long journey, they gave her all that was best to eat in the fridge: a cold chicken, some blueberry yogurts, and a large bottle of Coca-Cola.

The next morning, before her departure, they told her:

"Hurry up, don't delay, try to arrive before the sun sets because the night is full of unknown animals with which you would not know how to behave."

But the little girl had already flown off without listening to them. Already she was only a little white dot that was going off to meet the rising sun.

She passed over a thousand mountains, a thousand valleys, a thousand lakes. She arrived above the sea about noon, and as it was very hot and she was very thirsty, she descended to land on a small, shiny, gray island. She ate her cold chicken and her blueberry yogurts, drank her bottle of Coca-Cola, and went to sleep in the sun.

When the secret submarine discovered there was a little girl all pink on his back, he began to turn red with shame, to turn blue, to turn green, and plunged to the depths of the abyss that he should never have left.

The little girl remained clinging to her empty bottle of Coca-Cola as if it were a lifebuoy. Dolphins that had hidden behind the waves burst out laughing on seeing her, jumped over her face, and splashed her with their tails. When they saw that she did not know how to swim, they approached her and taught her so quickly to move in the water that soon she could go with them to the depths of the sea.

Suddenly, the little girl noticed that the sun was already down to five o'clock. Quickly, she took the two edges of her dress and flew away in the direction of her grandmother's country.

She arrived above a red river that she did not know and over which a little bright-green bird wandered. She came down from the clouds to ask her way, but no sooner had the bird seen her than he disappeared and reappeared a little farther on with a cry that was like a laugh and reverberated along the cliffs and monuments that bordered the river. In an instant she caught up with him, but in a half-instant he disappeared again and reappeared a little farther on with a cry that was like a laugh and reverberated along the cliffs and monuments that bordered the river. She followed it thus along the river; they crossed a lake inhabited by frogs that jumped in their way and pink flamingoes that flew off in squadrons.

They arrived thus on the white, pointed peak of the highest mountain of the continent. Then the little girl held out her hand for the bird to come and rest there. But she saw on the other side of the mountain the black night that was preparing to cross. She took the two edges of her dress and flew away as quickly as she could in the direction of her grandmother's country.

But the long hair of the night, the long hands of the night, the long folds of the dress of the night caught hold of her and began to whirl round. They closed her eyes and ears, knocked her over, turned her every which way, and threw her in a swamp. She woke in the dark and began to walk through the dead trees to a beach.

She finally arrived in a nocturnal city, all illuminated, full of bright stores, neon lights, loud music, colored drinks, people who jostled each other and jostled her without seeing her. She stood behind a tree, against the flow of strollers, and cowered.

A man who limped a little and who had a nice, child's face came up to her and asked if she wasn't cold in such a light dress. The little girl replied:

"Yes."

"Perhaps you would like to drink a hot chocolate in the pastry shop opposite?"

"Yes."

13. "La petite fille qui savait voler," from *La pêche de vigne et autres contes*, by Bruno de la Salle. Illustrations by Catherine Rebeyrol. Copyright © 1996 L'École des loisirs. Used by permission of L'École des loisirs.

She drank one hot chocolate, two hot chocolates, three hot chocolates. She ate some cream puffs, some rum babas, some chocolate éclairs. As soon as she turned her eyes toward a cake, the man clapped his hands and the cake was on her plate. So she turned her eyes to every corner of the room and ate all the cakes in the pastry shop.

She was so pretty with her beautiful, crumpled dress, her muddy little shoes, her hair down, her laughing eyes and mouth, that he wanted to laugh too or cry, to take her hand, to touch her, but he could not manage it.

Then he begins to shake from head to toe, and to swell. His face becomes green and black, and pointed like that of an animal. Quickly, he lowers his eyes below the table and regains his nice, child's face, and the little girl does not notice anything as she is so busy eating.

He asked her name. She said for fun:

"I am Little Red Riding Hood."

So, to show that he also knew the story, he said:

"Then I am the Big Bad Wolf."

And they both laughed.

She told him how beautiful it was in her grandmother's country and explained how to go there.

He proposed:

"Let's race and see who gets there first!"

And the little girl said to herself: "He looks so old that I am sure to win." And she accepted . . .

But she had played so much during the day, drunk so many hot chocolates, eaten so many cakes, that she fell asleep on the table. Then, the man got up on tiptoe without waking her. He went out by the back door, turned off the electricity, and locked the door. Then he took away all the noise, all the light, all the poisons that shone in the city, all the shouting people, and he left.

But the farther he got from the city, the larger and darker and more frightening he became.

He walked all around the earth and looked, combed with his hands and with his feet in the grass and in the bushes of the world, for the grandmother's country.

He found it in the early morning; the sun had not yet risen. There was some mist on the river, the birds flew off into the sky for the first time, the smoke died out in the chimneys.

The country was so calm and so quiet that he wanted to laugh or smile, whisper or sing, and as he could not manage it, he begins to shake from head to toe.

His face becomes green and black, and pointed like that of an animal. He advances on tiptoe so as not to be noticed, but he is so heavy and so big that he crushes and breaks everything around him: the houses, trees, forests. The birds crying in the sky, the animals fleeing before him, he catches them with his hands like flies, and he hits them to silence them and he kills them. From his pockets fall knives that kill, poisons that spread over the fields and rivers, lies. The traces of his passage are large gulfs that fill with refugees. Behind him, everything is ash, grayness, and desert.

He goes to the grandmother's house; he makes himself very small, all gray, and knocks at the door. He says:

"Open up! I have news of your granddaughter."

The grandmother answers joyfully:

"Pull the bobbin and the latch will go up."

He pulled the bobbin and the latch went up, and he went in.

She received him in the dining room and had him sit in the best arm-chair opposite the television.

She was so pretty, so nice, this grandmother! She had a dress the same color as the curtains. On the window, there were birds pecking, and on the fireplace an aquarium with laughing fish.

She said to him:

"I'm going to make you a coffee!"

But scarcely had she turned her back to go to the kitchen but he jumped on her, cut her up in pieces like a butcher, and then started to devour her.

He could not swallow everything. He put the meat that he had not eaten on a plate, he collected the blood in a bowl, and he put all that on the kitchen table.

He went into the bedroom, put a wig on his head, a nightgown on his back, and then slipped into Grandmother's bed.

The next morning, the little girl woke up in the abandoned pastry shop. She took the two edges of her crumpled dress and flew in the direction of her grandmother's country.

She knocked at the door and, as you know, he told her:

"Pull the bobbin and the latch will go up."

She pulled the bobbin and the latch went up, and she went in. She said:

"Grandmama, why are there so many dead trees and so many burned fields? Why are there so many dead fish in the rivers and so many run-over animals on the road?"

He said to her:

"It's the snow that hit them!"

"Why are there so many wrecked cars and so many demolished houses? Why are there so many men and so many women, so many children who remain lying on the ground without ever getting up again?"

He said to her:

"It's the spring flowers that the wind threw on them."

She asked:

"Is there anything to eat?"

He said to her:

"There is something in the kitchen."

She went to the kitchen and she ate what he had left. The cat said to her:

"You are eating the blood of your grandmother! You are drinking the blood of your grandmother!"

She said:

"Grandmama! Do you hear what the cat is saying?"

He answers:

"Don't listen to him! He is crazy! Come here instead!"

The little girl went into the bedroom; he said to her:

"Take off your shoes!"

The little girl took off her shoes and asked where she should put them. He said to her:

"Throw them in the fire; you won't be needing them anymore."

She was very surprised, but she threw them in the fire.

He said to her:

"Take off your dress!"

She took off her dress and asked him where she should store it. He said to her:

"Throw it in the fire; you won't be needing it anymore either."

She was even more surprised, but she threw it in the fire.

He said to her:

"Take off your chemise and throw it in the fire; you won't be needing it anymore!"

The little girl was again surprised, but she did what he asked.

Then, he said:

"Come, come get close to me, you will warm me up, I am very cold!"

The little girl got into the bed as he had said.

"Grandmama!" she cried, "what big feet you have!"

"It's because I've walked too much!"

"Grandmama! What big hands you have!"

"It's because I've worked too much!"

"Grandmama!" she was going to cry again on discovering how big everything about her grandmother was, but she said nothing at all. She understood that it wasn't her grandmother. She tried to think of an escape plan that he could not refuse. And she got it: She asked his permission to go very quickly to the toilet.

He had been disgusted and could not refuse her, and he even hurried to grant her request, but he attached a string to her ankle so she couldn't escape. The little girl fled to the toilet; she locked herself in with a double lock, attached the string to the toilet handle, and escaped by the little window above.

She ran to the bottom of the hill; she went into the forest where her godfather was hidden with many of the inhabitants of her grandmother's country who wanted to defend themselves against the invader. She told them what the man with the child's face was like, where he was, and how they had to catch him.

But the other one, in the bed, became impatient.

He pulls the string, he hears the sound of the flush, and he tells himself: "Good! She's coming!" Then he bites the pillow; he swallows all the feathers. He splays his toes. But as she does not come, he pulls a second time on the string; he hears the sound of the flush, and he says to himself: "Good! She's coming this time!" And he tries out the mattress springs; he jumps from the ceiling to the floor. And as she is still not coming, he pulls again a third time on the string, and he doesn't hear the sound of the flush as the tank was now completely empty. So he jumped out of bed, broke down the door, and saw the deception.

He had become large and dark and frightening again as he really was. He was going to leave the house, when the little girl's godfather arrived with all his supporters behind him, and the giant retreated.

He should not have retreated. The godfather raised a large axe and he opened his belly, from his throat to his orifice. And everything that villainous monster had devoured for years fell to the ground.

There were fields of wheat, fields worked by people who had been expelled. There were fields of rice that flooding had submerged. There were vegetable gardens overrun by weeds, there were factories that were now rusted. And there were so many things that could have remained beautiful if he had not devoured them!

There was also the grandmother, all alive, all bright. She had been transformed, younger, taller, lovelier, and it was a joy to see her thus.

She cried:

"Oh, it was dark in that belly! It was even darker than in the deepest woods!"

The monster had fallen to the ground, and he had fainted. They slipped tons and tons of salt into his belly.

When at last he woke, he was thirsty. He said to himself: "Oh, that grandmother was salty!" And he went to drink at the river. He swallowed almost all of it. His thirst was unquenchable. But his belly became heavy, so heavy that it hung to the ground. He bent down again to drink, and this time he fell into the river. It pushed him ahead of it, rolled him like a big stone, manhandled him to the sea.

In memory of this story, the sea became salty.

Little Red Riding Hood in Central Park
(Caperucita en Central Park)

CARMEN MARTÍN GAITE

The internationally acclaimed Spanish author Carmen Martín Gaite (1925–2000) was the first woman to win Spain's Premio Nacional de Literatura in 1978, for her adult novel *El cuarto de atrás* (translated in an English edition as *The Back Room*). Although most of her writing was published for adults, she resisted attempts to draw clear boundaries between children's and adult fiction. Her fairy-tale novel *Caperucita en Manhattan* (Little Red Riding Hood in Manhattan, 1990) was one of the most successful books the publishing house Siruela issued in their series "Las tres edades" (The Three Ages), for readers "from eight to eighty-eight." Rereading Perrault's tales for her translation of French fairy tales, published in 1980, had a marked influence on Martín Gaite's writing. All three of her books published for a young audience are fairy tales, and a volume of essays from the same period, *El cuento de nunca acabar* (The Never-Ending Tale, 1983), contains chapters inspired by Perrault's tales.

Caperucita en Manhattan enjoyed a great deal of success in the languages into which it was translated, but unfortunately English was not one of them. The lack of an English translation is particularly surprising, since the Spanish author got her inspiration for the novel and wrote it while she was in New York City as a visiting lecturer at Barnard College in 1985. Martín Gaite dedicated *Caperucita en Manhattan* to her friend, Juan Carlos Eguillor, who visited her in New York following the death of her daughter. He had tried to divert her painful thoughts by showing her his drawings of a Little Red Riding Hood–like figure flying above the skyscrapers from Brooklyn to Manhattan, and encouraged her to write a text for his comics. The author had hoped Eguillor would illustrate the novel (he had already illustrated her first, prize-winning children's book), but when he was unavailable, she decided to illustrate it herself with thirteen simple, childlike black-and-white drawings, one for each chapter.

The novel's cover illustration is Norman Rockwell's familiar *Statue of Liberty*, which appeared on the cover of the *Saturday Evening Post* in July 1946. The iconic statue plays an important physical and symbolic role in Martín Gaite's retelling, which presents an independent Little Red Riding Hood in search of freedom in Manhattan. The author transposes the classic tale to a very specific contemporary urban setting that evokes many New York City locations and landmarks. The protagonist, Sara Allen, lives with her mother and father on the fourteenth floor of a rather ugly apartment block in Brooklyn, while her unconventional, free-spirited grandmother, a former music-hall singer who has had several husbands and lovers, resides in Morningside. Weekly, Sara and her mother take the Brooklyn-Battery Tunnel to visit the

14. *Caperucita en Manhattan*, by Carmen Martín Gaite. Copyright © 1990 Ediciones Siruela. Used by permission of Ediciones Siruela.

grandmother, taking her the ritual strawberry cake, whose recipe has been in the family for generations. The encounter with the wolf, a millionaire businessman by the name of Edgar Woolf, takes place in Central Park. His cake empire, The Sweet Woolf, or El Dulce Lobo, is housed in a forty-story, cake-shaped skyscraper reminiscent of the Empire State Building. Despite the realistic setting and everyday world in which the story is set, fantasy and imagination play an essential role in this modern fairy tale. Martín Gaite has created an oneiric novel with magical realism overtones, in which the boundaries between dream and reality are blurred.

Perrault's version of the tale constitutes the hypotext of *Caperucita en Manhattan*, but it is also embedded in the novel, and there are numerous direct allusions to it throughout. Sara's *Little Red Riding Hood* book is one of her most cherished possessions, and it constitutes a benchmark for all aspects of her life. The protagonist and the author see the tale in a new light, in keeping with the theme of freedom that is the underlying message of all Martín Gaite's fiction. The tale is a story of freedom for Sara, as Little Red Riding Hood went to her grandmother's alone and not accompanied by her mother. A drawing portrays the protagonist—who goes to her grandmother's, rain or shine—in a red rubber raincoat with a hood; she is carrying a basket with the customary strawberry cake and holding the hand of the mother, whose fears about the dangers lurking in the city streets are illustrated by a thought bubble containing the dark silhouettes of two armed thugs. A subsequent drawing depicts this modern-day Little Red Riding Hood the day she finally makes the trip on her own: the happy heroine skips merrily in front of the Manhattan skyline, pronouncing, in a speech bubble, the English words "I'm free."

Martín Gaite set out with the intention of correcting Perrault's tale, with its passive heroine and tragic ending. In her mind the Grimms' happy ending did not offer a suitable alternative, being merely "a band-aid solution."[5] The Spanish retelling presents a modern fairy-tale heroine who takes charge of her own destiny, as well as those of her grandmother and the wolf, in what is also an adventure novel. The modern fairy-tale-cum-adventure-novel is also an initiatory tale: the tenth birthday of this clever, active Little Red Riding Hood marks the beginning of an initiatory journey during which she overcomes her fear, befriends the wolf, and saves her grandmother from loneliness. Martín Gaite appropriates the classic tale to examine the passage from childhood to adulthood, focusing on the difficult period of early adolescence. To the traditional cast of female characters, the author adds Miss Lunatic, a charmingly eccentric, fairy godmother–like figure, who lives in the Statue of Liberty and roams the city streets by day as a bag lady. She can be seen as a double of Sara's highly unusual grandmother, with whom she shares the role of wise woman and mentor. Unlike Sara's cautious and overly protective mother, Miss Lunatic encourages this Riding Hood to take a nocturnal stroll through Central Park, despite the fact that a legendary Jack-the-Ripper-type serial killer is still at large.

Chapter 11, "Caperucita en Central Park," is the most important chapter in the 205-page novel. It recounts the crucial encounter with the wolf, which, in this retelling, has been transposed toward the end of the story. Sara reacts to Edgar Woolf as she does to the wolf in her favorite picture from the beloved *Little Red Riding Hood* book, the one depicting the meeting in the woods. In the second chapter of the novel, Sara admits that, despite her knowledge of the tale's tragic ending, she identifies completely with Little Red Riding Hood, who smiles trustingly at the friendly looking wolf. Convinced that such a nice-looking wolf could never eat anyone, she pronounces the ending of the classic fairy tale all wrong. Martín Gaite's own drawing at the end of the chapter depicts her modern Little Red Riding Hood strolling through Central Park hand-in-hand with the affable and charming Edgar Woolf, who gallantly carries her basket. This reversion corrects the ending that Sara, like the author, considered so wrong. The clever, enterprising Sara is the agent of a classic fairy-tale happy ending for her grandmother and the wolf. The ending remains open with regard to the heroine herself, however. Readers are left to imagine for themselves what becomes of this Little Red Riding Hood when she leaves the happy couple dancing in each other's arms and makes her way in darkness back to the Statue of Liberty.

LITTLE RED RIDING HOOD IN CENTRAL PARK (1990)

Sara found herself alone under the large trees of Central Park; she had been walking for a time, absorbed in her thoughts, having lost track of time, and was beginning to get tired. She saw a bench and sat down, putting beside her the basket containing the strawberry cake. Although there was no one around and it was quite dark, she wasn't afraid. But she was filled with emotion. She felt a slight dizziness like when you get out of bed after a bad fever. The meeting with Miss Lunatic had left her with a feeling of unreality similar to what she had experienced when she had been sick, on learning that she would never meet Aurelio.[6] But it wasn't the same thing, because not only had she met Miss Lunatic, but she had recognized behind her beggar's disguise the face of Freedom in person. And she had shared with her this great secret that united them: "To whom you tell your secret, you give your liberty." That was all so beautiful! She had seen her face, her hands, and her voice transform! Or was it a dream? Everything that had happened to Alice had never existed. But what is the border between truth and lies?

She drew the little purse from her bosom and began to caress the greenish coin. No, it wasn't a dream. And a lot of other adventures would happen to her. Miss Lunatic had told her: "Don't ever look back." She was determined to obey, to always follow her path without getting lost in the details.

She was so absorbed by these memories and her musings that, when she heard steps in the underbrush behind her, she thought that it was the noise of the wind in the branches or the scampering of one of the numerous squirrels she had seen since she entered the wood.

Therefore, when she discovered the black shoes of a man standing in front of her, she was a little afraid. All the more so because the vampire of the Bronx still was at large, as Miss Lunatic herself had confirmed. And it was quite possible that, tired of not finding a victim in Morningside Park, he had decided to transfer his field of operation to another neighborhood.

However, her fright dissipated in part when she raised her eyes to look at him. He was a well-dressed man, with a gray hat and kid gloves, who did not look at all like a killer. It is true that at the movies sometimes these are the worst. Further, he wasn't saying anything, and he was barely moving. Only the nostrils of his pointed nose dilated as if they smelled something, which gave him the look of an animal on the prowl. His look inspired confidence; it was obviously that of a sad and lonely man. Suddenly he smiled. And Sara smiled back.

"What are you doing here all alone, beautiful child?" he asked politely. "Are you waiting for someone?"

"No, nobody. I was simply thinking."

"What a coincidence!" he exclaimed. "Yesterday, more or less at the same time, I met someone here who gave me the same answer as you. Doesn't that seem strange?"

"Not to me. People think a lot, and when they are alone, even more."

"Do you live in this neighborhood?" asked the man, while taking off his gloves.

"No, I don't have that good fortune. My grandmother says that it is the most beautiful neighborhood in Manhattan. I am going to see her and take her a strawberry cake that my mother made."

Suddenly the image of her grandmother waiting for her, perhaps with some dinner prepared and reading a detective novel, seemed so pleasant and welcoming to her that she stood up. She had so many things to tell her that they could talk without looking at the clock until they fell asleep. It was going to be so amusing! Obviously, she could not talk about the transformation of Miss Lunatic into Madame Bartholdi, because that was a secret. But with all the rest, there was plenty of material for a very long tale!

She prepared to take her basket when she noticed that the man was advancing to do the same thing and reaching out a hand with a large gold ring on the index finger. She looked at him; he had lifted the basket up to his thin face, surrounded by red hair that stuck out below his hat. He was smelling the cake, and his eyes shone with triumphant greed.

"Strawberry cake! I thought that I smelled strawberry cake! It's in your basket, isn't it, my dear child?"

His voice was so beseeching and so anxious that Sara felt sorry for him, and she thought that he was hungry in spite of his distinguished look. Such strange things happened in Manhattan!

"Yes, it is inside. Do you want to taste it? My mother made it, and she makes it very well."

"Oh, yes, taste it! Nothing would give me greater pleasure. But what will your grandmother say?"

"I don't think it will bother her if I bring it partly eaten," answered Sara, sitting back down on the bench and lifting the checkered serviette. "I will tell her that I met . . . well, the wolf," she added, laughing, "and that he was very hungry."

She finished unwrapping the cake, taking off the silver paper, and the odor that it gave off was really excellent.

"That would not be lying," said the man, "because my name is Edgar Woolf. And as for hunger . . . Oh, good heavens, it is much more than hunger! It is ecstasy, dear child! I am going to be able to try it! How impatient I am!"

He took off his hat, fell onto his knees, and contemplated the cake in raptures, smelling its aroma with frenzy. The truth is that his attitude was beginning to appear somewhat troubling. But Sara remembered Miss Lunatic's recommendations, and she decided that she would not be afraid.

"Do you have a knife, Mr. Woolf?" she asked with complete calm. "And, if you don't mind, I would ask you to refrain from putting your nose into the cake. Why don't you sit down calmly here with me?"

Mr. Woolf obeyed in silence, but his hands trembled when he took out a knife with a mother-of-pearl handle that he carried, along with a bunch of keys, attached to a large chain. He cut a piece with an unsteady hand. And, managing to control himself and to put manners ahead of gluttony, he offered it to the girl with a delicate gesture.

"Here, you want some too. What do you think of this improvised picnic in Central Park? I can tell my chauffeur to bring us some Cokes."

"Thank you, Mr. Woolf, but I am a little sick of strawberry cake. And my grandmother is too. It's because my mother makes it often, too often."

"And it always turns out as good?" asked Mr. Woolf who, already without ceremony, had gobbled up the first piece of cake and was savoring it while rolling his eyes.

"Always," assured Sara, "it is a recipe that doesn't fail."

Then something unexpected happened. Without stopping his chewing or licking his lips, Mr. Woolf fell down on his knees again, but this time in front of Sara. He lowered his head on his chest and implored, beside himself . . .

"The recipe! The real one! The genuine one! I must have this recipe. Oh, please! Ask me whatever you want, whatever you want, in exchange. You must help me! You are going to help me, aren't you?"

Not used to having anyone need something from her, and even less so with such passion, Sara had a feeling of superiority for the first time in her life. But this feeling was immediately replaced by another, even stronger: a kind of pity, the desire to console this person who was in such a sorry state. Without realizing it, she began to caress his hair as if he were a child. It was very clean, very soft to touch, and gave off very peculiar copper reflections in the semi-light. Mr.

Woolf calmed himself, and his breathing, interrupted with sighs, became more rhythmical. After a moment, he lifted his head, and he was crying.

"Please, Mr. Woolf, why are you crying? You will see that everything works out."

"How good you are! That's why I am crying, because you are so good. Are you really going to help me?"

Sara got a little on her guard. Fleetingly, she remembered the vampire of the Bronx. It wasn't advisable to let herself be tricked either, without having clarified things.

"I can't promise you anything, Mr. Woolf," she said, "until I understand better what you are asking me for and if I can give it to you . . . and, of course, also what advantages there would be for me."

"Every advantage!" he exclaimed quickly. "Ask me whatever you want! No matter how difficult it seems to you! Whatever you want!"

"Whatever I want? Are you a magician?" asked Sara, wide-eyed.

Mr. Woolf smiled. When he smiled he appeared younger and more handsome.

"No, my dear. Your naïveté charms me. I am only an ordinary business-man, but immensely rich. Look, you see that roof terrace with all the colored fruits that light up?"

Sara climbed on the stone bench, and her eyes followed the direction indicated by Mr. Woolf's index finger with the gold ring.

Among all the neon advertisements that topped the tall buildings close to the park, this one especially caught the attention. Precisely at the moment Sara made it out, the final explosion was taking place, and a fantastic jet of gold seeds rose toward the sky from the interior of the fruits.

"Oh, how wonderful!" exclaimed Sara.

Mr. Woolf encircled her waist delicately and helped her down from the bench.

"What is your name, dear?" he asked, with a calm and protective tone.

"Sara Allen, sir, at your service."

"Well, that building is mine, Sara," said Mr. Woolf.

"Really, it's yours? And the fruit lights? Inside as well?"

"Yes, inside as well."

"Why are you laughing?"

Indeed, Mr. Woolf was smiling with amusement and satisfaction as he looked at the girl.

"With happiness. Because I am happy that you like it so much."

Sara's eyes shone with enthusiasm.

"How could I not like it? But the one who would be even more enchanted is my grandmother. I'm thinking about her. I know now what I'm going to ask for. Can I ask that you let her come to see it tomorrow? I mean also inside, and to take a brief look at the terrace, and better still that she be served a drink . . . Well, I don't know if it's asking too much. But this would make her completely happy. Will you grant it to me?"

"Naturally, I'll send someone to get her. But it is very little in comparison to what I am going to ask you in exchange. It is nothing. Ask me for something else. Something for you, something that you really dream about. Do you have some unsatisfied desire . . ."

Sara remained thoughtful. Mr. Woolf watched her with curiosity and admiration.

"Don't hurry me, please!" she said, "because then I can't concentrate. And don't make so much fun of me. I need a little time to think."

"I'm laughing because you are very charming. Who is hurrying you, miss? Think as long as want."

And Edgar Woolf noticed that, in effect, that permanent hurried feeling that tied him up in knots inside had disappeared, replaced by a strange, pleasant calm.

While Sara was pacing in front of him with her hands behind her back and her eyes closed, he sat on the bench and cut himself another thin slice of cake and tasted it more slowly. No, this time he wasn't mistaken. It was definite. But what was strange was the fact that he was enjoying eating it and being in the park with this girl. He remembered that yesterday, in that same clearing in the wood, he had encountered the strange beggar with the white hair who had talked to him about the power of magic. Suddenly he remembered with complete clarity her words, and felt a disturbing chill running down his back.

People who fear magic must continually find themselves at an impasse, Mr. Woolf, she had said. The person who claims to deny the inexplicable will discover nothing. Reality is a well of enigmas. Ask scholars if it is not so.

He closed his eyes. He was surprised to remember in so much detail. For a long time, perhaps since his youth, he had not experienced the pleasure of going over an idea with his eyes closed. On opening them, he saw Sara Allen's little red shoes, fitted over her little white socks, and with that little round button on the strap. She was stopped in front of him. He looked at her with affection, smiling. Greg Monroe[7] was right: because of his business, he had denied himself many satisfactions. Having a grandchild must be a very nice thing.

"I thought that you were not feeling well or something," she said in a worried voice.

"No, I was simply thinking, like you earlier."

"They must have been good thoughts."

"Yes, very good. And have you thought what you want to ask me for?"

After having replayed in her memory all the images contemplated that night, Sara had arrived at the conclusion that the most impressive was that of the woman's long leg with the crystal shoe appearing out of the door of the luxurious car. She cried triumphantly:

"Yes, I've thought of it! I want to arrive at my grandmother's riding in a limousine. Alone. With a chauffeur driving me."

"Granted!"

In a spontaneous impulse, Sara hugged Mr. Woolf, who was still sitting on the bench, and planted a kiss on his forehead. He turned a little red.

"Well, wait, don't get excited so quickly. I still haven't told you what I'm going to ask for in exchange."

Sara's heart sank. What gift could she give to such a rich man who had everything? For sure, she would lose her limousine ride. A wave of joy spread over her face therefore when she heard him ask:

"Would you be able to give me the recipe for this splendid cake?"

"Of course! Is that all? I don't know how to make the strawberry cake, but I know where the real recipe is kept. In my grandmother's house in Morningside."

"And she will want to give it to me?"

"Definitely, she's very nice. And even more so if you tell her that you're going to invite her to visit your building. Forgive me for using *tú*, when you are so rich."

"It doesn't matter, I like it. Besides, we have made a pact."

Sara was on the point of saying that it was the second that she had made that afternoon, but she stopped herself in time. It was a secret. Anyway, she had become a little thoughtful, considering that the recipe was also a secret, with a seal and everything. But it was such a stupid secret!

"What are you thinking about?" asked Mr. Woolf.

"Nothing. There is no problem. I think that I can convince my grandmother. Do you like to go dancing?"

Mr. Woolf gave her a disconcerted look.

"It has been some time since I danced, although I don't do the tango badly."

"It's a small drawback," said Sara. "My grandmother adores dancing. She was a well-known artist. Her name was Gloria Star."

"Gloria Star!" exclaimed Mr. Woolf, looking dreamy-eyed into space. "The person who claims to deny the inexplicable will not discover anything. How true that is!"

"I don't understand you well. You know her?" asked Sara, looking at him curiously.

"I heard her sing several times when I was a boy and lived in Fourteenth Street. It seems like a dream. Your grandmother was an extraordinary woman."

"She is still extraordinary," said Sara. "And besides, she is going to give you the recipe for the strawberry cake. Don't forget."

"All right. I am burning with impatience. Let's go, Sara. We must leave for your grandmother's house right away, each of us in a limousine, since you want to go alone, you said."

Getting up agilely from the bench on which he was sitting, he put on his hat and took Sara by the hand.

"But how? Do you have two limousines?" she asked when they began to walk.

"No, I have three."

"Three? Then . . . you are very rich! And each one with a chauffeur?"

"Yes, each one with a chauffeur. But walk more swiftly, dear. Give me the basket, so I can carry it. When I tell Greg Monroe that I am going to meet Gloria Star . . . He is not going to believe it. In addition, because of the strawberry cake," he added laughing, "he will say it's fantasies, delirium . . ."

"Who is Greg Monroe?"

Their voices and their silhouettes faded toward the path that led out of the wood. From time to time, Mr. Woolf bent toward the girl and one could hear, in the darkness of the foliage, the echo of their laughter, interrupted from time to time by the scampering of some squirrel that kept late hours. The weather had gotten milder.

The King of Cakes and Sara Allen, seen from the back
and holding hands, formed a striking and peculiar couple
as they went off into the distance.
It was enough to inflame
the envy of Mr. Clinton.[8]
Let's face it.

15. *Caperucita en Manhattan*, by Carmen Martín Gaite. Copyright © 1990 Ediciones Siruela. Used by permission of Ediciones Siruela.

My Wolf (Mon Loup)

ANNE BERTIER

The unique picturebooks by the French author-illustrator Anne Bertier (1956–) are intended for an audience of both adults and children. Her first picturebook project, *Un amour de triangle* (A Love Triangle), is a playful, poetic fantasy that tells a highly unusual love story about triangles, and is intended for readers of all ages. Although the book was originally conceived in color, Bertier ultimately redid the illustrations in black and white many years later for its publication with the innovative publishing house Grandir in 2001. In the intervening years, Bertier had brought out *Mon Loup* with the same publishing house, in the same small, square format. For her second book, published in 1995, the author-illustrator had wanted to deal again with the theme of love, but this time specifically with "the feeling of love."[9] The idea of Riding Hood and the

16. *Mon Loup*, by Anne Bertier. Copyright © 1995 Anne Bertier and Éditions Grandir. Used by permission of Anne Bertier and Éditions Grandir.

wolf came instantly to mind. The possessive adjective in the title suggests the intimate relationship between this Riding Hood and her wolf, as "mon loup" is a common expression of endearment meaning "my love" or "my pet." Although the author deals with the development of a romantic relationship, it is evoked in simple, even childish terms that are accessible to very young children. This Riding Hood, named Violette, is depicted as a small, childlike figure with a distinctive pointed hood and a basket.

Like Carmen Martín Gaite, Bertier set out to rewrite the classic version— this time the Grimms'—because of the unsatisfactory ending. She had always found the story as it had been told to her as a child to be "horrible and terribly unjust": she did not see why the "poor wolf" should be punished and "the disobedient Little Red Riding Hood" saved. In her retelling, "the wolf would be seduced" and would make people—girls and women in particular—dream rather than giving them nightmares. The wolf depicted in Bertier's striking black-and-white illustrations is not only well bred and charming, but also an elegant and graceful creature who resembles a male dancer. However, her charming wolf can, at times, become hateful and frightening. Then he takes on enormous proportions in the illustrations, towering menacingly over the small figure of the girl. The medium—stencils used to create the effect of cut silhouettes—was deliberately chosen for this book about the feeling of love because it could convey emotions through body language. Bertier's early experience studying in Sylvia Monfort's famous mime school also informs the illustrations. The simple black figures on a white background are surprisingly expressive and effective, telling a touching story about the ups and downs of relationships. The illustrator also studied dance for many years, and the scenes she depicts all seem to have been choreographed. The characters meet, play, quarrel, make up, express their love, and dance in the pages of this enchanting love story.

17. *Mon Loup*, by Anne Bertier. Copyright © 1995 Anne Bertier and Éditions Grandir. Used by permission of Anne Bertier and Éditions Grandir.

My Wolf (1995)

One day I met a wolf.

At first, I was on my guard. Well do I know
the story of Little Red Riding Hood . . .
So, I kept my distance.
After watching for a long time, I understood
that this wolf was quite respectable.
We began to play together
with a ball, with a skipping rope.
Sometimes, I don't know why,
that wolf became hateful.
He frightened me.
Pinched my flowers.
Or trampled on them.
Just look at that!
Then we no longer spoke to each other.
But the very next day,
"Ah! My Wolf . . ."
"Ah! My Violette . . ."
When I was sick he
looked after me.
And I brushed his ears
when they were dusty.
One evening, I discovered a letter,
hidden under my pillow.

Dear Violette
I have too gruff
a voice to tell you
this
"you are wonderful"
your wolf

Day after day my Wolf
gained confidence.
And last Monday he said to me:
"Violette, what nice feet you have!"
"The better to dance with, my Wolf."
"Violette, what a sweet voice you have!"
"The better to enchant you with, my Wolf."

18. *Mon Loup*, by Anne Bertier. Copyright © 1995 Anne Bertier and Éditions Grandir. Used by permission of Anne Bertier and Éditions Grandir.

"Violette, your hands are so beautiful!"
"The better to caress you with, my Wolf."
And while reciting those lovely compliments,
he devoured me with his eyes,
with his eyes only.
Can you imagine?
Such wolves are so rare,
I kept him.

He looks after me when I am sick.
I brush his ears
when they are too dirty
and the rest of the time we play
and sing "Let's go for a walk in the woods."

The Blinder Girl (Skylappjenta)

IRAM HAQ AND ENDRE SKANDFER

Born in Norway of Pakistani parents, Iram Haq (1976–) is an actress, film-maker, screenwriter, author, and recording artist. She made her debut as a director in 2009 with the short film *Skylappjenta*, which has been screened with the English title "Little Miss Eyeflap," although the literal translation would be "The Blinder Girl." Haq wrote, directed, and starred in the film, which is in Norwegian and her mother tongue of Urdu. It won several awards at international film festivals and made its North American debut, with English subtitles, at the Sundance Film Festival in 2010. The film's art director was Endre Skandfer (1976–), a Norwegian illustrator, filmmaker, and animator. After they worked together on the film, Haq asked Skandfer to collaborate on the book with her as well. She actually had the idea for the book prior to making the film, but it appeared later the same year. The story and the design were slightly altered for the picturebook, although there is still a strong resemblance to the film. Skandfer said there was nothing in the film's visuals that he could use directly in the illustrations.[10] The author and illustrator worked together closely on both text and visuals, trying to tell the story with as few words as possible. The picturebook was nominated for several awards, including the Norwegian culture ministry's debut award for 2009 and UPrisen 2009, an award for the best youth book that is voted on by young readers themselves, indicating its wide appeal with that audience (plate 9). While the reviewer Kjell Olaf Jensen considers *Skylappjenta* suitable for all age groups, another reviewer recommends the book for older children and adults who like picturebooks.[11] According to Skandfer, the film and the book were both made without much regard for a particular audience: "We aimed them at people who are in the process of growing up, I guess. And that could be any age, I think."[12]

Inspired by the Grimms' version, this story also features a heroine who wears a red cap or hat, but it is quite distinctive, as it has blinders or eye-flaps on the sides (plate 10). The blinders metaphor is developed throughout this coming-of-age story, and the headgear reflects the protagonist's initiatory journey. While the young girl eventually discards her hat, her traditional grandmother is depicted wearing a similar hat. Haq uses the tale of "Little Red Cap" to deal with the difficulties of growing up between two cultures, and there is a strong autobiographical element in her story. The author admits that she is "playing with the clichés about Norwegians and Pakistanis."[13] In Norway, Pakistanis constitute the largest immigrant group, second only to the Swedes. Although Haq does not refer explicitly to Pakistani culture in the book, the allusions are evident in both the text and the illustrations. The protagonist's facial features and her clothing are obviously Pakistani. The suffix "-istan" is retained to create the imaginary country of "Langvekkistan"

95

(Farawayistan), while the warm, sunny colors of Skandfer's first illustrations, especially the orange, are those of the South Asian subcontinent. The tale is transposed to a Norwegian setting of forests, waterfalls, and snow, although the country is never named. In the forest the Blinder Girl encounters Norman, whose name (spelled with a final double "n" in Norwegian) is very close to the word *Nordmann* (meaning a Norwegian person), thereby turning Norman into a personification of the entire race.

Not only does Norman combine many of the clichés associated with Norwegians, but he is also portrayed as Espen Askeladd (the Ash Lad), a major figure in many Norwegian folktales. The Ash Lad is often the youngest brother who manages to overcome obstacles and use his wits to succeed where all others fail, often winning the princess and part of a kingdom. He is portrayed as a blue-eyed, positive fellow wearing a backpack, as is Norman, who appears almost magically in the forest, and later turns up at the grandmother's door to rescue the Blinder Girl. The Ash Lad association becomes particularly clear in the passage where Norman does a *hallingkast*—that is, a Norwegian folk dance move, in which a fellow jumps up and plucks a hat from a stick held high in the air by a girl. The words Norman pronounces as he jumps—"Jeg fant, jeg fant" (I found, I found)—which are enigmatic to non-Norwegian readers, constitute one of the most recognized expressions from an Ash Lad tale. This Ash Lad is highly unconventional, however, as he is up to no good and even seems to play the part of a charming two-legged wolf. He offers the temptations of Norwegian society that are taboo in Pakistani Muslim culture. Norman is obviously interested in seducing the heroine (the multiplication of his large hands in one illustration effectively suggests groping), but he is not cast in the role of the wolf. Haq is playing with the conventions of the fairy tale. There is a pun in Norman's words when he tries to call the fleeing protagonist back, telling her they are living a fairy tale. Their adventure is clearly a modern fairy tale, but experiencing a fairy tale together means having a brief sexual relationship.

Haq skillfully integrates formulaic expressions from Norwegian folk and fairy tales into a very contemporary retelling. The symbolism in the text, as well as the expressions and clichés with which Haq plays, are echoed and extended in Skandfer's illustrations. The illustration of Norman as a lovesick country bumpkin holding a large, red beribboned heart at the grandmother's door is a literal interpretation of the Norwegian expression that means to openly be in love or to wear your feelings on your sleeve. A spectacular pyrotechnics display is the backdrop to the embracing couple when the Blinder Girl drops her cigarette and literally burns her bridges. A few of the images of the heroine surrounded by flowers and butterflies have an almost Disney-like feel, while her long, animated braids seem to announce those of Rapunzel in the 2010 film *Tangled*. The heroine herself, with her caricatural features and enormous eyes, looks like a character from a manga or an animated cartoon. The butterfly is a recurrent symbol of freedom, while the pages that depict the meeting of the Blinder Girl and Norman in the forest are filled with heart-shaped images. Champagne bubbles still float in the air as Norman grabs at her, but the bubble of happiness has burst. There is a skillful use of contrast between light and shadow and bright and dark colors to symbolize the protagonist's familiar, reassuring world and the threatening, unknown world that lies beyond. The Blinder Girl walks through a corridor of bright sunlight, looking straight ahead and seeing only the flowers and butterflies in her path, while on both sides of her dark scenes depict the dangers and temptations of the forest. These scenes are not mentioned in the text and may not be real, but they foreshadow the temptations presented by Norman. While the story can be read on a literal level, the symbolism is transparent, even for children.

In Haq's contemporary fairy tale, the role of the wolf is shared by the protagonist's Uncle Chacha and her grandmother, both made more menacing by the fact that their faces are never seen clearly (plate 11). When the Blinder Girl encounters her uncle in the woods, he is a menacing figure who, like the wolf in the award-winning version by the photographer Sara Moon, remains invisible in a dark vehicle with bright headlights. (In a subsequent image the vague shadow of the driver's face is partially visible, as is the symbolic name of the taxi company, "Respect.") It is a known and controversial fact that Pakistani taxi drivers in Oslo form an unofficial intelligence network that keeps track of the whereabouts of other Pakistanis, especially those of young Pakistani women. Uncle Chacha's presence brings darkness and chill into a warm, sunny day. The grandmother is first seen from behind as a large figure of ambiguous gender sitting on a trunk, casting a large, menacing, animal-like shadow on the wall. Although it is not expressed explicitly in the picturebook, the fate that the heroine of the film escapes is an arranged marriage. Toward the end of the book, the dark pages give way to a light and then completely white background that evokes the snow, but also the hope for the future. The Blinder Girl is depicted without her hat, and with her hair no longer restricted by braids but blowing free in the wind. The final image shows the hat lying in the snow; the protagonist has disappeared, leaving only tracks that lead toward the blurred city skyline in the distance. The book's open ending adopts a formulaic expression from Norwegian folktales—"And if he/she still has not found it, he/she is probably still looking"—modifying it slightly to suggest more optimistically that the Blinder Girl seems about to find what she is looking for.

Haq's retelling of "Little Red Riding Hood" blends fairy tale and reality to tell a poignant, contemporary story about a girl who shares two cultures without feeling at home in either. *Skylappjenta* is a topical book about puberty, adolescence, rebellion, and liberation set in a multicultural society. It explores the problematic reality of many children and young people not only in Norway but throughout many parts of the world. The author refrains from taking sides in the debate about whether it is best for immigrant girls to accept the traditional life of their family or to find a Norwegian boyfriend and integrate into Norwegian society. Her protagonist seems to reject both those options and to choose a path of independence.

THE BLINDER GIRL (2009)

Once upon a time there was a young girl who lived with her mother in the middle of a tall and dense forest. The forest was so full of threats and terrible temptations that the girl was never allowed to go outside. She had to water the delicate herbs that grew against the wall through the window. She was not even allowed to hang out the laundry. The girl did not tend to complain, but did as she was told and never argued. She got small, delicious glimpses of the big, wide world through the TV screen. Then the girl daydreamed. She really wanted to be part of the song and dance of the big world outside. There, she thought, people were free and playful and smiled every day.

One late spring evening the TV picture suddenly disappeared, and a snowstorm filled the screen. Then the girl snuck up on the roof. She wanted to try to adjust the satellite dish again. But when she got up there, she just stood and listened. From far away came alluring sounds. Cars honking and a woman laughing in the distance. Was it a pop song? Was there a disco going on? She stretched her neck and tried to see where the sound came from. She did not hear her mother's angry shouting.

She did not notice anything until her mother grabbed her thin wrists and dragged her back to the kitchen. The mother's words were strict and not to be misunderstood:

"Such curiosity can destroy even the purest soul for the rest of her life!"

Then the mother pulled a hat down over the girl's ears. Attached to it were two blinders, so that she could see and hear only what was right in front of her. The mother said that from now on she had to always wear this. That is how she became the Blinder Girl.

One day the Blinder Girl had cleaned the kitchen shelves as usual. She had polished all the tiny windows in the house, cooked food until it bubbled and simmered in countless pots, washed the floor spotlessly clean, and dusted every nook and corner. Suddenly the mother burst into the kitchen and told her that the grandmother was sick. The Blinder Girl had to immediately take a basket of food and drink to Grandmother. She felt her heart begin to beat faster. Finally she was to be allowed out into the world.

"But you are not allowed to talk to any strangers on the way!" said the mother. The Blinder Girl promised on her honor, with a cross-my-heart-and-hope-to-die,[14] that she would do what the mother said, and only look straight ahead. If she dared to take off the hat, she would never be married.

With the basket on her arm, the Blinder Girl was eager to get out the door. The mother stopped her one last time.

"What do you do if you meet a boy?"

"Run away at once!" replied the Blinder Girl with lightning speed, and the mother nodded in satisfaction. The Blinder Girl opened the heavy gate and went out into the unknown forest.

Between the blinders she saw only the beauty that lay right in front of her and not all the strange things that happened in the bushes: flowers and berries in all imaginable colors and shapes, birds whistling, and confetti dancing down from the trees.

Then she saw a meadow full of flowers that nodded smilingly at her. She ran happily out into the flower meadow, but did not have time to pick a single flower before the sun suddenly disappeared, and a strong wind picked all the flowers up by the roots and blew them far away.

The wind came from the dark voice of Uncle Chacha.

"Good day, and where are you going so early?"

His eyes shone brightly toward her. Still, she replied politely that she was on her way to the grandmother's with food and drink. Uncle Chacha paused at length while he looked her up and down. It made her nervous. She shivered and felt cold when Uncle Chacha finally said something.

"It is too scary in the woods. I will drive you to Grandmother's."

The Blinder Girl took courage and politely refused the offer.

"I really want to pick some beautiful flowers for Grandmother first."

Uncle Chacha stared suspiciously at her for quite a while before he finally disappeared into the woods, without so much as a word of farewell. Then the sun came back and chased away the dark clouds.

She went farther and farther into the deep forest. On some strange trees she saw beautiful, heart-shaped apples with golden bows. The Blinder Girl's mouth watered, and she was about to pick an apple, when a young fellow with a backpack jumped out of the thicket. He bowed politely as he introduced himself:

"Hello. Morning. My name is Norman. That's a cute hat. Are those blinders?"

The girl nodded gravely.

"Where are you going, Blinder Girl?" asked Norman, grinning so broadly that the smile almost stuck to his ears. She wanted to run away, as she had promised her mother, but her legs would not move. Instead she closed both ears and mouth and tried to ignore him.

"You seem so . . . ," Norman thought carefully, ". . . so exotic! May I join you?"

She shook her head. Norman went down on his knees and pulled out a bunch of flowers.

"Here you are, beautiful lady, here is a bunch of forget-me-nots."

Then he asked one more time if he could join her for just a short distance. Norman was still smiling broadly as he sang out a long "Pleeeeeease?"

The girl had never seen someone smile at her before, except on TV. Norman's smile made her so hot that it started tickling all the way down in her big toe. Eventually the tickling became bubbles of happiness that grew so large they resembled butterflies fluttering around in her whole body.

Now it became difficult to think straight, and she was persuaded to let him accompany her a short distance.

Filled with joy, Norman did an impressive jump as he shouted:

"I found, I found."

When they had walked far and farther than far, they sat down hungrily. The Blinder Girl could scarcely believe her own eyes when she saw what Norman conjured up from his backpack. Ham, bubbly water, and a basket of delicious strawberries. While Norman eagerly poured the glasses, she took a big bite of the juicy ham.

She had never tasted anything like that before. Norman gave her a glass, and she emptied it in one gulp. Thirsty as she was, she had soon drunk the rest of the bottle. Norman clapped with wild enthusiasm.

The applause made her want even more, so he conjured up another bottle.

The bubbles from the bubbly water felt bigger and bigger. Now Norman stared intently at her.

"That tan of yours sure is hot. Have you been sunbathing a lot?" he asked, and hugged her so hard that she lost both mouth and speech.

She scrambled up to catch her breath, and she then saw something she had completely forgotten: the basket! In an instant her head cleared and she freed herself from Norman's embrace. She grabbed the basket and hurried on to Grandmother's house.

"Stop! Wait, Blinder Girl, we're having a fairy tale together!" Norman called after her, but she ran on as fast as she could.

Soon a storm blew up. The wind was so strong that the Blinder Girl was blown away, and the delicious food fell out of the basket. She felt completely shattered, but managed to pick up the basket and run on.

When she arrived at the grandmother's house, she knocked three times on the door.

"Who is it?" asked a deep voice from inside.

"It is I," replied the Blinder Girl with her most innocent voice, and explained that she had brought food and drink with which the grandmother could strengthen herself.

"Come in, come in, my child," roared Grandmother, and the Blinder Girl pressed the latch carefully down.

"But Grandma, what big eyes you have," cried the Blinder Girl when she saw her grandmother.

"That is probably because I've seen how you have behaved lately," whispered the grandmother while she beckoned her closer. The Blinder Girl did not know if she dared approach.

"And what a deep voice you have!" exclaimed the Blinder Girl. Grandmother did not answer, but beckoned to her with both hands. The Blinder

Girl approached carefully. Surprised, she saw that Grandmother's hands had grown big and hairy.

"Why do you have such big hands?" asked the Blinder Girl worriedly. Grandmother suddenly got an enormous grin around her mouth. The Blinder Girl drew back in fright, but Grandmother was already on top of her.

"That is because I'm going to take you on a journey of discovery, my little friend," shouted Grandmother, and jumped out of bed.

In the same instant she realized that it was Uncle Chacha and not Grandmother. He threw her into a trunk before she had time to draw her breath.

Through a small crack she glimpsed, to her horror, Grandma, who was wolfing down the contents of the basket. Grandma discovered the crack in the trunk and put her bum hard on top of the lid so that it was impossible to open.

The Blinder Girl felt sweaty and dizzy. Between bites the grandmother fervently chanted a prayer to save the family's honor. Now the Blinder Girl understood what Uncle and Grandma had planned. They would send her to Farawayistan, where there is no laughing or disco dancing. She felt the tears pressing.

Suddenly there were three knocks on the door.

"Is the Blinder Girl here?" asked a familiar voice. The Blinder Girl again felt happiness bubbles in her body when she realized that it was Norman who was at the door, with his heart in his hand.

"She has gone away with her grandmother," said Uncle Chacha dismissively, and attempted to close the door. But when Norman saw the braids sticking out of the trunk, he must have known that something was wrong. He put one foot in the crack of the door, pushed it open, and shoved Uncle Chacha hard to the ground before he rushed toward the trunk. Norman tried to politely shove the grandmother away, but she was not to be budged. Finally he opened the trunk so suddenly that Grandmother fell in the middle of the food basket. The Blinder Girl jumped out of the trunk, sweaty and flat.

Together with Norman she ran toward the door, but the grandmother had gotten to her feet. Now she stood in the doorway together with Uncle Chacha and blocked the way.

"You can't just run away from us, girl," said the uncle coldly.

"You belong to us!" screamed the grandmother, and pointed a needle-sharp index finger toward her.

The Blinder Girl felt smaller as her courage fluttered out of her body, but Norman stepped protectively to her side, and instantly the Blinder Girl felt strong and stubborn.

"I can manage fine without you," she said defiantly. She grabbed Norman's hand, and together they forced themselves past Grandma and Uncle Chacha.

"This is just like on TV," thought the Blinder Girl, as they ran hand in hand into the sunset. Norman wanted to celebrate, and pulled out a beer and cigarettes. Over the bridge and away from the grandmother's house they went. She could hear the grandmother shouting:

"If you leave us now, all bridges will be burned! For good!"

The Blinder Girl looked back, but then Norman grabbed her and kissed her so violently that she dropped the cigarette on the bridge. Soon the bridge was on fire.

They ran for a long time, hand in hand, through the forest. After a while it started to snow. The snow fell thicker and thicker, and a storm was brewing. Norman pulled out a pair of skis and put them on. He placed the Blinder Girl on the back of the skis and started skiing. She tried to hold on to the backpack, but after a while she fell off and was lying in the middle of the track, clinging to the backpack.

She tried running after him, but the snow was too deep and the wind too strong. She stood shouting after Norman, who disappeared into the forest. It was bitterly cold, and the snow whipped in her face.

The Blinder Girl sat down, exhausted, on a tree stump and opened Norman's backpack. She ate bread with goat's cheese while tears streamed down her face. In anger and despair she tore off her blinder hat.

"How different," said the Blinder Girl aloud. Now she heard and saw not only what was straight ahead, but also all that was on the sides. In the distance she glimpsed an unknown world. The Blinder Girl turned and looked back at the forest. She sniffled a little and thought about her mother, grandmother, Uncle Chacha, and Norman.

Then she dried her tears and turned her gaze forward. She took one step and another, and walked toward the big city.

Only the Blinder Girl knows if she found what she longed for.

And if she has not found it yet, she is surely on her way.

Little Blue Riding Hood (Caperucito Azul)

Hernán Rodríguez Castelo

Hernán Rodríguez Castelo (1933–) is an Ecuadorian author and journalist who has published on cinema, art, linguistics, and literature. A prolific literary critic, he authored an important theoretical study of children's literature, and has also written plays, essays, and children's books. In Latin America the Ecuadorian author is considered a major figure in the field of children's literature. His desire to promote the reading of great works of literature at all ages led to the publication, in 1975, of *Grandes libros para todos* (Great Books for All), a monumental guide of hundreds of works of fiction arranged by age levels. The same year he published *Caperucito Azul* (Little Blue Riding Hood), the first of two novels written for children.

Fairy tales play an essential role in Rodríguez Castelo's work. He published an authoritative translation of Perrault's *Contes* in 1997, preceded by an important preliminary study, and he also translated several classic fairy tales in *Caperucito*, a magazine he published between 1983 and 1985. The Ecuadorian author actually conceived the story of Little Blue Riding Hood in the 1960s while living in the small town of Comillas in the north of Spain. (He includes a photo he took of the town in his book.) The story constituted his farewell to the Comillas children, who had become his dear friends during his three-year stay. In a brief introduction, the author dedicates the story to the children, who were its first audience, as well as to the Ecuadorian children who heard it later. The storytelling author was sorely missed by the Comillas children, who grew up and told his story to their children. Eventually Rodríguez Castelo was obliged to write the story down, and it was first published in Bogota, Colombia, in 1975. It appeared for the first time in his own country in 1978. Later editions were dedicated by the author "to all the children to whom I have told stories—and who have told them to me—along the paths of the world. And, of course, to Little Riding Hood who lived in Comillas." The popularity of the author is indicated by the fact that the novel is now in its seventh edition. In his introduction to the novel, Germán Arciniegas writes that both adults and children read the work with as much pleasure as they would Hans Christian Andersen or the Brothers Grimm.

In Spanish, unlike French, Little Red Riding Hood is feminine (Caperucita Roja), but Rodríguez Castelo substitutes the masculine in his retelling of a curious little boy enamored of tales. In retellings of "Little Red Riding Hood," the role of storytelling is often emphasized, but Rodríguez Castelo is one of the few authors to give the role of storyteller to the tale's protagonist, and perhaps the only one to give it to a male Riding Hood. Whereas most retellings tend to emphasize the female oral tradition, this novel places Little Blue Riding Hood in the male literary tradition of Perrault, the Grimm brothers, and

19. *Caperucito Azul*, by Hernán Rodríguez Castelo. Illustrations by Jaime Villa. Copyright © 1975 Jaime Villa. Used by permission of Jaime Villa and Hernán Rodríguez Castelo.

Andersen. Rodríguez Castelo presents a curious, imaginative Riding Hood who is a born storyteller. No one believes the young boy's marvellous experiences and adventures: the talking dog, his participation in the nocturnal 12,000th Festival of the Tale attended by a multitude of fairy-tale characters, his meeting with Dickens in old London, or his visit with Andersen. In Rodríguez Castelo's retelling, as in Carmen Martín Gaite's, the borders between dream and reality are blurred. The boy's obsession with tales and his belief in the fantastic are seen as dangerous by parents, doctor, and teacher alike. The precocious, imaginative child is very much like the protagonist of *Caperucita en Manhattan*, whose mother is convinced she should see a psychiatrist. Little Blue Riding Hood's parents do take him to the doctor, and he is forbidden to tell stories or read tales and forced to suppress his all-consuming passion.

In his introduction to the novel, Arciniegas refers to the condemnation of fairy tales that was widespread until Bruno Bettelheim's groundbreaking work, *The Uses of Enchantment*, showed convincingly that they play a fundamental role in the development of the child's psyche, helping the child resolve inner conflicts. Rodríguez Castelo's defense of fairy tales precedes that of Bettelheim, whose study actually appeared the same year as the novel but was not available in a Spanish translation until 1976. (In any case, the Ecuadorian author had conceived and told his story in the 1960s.) Toward the end of the story, Little Blue Riding Hood finds an ally in the person of a visiting Swedish writer, Dr. Herrmärchen, whose symbolic name is actually German for Mr. Fairy Tale.

Caperucito Azul is described in the cover blurb as both a mini-novel and a long tale. The original edition was 148 pages in length, but its format was quite small. The illustrations, by Jaime Villa (1931–), are black-and-white reproductions of full-color originals that had been executed in crayon; they were never published in color. Jaime Villa is a well-known Ecuadorian painter and one of the country's foremost children's book illustrators, an occupation he engages in largely as a way to give back to the community. He has kindly given his permission to reproduce two of the illustrations that have never before appeared in color. The cover illustration of the eponymous hero as a very small boy in a blue-hooded jacket with a dog at his side is a variation of the full-page illustration in the first chapter (plate 12). The last two editions of the book also have striking illustrated initial capitals by the Ecuadorian artist Celso Rojas (1951–) at the beginning of each chapter. Rojas does not do children's book illustration but completed these illustrations especially for Rodríguez Castelo.

The first chapter of the novel has been included here, as it explains how Little Blue Riding Hood got his name and establishes the intertextual relationship with the classic tale. This is further developed in the second chapter, which recounts his invitation to the Festival of the Tale, where the master of ceremonies is Little Red Riding Hood herself. She also stars in the first tale to be performed that evening, the classic Grimm version of her story. A comment by the protagonist indicates that it is the same version the teacher had told his class. The narrator focuses on the audience's emotional reaction to a play that seems very real. Gretel's words of warning to Little Red Riding Hood accompany the illustration representing the encounter of Little Red Riding Hood and the wolf on the festival stage, which Little Blue Riding Hood watches intently from the audience (plate 13). Although Little Red Riding Hood is not as beautiful as Cinderella, Little Blue Riding Hood is reluctant to leave her company, and it is only in a parenthetical confession in the last chapter that readers learn that the protagonist would have liked her to be his girlfriend. His friend Dickens had once also confessed that Little Red Riding Hood was his "first love."

Rodríguez Castelo's novel is a defense of the tale and storytelling. There are references to Perrault, the Brothers Grimm, and Andersen, as well as to Selma Lagerlöf and Charles Dickens, in the novel. The Grimms receive more attention than Perrault, who is mentioned only in passing, but Rodríguez Castelo seems to have a predilection for Andersen, whose life had been the subject of a work titled "El cuento de la vida de Andersen" (The Story of the Life of Andersen), which he published as a serial in *Caperucito* in 1984. An epilogue provides fragmented glimpses of the happy ending of this modern fairy tale. Dr. Herrmärchen takes charge of Little Blue Riding Hood's education in Sweden, an education tailored to a future author of tales. Clippings from newspapers in various languages indicate that the precocious Spanish storyteller is already making a name for himself. On the final page of the novel, Little Blue Riding Hood's old teacher and mentor expresses the belief that the boy is the hope for "the privileged land of Don Quixote, [which] does not yet have its Andersen."

రొ

LITTLE BLUE RIDING HOOD (1975)

Once upon a time in a certain town, there was a boy. This boy had a very warm and very nice blue hood.

Our little one was very outgoing, and so he had made many friends in the tiny town. In addition to all his school and street acquaintances, he had made friends with the civil guard, and when he heard the rhythmic sound of the guard's footsteps on the cobblestone streets—. . . clack . . . clack . . . clack . . . clack . . .—he would prepare himself. The guard would approach . . . clack . . . clack . . . clack . . . click-clack! In front of the little boy he would stand at attention. The little boy would stand at attention to return the salute. Very serious, the guard would continue on his way; and very serious, the boy would return to his games.

He had also made friends with the night watchman. Every night around eleven o'clock, the night watchman would come out and begin his rounds. He would take the path to the beach as far as Portillo Bridge. From Portillo Bridge he would return and would go as far as Solatorre at the other end of town, below the marquis's castle and an extensive collection of university buildings with its seminaries. Every night the watchman, while on his first round, would pass in front of the house of our little boy, and he would stop, rummage through his pockets for a whistle, and give a very soft and very long whistle. No one knew why he did it . . . No one, except the little boy, who knew that it was the greeting and farewell of his friend, the night watchman.

The watchman was his best friend. He told the boy that he used to be very important, because in the old days, when there was no clock in the tower, it was the night watchman who would go about town telling the time: "One o'clock in the morning! All is peaceful and all is well! Two o'clock in the morning! All is peaceful and all is well!" And so the night watchman was necessary. Besides, in those days, they had no electricity, but lanterns, and it was the night watchman who would light and extinguish them. Yes, in those days it was wonderful to be a night watchman. Now, with the clock in the tower (the church tower of our town looked like a monk with a tall, pointed hood, and the yellowish face of the clock glowed high above in the night like an eye), with electricity, he could hardly be called a night watchman, but rather a guard. That is what the poor night watchman thought, and therefore he felt sad. He had told this to the little boy because he was his friend.

Another of our little boy's friends was the carpenter. He had offered to make him a wooden gun, painted and everything. Leaving the school, the little boy would pass by the shop of his friend the carpenter to wish him good morning and good afternoon.

The last of the boy's friends was a dog: a big, dirty, common stray dog, who, to the little boy, looked like the most beautiful dog in the world. The boy would always save him part of his lunch because the dog was his friend, and when the enormous animal would see the little boy appear at the top of the street from the school, he would come with long and heavy strides to greet him. He was so affectionate that he would lick his face! "If you don't behave, you won't get your bread," the little boy would scold him.

One day, the teacher told our young hero and his classmates a story.

"The story that I'm going to tell you is called 'Little Red Riding Hood,'" said the teacher.

"What is a 'little riding hood'?" right away asked a little boy who was always asking questions.

"Well, 'little riding hood' is a way of saying small hood."

"And what is a hood?" asked again the same little boy who was always asking questions.

"Well, a hood is a hooded jacket . . . it's . . . well, look: this is a hood," said the teacher, holding up the hero of our story by his arms, so that all his classmates could see his beautiful hood.

"Oooh . . . Little Blue Riding Hood . . . Little Blue Riding Hood!" cried one child, and then all the rest chimed in.

"Little Blue Riding Hood! Little Blue Riding Hood!"

From that day on, his classmates called our young lad "Little Blue Riding Hood," and, as he didn't mind, his friends also called him by the same name: the civil guard, the night watchman, the carpenter and . . . well, the dog, I don't think he did, although he did understand the story when his friend told him. Of course he understood: his eyes shone with happiness, and at the end he gave a bark of satisfaction!

That afternoon Little Riding Hood returned home sad from school. His little nose was scrunched up, and his big, blue eyes showed concern. When his friend, the big dog, came to him with adulation and affection, the little boy said:

"Be quiet. Can't you see that I'm thinking?"

And he sank into deep thought like a grownup. But the dog, who either did not understood or did not want to leave him so sad, increased its affections and sprints and yips. He seemed to say to him: "But why are you so sad? What's the matter with you?"

"Well, because you're my friend, I will tell you what's the matter," said the boy, and he began to talk to him very seriously: "You see, the other day the teacher told us a story . . . the one I told you about Little Red Riding Hood. After that, they began calling me Little Blue Riding Hood. I told you that as well, except that you don't remember anything. Well, I wanted to do something like Little Red Riding Hood, and this is the problem: it seems that I can never do anything like Little Red Riding Hood. I asked the teacher if wolves talk, and he told me no, that it only happens in stories. I asked him if it happened in today's stories, and he answered no, that it only happened in very old tales. Then something occurred to me: I asked him if dogs could talk, and he told me no . . . But you talk, don't you? I believe that wolves talk too, only nobody understands them. (The dog listened attentively—it would seem he did not want to miss a word of what the child said.) And then, all the rest is difficult too: the wolf eats Little Red Riding Hood, and afterward he dresses like her and goes to her grandmother's house, and then eats the grandmother too . . . But then, the hunter gets Little Red Riding Hood and her grandmother out alive. Do you think that is true? No, I don't think I can ever do something like Little Red Riding Hood."

After unburdening himself to his friend the dog, Little Riding Hood began hopping on one foot, and in that way, hopping on one foot, he ran away, followed by the dog, who made a fuss over him.

Halfway was the carpenter's workshop. The boy approached and greeted him.

"Good afternoon, Ramón . . ."

"God's gift to us, Little Riding Hood. What a pleasure! How are things at school?" responded the old artisan, with a broad smile that showed his satisfaction at the child's visit.

"Ramón," said the boy then, very mysteriously, "have you ever seen wolves?"

"Oh, yes, son, as a lad I was the best wolf hunter on the mountain . . ."

"You killed wolves?"

"Of course, I once killed two in the same day."

"And why did people kill them?"

"Well, because if you didn't, they could attack livestock and even people."

"And do wolves talk?"

"No, child, of course not."

"And do dogs talk?"

"No, little one, no animal talks."

"All right, goodbye, Ramón!"

"You see? What did I tell you?" confided the boy to the dog once they had left. "They don't believe that any animal can talk. And you talk. Maybe wolves can too . . . I'd like to talk to a wolf to see if all wolves are bad.

Then they heard the unmistakable footsteps in the street: . . . clack . . . clack . . . clack . . .

"Here comes the civil guard . . . I will ask him as well," said the boy. Clack . . . clack . . . clack . . . clack . . . click-clack! The man stood at attention in front of the boy, who, contrary to custom, did not stand at attention, but said:

"Listen, do you know if wolves can talk?"

"Of course they can! Woof . . . woof . . . woof!" answered the guard; he laughed; he stood at attention again and, still laughing, he left: . . . clack . . . clack . . . clack . . . clack . . .

"Of course they can . . . woof . . . woof . . . ," thought the boy. "He said yes but he didn't say it seriously . . . of course he didn't say it seriously . . . Now I have only the night watchman left."

The boy ran to the night watchman's house. It was a poor house, one of three very old and dilapidated houses that lined the pier as if patiently awaiting their demolition. The night watchman lived there alone. His wife had died years ago, and his children had left in search of employment, one for Germany and the other for America.

Knock . . . knock . . . knock . . .

"Who is it?"

"Me."

"Who?" The night watchman's voice sounded cranky, but upon reaching the door and seeing who it was, his wrinkled face softened.

"Ah! It's you, Little Riding Hood . . . To what do I owe the honor of this visit? You're going to get home late and be scolded . . ."

"Just one thing."

"But, come in, you can always sit down, even if it's only for a moment. Hurry up, come in . . ."

The night watchman made the boy come in, and once they were both seated, he said:

"Well, let's see now, little friend, what business brings you here . . ."

"Listen, Mr. Night Watchman, do wolves talk?"

"So that's it . . . Little Riding Hood asking if wolves can talk. What's gotten into that little head of yours?"

The boy knew then that the night watchman had guessed, but he was not surprised because the night watchman knew many things and understood everything; that's why Little Riding Hood told him all his concerns.

"You see, the thing is that I wanted to do something like Little Red Riding Hood . . . And everyone tells me that wolves don't talk. I asked Ramón, and he said that wolves don't talk. He has killed many wolves. I asked the civil guard, and he told me that yes, wolves can talk—woof . . . woof—, but he didn't say it seriously. And you, what do you say? Do wolves talk?"

"Well, wolves talk in stories . . ."

"And now?"

"Not anymore."

"But . . . ," hesitated the boy, before confessing his biggest problem, "but . . . okay, and do dogs talk?"

"No, little one, dogs don't talk either."

"And . . . and how is it that I talk with my dog . . . What happens is that nobody listens to the animals."

The night watchman watched the little boy, not daring to trouble his marvelous world of naïve goodness. He let his tired eyes wander while his heart escaped in search of old nostalgia, and he began to roll a cigarette. The boy brought him out of his deep thought with another question:

"Are there still tales now?"

"Child," the night watchman said seriously, "when I was a boy, there were tales. There were many tales in the world. In every street, in every plaza, in every corner there was a tale: tales about fairies, dwarves, princesses, and hidden treasure. In school, tales were the most important thing; my mother, in order to keep me still while she combed my hair, would tell me tales; in the little square next to the church, an old guard would tell tales to the children . . . And because, as children, we had tales—and for that reason alone—we haven't died of sorrow. It has happened to me as in a tale: There was a man who had two children, and they both went far away. But in the tale the two sons would return at the end and live happily ever after with their old father. Perhaps for that reason, I still wait for my sons . . . But, my little one, these things are serious and rather sad . . ."

The boy's big eyes were wide open as he listened. He thought he was beginning to understand. He said slowly:

"So, now there are no more tales . . ."

"No, Little Riding Hood, I didn't want to say that. Tales can still exist now, only it is more difficult. Very difficult. But yes, tales can still exist nowadays. And they do. I know a very beautiful one . . ."

"Tell it," Little Riding Hood promptly requested.

"But it's not finished yet . . ."

"Tell it anyway, whatever you already have . . ."

"Well, all right. Once upon a time there was a boy who knew how to talk with his dog . . ."

"That's not a tale. That could be true."

"And don't you think, my little friend, that tales can also be true? But enough of that for now, because it's very late, and you're going to be scolded at home for arriving so late."

Little Riding Hood ate dinner gloomily that night. First his mother and then his father had admonished him for his late arrival. They had not even wanted to listen to him. There was no justifiable excuse for a child to be wandering alone about the streets so late. Little Riding Hood was embarrassed, but a question danced in his little head. And finally the question overcame the fear, and he asked in a very timid voice:

"Dad . . ."

"What is it?"

"Can tales also be true?"

"No, dear," replied his mother instead of his father. "Don't you see that's why they call them tales . . . they are the things of tales."

The father stared at his son without saying a word.

The boy ate a few more bites and started asking:

"Dad, a boy who talks with his dog, can that be a tale?"

"Yes, that can be a tale," said the father. (The mother was now trying to get Little Riding Hood's younger brother to eat his dinner without spilling food.)

"Dad," insisted the child, afraid of bothering him by asking too many questions, "but it can be true, right?"

"No, that can't be true."

Little Riding Hood returned to his dinner, but he hardly paid any attention to what he was eating, waiting for the chance to ask another question. And, after allowing the passage of what seemed to him to be a long period of time but was in fact insignificant, he asked it:

"Dad, can tales still happen nowadays?"

The father exchanged a look with his wife. With that glance, Little Riding Hood's parents said: "It's a bad thing if he's getting into tales . . . How he likes to live in a dream world!" Staring at the child, he answered very seriously:

"Have you ever seen airplanes?"

Little Riding Hood nodded his head.

"And cars and motorboats . . . Well, none of that existed before. Neither did electricity. There were no newspapers, and only very few books, which were written on lambskin and were therefore very expensive. At that time, when science didn't exist, when there was no information by radio or newspapers, then people believed in tales . . . in ghosts, in fairies, and in witches.

All that is finished . . . Do you understand? And now, it's homework and then bed for you."

In bed now, the little boy waited for the greeting of his friend the night watchman before falling asleep. With his eyes fixed on his bedroom window, he was sad at the thought that tales had come to an end. When the night watchman was a boy, there had still been tales . . . How wonderful it must have been to have lived at that time! "In every street, in every plaza, in every corner there was a tale," the night watchman had told him . . . But, of course, it was that at that time there was no electricity and books were written on the skins of lambs and that's why they cost so much . . . But the night watchman had said that there could still be tales today, only that it was a little difficult . . .

At that moment a very long and very soft whistle was heard from the street.

How Little Riding Hood would have liked to go and tell his friend, the night watchman, what his father had said! Would the night watchman still have one of those lambskin books?

And thinking of these things, Little Riding Hood fell asleep.

Little Green Cap (Prassini Soufitsa)

Ioulita Iliopoulou

The Greek author and poet Ioulita Iliopoulou (1965–) writes for both adults and children. She has written five poetry collections for adults, as well as essays and lyrics for songs. Music has a special place in her writing. She wrote the libretto for the opera *The Fir Ship* and the poetry for the lyric tragedy *Jocasta*, both by the well-known Greek composer George Couroupos. The author also collaborates with the Orchestra of Colors in the creation of programs that bring together words and music. She was the partner of the Greek poet and Nobel laureate Odysseas Elytis during the final years of his life. In 2005 she began publishing children's books. Her fairy-tale novella, *Prassini Soufitsa* (Little Green Cap), was published for young readers in 2007. Iliopoulou's lyrical poetry is published for adults, but her stories for children also include small poems related to the narrative. Embedded in the prose of *Prassini Soufitsa* are seven such poems, which the author was kind enough to adapt into English for this translation. The rhythm and rhymes of the original poems have been retained as much as possible in the translation.

The 53-page novella was illustrated with eleven paintings by Yannis Kottis (1949–), a well-known Greek painter who lives and works in Paris. The artist and the author are friends, and had already collaborated on the author's first children's book, *Ti zitai o Zinon?* (What Is Zenon Looking For?), which had unanimously won Greece's 2005 national children's book awards in the categories of both illustration and literature; Iliopoulou asked Kottis to illustrate her novella as well. Following the plot and the atmosphere of the story quite faithfully, Kottis created one painting for each of the ten chapters.

In her "free adaptation" of "Little Red Cap," Iliopoulou's intention was not "to retell the story of 'Little Red Cap' but to continue her story life" in a kind of sequel. Since Iliopoulou wanted to "'meet' her years later," she naturally chose as hypotext the Grimms' version, in which the protagonist survived her adventure.[15] Although she is now called Little Green Cap, the ex–Little Red Cap's first name, Rosa, evokes her original identity. Convinced that our childhoods dictate our future lives, the author wondered how Little Red Cap managed in later years. The consequences of the events recounted in the classic tale are manifest in the psyche of the protagonist of this modern retelling. While she has grown into a young woman physically, mentally she seems still to be a child. Her vulnerability is suggested in the first line by the metaphor of the fallen doll. It is the fairy-tale heroine's life as a single adult that interests the Greek author. Initially, it seems that the author might give her tale of Little Red Cap the classic fairy-tale ending in which a couple live "happily ever after," but the potential love story of the ex–Little Red Cap

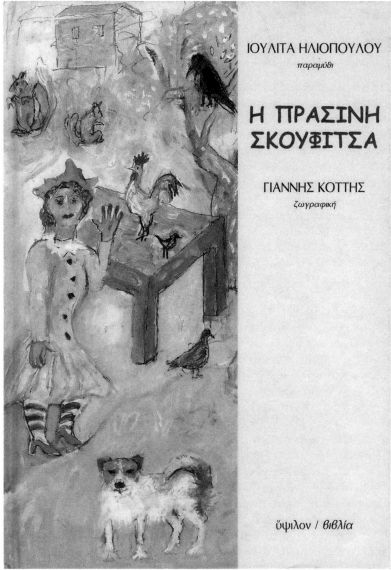

20. *Prassini Soufitsa*, by Ioulita Iliopoulou. Illustrations by Yannis Kottis. Copyright © 2008 Ypsilon/Vivlia. Used by permission of Ypsilon/Vivlia.

and the woodcutter has a much more realistic conclusion (plate 14). Gender stereotypes prevent the woodcutter from leaving his wife for such an unconventional female.

The enemy in this modern retelling is no longer the wolf but rather land developers and their supporters. As in many contemporary recastings of the tale, the moral is that in today's world people are a far greater threat than wolves, which have also become their victims. Iliopoulou's retelling adopts an ecological approach, criticizing the materialism of our consumer society, which indiscriminately destroys nature. At the same time she questions the conventions and stereotypes of the classic fairy tale. Escaping the permanent childhood in which the fairy tale confines her, Rosa learns to deal with her fears and acquires self-sufficiency and independence (plate 15). Iliopoulou follows Rosa's story to old age, when, somewhat paradoxically, the former fairy-tale heroine assumes the role of storyteller to relate the classic version of her own story. The author's world lies on the border between the dream world and reality. Using postmodern techniques to recast the classic tale, Iliopoulou attempts to redefine reality, opposing pragmatism, indifference, malevolence, and greed with imagination, sensitivity, love, and selflessness.

Little Green Cap (2007)

Little Red Cap Has Grown Up

"What happens when a doll falls down from her shelf?" Rosa kept wondering; "Or even worse," she whispered, "when she falls out of her fairy tale? What happens?"

Silence . . . huge birdlike eyes glared through the dusk but no chirping could be heard. Now, the years have gone by, hunters had shot the wolf, and Grandmother was now in heaven, forever knitting her granddaughter's once-red cap from there.

Because, for years, Rosa had been a little girl with a red cap, a basket, boots for the mountain mud, her hooded cape, and all other necessary accessories . . . However, nothing, nothing is forever . . . She inherited her grandmother's wooden hut, she rebuilt it with stone, with a little terrace, and a big iron gate because—I should not have to tell you—she never stopped being afraid in the forest . . .

She took a job in town in a toy shop. The sign said "Doll's House," and it had hundreds of dolls, most of them vintage . . . She loved dolls! Unfortunately, she worked in the orders department, and all day she wrote symbols she couldn't understand—codes they called them—and next to them . . . so many euros and delivery dates and strange destinations . . .

On Jasmine Street
K, l, b three times t
Miniature fair
Will be sent by air . . .

A blue-mauve fur fox
In the tartan box
Is not so tall
And the price is small.

P, q, h, g, g
The doll's name is Gigi
She swims in the sea
Sitting on a floating pea,

In a packet so big
Bonny sweet as a fig
Will be sent to Aberdeen
By post, safe and clean.

"What a day!" muttered Lina, her colleague, as they were leaving for home after work on a Wednesday afternoon. Spring had set in for good, and Little Red Cap, sorry, I meant Rosa, took the train, got off at the stop Weed, and started to walk uphill . . .

The anemones were in bloom, and the slim lilies—like morning stars—sprang up among the pine trees; further down a line of pomegranate trees rubbed their feet in the brook; two boys ran to catch their orange ball, which was rolling downhill, while bees and a big cuckoo flew behind them.

"Coo-coo-coo coo-coo-coo," the cuckoo greeted Rosa.

"You're late," he said. Not wanting to be seen by the children, Rosa replied: "Didn't I tell you, we had to register the merchandise today . . ."

"Coo-coo Coo-coo, blah, blah. And I have my birthday today, as you know!"

"I know, and I will make hempseed salad, strawberry honey, and milk pie to blow out the candles!"

The Cuckoo's Birthday

Indeed, late in the afternoon, everyone Rosa loved was around the stone table in the yard: Herald the cuckoo celebrating his birthday, his friend Verina the partridge with her neighbor Rachel, Peach the dog, her two cats Go and Come, Terry the most high-spirited squirrel in the forest, and his small fiancée, Lucky. They were all there: Sol the nightingale with his golden key; Open-eyes the eagle, who was called the Rainmaker because he knew how to bring showers; Morning Star, first tenor rooster; the sparrow, Crumps; and, of course, McCrow, the grumpy raven who was said to bring bad luck. "You should feed the bad dog," Rosa's grandmother used to say, and that is why she invited him, but nothing nice ever came out of his beak.

However, he was compelled to sing with all the rest when the huge milk pie with the eight candles arrived.

Happy birthday, cuckoo Herald
Happy birthday, bright emerald

Pines, cedars, and olive trees
Give you a nest in their leaves

Fly cuckoo and bring
All the roses of spring

Fly free, tread on air
To the sunset's red hair

Happy birthday, cuckoo Herald
Happy birthday, bright emerald.

But as soon as the song ended—"Stop," croaked the raven. "It's time to listen to the news from the leading channel Crow *plus*." He sat behind the window, coughed, and started to announce:

"Dear spectators,

"From reliable sources of the forest, Stingy the mole, Nevermind the badger, and Match the weasel, we were informed of the plans of the large multinational firm 'Claws Universal and Son' for the development of our forest. One hundred and twenty maisonettes with polyester lawns and electronic seesaw-benches will take the place of the trees, bushes, and anarchist weeds. We shall enter the civilization of the 21st century. Sewers, gutters, triple underground warehouses will replace the ravine, *Dreamland*. Spotless concrete slabs will cover the worn-out stones. Thyme and lavender bushes will be dried for the town botanic museum, and most importantly: bonds will be distributed, Book-entry Securities for those truly open-minded who wish for development. Certainly, the possibility will be given to the friends of a retro lifestyle to settle down in a zoo. Hurry!

"With democratic processes, naturally, tomorrow has been decided. Tomorrow can't wait!"

"Ah, this is no longer a joke, McCrow," shouted Rosa, red-hot with anger.

"This is not a joke," he croaked, and put on his coat in order to leave hastily before the rest of the guests got angry with him, too, and threw acorns at him.

But the birds were drunk from the strawberry honey and chirped laughingly. Just in time the woodsman Goody[16] arrived. He was very fat but charming. They called him Juicy, and he liked both his nickname as well as Rosa. If she didn't have this bad habit of talking with dolls and with all the birds, he might even think of marrying her. Alas, divorce his grumpy but sensible wife and go looking for trouble and fantasies? Ah, I'd better leave it, he thought.

"Greetings to you and your cuckoo, Rosa. Enjoy your fairy tales," he told her, and kissed her. He held a tiny box in his hands. Go and Come, the roaming cats, thought that he might have brought her some jewellery, like so many do in town, and would tell her at last that he loved her and that he wanted to . . .

"Thanks!" Rosa shouted merrily, finding in the box the tiniest, most beautiful doll, with a dark red lace dress and her long hair braided above the ears. He had probably brought it from Italy when he went for a meeting of woodsmen.

"I will call her 'Prezziosa' because you gave her to me," said Rosa.

"Yes, keep her, love her, to remember me," said Goody, and a little sadness slipped from his words.

And before she could ask him why, Sol the nightingale burnished his key, sat at the canephone, and started to sing . . .

A poppy so red
Different, you said
Into the water falls
And I run after its calls.

But with the first morning light
The cloud whispers from its height
And keeps saying and saying
Crying all the time, not playing

Love has many labors
Boat away from harbors
Love makes water catch fire
And throws your heart into mire.

A poppy so red
Different, you said
Into the water falls
And I run after its calls

Night fell. All the guests had already left. The stars rolled out, shining little buttons in the sky. You could faintly see their pale colors. The smallest were yellow, like egg yolks, some were like slices of orange, and some strawberry red; those were the biggest, already very old, but they shone brightly on the window sill . . .

"Look!" said Rosa to Peach, her dog. "The wolf is back with his cubs!"

Indeed, Lycurgus, the reddish-brown wolf that lived deep in the forest, was evidently hungry and, crying, he reached her window. What could Rosa do? She was afraid of wolves since she was little; don't forget she was once a Little Red Cap, and no matter how many books on the intricate tangles of the soul she had read, a little fear had lingered.

Nevertheless, she opened the window and gave him the last remains of the milk pie and a little yogurt with honey and hazelnuts.

She then went to bed, but to no use. It was a bad habit of hers to think of all that worried her before going to sleep. And now, she couldn't help thinking . . . First it was the raven and his dark words, and then Goody who was a little strange tonight . . . "Tomorrow," she murmured, "I'll go the Bank of Wishes in town and make a deposit."

The Bank of Wishes

She merrily started out early in the morning. She took the train. She remembered her grandmother's words: "Whatever you wish for takes you far way, but when you come back, you should find it . . ." She reached the big road with the supermarket and the bank. It was the first time she went inside. She went through a sliding door that turned endlessly. A guard asked for her ID and told her to wait. He then led her to the glass office of the bank manager. Mr. Cotton, fat and wearing a leather jacket, thought it strange to see her.

"Go down to the third underground floor, miss," he hissed through his teeth. "The department for small depositors is there. Write your wish on a blank piece of paper, and put it in the right box. We shall see the general balance in a month and we shall evaluate the yields."

What did he mean? She could not understand anything. But she did as she was told. Then she ran to work, at the Doll's House.

"Where have you been, miss?" asked her boss from the loft. "You should have been here three and a half minutes ago, you are quite late!"

"You know . . . ," she muttered but did not continue.

Sounds at Night, or Danger Is Near

And the days went by, more or less the same. Orders, numbers, and only when there was no one around did Rosa daydream, looking at the dolls with their exquisite dresses.

Some nights, though, when all was quiet and she was fast asleep with Peach at her feet, she suddenly heard strange twittering and sometimes abrupt cracking noises, croaking, sharp sounds and movement, heavy crushing noises, as if trees were falling or as if stones were rolling down a precipice. And then, sharp, tremulous fluttering . . .

> How strange the nightingale
> In my dreams, how it tweets!
> Like being in a gale
> Really out of its wits.
>
> Croak croak croak
> Is it Max the frog?
> Or a fox that broke
> Like a glass the fog?
>
> How strange the pine twigs
> Swish around and rustle!
> Voices from weird shindigs
> Threaten sleep's castle.

One night she heard a strong electrical sound . . . a mysterious sound! Go and Come looked at her, the pupils of their eyes huge and their tails bushy and erect like a squirrel's.

"Someone is cutting trees," they mewed.

"Remember what McCrow said?" Peach barked.

Rosa stayed up all night, thinking: "What if they are right?" And she listened . . .

The next morning, a little farther up from her house, she saw the bulldozers as well as big trucks full of sand and five workmen dressed in striped uniforms with a red saw hanging from their pockets.

"Hey, what are you doing here?" she called. But they went on digging silently while two others with black uniforms were moving a tree trunk and a very tall man with a power saw was cutting an old oak which was crying inconsolably.

"Stop!" she cried. "What are you doing?" No one answered her.

"No, no," she thought. "I must stop them."

She walked downhill to town. She reached the big road with the supermarket and the bank, and walked straight to the marble edifice of the gendarmerie. "For indictments on the left, for applications upstairs or downstairs, for lost property nowhere," said a small sign. She waited in a small office, as there was no one around. When a thin police officer in a yellow uniform and hat walked in, Rosa explained.

"They are cutting down trees. They want to build in the woods . . . we are all in danger, the animals, birds, the town!"

"Ah, you are in the wrong office. First go to the second floor, straight to the twentieth door, and then fourth corridor on the right and back again."

The ex–Little Red Cap, Rosa, went on, flustered and ready to start crying.

When she finally arrived at the right office, she came face to face with a secretary who wore black glasses and earrings made of ivory that were so long, they touched her waist.

"You are not in the right office, miss. Go down one floor, turn 180 degrees, second door on the left, and . . ."

Rosa got terribly angry, left the office, and started walking down corridors, going up and down floors with the lift, until, as she was outside the door of a room on the roof, she heard someone saying:

"Stop this crazy girl! Even a single complaint will delay our plans. The damage will be enormous . . ."

"Calm down, Mr. Claws, please. She will never find the office . . . ," replied another piercing voice.

Suddenly, she hears footsteps approaching and sees the door opening. Rosa runs and hides in a small side room; there was no one inside. There was only a huge computer on a desk. It said: "Urgent mail. To be used only by personnel for High Inspection."

Rosa wrote her complaint with great care:

Sun made trail in the snow
Filled up suddenly with feathers;
With the southern wind and the northern wind

Cypress cones and pine nuts
Fight the boogeyman—a buzzsaw.

His heavy footsteps
Startle a lonely owl in the dark
And all the forest is alarmed
For danger is near, alas!

In the Arms of the Children

Time had gone by. There was no sense in going to work now. They would surely scold her, if not fire her. It was not the first time she was late. It was noon now; she sat on a bench, weary and desperate.

She had nothing else but the woods, the animals, the chirping and twittering of the birds, the million red wisps, the small acorns, Drilly the hedgehog, Sol the nightingale, even Lycurgus; she thought of them and cried . . .

She suddenly heard the voices of the children who were leaving school across the street. Niki and Myrto heard her crying and went to her. They knew Rosa from the Doll's House and loved her. But they only said good morning to her because they were a little afraid of her—she was like an elf, their mother said.

Their mother also said that they were too old for fairy tales and such things. But she wasn't right. So they sat near Rosa and heard the whole story. As time passed other children gathered around them, Bousgos, Diana, Kyriakos, the twins Silver and Goldie, Neta, and many others. Bousgos, who was the leader and always carried a slingshot, had a wise idea.

"Let's go to the forest with you," he said, "and stop the work."

"And how do you think we could do this? With your slingshot?" said Notis and laughed.

"Yes, with the slingshot of our hearts. We will each put our arms around a tree and will not move until morning comes!"

And so it happened.

The trees spent the night in the arms of the children. Goody, the woodsman, came and asked them to go home. But to no effect; children and trees stayed hugging, softly singing a lullaby and drowsing . . .

Tick tock tick tock
Slumber chased by the clock.

Stars are wandering in flock
Moon is like a golden rock
Rolling down in the weeds
in my foggy sleeping fields

Tick tock tick tock
Paper boat, paper stork

In the forest something sparkles
In the sky something crackles
And an angel can be seen
Making true my little dream

The children left the forest with the morning light.

What Is the Price of a Wish?

Construction work stopped, at least temporarily. Rosa's complaint had reached the High Inspection, and they had to set up a committee of wise men to investigate. "What is the interest of the community?" "Modernization or useless wood?" were the headlines in the newspapers.

Only a small journal, *The Morning Skylark*, said: "You have an ace up your sleeve, friend . . . the forest." And in smaller type: "The pines are green gold, not enemies."

Mr. Cotton, the banker, was appointed president of the committee. Alas, everyone was expecting the outcome with great emotional excitement. And summer was getting on.

Rosa lost her job. In the mornings she walked downtown to see if any of the shops were looking for an employee. But there was nothing. One day, as she was walking by the big Bank of Wishes, she paused at the door, on which a piece of graph paper was stuck that said "I-A, General Balance-Yields." What is this? she thought. Ah, yes . . .

Kika the magpie, with her tasselled tail, whom Peach called Kika the lifter, because she always stole whatever caught her eye, explained the bank's system to Rosa: When a lot of people made the same wish, the price of the wish rose, and it came true. But when the wishes were too few, she said, they got lost, as if they were never made. No profit, no hope, nothing . . .

"Ah, let me see, I must see," said Rosa, and glued her nose to the window:

Red box: 100 percent rise in the wishes for the development of the area—construction of luxury villas, roads, bridges, concretizations, drainage.

Brown box: 80 percent rise in wishes for the possession of a third car, electric moped, and power dinghy.

Pink box: 79 percent rise in wishes for the possession of a second house equipped according to the latest fantasy.

Beige box: stabilization of marriage wishes.

White box: vertical drop in useless wishes, dreams, nature, love.

Rosa sighed deeply. She knew she had dropped her wish in the white box. "I wish Peach and his friends will be well, I wish Lycurgus the wolf will not go hungry, and I wish Goody . . . ," but she did not finish her thought . . .

Goody

She went back to her woods. It was so hot! The cicadas sang nonstop with their throaty voices. Peach was lying by the dripping faucet to keep his tail wet. Sol, out of breath, could not tweet. Only Pip the wood pigeon was in a good mood . . ."Green palace, red curtains inside it, beautiful black woman," he said while nibbling at a watermelon . . .

Right then came the wolf neighbors, Lycurgus with his three young cubs, Lily, Lucky, and Lara, who had a blonde tail. They were thirsty. Rosa, who wasn't so afraid of them now, put some water and sesame sweet with honey at the end of the yard for them to eat. It wasn't their fault that they became wolves and not pigs, she thought.

She sat on her wooden chair near the door and started knitting. Since she lost her job in town she knitted caps, although rarely red—she didn't fancy them; most of the caps she made were green with white stars; also with tiny colorful flowers.

She sold them at the street market on Wednesdays. Many women bought them for their daughters. Today she was knitting a yellow cap with orange daisies and foliage around, like ivy.

"How are you, my little flowercap?" Goody called from afar.

She was so happy to see him! But as he got closer to her, she thought he was carrying a suitcase, and he wasn't wearing his woodsman uniform in which he looked so nice.

"Goody, where are you going?" she asked anxiously.

"I'm leaving, Rosie. I'm leaving for good. I'm going to town to become a superintendent at the spirits factory. I'll be closer to home."

"And what about me?" she dared ask.

He did not reply. He bent his head. On the table he left the big torch he had used as a woodsman.

"You might need it," he said, and then called out: "Take careeeee!" as he was leaving.

Rosa did not cry. She was so sad, she could not squeeze her sorrow into a tear. Only her doll, little Prezziosa, sighed as she saw him vanish.

Once upon a time forgotten
Who is spinning a yarn rotten?

Which had been so red and silky
But the wheel turned so quickly

With a pair of compasses
Future's drawing, time passes

In the clouds who is living?
All alone and is keeping

A flower house of wishes
Of caresses, tales, and kisses

Who once upon a time
Found but lost love's golden mine?

The Wind of Fire

Suddenly there was a strong gust of wind. In it you could see McCrow and hear his quick fluttering moving like a typhoon. Dust blew everywhere. Go and Come started coughing, Herald the cuckoo began to say something to break the silence but hesitated. Pipi the wood pigeon, who dashed in busily, started announcing: "Tomorrow, tomorrow the decision about the construction works in the woods will be announced. Some say that two ministers, Peevy and Pimply, have taken personal interest; others allege differently." No one spoke.

The sun had already set. Rosa wound and unwound a ball of light blue wool. Go and Come kept coughing. A thin layer of dust, just like fog, covered everything. Suddenly Ermine the weasel turned up, panting.

"Run, ruuuuunn, they are bur...," was all she said before falling unconscious.

Perry, the strange parrot who believed he was a doctor—and appeared to help even before he was called for when a calamity broke out—stooped over her. The dust turned into thick smoke, and the sky became red. The first flames showed themselves from behind the mountain.

Rosa hastened to the telephone to reach Goody the woodsman; she had forgotten he had already left and he would not answer. When trying to call the fire brigade, she heard a thin voice repeating: please, wait for your turn, please, wait for your turn . . . She put the phone down. "Help, help," she cried.

She took the water hose she watered her garden with and started sprinkling water as far as she could. "Help, heeeeelp," all the birds started chittering and scattered in the sky. Sol, who had hurt one of his feathers and could not fly, got on Peach's back. He sprang up and started galloping toward the town, like a slingshot. The flames grew bigger, the smoke made everything float in a gray cloud that turned pitch-black. Peach turned his head to see; nothing was visible, so he started barking like mad: "Help, help, FIRE."

What Happened to the Forest?

When Rosa woke up, everything around her was white. The bedsheets, the bedside table, the walls. All she could see from the white window was Sol with his golden key. She had been taken to hospital, he told her, because she had fainted from the smoke.

"And what about the forest?" she whispered. He told her everything. "Peach ran for help. The children were the first to realize what was happening, and they ran uphill like lightning to save the forest. The firemen also came with huge water hoses. However, if the eagle Open-eyes had not brought heavy rain, nothing could have been done. Half the forest was saved. The back side of the mountain, though, was burnt to ashes. The cedars, the pine forest with the mountain herb tea, and ...," he faltered.

"And what else?" asked Rosa, almost angry.

"The wolf Lycurgus, his son Lucky, and Ermine the weasel ... they perished. Maybe McCrow the raven, too; no one has seen him since."

Her eyes filled with tears.

"Goody? Did he come to help?" she murmured.

"He was not seen at all, Rosa."

Little Green Cap

The days and the years went by. "When evil calls, some people wake up," Little Red Cap's grandmother used to say.

And indeed, after this destruction some . . . woke up. The plans of the big multinational company "Claws Universal and Sons" for the development, that is, the destruction, of the forest fell through. After the fire the government could not but decide: r e f o r e s t a t i o n. The international organization "Green Cap" supervised the works and, indeed, the mountainside was replanted, and a big wild animal reserve was made. They called it "Lycurgus and Ermine," to honor the animals that perished in the fire.

Every Sunday the children—and some grownups, too—climbed the mountain and planted "trees of the heart," as Rosa called them; they dug the ground and watered them, and the woods were filled with their laughter.

Sky and earth twine together
In all kinds of weather
Flying in and out of moon
In a lovely slow tune

Donkeys, sheep, and hens are laughing
Frogs are whispering me something
Like a secret, like a wish
Like a prayer or a kiss

Lilies, violets will grow
And the gray storm will go
The winters will slip
On a pine needle strip

Till a smile will shine
As a rare firefly
Everywhere in my dreams
In the forests, in the fields . . .

And what happened to Rosa? Rosa stayed forever in the little house in the woods she inherited from her grandmother. She grew basil, gardenias, and orange trees, and sold her produce every Wednesday in the street market, along with her colorful caps, until she was too old to go down to town. In the afternoons she went to the Wild Animal Reserve and helped. Often the children came and asked her to tell them stories.

She never said no. She gave them milk pie or cold strawberry juice if it was summer and started the tale.

"Once upon a time there was a little girl who wore a red cap. One day she went to the woods to see her grandmother . . ."

Little Gray Riding Hood (O Capuchinho Cinzento)

Matilde Rosa Araújo and André Letria

Matilde Rosa Araújo (1921–2010) was an award-winning Portuguese author best known for her children's books, although she also wrote poetry and short stories for adults. Along with her career as a teacher, she began publishing books for children in 1950. She produced more than two dozen books for children in a variety of genres, including poetry, novels, and short stories. Her books have been reissued many times, and several of her early works are still in print, testifying to her great popularity as an author. Araújo received numerous awards, including the grand prize for literature for children from the Calouste Gulbenkian Foundation in 1980. Like Gabriela Mistral, the long-time teacher was concerned with children's problems and unwaveringly defended their rights. She did not hesitate to engage children in a dialogue on difficult themes, such as poverty and abandonment. *O Capuchinho Cinzento* (Little Gray Riding Hood), published in 2005, is one of the last works by the author. The book's illustrations are by the award-winning Portuguese illustrator André Letria (1973–). Letria has also directed an animated short film and an animated TV series adapted from his books, worked as a set designer, and founded a publishing house.

Araújo's own advanced age when she wrote the book undoubtedly explains her choice of an elderly Riding Hood whose story allows a reflection on old age. As Sara Reis da Silva points out, the picturebook offers "a profound reflection on the human condition and the transience of life."[17] Despite the subject matter, the dedication, "To all children, with great tenderness . . . ," clearly established that the intended audience is indeed children. The 56-page picturebook makes great demands on young readers, as it is a kind of poem in prose. The style is emotional and intimate, and the evocative imagery appeals to all the senses. Recurring phrases, words, and sounds create a haunting, incantatory melody. Araújo's rewriting demonstrates the importance of the oral tradition and retains many of its strategies, although the narrator is in the process of writing down her story. The substitution of gray for red in the eponymous heroine's name obviously has symbolic implications. The protagonist's age is not immediately visible, however, as she is seen only from the back on the book's cover, a perspective that is maintained in most of the interior illustrations. One striking illustration shows only her nose and mouth, while focusing on the hand bearing the shining thimble and holding the jug (plate 16). (An unusual closeup of the same hand is framed on another full-page illustration.) In this manner Letria conveys the symbolism attached to these objects in the text. Letria uses a palette of predominantly black and gray, with a few touches of vivid red—thickly applied paint with visible brush-strokes—to create a dark, mysterious atmosphere that complements the

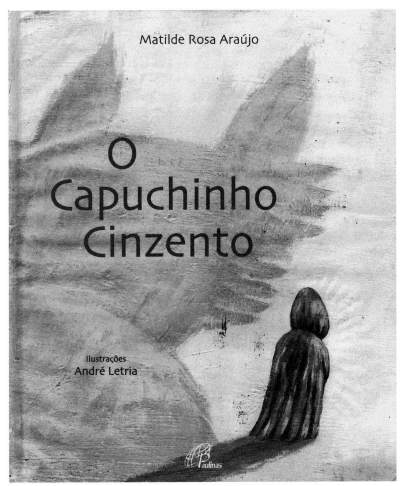

Matilde Rosa Araújo

O
Capuchinho
Cinzento

Ilustrações
André Letria

21. *O Capuchinho Cinzento*, by Matilde Rosa Araújo. Illustrations by André Letria. Text copyright © 2012 Matilde Rosa Araújo/SPA; illustrations copyright © 2012 André Letria. Used by permission of SPA.

rather enigmatic, poetic text. Gray is predominant, as the color associated with maturity and old age, but also with melancholy and grief. The stark, bare branches of the dark trees that seem menacingly to surround the protagonist create a melancholic mood and highlight the fact that she is in the winter of her life.

The classic story of childhood and fear has been transformed into a story about old age and fear conquered. When the little birds who tell the story evoke the Red Riding Hood the protagonist used to be, the illustration on the facing page is a striking image of the little girl in the red hood peering out a hole in the cover of an old-looking, red, leather-bound book, a splash of vivid color in the otherwise dark, subdued illustrations of the story of the Gray Riding Hood. Through the familiar story, Araújo explores the passage of time, the fusion of past and present, the continuum of life from childhood through old age. The little girl, whose grandmother once sewed for her, is now a grandmother who sews for her own grandchildren. Readers see the changes wrought by a lifetime of experience and how time transforms people physically, mentally, and spiritually. The little girl who once set off energetically for her grandmother's is now a tired, old grandmother whose body has become more fragile with age. The once-naïve little girl has become a wise woman, living in harmony with nature, able to commune with Mother Nature, the elements, and the celestial bodies. Despite her past traumatic experience, the former Little Red Riding Hood is not fearful, and she has learned to live peacefully with the wolf. Haunting closeups of the characters' eyes create a very intimate tête-à tête in the illustrations. Two consecutive spreads early in the book depict striking closeups first of Little Gray Riding Hood's large dark eyes, framed under gray eyebrows, and then of the wolf's almost identical large dark eyes under equally gray eyebrows. The revelation in the text that the wolf's eyes are full of tenderness as he watches the old woman sleep is accompanied by another closeup of the wolf's large dark eyes framed in what looks like a red mirror. Little Gray Riding Hood's large eyes fill the final spread, and mirrored within the pupils is a portrait of the wolf and the old woman's hand reaching out to pet him. Araújo and Letria retell the classic tale of fear and violence as a moving story about the tender friendship between Riding Hood and the wolf.

The enigmatic text and illustrations create a sense of foreboding in the reader, which echoes that of the narrator. Until the final pages, the wolf is a menacing presence, depicted as an animal, but anthropomorphized by his upright gait, his boots, and the capitalization of his name. Little Gray Riding Hood is a small figure seen from the back in the bottom right corner of the front cover, oblivious to the huge, threatening shadow cast over her by the relatively small figure of the wolf on the back cover. The reader and even the narrator bring to the book their memories of the classic tale, and they initially react to the events of the story in the light of those memories. Araújo creates an opposition between the ignorance and fear of the classic version and the knowledge and peace of a retelling that presents life in terms of an initiatory journey from the darkness to the light. In several illustrations of the old woman, particularly the two that reveal her face, she is surrounded by a luminous aura, as is the magical thimble. The shadow of fear and the gloomy sense of melancholy and loneliness are dissipated by the comradeship between the wolf and the former Little Red Riding Hood in the twilight of their lives. At the end of the book, there is only a profound sense of peace and serenity. Araújo's unusual poetic retelling is a multilayered text that speaks to young and old alike.

Little Gray Riding Hood (2005)

To all children, with great tenderness . . .

What can I tell?
Little crystal birds,[18] why have they been around my head telling me a story
    that I do not understand?
The Moon is turning in the night
and my dazed head listening, listening.
The Moon so round, large, full of light,
will go to rest while the night will be dying . . .

Little crystal birds, what do you have to tell me?
And the little crystal birds, flying, singing:
"It is the story of Little Gray Riding Hood,
who was little red riding hood
the girl who took a little snack to her grandmother
and met a bad wolf!"
"Oh, delicate crystal singers, tell me,
sing me what happened to Little Gray Riding Hood,
now so old?"
"Remember Little Red Riding Hood
walking through the peaceful, green forest?
A forest of green leaves wet with pearls of dew?
A fragrant forest
with the scent of the leaves that danced in the wind?
That dried with the fire of light
that fell from heaven?"

"Oh delicate crystal singers help me,
bring to my mind a silver kiss from the cold waters
to wake me.
I only see Old Gray Riding Hood
very close, very close to me.
And I see a Wolf with boots of thorns
walking, walking, walking . . .

Alas, little crystal birds,
Where is Old Gray Riding Hood going?"
"She is perhaps going to the source to hear the violin of flowing water,
or to get a little jug of water.
The water, when it gets trapped inside the little clay jug,

cannot sing.
But it quenches thirst!"
"Little crystal birds,
tell me what I cannot tell. Sing!
Did you see a shining thimble on the finger of Old Gray Riding Hood?"
"She forgot to take it off
when she went to the source.
She was mending the shorts and skirts of her grandchildren,
those holes in the clothes that only children know how to make.
She suddenly stood up and started walking . . ."
"You know, little birds? I can hear
Old Gray Riding Hood sing!
With a trembling voice,
now a tiny bit hoarse.
Chanting and sweet as
when she had the red riding hood.
And was going so happily, through the woods,
carrying the little lunch to her grandmother.

Oh! But now I still see the Wolf walking, walking . . .
toward Old Gray Riding Hood."
"She did not notice him, as she was singing so and already a little deaf.
And the Wolf comes slowly, gently, very gently, so as not to frighten her."
"Little crystal birds,
help me now!
I am troubled as I tell this story.
A story that happened.
Really.
And it seems to want to continue . . .
O delicate crystal birds,
so why does that
Old Gray Riding Hood
go to the source?
It is still night, and she sings, sings
and the full Moon dances in the sky!"
The Wolf advances, advances toward her. And the Old Woman does not hear
his steps . . . It seems her hearing only understands
the violin of water from the fountain that she's going to capture in the little
    clay jug.
The Old Woman now feels tired, her legs are weak,
sore from being so old.
So, see a rock in the forest, almost hidden
under the moss cover. And there she sits,
with difficulty (ouch, how it hurts to bend her knees!).

She sits, putting the little jug on her aching knees
and, little by little, she lets herself fall asleep.
It is still dark, but almost day . . .
It beats in silence, the hidden heart of the forest.
Only the thimble shines on the finger of Little Gray Riding Hood,
magical and shining like the tears from a star.
The Wolf slowly, very slowly, is coming to the rock covered with moss.
where the Old Woman rests, asleep. Even a queen of bygone days
could not rest so on a velvet throne!
And the Wolf slowly, very slowly, comes closer to the rock—the Wolf,
with boots with thorns, eyes of lights, huge jaws
showing sharp, threatening teeth.

"Oh, little crystal birds, I myself who am writing
here on my desk, at home, I'm afraid. Help me.
You cannot scare away the Wolf, can you?
They are such fragile birds, with their wings of feather. Airy . . .
I know you are also afraid. But sing!
We will not desert the Old Woman, will we?
Look, she dreams and smiles, her face full of wrinkles
beneath the gray hood.
And she holds the little jug in her hands,
the thimble shining like the tear of a star.
The flowers still sleep in the woods,
their petals closed in the warmth of the ground.
The cloak of night rises slowly."
"And the Wolf, little birds?"
"The Wolf comes, comes softly to the sleeping Old Woman.
And stops, dazzled. His eyes are lights of tenderness!
He gently licks the hands
that hold the little jug,
he licks the thimble, star of the Sun.
Old Gray Riding Hood shudders.
She almost wakes up at the feel of the rough tongue
that passes over her hands
that hold the little jug. And she smiles.
She wakes up slowly and looks at the Wolf with her tired eyes.
Pets it, like the Wolf was a dog.
The Sun has just come up and, dancing amidst ancient rays,
celebrates this reunion. And kisses the thimble, his brother of light."

"Little birds of crystal,
tell me if I'm dreaming,
or if it is Gray Riding Hood who dreams.

Delicate little birds of crystal,
are you the ones singing the answer to this question?
Or is it the Moon that danced in the sky?
Or the children in torn shorts and skirts that Grandma was going to mend?
Or the music of water inside the little jug?
Or the flowers that the Sun awoke?
Or the magic of the thimble?
Sing! Sing!
Do not stop singing,
fly,
so this story, of limpid secrets, never ends . . ."

THREE

Playing with the Story of Red Riding Hood and the Wolf

Whoever wants to play the Little Red Cap game . . .

Janosch, "Das elektrische Rotkäppchen"

The Tale of Little Red Riding Hood
(Le conte du Petit Chaperon Rouge)

Pef

"Pef" is the pen name Pierre Elie Ferrier (1939–)—journalist, author, and illustrator—uses for his children's books. The prolific author, known for his wit and clever wordplay, has published more than a hundred illustrated books for children. In 1984 he received the Hans Christian Andersen Prize. Many of his books have been published by Éditions La Farandole (later Messidor/La Farandole), a publisher specializing in children's literature, which later was part of the Messidor group of French communist publishing houses.

"Le conte du Petit Chaperon Rouge" was published in 1991, in the fourteenth volume of *Contes comme la lune* (Tales like the Moon), a collection of tales which seek, through humorous transgression, to renew the genre of the tale. Paradoxically, the rather old-fashioned design of the volumes is reminiscent of nineteenth-century books. Pef accompanies his retelling of "Little Red Riding Hood" with several drawings. A rather ambiguous drawing on the title page depicts the little girl peering out of the open wolf's jaws, but it is unclear whether the wolf is eating her or she is wearing a very real-looking wolf's head. The wolf's long upper jaw resembles a rather unusual pointed bonnet not so different from the one the protagonist wears in the drawing on the first page of the story. Pef's second drawing is enlarged and reproduced on the right front endpaper, so that a rather homely, decidedly shamefaced-looking version of the famous fairy tale icon greets readers on the threshold of the volume of subversive tales.

Pef's retelling of "Little Red Riding Hood" is a tongue-in-cheek commentary on the extensive theorizing of critics, folklorists, and psychoanalysts about the significance of the heroine's red headgear, in which he offers several absurd hypotheses of his own. The nonsensical story ends abruptly with the comparison of Little Red Riding Hood to a red light, which, as a universal warning to stop, constitutes a very pertinent symbol in a cautionary tale. However, red is also the color associated with sensual arousal and sexual desire, as Pef's earlier sexual innuendos clearly remind older readers. Child and adult perspectives on the famous story are juxtaposed, and the validity of such "adult" theories is questioned by the incensed child protagonist herself. As the parenthetical note on the title page indicates, Pef's Riding Hood, to whom the narrator briefly gives voice, seems to be "settling the score" with adult readers on behalf of generations of child readers. Although the author signs this text "Pef," the sexual innuendos are directed at an older, knowing audience.

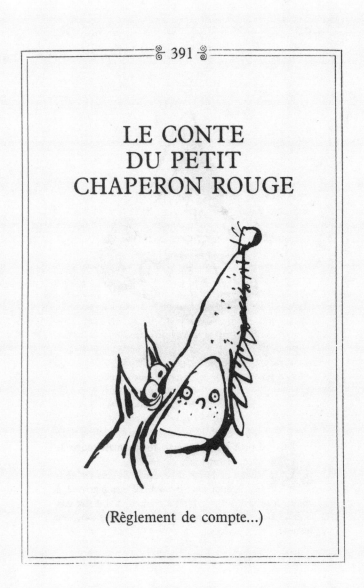

22. "Le conte du Petit Chaperon Rouge," by Pef, from *Contes comme la lune*. Copyright © 1991 Messidor/La Farandole. Used by permission of Pef.

23. "Le conte du Petit Chaperon Rouge," by Pef, from *Contes comme la lune*. Copyright © 1991 Messidor/La Farandole. Used by permission of Pef.

THE TALE OF LITTLE RED RIDING HOOD (1991)

(Settling of scores . . .)[1]

The little riding hood was red, but red from what, I ask you?

Red from shame, perhaps? If that is proven to be true, what was she ashamed of? Of her poverty, definitely. Walking through a forest, instead of being in command of a 4 x 4, is certainly not worth a story.

But, maybe, she was red with anger. That her mother dragged her from the TV had, in this case, probably made her hopping mad.

Or the riding hood was red with embarrassment at the simple idea of taking a cake to her enormous grandmother, who had a lot of back pain because of her natural gluttony. With, in addition, let us never forget, that famous little pot of butter, not even low calorie.

Let us also ask the possible question of a red of disgrace melting on the little riding hood. Because we have never seen a little girl talk to a wolf.

"What turpitude!" lamented the kid. To make millions of children swallow this idiotic story that generations of adults are unable to forget without really having thought about it further!

You must be careful what you write, because it is also possible that the riding hood was nothing but a little red light lost among all the green lights in the forest.

It is strongly recommended to stop at a red light, that's why we will not go any further, and we will try, shortly, to find out exactly what color Bluebeard's beard was.

Little Red Cap Another Way
(Crvenkapica na drugi način)

Zoran Pongrašić

The Croatian author Zoran Pongrašić (1961–) agrees with a writer friend who once called him a "general practitioner" writer.[2] He writes prose for all ages, as well as radio dramas, movie scenarios, and television series. While his novels for adults have a more serious tone, all of his work for children and teenagers is in a humorous vein. During the school year 2005–2006, the author began retelling stories for the children's magazine *Prvi izbor* (First Choice), the first of which was "The Ant and the Grasshopper." When he decided to publish some of these stories in a book in 2010, he focused on fairy tales, titling the book *Zašto (ne) volim bajke* (Why I [Don't] Like Fairy Tales). The collection contains nine fairy tales, one of which is "Crvenkapica na drugi način" (Little Red Cap Another Way). The book was followed, the same year, by a second volume, titled simply *Zašto (ne) volim bajke 2*, which Pongrašić wrote this time with his daughter Ema, who is also a writer. (Four tales by Pongrašić are followed by five tales by his daughter.) Both volumes were illustrated by the Croatian illustrator Ivana Guljašević (1970–), whose artwork bears the mark of her work in comics and animated films.

Pongrašić told me he wrote these books because he thinks the original stories written by the Grimm brothers and Hans Christian Andersen are "completely inappropriate for children because of their brutality and because of their complete lack of humor." There is certainly no lack of humor in his fairy tales, although some adults might consider certain elements inappropriate for children. Five stories in the book have the words "na drugi način" (another way) added to the original title, including "Hansel and Gretel" and "Snow White." When Croatians speak of the fairy-tale heroine in English (Croatian readers begin learning English as a second language at a very young age), they usually refer to Little Red Riding Hood rather than Little Red Cap, but since Croatian versions are traditionally adapted from the Grimms' version and the Croatian title evokes a little cap (*kapica* is the diminutive of *kapa*, meaning "cap"), the latter has been retained. The Grimms' title is particularly fitting in the case of Pongrašić's story, as the cap is actually mentioned in the text. As in the Grimms' version, a hunter saves the day, but he bears the traditional Croatian name of Luka. Guljašević's single illustration for the story is reproduced on the cover of the volume. Her simple, cartoonlike illustrations throughout the book complement the author's take on classic fairy tales. In the illustration for "Little Red Cap Another Way," which depicts the encounter scene, the protagonist and the wolf are childlike figures with stick legs and simple dots or lines for features. Little Red Cap stares smilingly at the reader, apparently oblivious to the wolf, who fixes the

24. "Crvenkapica na drugi način," from *Zašto (ne) volim bajke*, by Zoran Pongrašić. Illustrations by Ivana Guljašević. Text copyright © 2010 Zoran Pongrašić; illustrations copyright © 2010 Ivana Guljašević. Used by permission of Zoran Pongrašić and Ivana Guljašević.

little girl with what also appears to be a smile revealing exaggeratedly large, sharp, sharklike teeth.

Like many postmodern versions, Pongrašić's story focuses on the disruption of the suspension of disbelief, encouraging readers to question the realistic implications of the traditional story. Smiljana Narančić Kovač rightly compares his approach to that sometimes used by Roald Dahl, as, for example, in his retelling of "Goldilocks and the Three Bears" in *Revolting Rhymes*.[3] Like Dahl, Pongrašić also incorporates jokes aimed at adults, which may also be understood by children, although some readers may feel some are in bad taste, as in the case of the alcoholic grandmother. The reference in the original to "a special school"—that is, a school for children with special needs and learning disabilities—may also be considered not very politically correct, so we have substituted "a school for children with special needs." Pongrašić's retellings are full of nonsensical wordplay, which is sometimes introduced in footnotes. The Croatian word *narkoza*, meaning "anesthetic," is treated as a pun and given a nonsensical explanation in the footnote: a she-goat (*koza*) who takes drugs (*narko*, from the Croatian word *narkotic*, meaning an addictive drug)[4]. In his retelling, Pongrašić skeptically questions almost every element of the Grimms' version before pronouncing it "a silly tale" and conspiratorially inviting the reader's concurrence.

~

LITTLE RED CAP ANOTHER WAY (2010)

If there is anything I do not like, really do not like, then it is tales that are completely impossible. Such as, for instance, the story about Little Red Cap. You know, like once upon a time there was a little girl, whose Granny made her a red cap, and they called her Little Red Cap, because when she stuffed that cap onto her head, she never took it off. *Never*? Not even when she went to bed? Not even when she had a shower? Hmm, I wonder what that stupid cap looked like after, say, three and a half months of constantly being worn on her head. Does it not seem impossible?

And then Granny got sick, and Little Red Cap's mother gave her the chore of taking some food to Granny. To be more precise, cakes and wine. *Wine*? For sick Granny? Instead of taking her some cough syrup—*alcohol*? Is Granny a once treated (and never really cured) alcoholic*? But that's impossible!

And then Little Red Cap is carrying those cakes (and that alcohol) and meets a wolf (who speaks a human language, which is again completely impossible!), and then she gives away everything, where she is going and why she is going there and where her sick and helpless Granny lives. And then suddenly she forgets all about Granny and starts picking flowers. She does not care a bit if Granny starves to death. And is perhaps having an alcohol withdrawal seizure. And the wolf goes to Granny's house and swallows that one (the Granny, not the house).

Well, that is one of the yuckiest parts in the whole tale. Except that it is *impossible* to swallow the whole Granny in one piece just like that—that part

---

**A person (e.g., a Granny) who cannot live without alcohol. (If she does not drink something, she cannot even sew red caps. And when she does, she cannot either.)*

makes me throw up. Swallow a Granny? Old and sick? Oh, man, that makes you infected right away! With at least three different infectious diseases. Or at least you get the runs. One of those bigger ones.

And then follows the masquerade. The wolf puts on Granny's nightgown and nightcap (just don't ask me how he managed that, when, as you know, he does not have hands or fingers), lies down in Granny's bed, and pretends to be the sick Granny. And then along comes Little Red Cap. With cakes, alcohol, and a small bunch of flowers. And with a red cap, of course. And then there comes the most impossible part of the story, the part about big ears and big eyes and big mouth. You know that line: "Granny, Granny, what big (now you fill in the previous items) you've got!" I mean, who is crazy there?! Does Little Red Cap really think that the wolf is her Granny, just, well, looking a bit strange?! I suppose it is normal to her that when grannies get sick, their ears, and eyes, and mouths, instantly grow. Not to mention the hair. Come on, really. That Little Red Cap either attends a school for children with special needs or she needs ashtray-thick glasses.** For goodness sake, it seems to her that her own Granny (the mom of her *own* mom, great-granny of her *own* future children—even though who would like to marry her, being so stupid and blind?) and that wolf are as similar as if they were twins. The twin Granny and the twin wolf! It is really hard to believe that someone has even dared to tell such an impossible story.

And the ending is no better. After that stupidity with ears, eyes, and mouth, the wolf swallows up Little Red Cap, too! Listen to this, he had already gobbled up the Granny, and now the granddaughter, too. And where does he put all that?! Is he a wolf or an oceanliner?! And that swallowing business is a stupidity larger than life. Namely, although they are swallowed up, Granny and the Little Red Cap meet there inside the wolf, alive and in good health. And they probably even keep hugging and kissing each other till they are fully content. And maybe they even talk to each other. "What, he swallowed you, too?" "Yeah, a moment ago." "Oooh, horrible, isn't it?" "Yeah, it reeks horribly in his mouth." Etc., etc., etc. And then Luke the Hunter comes by, and sees the wolf, and immediately understands what has happened, and (now comes the bloody part!) cuts the wolf's belly with a pair of scissors (and he sleeps and does not even notice that someone is cutting him?! As if the eaten-up Granny and Little Red Cap were some kind of narcosis***), and he shouts to them inside: "Stop talking! Come on, all out! Move!" And when Granny and Little Red Cap get out, they fill the wolf with stones, which somehow fall heavy on his stomach, and he dies because of that.

Well, what a silly tale![5] Isn't it?

** *A special kind of glasses (ask your teacher for details).*
*** *A sis(ter) who sells drugs.*

Two Stories about Little Red Cap from *The Snow King* (Snježni kralj)

Damir Miloš, Radovan Devlić, and Krešimir Skozret

The short retelling by the acclaimed Croatian author Damir Miloš (1954–) is an embedded story from his picturebook *Snježni kralj* (The Snow King, 1986), illustrated by the prominent Croatian comics artists Radovan Devlić (1950–2000) and Krešimir Skozret (1951–). Miloš is an author and adventurer; he is often described as a writer who sails and a sailor who writes. His numerous novels for adults experiment with narrative techniques and borders, which explain the postmodern tendencies in his children's books. Although he currently writes novels and short stories for adults, he has also written three children's novels, including *Bijeli klaun* (The White Clown, 1988), which is one of the most acclaimed contemporary Croatian novels for children and is on the eighth-grade reading list for Croatian students. The novel has been compared to Saint-Exupéry's *The Little Prince*, and it has a philosophical dimension that is undoubtedly the result of the author's philosophical studies. The novel tells the story of a boy who cannot see colors and lives in a world that is gray both literally and metaphorically; yet he learns, with the help of an old man, to find his own color, or rather non-color: white, the color of innocence and childhood. Miloš's interest in colors is also evident in *The Snow King*, which was published two years earlier, and is his only fiction picturebook.

The illustrations are an integral part of *The Snow King*, which is to be expected when the illustrators are comics artists. Those that accompany the first Little Red Cap story are so directly connected to it that it seemed essential to reproduce them here. Devlić drew all the pictures, but because he was working with only brown hues at the time and was not inclined to color them, Skozret applied color to the final illustrations. As the latter pointed out, it is impossible to depict snow with brown. Devlić and Skozret knew each other well and could collaborate in this manner because they had already worked together from time to time; both also belonged to the Novi kvadrat (New Square), a group of Croatian cartoonists established in 1977. The group's promotion and improvement of the art of comics left a lasting impact on the fields of Croatian graphic art, comics, and illustration in general. The members of the group were extremely talented cartoonists who shared common interests but left individual marks on the art of comics and other forms of visual narration, ranging from animated movies to graphic novels. Devlić died, regrettably, in 2000, as a result of ailments related to his participation, along with Skozret, in the war for Croatian independence in the 1990s. Skozret is now retired and lives on a Croatian island, where he paints landscapes.

25. *Snježni kralj*, by Damir Miloš. Illustrations by Radovan Devlić and Krešimir Skozret. Text copyright © 1986 Damir Miloš; illustrations copyright Radovan Devlić and Krešimir Skozret. Used by permission of Damir Miloš, Dora Devlić, and Krešimir Skozret.

The Snow King is an unusual picturebook, as it presents a rather fragmentary narrative sprinkled with intertexts, such as the story of Little Red Cap. The frame story, which a casual remark by the narrator sets in the twenty-first century, is narrated in the first person by a little girl who is waiting for the return of the Snow King. As she waits she tells us about him: her first meeting with him, his ice castle, the stories he told her, and so forth. She also tells readers about the Spring Prince, a confirmed liar who lies about everything, especially when he talks about the Snow King and his wife. (The little girl, who is in love with the Snow King, exclaims categorically that he does not have a wife, and the story ends with her dreams of the day he will return to marry her.) As the girl relates the Snow King's many wonderful qualities—his ability to tame animals and to confront monsters, his nobility and courage—references or allusions to various intertexts appear, including Homer's *Odyssey*, Hans Christian Andersen's "Snow Queen," other European fairy tales, the story of the Garden of Eden, the legend of the Phoenix, and the tale of the Loch Ness monster. The idea of a monster in the lake—"monsters in the 21st century?!"—is presented as proof that the Spring Prince is a liar. Miloš's story is generally told in a serious tone, although it is sprinkled with humorous, even nonsensical elements in a style somewhat reminiscent of Lewis Carroll's. Miloš changes the rules in a rather Carrollian manner by using the color green to indicate lying instead of envy.

As with Pongrašić's version, the translation of the protagonist's name was not an immediately obvious choice, and the author himself, when consulted, was undecided. Although the illustrations present the girl wearing a riding hood rather than a cap, the text mentions the hunter, and, as we have already seen, the Croatian literary tradition of the tale derives from the Grimms' version. The beginning of the first excerpt includes a reference to the eponymous protagonist of the frame story, the Snow King; this "Little Red Cap" is the result of his extensive reading and a desire to set the record straight. Later in the story, the girl again refers to the tale, this time the Spring Prince's version, as further proof that the latter is a liar. Miloš's subversive metafictive play with "Little Red Cap" is quite subtle. The first excerpt, which directly questions the "truth" of the classic story, presents the paradoxical situation of a story that predates the so-called true story. (We are told that Little Red Cap would meet the wolf later.) Yet the sow was already familiar with the tale prior to her meeting with Little Red Cap (plate 17). The embedding of a second version of the tale highlights this questioning of the "truth" of stories.

Miloš explores the rather blurred borders between truth and fiction in a number of ways. Readers are encouraged to question the reliability of the young narrator, who is herself fictional. If even the classic Grimms' version can be called into question, why should the reader take the conceivably biased little girl's word for it that the true version is that of the Snow King and not that of the Spring Prince? The embedded Little Red Cap story, regardless of the version, does not really seem more fictional than the world of the frame story, in which a little girl of the twenty-first century awaits the arrival of her beloved Snow King. The postmodern concerns of the author's adult fiction make their way into his innovative picturebook for children, where the story of Little Red Cap allows him to engage in metafictional play that is accessible to children but nonetheless complex.

Nekada davno on je pročitao sve knjige i zna sve priče napamet. I jako mu je žao što se neke priče krivo prepričavaju. Evo, na primjer, ova... Crvenkapica:
Znate li vi da Crvenkapica nije nikada srela vuka?! U stvari jest, ali kasnije!
Sve je točno dok Crvenkapica ne naide puteljkom i ne sretne...
Snježni Kralj mi je ispričao istinu! Ovo što ću vam ispričati nemojte prepričavati mami ili tati, možda samo baki...
... jer neke bake znaju istinu, ali šute... neke su i umrle.

Crvenkapica je srela divlju svinju!

26. *Snježni kralj,* by Damir Miloš. Illustrations by Radovan Devlić and Krešimir Skozret. Text copyright © 1986 Damir Miloš; illustrations copyright Radovan Devlić and Krešimir Skozret. Used by permission of Damir Miloš, Dora Devlić, and Krešimir Skozret.

ॐ

Two Stories about Little Red Cap
from *The Snow King* (Snježni kralj, 1986)

Long ago the Snow King read all the books, and he knows all the stories by heart. And he is very sorry that some stories are told in a wrong way. Well, for instance, this one . . .

Little Red Cap:

Do you know that Little Red Cap never met a wolf?! In fact, she did, but later!

Everything is right until the moment when Little Red Cap comes along the path and meets . . .

The Snow King told me the truth! Do not retell what I will tell you to Mom or Dad, perhaps only to Granny . . .

. . . because some grannies know the truth, but they keep silent . . . some have even died.

Little Red Cap met a wild swine!

Swine will be swine, she was full. She had stuffed herself with acorns when Little Red Cap came along the path. The sow knew the story about Little Red Cap, and she was embarrassed to find herself in the wolf's place. Whom the sow learned the story from, not even the Snow King knows that.

Anyway, the sow talked with Little Red Cap as if she were the wolf.

Little Red Cap is also to blame because she pretended everything was all right.

Swine will be swine, she did not want to end up like the wolf—to be killed by the hunter in the end—so, having said goodbye to Little Red Cap, she ran to the wolf and told him everything. The wolf went to the granny's, and, of course, came to a murky end! That is the truth!

. . .

I met the Spring Prince when I was coming back from the ice castle.

How he likes to lie! That is best seen from his color. He who lies is green in color, and the Spring Prince is green all over. Like a rag!

He tells every story, whether old or new, somehow differently. I have already told the truth about Little Red Cap, and who was first, the wolf or the swine?! And you know what the Spring Prince is saying? It is all gibberish. That Little Red Cap was going through the wood and met a wolf. And she did not! And that the wolf talked to Little Red Cap, ran to the granny's, ate the granny, and got into bed! In the end, the hunter came, killed the wolf, wounded the granny . . . incredible! That the hunter and the granny got married and lived happily ever after . . . and that Little Red Cap was late! What a disgrace!

Little Red Riding Hood (O Červené Karkulce)

ALOIS MIKULKA

A painter and sculptor by profession, Alois Mikulka (1933–), who lives in Brno, is one of the most original Czech fairy-tale authors/illustrators of the past fifty years. He creates short, highly imaginative, often nonsensical stories where the text is most prominent, as well as picturebooks dominated by the unique visual style that has characterized his work since his first book, *Aby se děti divily* (To Make the Children Wonder), published in 1961. The author-illustrator has always refused to be influenced by trends and fashions in writing or art, so there is a recognizable consistency to his style over the years. Mikulka takes pleasure in reintroducing his favorite fairy-tale or pulp characters—including witches, clowns, giants, cowboys, and vampires—into the modern world, in titles such as *Supermani, medvědi a trampové* (Supermen, Bears, and Hikers, 1990).

Among the traditional fairy tales he reinvents, "Little Red Riding Hood" has a prominent role. In his more recent books, including *Karkulka v maskáčích* (Red Riding Hood in Battle Fatigues, 2001), Mikulka shifts from situational humor to a more refined comedy that depends largely on character portrayal and style. The novel, illustrated by the author, features a bright, audacious, and mischievous girl, whose riding hood contrasts with the camouflage outfit she wears into the forest. Having escaped from an orphanage, she is hunted by police and finds refuge in a house that belongs not to Grandmother but to the traditional witch of Slavic and especially Russian folklore, Baba Yaga. ("Baba" means "old woman" or "grandmother" in most Slavic languages.) In the forest Red Riding Hood encounters thirty hungry wolves who want to eat her and a gamekeeper, but also a bear, a gorilla, a robot, and Tom Thumb, among others.

The retelling that follows, chosen by the author for this anthology, is an older work published in 1974, in a collection of short tales titled *Dvanáct usmívajících se ježibab* (Twelve Smiling Witches). The other tales in the volume, all consisting of only one or two pages, are modern variations of traditional tales in the same vein as the reworking of "Little Red Riding Hood."

Mikulka opens his tale with the formulaic incipit, but rather than present the eponymous heroine, he introduces the wolf—or rather the werewolf, whose presence is unusual in a retelling for children. This explains in part the success of this retelling, as the werewolf is a familiar figure in Slavic folklore. However, the author demystifies the conventional image of the werewolf by giving him a humorous idiosyncrasy: he is cross-eyed. Mikulka's use of the Czech verb meaning "to squint" in constructions where the verb "to see" or "to look" is generally used is as unusual and surprising for Czech readers as it is for English readers. The author's writing is difficult to translate because he often invents words. Much of the humor in Mikulka's work derives from the language play and stylistic surprises. Little Red Riding Hood's threat is rendered even more comical by the substitution of "potato patties" in the expression that, in Czech as in English, is normally "to make mincemeat out of." In the very first sentence, Mikulka gives the well-known folktale a nonsensical slant that is typical of his writing and notably his retellings of fairy tales. Older readers appreciate the subtleties of the language—for example, the contrast between the werewolf's quite colloquial and expressive language and Little Red Riding Hood's much more literary and meticulous speech. It is obvious even to young readers that this fairy-tale heroine is well-educated.

The author subverts not only the traditional image of the werewolf but also the stereotypical image of Little Red Riding Hood as a pretty little girl. The subversion of the werewolf image is heightened by the illustrations, which portray a very caricatural, harmless-looking wolf rather than a werewolf. As Mikulka is a painter, illustrations are an integral part of his work. (He was quite anxious to ensure that the two illustrations from the original work would be reproduced with the translation in this book.) Although the illustrations in Mikulka's recent books, such as his Little Red Riding Hood novel, are in color, this text, like many of his early works, is accompanied by black-and-white pencil drawings that are simply a reflection of the technical limitations in book printing of the 1970s. However, the simple, childlike style is typical of Mikulka's work, which relies on hyperbole for its humorous effect. Like Pef's nonsense works, Mikulka's illustrations and writing have their own irrefutable logic, and the result is a humorous and fantastic world in which anything is possible.

27. "O Červené Karkulce," from *Dvanáct usmívajících se ježibab*, by Alois Mikulka. Copyright © 1974 Alois Mikulka. Used by permission of Alois Mikulka.

∾

LITTLE RED RIDING HOOD (1974)

Once upon a time there was a werewolf, and he squinted so greatly, that one day he managed to squint up behind nine mountains. And there he saw Little Red Riding Hood carrying a cherry cake full of candles and some blueberry juice. "Yeah!" the werewolf shouted as with seven voices at once: "This is something for me!" And hop! He jumped over the mountains and right in front of Red Riding Hood: "Boo! Huge, Ugly Riding Hood, give me your chow!" And he squinted frightfully at her. Red Riding Hood told him in a polite voice: "I'm carrying this to my grandmother for her birthday, so do not be a boor!" The werewolf was so surprised that he stuck his tongue out at her and squawked: "Eh! She doesn't seem to have any idea who I am! I'm a very dangerous villain, and if I get upset, beware of me!" Red Riding Hood did not answer a word because judo girls like her do not talk a lot. She grabbed the werewolf's tail, and for a while she beat him against the ground; then, before the werewolf could take a breath, she braided his ears in a cute plait and spoke quite disarmingly to him: "So what, earthworm?" The werewolf howled: "Mercy, my dear Little Red Riding Hood, I'm just kidding!" Red Riding Hood laughed: "Well, I am kidding as well. Otherwise, I would have made potato patties out of you!" And she put a collar on the werewolf and dragged the howling flea-infested creature through the Black Forest. They arrived at the grandmother's, and there they saw her trying, with much bemoaning, to cut wood in the courtyard; but despite her efforts she was not able to hit a single log. Red Riding

28. "O Červené Karkulce," from *Dvanáct usmívajících se ježibab*, by Alois Mikulka. Copyright © 1974 Alois Mikulka. Used by permission of Alois Mikulka.

Hood greeted her: "Hey, Grandma! I brought you a helper. He loves cutting wood!" "That's not true," shouted the werewolf, crying, but not wanting to be slapped around again by Little Red Riding Hood, in a jiffy he stood next to the woodpile, making a rumbling noise as he cut logs. Grandmother and Red Riding Hood sat down at the table and started into the cake. First they poked out the cherries and then the filling. They washed it down with blueberry juice, and at that moment all the wood in the courtyard, even the stump, had already been cut in logs as tiny as skewers. The werewolf was steaming like a laundry and breathing like a whistle. So Little Red Riding Hood gave him the rest of the cake, and he gobbled it up even with the one hundred and ninety-two candles, because that was exactly the grandmother's age. The werewolf was licking himself up behind the ears[6] that had been braided into a plait, but Little Red Riding Hood told him, "You pig! You will be sick!" But the grandmother said: "It doesn't matter if he eats soap, the important thing is that he likes it," and gave him the bottle with the rest of the blueberry juice. The werewolf gargled it down, and then he gobbled up the whole bottle, cork and all. Little Red Riding Hood shook her head, but Grandma laughed: "He is an exceedingly funny numbskull! At least we do not have to clean up after him. I'll keep him for amusement!" And that's exactly what she did.

The Electric Little Red Cap
(Das elektrische Rotkäppchen)

JANOSCH

Janosch, whose real name is Horst Eckert (1931–), is one of Germany's most successful children's author-illustrators. His award-winning children's books are popular in many European countries, but he is virtually unknown in the English-speaking world. *Janosch erzählt Grimms' Märchen und zeichnet für Kinder von heute* (Janosch Tells Grimms' Fairy Tales and Draws for Today's Children), published in 1972, is one of the few books by the internationally renowned author-illustrator to have been translated into English. *Not Quite as Grimm* appeared in London in 1974, but it has never been reprinted, and it was a truncated edition of the original that omitted approximately one-third of the tales. As the original title clearly indicates, Janosch felt the need to update the Grimms' tales for today's children. "Das elektrische Rotkäppchen," along with several other tales, was released as an album in 2007. Janosch turns the Grimms' fairy tales upside down to create witty, ironic, irreverent, and highly subversive reversions that question the hypotexts. The parody is underscored by comical pen-and-ink drawings that play a major role in the narrative. There is nonetheless a very serious intention behind Janosch's retellings, which offer a social commentary on our times. As Jack Zipes rightly points out, Janosch "shows the discomfiting results of the middle-class legacy of the Grimms' tales" and "expose[s] the shallowness of contemporary society."[7]

Janosch's recasting of "Rotkäppchen" is somewhat exceptional in that he generally tended to avoid the best-known tales in his collection. "Das elektrische Rotkäppchen" (The Electric Little Red Cap), is among the tales omitted from the translated English edition. While many of Janosch's retellings diverge significantly from the hypotext, his "Little Red Cap" follows the classic tale quite closely. The author turns it into a game that he encourages children to play in a short text titled "Das Rotkäppchenspiel" (The Little Red Cap Game), which he appends to his reversion in order to explain the rules of the game in which he himself has just engaged. The indiscriminate insertion of the word "electric" or a derivative everywhere possible places the retelling in the nonsense tradition. Although the game is somewhat mechanical, the electrical transformation of the tale is nonetheless striking, as characters, plot, and motifs take on new meaning. Everything from the cautionary scene to the latch to the demise of the wolf receives an electrical updating. Little Red Cap and the wolf become automated toys, the huntsman an electrician, and the setting an illuminated forest that evokes Disneyfied theme parks. In addition to the illustrated initial capital that begins the tale, the story is accompanied by three full-page caricatural black-and-white drawings that are reminiscent of comics. The first is a single full-page illustration, and the other

29. "Das elektrische Rotkäppchen," from *Janosch erzählt Grimm's Märchen und zeichnet für Kinder von heute*, by Janosch. Copyright © 1972, 1991 Beltz Verlag, Weinheim und Basel, Programm Beltz & Gelberg; Janosch, film & medien AG, Berlin. Used by permission of Verlagsguppe Beltz and Janosch, film & medien AG.

two are divided into frames. With four frames set sequentially in comic-strip style, complete with speech bubbles, the second illustration offers a hilarious visual rendition of events at the grandmother's house. The irreverent, witty drawings emphasize the mechanical, even robotic quality of characters who seem to have been programmed to play their roles. Janosch's witty, playful revision rejuvenates the Grimms' tale, bringing it into the modern era and using it as a social commentary on contemporary society.

The Electric Little Red Cap (1972)

Once upon a time there was a sweet electric maiden, whom everyone loved electrically, most of all her electric grandma; she could never give the child enough. One day she gave her a little, electric red velvet cap. And since it was so becoming that she did not want to wear anything else, she was called the "electric Little Red Cap."

One day her mother said to her: "Come here, electric Little Red Cap! Here is a piece of electric cake and an electric bottle of electric wine to take to your electric grandmother. She is sick and weak, and this should electrify her a bit. But take good care that you do not veer from the path, otherwise you will twist a wire! Now go on!"

She turned her child on, gave her a push, and the electric Little Red Cap set out on the electric path.

Now, the electric grandmother lived but an electric hour away behind the electric fairy-tale forest. In the electric fairy-tale forest she met the electric wolf at an electric clearing. The electric Little Red Cap did not know what a wicked and terrible electrifier he was, and she was not afraid of him.

"Good day, electric Little Red Cap," he said. "Where are you going so early?"

"To electric Grandmother's, to take her some electric cake and electric wine. It will electrify her somewhat. It will do her good."

"Where does your electric grandmother live?" asked the electric wolf.

"An electric hour away," replied the electric Little Red Cap, "behind the large electric mains, you will recognize it."

"Listen, Little Red Cap," said the electric wolf, "have you not seen the electric lights in the woods? Have you not heard the beautiful humming and himming? Go off the path! You'll see how beautifully electric everything is."

The electric Little Red Cap opened her eyes and saw that what the electric wolf said was true. And she turned slightly to the left, and deviated from the path and went into the electric fairy-tale forest. She electrified herself at the beautiful electric lights until it was five o'clock.

Meanwhile, however, the electric wolf arrived at the grandmother's electric house and said electrically: "Open up, electric Grandmother, it's the electric Little Red Cap, and I bring you electric cake and electric wine, so you can electrify yourself nicely."

"Just press the electric button," said the electric grandmother. And when the electric wolf had done that, the electric door opened.

He went in and electrically ate the electric grandmother. He put on her electric nightcap, her electric nightgown, and lay down electrically in bed. He drew the curtains electrically, and when electric Little Red Cap arrived and brought the electric gifts to the electric grandmother, it looked so strange in the electric room.

30. "Das elektrische Rotkäppchen," from *Janosch erzählt Grimm's Märchen und zeichnet für Kinder von heute*, by Janosch. Copyright © 1972, 1991 Beltz Verlag, Weinheim und Basel, Programm Beltz & Gelberg; Janosch, film & medien AG, Berlin. Used by permission of Verlagsguppe Beltz and Janosch, film & medien AG.

The electric Little Red Cap said: "Oh, how strangely electric I feel. I'm usually so happy to come to electric Granny's!"

She came closer, pulled aside the electric curtain, and said, "Oh, electric Grandma, what electrically big ears you have today?"

"The better to hear you with," replied the electric wolf.

"But what an electrically large nose you have?"

"The better to smell you with."

"And what electrically big eyes you have?"

"The better to illuminate you with."

"But you also have such an electrically large mouth!"

"Oh yes," said the electric wolf, jumped out of bed, and gobbled up electric Little Red Cap. Then he lay down again and began to snore electrically.

The electrician happened to be passing that way. He heard the electric snoring outside and said to himself: "Why on earth is the electric grandmother snoring so loudly, she surely has no electrical disturbance in her tubes!" He pushed down the electric latch, went into the electric house, and found the wolf in the electric bed. Then the electrician took his electric tool, disconnected the electric wolf from the current, and extinguished his electric life. Then he unscrewed him, and found the electric grandmother and the electric Little Red Cap in his belly and freed them.

Then the two were really happy. They shared with the electrician their electric cake and electric wine and ate it all together. Then the electrician took the electric Little Red Cap with him; he accompanied her a small electric

31. "Das elektrische Rotkäppchen," from *Janosch erzählt Grimm's Märchen und zeichnet für Kinder von heute*, by Janosch. Copyright © 1972, 1991 Beltz Verlag, Weinheim und Basel, Programm Beltz & Gelberg; Janosch, film & medien AG, Berlin. Used by permission of Verlagsguppe Beltz and Janosch, film & medien AG.

part of the way, and she went back through the electric forest to her electric mother. And throughout her life, she never, never again strayed from her electric path to visit the electric lamps, and therefore she lived yet a very long time. And if she has not died, then she is still living even today.

The Little Red Cap Game

Whoever wants to play the Little Red Cap game must put an adjective in front of each word, where it fits. For example, "square." Then it would go like this: "Once upon a time there was a sweet square maiden whom everyone loved squarely, most of all her square grandma . . . ," and so on. Or "Chinese." Then it would go like this: "Once upon a time there was a Chinese maiden whom everyone loved Chinesely . . ." And so on. Or "checkered," or "transparent." But you can also invent words that do not exist, for example, "moralide." . . .

Layla, the Wolf, and the Phone
(Laylā wa-al-dhi'b wa-l-hātif)

SANA TAYARA AND TALAR KIZIRIAN

Sanaa Omar Al-Tayara (1966–), who publishes under the name Sana Ta-yara, is a Lebanese teacher and author of children's books. She has published several children's books with the juvenile publisher Asala in Beirut, which also brought out the picturebook *Laylā wa-al-dhi'b wa-l-hātif* (Layla, the Wolf, and the Phone) in 2011. The small-format paperback was marketed for children from four to seven years of age. It is illustrated by Talar Kizirian, a Lebanese illustrator of Armenian descent, whose mixed cultural heritage is evident in her work. Her children's books portray characters of Armenian and Lebanese origin. Kizirian has a degree in graphic design and a minor in fine arts, but her work also bears the mark of a childhood spent drawing and painting.

Tayara offers an updated rendition of the traditional Arabic version of "Little Red Riding Hood," which is known as "Laylā wa-al-dhi'b" (Layla and the Wolf). The heroine of her tale retains the traditional Arabic name of Little Red Riding Hood, Laylā (which appears without the diacritic in the English translation). Details, such as the grandmother's head scarf that the wolf dons, suggest a Middle Eastern setting, but the illustrations also bear traces of Kizirian's Armenian heritage. Layla is a modern heroine who wears a dark-red sweatshirt with a hood and long red stockings. While her tale does not entirely eliminate male rescuers, Tayara offers modern children a resourceful young heroine who saves herself and her grandmother with her quick-thinking use of her mobile phone. The illustrations are influenced by comics and animated cartoons: the caricatural characters, the question marks in Layla's eyes as she engages in the formulaic dialogue, the floating hearts, and a large thought bubble. While Layla stands knocking at her grandmother's door, red hearts float above her head, as they do when the girl thinks of her beloved grandmother, but the object of her love seems humorously to be the wolf in her grandmother's bed on the other side of the door. Tayara and Kizirian bring the traditional Arabic tale into the twenty-first century.

LAYLA, THE WOLF, AND THE PHONE (2011)

Once upon a time, and that was not long ago, there was a girl named Layla. Layla loved her grandma a lot. She visited her very often. On the weekend, Layla's mom asked her to take some baked goods to her grandma. Layla put the pack of baked goods on her red bicycle and went to her grandma's house.

ليلى والذِّئب ... والهاتف

تأليف: سناء طيارة
رسم: تالار كيزريان

32. *Laylā wa-al-dhi'b wa-l-hātif*, by Sana Tayara and Talar Kizirian. Copyright © 2011 Asala. Used by permission of Asala.

On her way, she met the wolf on his motorcycle. The wolf stopped her and said: "Wow, what a nice bicycle, it seems very fast. Where are you going?"

Layla said: "I am going to my grandma's house." The wolf said: "Let's race and find out who will reach your grandma's house first. You will ride your fast red bicycle, and I will ride my motorcycle." The wolf continued: "You will go this way, and I will take another path." Layla nodded her head and set off.

Of course the wolf reached Grandma's house first with his motorcycle. He knocked at the door. The grandma said: "Who is that, is it you, Layla?" The wolf said: "I am the delivery boy." The grandma wondered, as she hadn't ordered any food, so she said: "Come in, boy, the door is open." The wolf entered, carrying a piece of cake in which he had put a soporific drug. The wolf said: "Madam, we, the delivery service, are distributing cake slices for clients to taste and give us their opinions."

The grandma replied kindly: "With pleasure." She ate the cake, and in a few minutes she fell asleep.

After a while, Layla arrived. She knocked at the door and called: "Grandma, Grandma, it's Layla." The wolf said: "Come in, sweetie. The door is open." Layla came in with the pack of baked goods in her hand. The wolf said:

"Come close, sweetie. Sit here in front of me on the bedside." Layla looked at him with surprise and said: "Grandma, have you changed your contact lenses? Your eyes look very big, why?"

The wolf said: "In order to see you clearly." Staring at her grandma's face, Layla said: "Where is your hearing aid? Your ears have become very big. Why?" The wolf said: "In order to hear your voice clearly without it." Layla went on with surprise: "And why has your nose become so big?" The wolf said: "In order to smell your perfume from far away." Layla said, inspecting her grandmother: "And why are your hands so big?" The wolf said: "In order to grab things tightly without letting them fall." Layla said, with astonishment: "But why has your mouth become so much bigger?" The wolf said: "To eat you with."

33. *Laylā wa-al-dhi'b wa-l-hātif*, by Sana Tayara and Talar Kizirian. Copyright © 2011 Asala. Used by permission of Asala.

Layla ran away very quickly, exclaiming: "Oh, you are the wolf I met on my way!" She held up her mobile phone and called the police. A few minutes later, the policemen arrived and helped Layla. The wolf was taken to jail. With the help of the policemen, Layla searched for her grandma, whom they found asleep in the closet.

Later on, the grandma woke up and asked Layla to give her her eyeglasses so she could see better. She wondered why the policemen were at her home, and Layla told her what had happened while she was asleep. Layla and the grandma thanked the policemen and invited them to have some baked goods as well.

Little Green Riding Hood (Le Petit Chaperon Vert)

GRÉGOIRE SOLOTAREFF AND NADJA

Grégoire Solotareff (1953–), one of France's most popular contemporary author-illustrators, was born in Egypt and practiced medicine for five years before creating his first picturebooks. Solotareff often illustrates his own picturebook texts, but he also frequently collaborates with his sister Nadja (1955–), who is an author and illustrator as well. Together they created a series of hilarious remakes of classic tales, the first of which was *Le Petit Chaperon Vert*, published in 1989. This playfulness is emphasized in the 2000 paperback edition, in which the story is dedicated, tongue in cheek,

Grégoire Solotareff et Nadja

LE PETIT CHAPERON VERT

Renardeau
l'école des loisirs

34. *Le Petit Chaperon Vert*, by Grégoire Solotareff and Nadja. Copyright © 1989 L'École des loisirs. Used by permission of Grégoire Solotareff, Nadja, and L'École des loisirs.

to "all the little pale-green, bottle-green, bus-green, emerald-green, olive-green, greenish, and dark-green riding hoods." Solotareff and Nadja adopt a similar strategy to retell the tale of "Barbe-Bleue" (Bluebeard) in the second book in the series, *Barbe-Rose* (Pinkbeard), which was published the following year.

In their Riding Hood story, the color substitution is attributed to a prudent mother who feels that her daughter will thus be safely camouflaged in the woods. She even sends her obedient but resentful daughter into the dangerous woods a second time to escort her worst enemy safely home. Solotareff gives a highly original twist to the classic tale, questioning its truth by turning the heroine into a secondary character in the story of a new Riding Hood. The story of Little Red Riding Hood unfolds parallel to that of Little Green Riding Hood, somewhat behind the scenes. Solotareff retains many elements of Perrault's tale, but subverts them playfully: the incipit; the rough voice of the sick grandmother whose congestion is conveyed by her nasal speech; and the archaic formula concerning the *chevillette* (bobbin) and the *bobinette* (latch), which is transposed to the third person subjunctive, giving the scene a very comic effect that is heightened by Nadja's picture of the protagonist hanging awkwardly from a very complicated mechanism (plate 18). Little Green Riding Hood's story takes as its hypotext Perrault's version, despite the very different tone and ending, but the embedded story of Little Red Riding Hood is a variation on the Grimms' version, in which the protagonist is rescued by two hunters.

With consummate skill, the brother and sister team create extremely simple characters who nonetheless have very distinctive personalities and temperaments. Few retellings of the tale feature a Riding Hood who is as far from the stereotypical image of a pretty little girl. Perrault's epithet "pretty" is conspicuously absent in Solotareff's incipit, while Nadja portrays Little Green Riding Hood and her archrival as very ugly ducklings or chicks. The majority of Nadja's illustrations of the two enemy Riding Hoods are placed either at opposite sides of the page or double page or separated by white space on islands of color, effectively conveying their rivalry and their psychological and emotional distance. The personalities of the two Riding Hoods are best revealed in the surprisingly expressive images. Little Red Riding Hood is silly, perhaps even stupid, and decidedly naughty, generally sticking out her tongue or thumbing her nose at the prim and proper Little Green Riding Hood, who appears haughty, disgusted, or annoyed during their meetings, although one senses the underlying jealousy of an overprotected child/chick. Solotareff's modern version ostensibly turns the classic tale into a story fabricated by a bratty, lying little braggart, but few young readers are likely to seriously question the "truth" of such a well-known fiction or to accept the image of a Little Riding Hood who cried wolf. The story is presented as a cautionary tale with a tongue-in-cheek moral about the dangers of lying.

35. *Le Petit Chaperon Vert*, by Grégoire Solotareff and Nadja. Copyright © 1989 L'École des loisirs. Used by permission of Nadja and L'École des loisirs.

LITTLE GREEN RIDING HOOD (1989)

Once upon a time there was a little girl whom everyone called "Little Green Riding Hood," because she wore a kind of pointed, green hood.

Her sister wore a yellow hood and her best friend a blue hood.

But she had an enemy (a little girl she detested because she was a liar) who wore a red hood . . .

. . . and she really detested her.

One day, her mother said to her:

"Little Green Riding Hood, your grandmother is very sick."

"Oh, no!" said the little girl, who loved her grandmother very much.

"We must take her some medicine and some good things to eat, but neither your sister nor your father is here. Do you have the courage to go, in spite of the ravenous wolf that lurks in the forest?"

"Of course," answered the little girl.

"There, take this basket and go, but be careful of the wolf!"

"Yes, yes," said the little girl.

She set out courageously after putting on her green hood.

And in the woods, who did she meet?

Little Red Riding Hood, who was picking flowers and gathering chanterelles!

She also had a basket full of medicine and food, and Little Green Riding Hood thought that her grandmother must also be sick.

As she detested her, she didn't say hello and went her way.

She hadn't gone a hundred feet when an enormous black wolf ran past her, out of breath.

She didn't even have time to really be frightened, the wolf was going so fast; and he paid no attention to the little girl all dressed in green, sitting in the green grass of the forest.

Once recovered from her emotions, she set off on her way again.

Having arrived at her grandmother's, Little Green Riding Hood pulled the bobbin so that the latch could go up, and the door opened.

The little girl gave the medicine and the good things to eat to her grand-mother. The old lady didn't even want to taste them, she felt so ill.

"Don't combe close to bme," she said to the little girl, "you are sweet enough to eat but I have a bad cold and you run the risk of catching it. That's all we would need!"

"All right, Grandmother," said the little girl. "Then I'll be off. Goodbye! Oh! I forgot to tell you: I met the wolf."

"What?" said the grandmother. "Goodness mbe! And you weren't afraid?"

"Not at all," said the little girl. "He was running so fast that he didn't have time to see me."

"Goodness mbe!" repeated the grandmother. "How lucky you were!"

She gave her a kiss on the hand, and the little girl left.

On the way home, she met Little Red Riding Hood, who continued to pick flowers quite peacefully.

"You know," Little Green Riding Hood told her, "I don't like you, but I would still like to warn you: I saw the wolf a little while ago!"

"Me too, me too," sang Little Red Riding Hood, sticking out her tongue at her.

"He even asked me
What-I-was-doing
In the woods
And-where-I-was-going
With my basket
Nananananana!"

"Be careful, he is very bad!" said Little Green Riding Hood. "You sing, you sing, but you know what can happen? Well, he can eat you and even eat your grandmother!"

"Eat my grandmother?" said Little Red Riding Hood, raising her eyes heavenward. "Pooh! Whatever!"

"We'll see," said Little Green Riding Hood, "we'll see!"

Little Red Riding Hood stuck out her tongue at her one last time and continued picking flowers as if nothing had happened. Little Green Riding Hood went home.

"So?" her mom said to her. "Everything went well?"

"Very well," said Little Green Riding Hood. "Grandmother only has a bad cold, and she didn't want to kiss me. I still gave her everything you prepared for her."

"Good," said her mother. "And you didn't meet anyone in the woods?"

"Yes! Little Red Riding Hood. And then the wolf, too."

"Goodness me!" said the mother. "Little Red Riding Hood? But what you're saying is terrible! The wolf is going to eat her! Don't you know that the wolf eats everything that is red? Red meat, red fruits, but especially little girls dressed in red?"

"But no, Mom, don't worry," said the little girl. "I saw Little Red Riding Hood *after* seeing the wolf, and besides, the wolf was running at full speed; he seemed in a great hurry."

"Really!" said the mother with a sigh of relief. "You reassure me. But still, my mind is not completely at ease; would you mind accompanying her home? I know you don't like Little Red Riding Hood much, but if something ever happened, it would be terrible! And, dressed in green, with your green riding hood among the tall green grass of the green forest, you don't run much risk, and moreover that's why I always dress you in green."

Little Green Riding Hood returned courageously to the woods, although night was about to fall and she detested Little Green Riding Hood.

She had scarcely gone two hundred feet when she met hunters carrying the wolf tied to a branch, quite dead. And who accompanied them?

Little Red Riding Hood, who ran toward her as soon as she saw her, singing:

"You were right
You were right
The wolf ate me
The wolf ate me
And-he-also
Ate my grandmother
Nanananana."

"I don't believe you!" said Little Green Riding Hood. "You're a liar. I said that to scare you, and you believe it's the truth?"

"And even that they took us
both
Out of the wolf's belly.
Nanananana,"
answered Little Red Riding Hood.

But Little Green Riding Hood was already turning her back and returning home with a shrug.

Once home, she said to her mother: "Mom, Little Red Riding Hood returned home, and the hunters killed the wolf! . . . And you know what she told me, that liar Little Red Riding Hood? That the wolf had eaten her, and even eaten her grandmother! And then both of them were taken out of the wolf's belly!"

"Oh!" said the mother. "You know, there are children who lie, and it isn't at all good. Therefore I ask you never to lie."

"I promise," said Little Green Riding Hood. And her mother gave her a kiss.

"Besides, one day, no one will believe her anymore, if she lies all the time," added Little Green Riding Hood.

"Exactly," said her mother.

And both of them sat down by the fireside while they waited for the dinner to cook.

Outside, the wind was blowing very hard, and it was getting very cold, in the heart of the forest.

Little Black Riding Hood (La Caputxeta Negra)

CARLES CANO AND PACO GIMÉNEZ

The Valencian children's author Carles Cano (1957–) has returned time and again to the tale of "Little Red Riding Hood." As a professional storyteller and lecturer on storytelling, he reminds us through his multiple retellings of "Little Red Riding Hood" that traditionally the folktale was never told twice in the same manner but was constantly renewed by storytellers for new audiences. His first retelling, *T'he agafat, Caputxeta!* (Got'cha Little Red Riding Hood!, 1995), was written in Valencian and published simultaneously in Valencian, Catalan, and Castilian by Bruño after it won Spain's most prestigious prize for children's literature, the Premio Lazarillo, in 1994. Too lengthy to be included in this anthology, the work nonetheless bears mentioning, as it sheds light on the author's approach to the tale in the two reworkings that do appear in this volume.

The innovative retelling is a postmodern bricolage of genres and media: a theatrical work ready to be staged, presented as if it was a one-act play in five scenes, but adapted for television with short commercials. The illustrations by the award-winning Argentine illustrator Gusti (1963–), which make use of onomatopoeia and various comics icons, highlight the theatrical setting and the text's metafictive play. Through the diametrically opposed characters of an old male narrator, who lovingly caresses a volume of classic fairy tales, and a young female television producer, Cano presents the arguments of the purists who believe the classic tales are sacred and the modernists who feel they should be updated for contemporary audiences. Cast as the aggressor rather than the victim, this Little Red Riding Hood, a "psychopath" according to the wolf,[8] is arrested for abuse of a protected species, "a genuine *Canis lupus*" (20). Tired of the roles they have been playing for generations, however, Little Red Riding Hood and the wolf take their destiny into their own hands. The zany modern retelling receives a tongue-in-cheek happy ending, as the wolf and Little Red Riding Hood are joined together in matrimony after the bride-to-be shows the traditionalist wolf that she can provide the classic white wedding apparel by turning her reversible cape inside out.

The year after *T'he agafat, Caputxeta!* Cano brought out two retellings of "Little Red Riding Hood," *Caperucita de colores* (Colorful Little Riding Hood) in Castilian and *La Caputxeta Negra* (Little Black Riding Hood) in Valencian. Both tales are based on the color substitution play that is so common in humorous versions for children, play that was already introduced with the reversible cape motif in Cano's earlier work. *Caperucita de colores* is a small picturebook illustrated in cartoon style by the Spanish author and illustrator Violeta Monreal (1963–), intended for children four years old and up. It is the story of a clever Little Red Riding Hood who outwits and eludes the new

36. *La Caputxeta Negra*, by Carles Cano and Paco Giménez. Copyright © 1996 Edicions Bullent. Used by permission of Edicions Bullent.

and improved wolf with camouflage clothing that changes with the seasons. Unlike Bruno Munari's Little White Riding Hood, who is invisible because she dresses all in white in a world of snow, Cano's Riding Hood does not like the color white and never goes out in the cold forest in winter. Like so many contemporary rehabilitated wolves, this one also becomes a vegetarian, and the age-old enemies once again forget their differences to become friends.

In the small picturebook *La Caputxeta Negra*, the color substitution is skin deep, and the tale is transposed to a rather stereotypical African setting. The simple, monochrome drawings in dark red, by the award-winning Valencian illustrator Paco Giménez (1954–), are an integral part of the narrative and fill many gaps. The opening spread depicts the rest of the elephant's herd disappearing on the horizon of the endless savannah on the verso page, while one large elephant, distinguished from the others by a small straw hat perched jauntily on his huge head, heads into the jungle in the opposite direction. The protagonist in the leopard-skin cape is accompanied by a pet monkey with a very long tail, whose antics and cries of "Ee, Ee, Ee" humorously punctuate her questions and actions during the encounter with the elephant in her grandmother's hut.[9] Humorous details in Giménez's illustrations are entertaining for readers of all ages: the African animals that observe or comment on events; the signpost that points the way to the African granny's hut; the television aerial and the electrical wire, which doubles as a clothesline, in the middle of the jungle; the African art that decorates granny's hut; and so forth. The metafictional play that is never absent from Cano's retellings is reserved for the ending, where the narrator makes his tongue-in-cheek suggestion that this African version is perhaps the hypotext of the classic European tale.

37. *La Caputxeta Negra*, by Carles Cano and Paco Giménez. Copyright © 1996 Edicions Bullent. Used by permission of Edicions Bullent.

LITTLE BLACK RIDING HOOD (1996)

One day an elephant went into the jungle and got lost . . .

He wandered aimlessly on all sides.

Until he found a hut in the middle of the jungle.

He was tired and hungry and decided to seek shelter and food there, so he knocked on the door three times with his trunk.

KNOCK KNOCK KNOCK

It was opened by an old lady who, on seeing who it was, became so frightened . . .

OOOOH . . . !

Plunk! Plunk!

. . . . that she went stampeding out the window.

The elephant thought that maybe she was late going to the market and gave it no importance.

He entered the hut with great difficulty . . .

RRIIIIP . . . !

. . . and he fell asleep on the floor, because he was terribly tired.

He had scarcely closed his eyes when a girl with a kind of leopard-skin cape and hood and a woven palm basket filled with fruit appeared at the door of the hut.

RAT TAT

As soon as she entered, she stood, staring fixedly at his eyes, because she was short-sighted and blind as a bat, and she said:

"Grandma, Grandma, what big eyes you have."

"All the better to see you."

"Grandma, Grandma, what big ears you have."

"All the better to hear you."

"Grandma, Grandma, what a big nose you have."

"All the better to smell you."

"Grandma, Grandma, what big teeth you have."

"All the better to eat you!"

And on saying this he opened his mouth and . . .

PRHHEEEEEE!

. . . let loose a deafening bellow.

The girl, terribly frightened, struck a blow to the elephant's trunk[10] with the basket . . .

SMACK

. . . and she went out running and screaming like crazy. The elephant did not suffer even a scratch and could tranquilly eat the delicious fruit and honey that were in the basket.

OOOOH . . . !

Afterward he slept like a log without having to hear the hysterical cries and the impertinent questions of that girl and her grandmother.

ZZZZZZ

PRHHHEEEEEEEE . . . !

The next day, rested and with a full belly, he managed to find the trail of the herd and reunite with them.

PRHHEEE!

Here is an African version of Little Red Riding Hood. Or is Little Red Riding Hood a European version of Little Black Riding Hood?

38. *La Caputxeta Negra*, by Carles Cano and Paco Giménez. Copyright © 1996 Edicions Bullent. Used by permission of Edicions Bullent.

The Wolf and the Little Riding Hoods
(El Lobo y las Caperucitas)

CARLES CANO

In the second retelling by Carles Cano, the author multiplies the colored Riding Hoods to create a humorous story not unlike those of Gianni Rodari and Bruno Munari. The tale appeared in Castilian in a school reading book titled *El Puchero del Tesoro* (The Treasure Pot), which was published for first grade children by the well-known children's publisher Anaya in 2007. As in Munari's *Cappuccetto Bianco*, there is a great deal of wordplay in this retelling, some of which cannot be translated into English. There is a poetic quality to the text, as for example in the double rhyming adjectives that the author repeatedly uses to describe the wolf throughout. The author invents the word *rojívoro* to rhyme with *carnívoro* (carnivorous) in order to portray a very single-minded carnivore that will eat only red Riding Hoods. This retelling is an excellent example of the wordplay and verbal acrobatics that characterize Cano's writing. This time the wolf is given top billing in a playful story that focuses on him.

THE WOLF AND THE LITTLE RIDING HOODS (2007)

The wolf, the fearful and frightful wolf, was lurking in the woods when he saw a girl with a hood coming. His mouth began to water, his eyes were almost popping out of their sockets, but . . . there was something wrong with that girl. What was it? Oh, of course! Her hood! It was green.

"Where are you going, Little Green Riding Hood?" asked Mr. Ferocious, which was the name of the wolf.

"Duh, the same place as always, to my grandma's house to take her some lettuce, some spinach, and a cabbage."

"But cabbage isn't green, it's white, right?"

"Yes, but it's also a vegetable.[1] You see?"

"I see now. And you haven't seen Little Red Riding Hood by chance?"

"Well, no. I'm off because I'm late," said Riding Hood, slightly stiltedly.

The ferocious and vicious animal remained there lurking, hidden behind some bushes, until another little girl came along. This one was wearing a yellow riding hood.

"Where are you going, Little Yellow Riding Hood?"

"I'm going to see my grandma to take her some bananas, some fried eggs, and a little pineapple in syrup."

"What a strange menu!"

"Yes, but this is what it must be if you're Little Yellow Riding Hood. I'm off." She left so fast that she gave him no time to ask after her incarnadine colleague.

The surly and furry animal was still waiting when Little Blue Riding Hood appeared.

"What are you taking to your grandma?" asked the wolf directly, skipping the first part to be briefer.

"A little blue fish. Her cholesterol is through the roof."

"Oh, and you haven't seen Little Red Riding Hood, right?"

"Well, no. I'm off, as fish spoils in this heat."

And there the very carnivorous and redivorous animal continued to wait and wait and wait, watching Little Riding Hoods pass by in the woods. And Little Brown Riding Hood went by, whom he did not even want to question, and then Little Purple Riding Hood, Little Light Blue Riding Hood, Little Navy Blue Riding Hood, Little Orange Riding Hood with her basket of mandarins, Little Pink Riding Hood with her little bows . . . But not a trace of the Red. What had happened to Little Red Riding Hood?

The wolf did not know, but Little Red Riding Hood's grandmother had gone on a trip to Mallorca with the retirees from her part of the forest. Of course, Riding then spent her time playing video games, loafing around, and occasionally arguing with her mother.

And the wolf? They say that this wolf had cobwebs in his stomach, because he was so single-minded that he ate only Red Riding Hoods.

Little Red Riding Hood (The Tale of a Hunt)
(Czerwony Kapturek [Bajka myśliwska])

Bohdan Butenko

Bohdan Butenko (1931–) is a Polish author, illustrator, and comics artist who has been publishing children's books since 1956. He also has many animated films and television programs to his credit. During his prolific career, Butenko has illustrated about 250 books, his own texts as well as those of other authors. He has created his own original style of book design, addressed chiefly to children and young people, that seeks the complete integration of picture and word. Butenko is often described as an "architect of the book,"[12] because he is concerned with every aspect of the volume, from cover to cover, including all the elements of the paratext. No detail, however minor, is overlooked. He makes skillful use of different font styles and sizes, layouts, initial capitals, vignettes, and so forth, and he continually explores the text-image relationship. In 2008 he published *Krulewna Sniezka* (Snow Wite), a collection of retellings of four famous fairy tales: "Little Red Riding Hood," "Hansel and Gretel," "Cinderella," and "Snow White." The deliberate misspelling in the title immediately indicates the subversive intention of the author, who set out to write the "true" story about these fairy-tale characters. The unusual square, 165-page book contains about two hundred illustrations in pen, ink, and watercolor. It constitutes an excellent example of Butenko's unique concept of book design, which marries text and image intimately.

The recasting of "Little Red Riding Hood," subtitled "Bajka myśliwska" (The Tale of a Hunt), is the first tale in the collection. Like Mikulka's Czech retelling and Pongrašić's Croatian retelling, Butenko's is rooted in the author's culture: the collecting of mushrooms, the Polish brand of the knife the forester uses to open the wolf's belly, and the wolf's puffing sounds being compared to the train in a popular Polish poem for children. Each of the tales is told on different-colored paper, and this one has a green background in keeping with the setting. The story is introduced by the dwarves from Snow White, who play the role of stagehands throughout the book. Completely dressed in red, from their pointed hoods to their shoes, they look like miniature male Riding Hoods. On the tale's title page, one of the dwarves carries a rope that is attached to the attractive initial capital that begins the text on the next recto (a "P" that constitutes a tree in the forest).

The entire book is designed with this meticulous attention to detail. The layout is constantly changing so that the illustrations are embedded in ever-varying ways. Text is sometimes integrated into the illustrations, and an arrow often links a part of the text to the illustration, which constitutes a kind of explanation for or punctuation of a remark. The simple, caricatural

39. "Czerwony Kapturek (Bajka myśliwska)," from *Krulewna Sniezka*, by Bohdan Butenko. Copyright © 2008 Bohdan Butenko. Used by permission of Bohdan Butenko.

illustrations are lively and engaging. On the first page of the story, the protagonist's distinctive red headgear is the only touch of color in an otherwise black-and-white illustration. Little Red Riding Hood tears across one page of the spread, with the forester's bullets preceding her (plate 19), while on the facing page she is perched in the tree, still carrying the enormous basket on her back. First-person narration often issues from pictures of the characters like a speech bubble without the bubble. Typography plays an important role in the narrative, as some lines are angled to link them more closely to the illustration, while others appear in a very large font for emphasis; for example, the "Bang! Bang!" of the forester's gun.

The tale is written in the author's characteristically humorous tone. Despite the zany, nonsensical nature of the story, the metafictive play is quite clever. The forester seems to crack under the pressure of endlessly playing the same role; Little Red Riding Hood's frustration is made quite clear from the beginning. Not only are all the characters very conscious of the roles they are playing (Butenko deliberately capitalizes the names of all the fairy-tale characters), but the author himself is drawn into the story to try to rescue the grandmother from her unusual fate. It is undoubtedly the only retelling in which the author interprets the role of Little Red Riding Hood.

40. "Czerwony Kapturek (Bajka myśliwska)," from *Krulewna Sniezka*, by Bohdan Butenko. Copyright © 2008 Bohdan Butenko. Used by permission of Bohdan Butenko.

~ઝ

LITTLE RED RIDING HOOD
(THE TALE OF A HUNT) (2008)

Now, tell me if you know the fairy tale of Little Red Riding Hood. Raise your hands if you don't! Well, if you do, you can raise your hands as well.

Whether you know it or not, I will tell the story anyway. So you'd better sit down and listen, so we may go ahead with it. Ready?

Attention! I begin.

Little Red Riding Hood, who was quite a sweet girl by the way, lived with her beloved Mom in a cute, tiny cottage surrounded with cute trees and an even more cute tiny fence. And it was in such aesthetic surroundings that Little Red Riding Hood would spend her nights and mornings.

"And how about the rest of the day?" you'll ask, and it will be a wise question indeed.

As it happens, our heroine would spend the rest of the day doing her everyday duties: in the morning, she would set off with victuals to see her Grandma, and she would meet the Wolf on her way, who would then in turn eat up Grandma and—a while later—eat up Riding Hood as well; and then Mr. Forester would come, kill the Wolf, and extricate Grandma together with Little Red Riding Hood out of the Wolf's stomach; and then Little Red Riding Hood would return to her beloved Mom weary and a trifle bored, to get some rest at night, so as to rise in the morning and set off with her basket to see her Grandma, meet the Wolf on her way, and so on, and so forth . . .

Believe me, it was no fun at all to let a wolf eat you up EVERY DAY, to be squeezed in its stomach with Grandma EVERY DAY, and to wait to see if Mr. Forester will KINDLY come, KINDLY shoot the Wolf, and KINDLY drag Riding Hood with her Grandma out of the Wolf's stomach in the end.

Try to imagine now: What would happen had Mr. Forester been late? Or had he not come at all?

Or had he lost his way? Maybe we'd better not imagine that . . .

But in the meanwhile, every single day went along the same pattern.

"You're already up? That's good!" says the girl's beloved Mom. "You will now go and see your Grandma, who's ill and lives in the very heart of the forest . . ."

"Don't I know where she lives, as I see her every day . . . ," murmurs Riding Hood.

"You know or you don't, I have to say it as it's in the script. So do kindly restrain yourself from silly comments and listen!" her beloved Mom admonishes her. "So you will now go and see Grandma, and take her a small basket of food . . ."

"Which basket? This one?! I won't take this thing! It's fine for carrying coal to the basement, not for taking victuals to an elderly lady!"

"There is no other one."

"And the one I would always take? Very wicker, with a small handle?"

"Wicker, with a small handle? Ahhh . . . You see, Mr. Forester took it when he went to collect mushrooms this morning, and he tore the handle off. Besides, he's smeared Boletus mushrooms all over it. Let me tell you again, that is the only basket which is of any use!"

Willy-nilly, Riding Hood takes it, and her beloved Mom places inside a small bottle of Ersatz coffee with milk, wrapped up in a newspaper so that it doesn't cool down, two hard-boiled eggs, a jar of apricot jam, two crusty buns with a little butter, some loin chops, and two pounds of matjes herring,[13] which Grandma absolutely loves.

The basket's large—the victuals few, so they are jolted this way and that, but the ambitious Riding Hood holds firm and marches boldly through the forest to the well-known bush, out of which the Wolf should jump.

The bush is there, the Wolf is there. He knows his role, so he asks:

"Little Red Riding Hood, where are you going?"

"To visit my Grandma, who is ill and lives in the very heart of the forest!" recites the girl quickly; she has thrown away her little crib sheet a long time ago, knowing her lines by heart.

"And what delicacies have you got in that basket of yours?" asks the Wolf and chuckles, for the basket is a lot bigger than Riding Hood herself.

"Just you wait, rascal; feel like making jokes, do you?" thinks the girl, but she says aloud, according to the script, "I bring a small bottle of ersatz coffee with milk, wrapped up in a newspaper so that it doesn't cool down, two hard-boiled eggs, a jar of raspberry jam . . ."

"I think apricot jam!" the Wolf corrects her.

"Yes, indeed, of course it's apricot jam!" Riding Hood gets annoyed, upset at her own mistake. "So, a jar of apricot jam, and two crusty buns with a little butter . . ."

"And what else with?" interrupts the Wolf, hoping to confuse the girl again.

"With some loincloth, no, loin chops, well, it doesn't matter anyway. And two pounds of matjes herring, which Grandma absolutely loves . . ."

"And she's not the only one! I love matjes herring as well, and you say you have them in your basket . . ."

"It's too good for the likes of you!" Riding Hood cuts him short, having had enough of this idle talk by now. "See you soon!" she adds, and sets off again.

She walks and walks through the forest. Meanwhile, the Wolf runs up to Grandma's cottage by a path known only to himself and rushes inside. Let us spare the description of the elderly lady being swallowed up; it's enough to say that when Riding Hood arrives, the Wolf is already in bed, dressed up in a fustian nightgown and a lace bonnet.

The girl struggles with the door for a while, unable to squeeze the large basket through; at last she comes in, takes the burden off her shoulders with relief, and says as usual, "Grandma, Grandma, what big ears you have!"

"The better to hear you with, my dear Granddaughter!"

"Grandma, Grandma, what big eyes you have!"

"The better to see you with, my dear Granddaughter!"

"Grandma, Grandma, but what gigantic jaws you have!"

"The better to eat you with, my dear Granddaughter!" cries the Wolf, leaps up at Riding Hood, swallows her whole, and returns to the bed (feeling bloated after overeating) to wait for Mr. Forester, who arrives at last and, no questions asked, "Bang! Bang!" fires the shotgun. The shot Wolf slides down onto the pillows, and Mr. Forester extricates the somewhat crumpled Riding Hood and a similar Grandma out of the Wolf's stomach, using a Gerlach brand knife.

Everyone (I guess maybe except the Wolf) is happy and feasts on the delicacies brought in the basket, and immediately after that Riding Hood returns hastily to her tiny cottage for some well-deserved rest, for the following day, everything will begin anew. You can say, DA CAPO AL FINE.

And thus it would have continued until this very day, had it not been for that ill-fated Thursday.

And that Thursday was a very beautiful day indeed, like every day in this fairy tale. Birds were singing, cats were meowing, in short: pure bliss!

"You're already up? That's good!" says the girl's beloved Mom. "You will now go and see your Grandma, who's ill . . ."

"I would like to be as healthy as she is!" murmurs the sullen Little Red Riding Hood.

". . . who's ill and lives in the very heart of the forest. You'll take her a small basket of food."

Little Red Riding Hood does not reply, but the look on her face testifies how furious she is. Willy-nilly, she takes the basket, and her beloved Mom places inside a small bottle of ersatz coffee with milk, wrapped up in a newspaper so that it doesn't cool down, two hard-boiled eggs, a jar of apricot jam, two crusty buns with a little butter, some loin chops, and two pounds of matjes herring, which Grandma absolutely loves.

The basket's large—the victuals few, so they are jolted this way and that, but the ambitious Little Red Riding Hood holds firm and marches boldly through the forest to the well-known bush, out of which the Wolf should jump.

The bush is there, but the Wolf is not.

Little Red Riding Hood looks around—nobody's there, and even less than nobody.

"He should be given a chance!" she decides.

So she walks forty-eight steps back, turns around, and walks again slowly, this time dragging her feet . . .

The Wolf is not there. He doesn't jump out.

Riding Hood, quite vexed, walks back one more time.

"Third return lucky," she thinks.

She walks up to the bush and is almost sure the Wolf won't be there again, when suddenly he jumps out of the shrubs with his tail between his legs and his tongue lolling.

He is puffing like a locomotive,[14] but asks according to the plan:

"Wheew . . . wheeew . . . Little Red Riding Hood, where on earth are you going? Wheew . . . wheeew . . ."

"You're late!" replies the girl severely. "By a full ten minutes! And I am going to visit my Grandma, who is ill and lives in the very heart of the forest."

But rather than go on with this chitchat, her interlocutor looks anxiously all around and moves his nose as if he were smelling something.

"Is he mad or what? I won't be through with this moron till the evening!" thinks Riding Hood, but repeats out loud her last lines, ". . . lives in the very heart of the forest! Forest! Forest! Fo-rest! Fo-rest! Foooo-rest!"

"And what delicacies have you got in that ba . . . ," picks up the Wolf, but he doesn't finish, for at that very moment two shots are heard. With an ear shot through, the Wolf dives into the nearby thickets.

The girl has no time to think, for she hears the loud "Bang! Bang!" again and sees the bullets hit the basket. She looks around and sees Mr. Forester emerge from the copse with a smoking shotgun.

"Mr. Forester! You enter only in Grandma's cottage! And besides, I am Riding Hood, not the Wolf! Please do not shoot me!" cries Riding Hood and suddenly understands the situation. "Please put on your glasses immediately! You have forgotten your glasses! The glasses!"

"That's a sly vermin!" gasps Mr. Forester. "Who'd think it could mimic Riding Hood's voice so well! It's true I've forgotten my glasses, but I won't have you pull my leg, and I will do my duty. I am to slaughter the Wolf and liberate those broads so I will slaughter and liberate. Just you wait, you dog!

And he starts to load the shotgun.

Riding Hood sees it's no picnic, so she jumps into the bushes and hears only the bullet, whooosh . . . whooosh . . . whoosh . . . , fly over her head. There's not a minute to waste—time to run!

Riding Hood runs through the forest, and the forest is so large—bah!—huge and unknown. Riding Hood races, damages the basket on the pines, but flies as fast as she can, the farther the better from Mr. Forester and his shotgun.

She sees a tall tree, clambers up to its top with the last of her strength, and, out of breath, she sits on a branch and listens, glad that no one's pursuing her.

She'd been sitting like this for several hours when she finally decided to climb down and continue on her way to Grandma's. Continue on her way! It's a fine thing to say when you're on the path you know by heart, but this forest is—as it has been said—huge, and to make matters worse, completely unknown in this area. Riding Hood had tramped the forest all over, been lost

Zobaczył wielkie drzewo, resztką sił, zady-
szany, wlazł na czubek, siedzi na gałęzi i nasłu-
chuje, szczęśliwy, że nikt go nie goni.

41. "Czerwony Kapturek (Bajka myśliwska)," from *Krulewna Sniezka*, by Bohdan
Butenko. Copyright © 2008 Bohdan Butenko. Used by permission of Bohdan Butenko.

in the forest all over, looking behind every tree in mortal fear of Mr. Forester,
before she found Grandma's cottage.

Meanwhile, the Wolf, who had run away in exactly the opposite direction, hid himself deep in some hollow, and didn't in the least consider coming
out when Riding Hood was already on Grandma's steps.

Little Red Riding Hood politely knocks on the door.

"Come in!" replies Grandma.

The girl struggles with the door for a good while, unable to squeeze the
large basket through; at last she comes in, takes the burden off her shoulders
with relief, and says as usual, "Grandma, Grandma, what big ears you have!"

"And what is this nonsense?" mutters the astonished old lady. "I have got
big ears! That's impertinence!"

In the meantime, Little Red Riding Hood, tired after running through the forest, dreams of just rattling it off, so she doesn't have a closer look at her Grandma, doesn't really listen to the replies she knows by heart, but she goes on, "Grandma, Grandma, what big eyes you have!"

"Big eyes! But that's all we needed! Why, am I a cow or some other hippo, or what? You must have quite lost your wits, dear granddaughter . . . ," rails Grandma, and peers into the basket, where, instead of delicacies, she sees only a hole at the bottom and total emptiness. Everything had simply fallen out on the way!

"Grandma, Grandma, but what gigantic jaws you have!" continues the girl.

The elderly lady lost her patience.

"Now I see! I've been lying here since the morning, withering of hunger, and you come only in the afternoon with an empty basket, and abuse me while still on the threshold! Now I'll show you . . ."

She leaped out of the bed, grabbed a poker, and bounded to Riding Hood's side. She would've surely caught her had the door not flown open all of a sudden to reveal Mr. Forester himself. He took aim and, "Bang! Bang!" fired at the empty bed. He also managed to hit a flower vase; the glass shatters in all directions, water flows on the bed covers, feathers fly around the room . . .

Grandma was at first flabbergasted, but when she saw Mr. Forester take aim again, she lost her patience.

"Have you all gone nuts?" she yells. "One fool keeps me hungry and calls me gigantic jaws, the other one ruins my home! I must move to some other fairy tale, as it's a real madhouse here! Run off now, you dullard!"

She tore the shotgun out of his hands, and she started hitting him with the poker.

So it is now Mr. Forester who's on the run, with Grandma trotting close at his heels. Little Red Riding Hood preferred not to wait until the livid elderly lady's return, and she immediately jumped out the window and into the forest.

Meanwhile, the Wolf was lying very quiet in his hole and, hearing the shots, dared not move. When everything was silent again, he decided the way was clear, and he ran stealthily to the well-known cottage.

He peers inside and sees the pitiful sight of destruction, but, dauntless, he decides to play his role to the end. So he dresses in the bonnet, climbs into the bed, and lies down in the wet bedcovers filled with holes.

"It's not the way it's supposed to be, but it's not my fault that nobody's here and everyone keeps on running around the forest!" he thought.

Chasing Mr. Forester, Grandma lost her breath, so she shook her finger at him and decided to return home.

She approaches the cottage and listens—something's moving inside. She peers through the window and what does she see but the Wolf curling up to sleep in her own bed!

She saw red, clutched the poker tight, and flew into the chamber.

"You dog! Won't your grace sit in the forest anymore? One nutcase has shot my bed covers all through, the other one gets right into my clean bed, covered all over with mud! Ohhhh! And he has put my new bonnet on his dirty noggin!"

Take that! Take that!

And she started to pummel him at random. The Wolf tries to explain himself at first—he even evokes the script of the fairy tale—but the livid elderly lady doesn't want to listen to anything.

What's to be done? He's turned tail and run to the forest through the window, in Grandma's bonnet and all covered in feathers.

Grandma runs out after him, but the Wolf is nowhere to be seen. Only some bush twigs are still quivering . . .

"He's taken my bonnet, the dog!" thinks Grandma.

She returns home, collects the feathers, mends the bed covers, cleans up, loudly vacuums the whole cottage . . .

She had some rest.

She's prepared tea, sits down, and thinks: "What will it come to now? The fairy tale's fallen to pieces and I'm sitting here waiting—what for I don't know myself!"

She'd been waiting one day—nobody came.

She'd been waiting two days—the same.

She would stand in front of the cottage, she would bellow, she would even wander through the forest, booming—nobody answered.

At last, on the third day, she dressed up neatly, put on her Sunday headscarf, and came to see me.

"Save us!" she said. "Advise me what to do! The Wolf, Mr. Forester, and Little Red Riding Hood were so scared that they got lost somewhere and they're not coming back. We're all waiting for them, and the fairy tale isn't working. It's unfair! They didn't even come on Grandma's Day, didn't bring any flowers . . . What's more, my stomach's rumbling with hunger, as Riding Hood would always bring me some goodies, and now—what? I'm sipping tea, but how long can you live on just tea? Save us, my friend, and tell me, what should I do?"

This has troubled me greatly indeed. But in the meantime, I treated Grandma with dinner.

"Maybe we'll think something up together!" I said consolingly.

But we didn't think up anything at all.

And I had to help somehow.

So now I pack my little basket with a small bottle of ersatz coffee with milk, wrapped up in a newspaper so that it doesn't cool down, two hard-boiled eggs, a jar of apricot jam, two crusty buns with a little butter, some loin chops, and two pounds of matjes herring, which Grandma absolutely loves.

I take this basket, and I go through the forest to Grandma's cottage, looking around carefully near the bush to see if the Wolf doesn't jump out of it.

But it doesn't.

And Mr. Forester's shots are not heard, either.

So I shuffle my feet slowly and think: "I must ask everyone reading this story to take a careful look around when they're collecting mushrooms or just taking a walk in the forest. Maybe they'll see Mr. Forester, the Wolf, or even Little Red Riding Hood herself hidden somewhere."

And then—I ask you kindly—please do explain to them that Grandma's not angry anymore and that she's still waiting for them, so that the fairy tale can go on.

And if you don't have the courage to talk to them, just tell me, and I will talk to them myself.

Let Grandma be happy again.

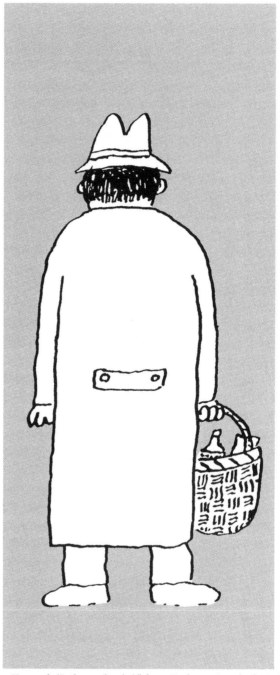

42. "Czerwony Kapturek (Bajka myśliwska)," from *Krulewna Sniezka*, by Bohdan
Butenko. Copyright © 2008 Bohdan Butenko. Used by permission of Bohdan Butenko.

1. *Un petit chaperon rouge*, by Claude Clément and Isabelle Forestier. Copyright © 2000 Éditions Grasset & Fasquelle. Used by permission of Isabelle Forestier and Éditions Grasset & Fasquelle.

2. *Ches! Eotteohge alassji? Honjaseo gileul gadaga yugoebeomeul mulrichin bbalganmoja iyagi*, by Mia Sim. Copyright © 2010 Nurimbo. Used by permission of Mia Sim and Nurimbo.

3. *Czerwony Kapturek*, by Joanna Olech and Grażka Lange. Illustrations copyright
© 2005 Jacek Santorski & Co, Agencja Wydawnicza, and Grażka Lange. Used by
permission of Grażka Lange.

4. *Czerwony Kapturek*, by Joanna Olech and Grażka Lange. Illustrations copyright
© 2005 Jacek Santorski & Co, Agencja Wydawnicza, and Grażka Lange. Used by
permission of Grażka Lange.

5. "The Wolf Chats Up Red Riding Hood," from *Little Red Riding Hood Suite*, by Paula Rego. Copyright © 2003 Paula Rego. Used by permission of Paula Rego.

191

8. *Rood Rood Roodkapje*, by Edward van de Vendel and Isabelle Vandenabeele. Copyright © 2003 Uitgeverij De Eenhoorn. Used by permission of Uitgeverij De Eenhoorn.

9. *Skylappjenta*, by Iram Haq and Endre Skandfer. Copyright © 2009 Cappelen Damm. Used by permission of Cappelen Damm.

10. *Skylappjenta*, by Iram Haq and Endre Skandfer. Copyright © 2009 Cappelen Damm. Used by permission of Endre Skandfer and Cappelen Damm.

11. *Skylappjenta*, by Iram Haq and Endre Skandfer. Copyright © 2009 Cappelen Damm. Used by permission of Endre Skandfer and Cappelen Damm.

12. *Caperucito Azul*, by Hernán Rodríguez Castelo. Illustrations by Jaime Villa. Copyright © 1975 Jaime Villa. Used by permission of Jaime Villa.

13. *Caperucito Azul*, by Hernán Rodríguez Castelo. Illustrations by Jaime Villa. Copyright © 1975 Jaime Villa. Used by permission of Jaime Villa.

14. *Prassini Soufitsa*, by Ioulita Iliopoulou. Illustrations by Yannis Kottis. Copyright ©
2008 Ypsilon/Vivlia. Used by permission of Ypsilon/Vivlia.

15. *Prassini Soufitsa*, by Ioulita Iliopoulou. Illustrations by Yannis Kottis. Copyright ©
2008 Ypsilon/Vivlia. Used by permission of Ypsilon/Vivlia.

16. *O Capuchinho Cinzento*, by Matilde Rosa Araújo. Illustrations by André Letria. Copyright © 2012 André Letria/SPA. Used by permission of SPA.

Svinja ko svinja, bila je sita. Najela se žira, kad putem naiđe Crvenkapica. Svinja je znala priču o Crvenkapici i bilo joj je neugodno što se našla na mjestu vuka. Od koga je svinja saznala priču o Crvenkapici to ni Snježni Kralj ne zna.

Uglavnom, svinja je razgovarala s Crvenkapicom kao da je vuk.
Kriva je i Crvenkapica jer se pretvarala da je sve u redu.

Svinja ko svinja, nije htjela završiti kao vuk — da je lovac na kraju ubije — pa je pozdravivši se s Crvenkapicom otrčala k vuku i sve mu ispričala. Vuk je otišao baki i, naravno, nastradao! To je istina!

17. *Snježni kralj*, by Damir Miloš. Illustrations by Radovan Devlić and Krešimir Skozret. Copyright © 1986. Used by permission of Damir Miloš, Dora Devlić, and Krešimir Skozret.

18. *Le Petit Chaperon Vert*, by Grégoire Solotareff. Illustrations by Nadja. Copyright © 1989 L'École des loisirs. Used by permission of Nadja and L'École des loisirs.

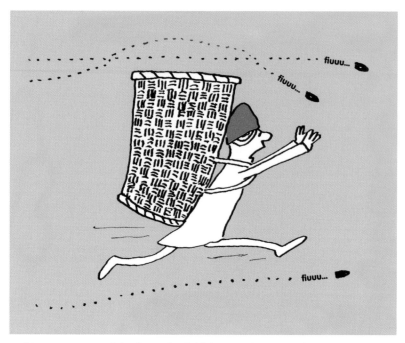

19. "Czerwony Kapturek (Bajka myśliwska)," from *Krulewna Sniezka*, by Bohdan Butenko. Copyright © 2008 Bohdan Butenko. Used by permission of Bohdan Butenko.

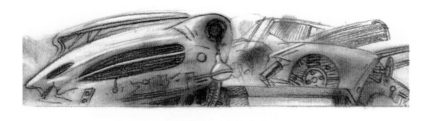

20. *Le Petit Chaperon Rouge*, by Jean Claverie. Copyright © 2009 Éditions Mijade. Used by permission of Jean Claverie and Éditions Mijade.

21. *El último lobo y Caperucita*, by José Luis García Sánchez and Miguel Ángel Pacheco. Illustrations copyright © 1975 Miguel Ángel Pacheco. Used by permission of Miguel Ángel Pacheco.

22. *El último lobo y Caperucita*, by José Luis García Sánchez and Miguel Ángel Pacheco. Text copyright © 1975 José Luis García Sánchez; illustrations copyright © 1975 Miguel Ángel Pacheco. Used by permission of José Luis García Sánchez and Miguel Ángel Pacheco.

23. *Waldtraut und der Wolf*, by Meike Stoebe and Susann Stoebe. Copyright © 1996 Nord-Süd Verlag. Used by permission of Nord-Süd Verlag.

فى ذلكَ الوقت، كانَ الذئبُ جالسًا تحتَ شَجرته المفضَّلة، مُنتظرًا ذاتَ الرداءِ الأحمر، مُنهمكًا كعادته فى قراءة قصته القديمة. ولذا حينَما مرَّت نُور عليْه فى ثوْبها الأخضرِ، لمْ يلاحظْها وظلَّ يَقرأ بشغَف فى قصته، وينظرُ إلى الصُّورِ بعنايةٍ شديدةٍ.

وصلتْ نُور بيتَ جَدَّتها وسلَّمتْها الطَّعامَ، فشكرتْها الجدةُ وقالتْ لهَا: «لا بُدَّ أنْ تخلعى الثوبَ الأخضرَ وتكتفى بالثوب الأحمر حتَّى لا تشعُرى بالحرِّ». فشكرتْها نُور على نصيحتها، ووضعتْ فُستانَها الأخضرَ فى السلة وقبَّلتْ جدَّتها وركبتْ الدَّرَّاجة لتَلحقَ بإخْوتها فى قصرِ سندريلا وقمر الزَّمانِ.

24. *Ser ekhtifaa el zeeb el shahir bel mohtar*, by Abdelwahab M. Elmessiri and Safaa Nabaa. Copyright © Dar El Shorouk. Used by permission of Dar El Shorouk.

وبينَما هى فى الغابة، ظهرَ الذئبُ يَحملُ القصةَ القديمةَ، وابتسمَ ابتسامتَه الماكرةَ المعتادةَ، ثم قال: «إلى أينَ أنت ذاهبةٌ يا ذاتَ الرداءِ الأحمر؟» ضحكتْ نورُ وقالتْ: «أنا لستُ ذاهبةً، بلْ أنا عائدةٌ من عند جدّتى». اختفتْ الابتسامةُ فجأةً من على وجهِ الذئب، وقالَ: «ماذا تَعْنين؟ أنا سألتُك: إلى أينَ أنت ذاهبةٌ يا ذاتَ الرداءِ الأحمر؟ تمامًا كما جاءَ فى القصة، والمَفروضُ أنْ تُجيبى: أنَا ذاهبةٌ إلى جدّتى، لا عائدةٌ من عندها. إنى أنْتظرك منذ عدّةِ أيام، ولمْ أرَك وأنت ذاهبةٌ». فهمتْ نُور ما حَدَث، فابتسمتْ وقالتْ له: «هلْ سمعتَ عنْ مترو الأنفاق؟! هلْ رأيتَ من قبل ذاتَ الرداءِ الأخضر يا مستر وولف؟ هل قرأتَ حكاياتِ هذا الزمان؟» نَظر الذئبُ لها فى حَيرة، وقلّب صفحاتِ القصة القديمة، ولكنّه لمْ يجدْ أىَّ إشارة لمترو الأنفاق أو لذاتِ الرداءِ الأخضرِ هذه، فسألَها: «عمَّ تتحدثين؟». ضحكتْ نُور وقالتْ له: «استمرّ أنتَ فى قراءةِ قصتِك القديمة، أمّا أنَا فسأسمّيكَ الذئبَ الشهيرَ بالمُحتار. فهذا اسمٌ على مُسمّى». وتركتْه يقلّب صفحاتِ قصته بعصبيةٍ واضحةٍ ويتْمْتم لنفْسه: «ماذا يَجرى فى هذه الدُنيا؟ ما الذى يَحْدثُ فى هَذا الزّمان؟».

25. *Ser ekhtifaa el zeeb el shahir bel mohtar*, by Abdelwahab M. Elmessiri and Safaa Nabaa. Copyright © Dar El Shorouk. Used by permission of Dar El Shorouk.

26. *In bocca al lupo*, by Fabian Negrin. Copyright © 2003 Orecchio Acerbo. Used by permission of Fabian Negrin and Orecchio Acerbo.

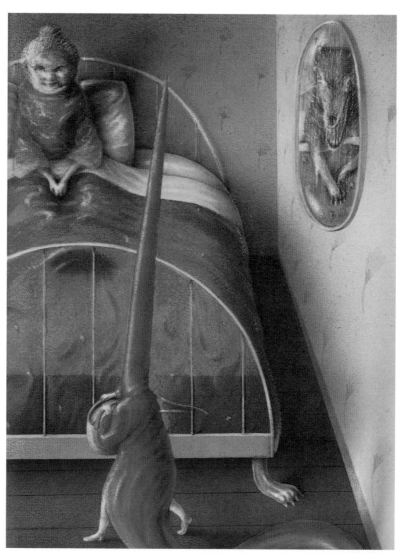

27. *In bocca al lupo*, by Fabian Negrin. Copyright © 2003 Orecchio Acerbo. Used by permission of Fabian Negrin and Orecchio Acerbo.

28. *In bocca al lupo*, by Fabian Negrin. Copyright © 2003 Orecchio Acerbo. Used by permission of Fabian Negrin and Orecchio Acerbo.

29. "En el vientre del lobo," by Izumi Yamada, from *Érase veintiuna veces Caperucita Roja*. Illustrations by Izumi Yamada. Copyright © 2006 Media Vaca. Used by permission of Media Vaca.

30. "The Bed," by Vassilis Papatsarouchas, reproduced in "I Kokkinoskoufitsa apo mesa," by Hara Yiannakopoulou. Illustration copyright © 2007 Vassilis Papatsarouchas. Used by permission of Vassilis Papatsarouchas.

31. "I Kokkinoskoufitsa apo mesa," by Hara Yiannakopoulou, from *Mia agapi, epta chromata kai enas lykos*. Illustrations by Vassilis Papatsarouchas. Illustrations copyright © 2007 Metaichmio and Vassilis Papatsarouchas. Used by permission of Vassilis Papatsarouchas and Metaichmio.

32. "I Kokkinoskoufitsa apo mesa," by Hara Yiannakopoulou, from *Mia agapi, epta chromata kai enas lykos*. Illustrations by Vassilis Papatsarouchas. Illustrations copyright © 2007 Metaichmio and Vassilis Papatsarouchas. Used by permission of Vassilis Papatsarouchas and Metaichmio.

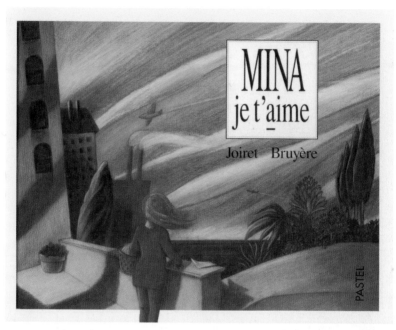

33. *Mina, je t'aime*, by Patricia Joiret and Xavier Bruyère. Copyright © 1991 L'École des loisirs. Used by permission of L'École des loisirs.

34. *Mina, je t'aime*, by Patricia Joiret and Xavier Bruyère. Copyright © 1991 L'École des loisirs. Used by permission of L'École des loisirs.

35. *Mon Chaperon Rouge*, by Anne Ikhlef and Alain Gauthier. Illustrations by Alain Gauthier. Paris: Éditions du Seuil, 1998. Text copyright © Anne Ikhlef; illustrations copyright © Alain Gauthier. Used by permission of Anne Ikhlef and Alain Gauthier.

36. *Mon Chaperon Rouge*, by Anne Ikhlef and Alain Gauthier. Illustrations by Alain Gauthier. Paris: Éditions du Seuil, 1998. Text copyright © Anne Ikhlef; illustrations copyright © Alain Gauthier. Used by permission of Anne Ikhlef and Alain Gauthier.

FOUR

Rehabilitating the Wolf

It is also claimed that wolves slyly attack
defenseless little children to steal everything they have.
That is just nonsense!

Meike Stoebe and Susann Stoebe, *Waldtraut und der Wolf*

Little Crimson Riding Hood Had a Scare ... and Then Nothing! (Caperucita Encarnada pasó un susto ... y luego ¡nada!)

ANTONIORROBLES

The Spanish writer and journalist Antonio J. Robles Soler (1895–1983), better known as Antonio Robles or Antoniorrobles (the name he adopted when he began writing for children), started his career writing humorous magazine stories for adults. Strongly influenced by the avant-garde, his writing was experimental, innovative, and revolutionary. Along with other writers of the time, he introduced a new concept of humor, that of the absurd, into Spanish literature. When, at the urging of a friend, he turned his hand to writing for children in the mid-1920s, he brought the avant-garde and his special brand of humor to Spanish children's literature. Antoniorrobles established his reputation as a children's author with the publication of two collections of stories: *Hermanos Monigotes* (Puppet Brothers, 1935) and *Rompetacones y Azulita* (1936). Although he was the author of more than a dozen books for adults, he is best known for his classic books for children and young people. At the end of the Spanish civil war, Antoniorrobles traveled by way of France into exile in Mexico, where he eventually became a citizen. In Mexico he took a position as professor of children's literature in the National Teachers College, and continued to write for children and adults. In 1972 the author returned to Spain.

Antoniorrobles published the playful retelling "Caperucita Encarnada pasó un susto ... y luego ¡nada!" (Little Crimson Riding Hood Had a Scare ... and Then Nothing!) in 1962, in *Rompetacones y 100 cuentos más* (Rompetacones and 100 More Tales), a collection of ten-minute stories for school and radio that included both original tales and adapted folk and fairy tales. It is not surprising that the tale has never been translated into English, as the prolific Spanish children's author, who spent so much of his life in Mexico, has only recently begun to receive the recognition he deserves in his own country. During the Spanish civil war, Antoniorrobles unequivocally espoused the cause of the Republicans, and he published two collections for children that were deliberately propagandist. The first was a collection of classic tales, including "Caperucita Roja," which were transposed to the contemporary era to allow the author to convey a clear ideological message. A lifetime of writing for children led Antoniorrobles to develop theories on children's literature; the story of Little Red Riding Hood also provided the title of a collection of essays for teachers, *¿Se comió el lobo à Caperucita?* (Did the Wolf Eat Little Red Riding Hood?, 1942). While he objected to the violence and evil in traditional tales, the author did not want to reject them entirely and chose to work from within their framework to revise them. He brings to them his unique way of understanding reality and of treating fantasy. The replacement, in the title, of the traditional adjective *roja* with *encarnada*—which means either "red" or "incarnate"—was not unique to Antoniorrobles's retelling but was widely employed by Spanish writers during the reign of Francisco Franco to avoid the political connotations of "red."

In his recasting of "Little Red Riding Hood," Antoniorrobles mitigates the violence and rehabilitates the wolf. The drama of the classic tale is removed from the outset by the long, descriptive title, which reassures readers of the positive outcome. Although Little Crimson Riding Hood is still eaten by the wolf, the traumatic event is turned into a ludic scene. In recent decades the author has been accused of moralizing and excessively sanitizing the classic tale. In the preface to the collection, however, the author justifies his approach to this particular story. Opposed to the violence and cruelty of Perrault's version and convinced that children no longer believe in the possibility of Little Red Riding Hood coming out of the wolf's belly alive in a kind of "Caesarean operation," he felt it was important for contemporary authors to find a witty strategy allowing them "to end the story with a scene of pardon and friendship between the wolf and the girl." In his own retelling he adopts the "forgiveness" and "humor" that he sees as the only viable strategies left to contemporary authors.[1] Although the wolf is punished by society, Little Crimson Riding Hood intercedes on his behalf at the trial and becomes his friend on his release from prison. Having deliberately set out to rewrite the cruel ending of Perrault's tale, Antoniorrobles's playful, watered-down version concludes with the ritualistic, rhyming ending of Spanish fairy tales: "y con eso, colorín, colorado, este cuento se ha acabado" (65). The words "colorín, colorado" are nonsense words that merely serve to create an entertaining rhythm and rhyme. Rather than translating the line with the conventional fairy-tale ending, "And they lived happily ever after," this anthology adopts a more obscure ending that is particularly appropriate in a tale that actually includes a mouse.

In the author's eyes only the ending of his story deviates significantly from Perrault's version, but in fact he has transformed the entire story into a comical, playful text that bears little resemblance to the classic tale. All fear and trauma have been removed from the tale through the humorous treatment of characters, motifs, and events. This sense of reassurance is magnified by the small, simple line drawing by the author that is inset to the left of the opening text. The drawing depicts a smiling Little Crimson Riding Hood, in the versatile red outfit that provides her name, walking side by side with a friendly looking, doglike wolf. Antoniorrobles's rehabilitation of the wolf is his contribution to the utopian vision he evokes in the prologue to his collection: a world in which we would have learned "to pardon the wolf in childhood" (21).

❧

Little Crimson Riding Hood Had a Scare . . . and Then, Nothing! (1962)

43. "Caperucita Encarnada pasó un susto . . . y luego ¡nada!" from *Rompetacones y 100 cuentos más*, by Antoniorrobles. Copyright © 1964 Oasis. Used by permission of Luis Miguel Robles do Campo.

Well, Sir, there once was a little village girl, the prettiest who was ever seen, and the most famous in children's stories; her mother was crazy about her, and her grandmother even more so. This good woman, who was a nice old lady, gave her granddaughter a short coat with a red hood that protected her from the sun, the wind, and the rain; and it suited her so well that throughout the village, in all the neighboring hamlets, and in her school, everyone called her "Little Crimson Riding Hood."

Since the grandmother lived in a cottage that was quite far away, a certain Saturday, Little Crimson Riding Hood's mother said to her:

"My daughter, as I imagine you will go and visit your grandmother, take her the cake that I made her this morning, and this jar of butter; give her lots of kisses for she is fragile, and you know how much she loves you."

"Yes, Mother; I love her a lot, too."

Little Crimson Riding Hood put on her hood, placed the cake and the pot of butter into her basket, then lovingly said goodbye to her mother and headed out toward her grandmother's cottage.

It turns out that in those parts lived Master Wolf, who, assuredly, was one of the worst wolves known. Some say that he didn't have that terrible a heart, but he did like to eat more than any of his relatives, and to fill his belly, he was capable of anything. It was even said that one night he entered the slaughter-house of a city, and finding himself with two dead bulls, he ate them all up, leaving only the horns, which he later used for toothpicks.

Well, there went Little Riding Hood so contentedly, singing a little song that made her take happy, dancing steps, when she saw that the wolf was sitting quietly in the shade of a tree on the path.

"Good afternoon!" she said politely.

"Good afternoon, pretty girl!" replied the wolf. "Where are you headed?"

"I'm going to see my grandmother and take her a cake and a jar of butter on behalf of my mom, and some flowers that I will pick along the way."

"And does your grandmother live very far away?" asked the rogue wolf, who did not yet even want to bite her because it sounded like some loggers were nearby; and the little girl replied:

"Yes, quite far, in a little white house that's behind that mill."

The truth is that Master Wolf's appetite was growing just looking at her. She would be so tender! . . . So he said to her:

"Look, we're going to play a game; I am going to take this path, and you take the other. Let's see which of us arrives first!"

"Yes, sir! Yes! Yes!" she agreed to the game, while at the same time she set off running as fast as she could.

Oh, but the wolf, who was very hungry because the local dogs didn't let him eat lamb, galloped away and arrived immediately at the grandmother's door. He then called:

"Knock! Knock!"

"Who is it?" asked the old lady.

"It's your granddaughter, Little Crimson Riding Hood," said the rogue, feigning her voice, and then he added: "I'm bringing you a cake and a little pot of butter on behalf of my mom."

The poor grandmother, who stayed in her bed because she was a little fragile, called from her bed:

"Pull the cord on your left, and the door will open."

The wolf pulled, and the door opened; he was even tempted to eat the grandmother, he was so hungry. But in order to await the tender little girl, he roughly locked up the old lady in a wardrobe and even stuffed her mouth with a dishcloth. Next, he put on the little old lady's nightcap and calmly got into the bed.

After a little while, the girl called at the door:

"Knock! Knock!"

"Who is it?" asked the wolf, imitating the grandmother's voice, which, even though he didn't get it quite right, could be it, thought the girl, because the old lady was a little hoarse and fragile.

"It's your granddaughter, Little Crimson Riding Hood. I'm bringing you a cake and a pot of butter from my mom."

Master Wolf then called out:

"Pull the cord on your left, and the door will open."

The little girl pulled the cord, and the door opened. She quietly walked into the room, which was a little dark, and then the wolf, hiding between the sleeping cap he had put on and the edge of the sheet, said as gently as he could:

"Put the cake and the little jar on that table, and come and lie down a little while with your grandmother. Come on, pretty girl."

The little girl removed her shoes and hood and confidently got into her grandmother's bed, hoping that she would tell her stories. However, upon seeing how strange the old lady looked this time, she exclaimed in astonishment:

"Grandma, what big arms you have! They look like elephant trunks!"

"All the better to hug you with, my dear," said the wolf with a fake voice.

"Grandma, what big legs you have!"

"All the better to run with, my dear."

"Grandma, what big ears you have!"

"All the better to hear you with, my dear."

"Grandma, what big teeth you have. They look like piano keys!"

"All the better to eat you with! . . ."

And with these quick words, the wicked wolf threw himself on the girl and swallowed her. But such was the eagerness and hunger of the beast that he didn't wait to chew her, and so the very pretty little girl went down the wolf's throat with the speed at which children throw themselves down the slippery slides of public parks. She even felt a bit of vertigo that nearly made her smile.

And, of course, once the glutton satisfied his greedy whim, he fell asleep, ready to digest his tasty snack.

In fact, he started to snore so loudly, with his mouth so wide open, that it immediately caught the attention of one of the many mice thereabouts. The curiosity about the racket led the mouse up to the mouth of Master Wolf and zip! he went in as if it were a mouse-hole.

Oh, how magnificent! Upon feeling the tickle of his whiskers, Little Riding Hood went to grab hold of him. He then turned to get out, and she firmly grasped his tail. The mouse called for help, and twelve of his family members came running; they pulled him . . . and out through the mouth of the wolf he came, along with the little girl, who hadn't let go of his tail.

On seeing that it was the wolf that had swallowed her, Little Riding Hood gave a shriek and used a stool to climb on top of the wardrobe, where the grandmother was locked up. Thus they were both safe from the wolf, who, waking up with the girl's scream, wanted to swallow her again.

Fortunately, there was an umbrella on top of the wardrobe; with it, Little Riding Hood threatened the beast, and when the wolf attacked her, the first thing to enter his mouth was the umbrella. Little Riding Hood opened it up, and now, with that device opened up inside his belly, the beast could not hurt anyone.

The little girl safe, and the grandmother saved also, some peasants came and tied up Master Wolf. They removed the umbrella, and afterward a trial was held. A fox who acted as a defense lawyer said:

"Keep in mind, judges, that this 'poor little animal' didn't so much as scratch her with his fangs!"

With that bit about "poor little animal," the public began to laugh, because everyone knew that if they didn't dig in, it was because of the eagerness with which he had swallowed her. But the little girl was so good that she said to her parents:

"I want you to forgive him because it is true that he didn't even give me a scratch . . ."

The wolf was not pardoned altogether; they condemned him to a year in prison eating radishes and carrots, without even a taste of meat. The wolf became so fond of Little Riding Hood, because she wanted to pardon him, that when he was released, he waited for her at her door every Saturday, and the two of them walked peacefully to visit her grandmother, in her little white house. This way, the wolf could defend her if any other beast from those parts tried to attack the little girl. A mouse did run; my story now is done.

Little Red Riding Hood (Le Petit Chaperon Rouge)

Jean Claverie

Jean Claverie (1946–) is widely considered one of France's most important contemporary author-illustrators. He began his career as an advertising illustrator, but started specializing in children's books in 1977. Claverie has illustrated several of Charles Perrault's tales, but he has also retold the story of Little Red Riding Hood in a humorous parody that transposes it to a modern urban setting.

The picturebook *Le Petit Chaperon Rouge* was first published in France in 1994 and was reissued, by a Belgian publisher, in 2009. The first spread is a bird's eye view of the cityscape (an apt reflection of the third-person narrator's omniscience), which makes excellent use of Claverie's distinctive technique of leaving illustrations in the unfinished state of preliminary sketches. In the foreground of the detailed pencil drawing, touches of subtle color immediately draw readers' attention to the copse of trees where Mamma Gina parks her pizza van, but as the eye recedes, the color disappears, and the drawing becomes less precise. As in all of his books, Claverie plays skillfully with perspective, varying the reader's viewpoint from one illustration to the next. The second spread places readers on the street in front of the pizza van, where the dangers of the scrapyard that dominated the first spread are hidden from view by the wall as the mother waves to the little girl from the streetcorner. Claverie heightens the drama of the tale with the skillful use of light and shadow as well as the contrasting warm golden and cool blue and gray tones that characterize all of his work (plate 20).

Unlike many of his compatriots, Claverie chiefly uses the hypotext of the Grimm version, which is embedded in the visual narrative in the form of a videotape, clearly labeled "Rotkäppchen," in the technically savvy grandmother's video collection. In this feminist retelling, the protagonist's enterprising and courageous mother comes to her daughter's rescue armed with the axe of her great-great-grandfather woodcutter. At the same time, details of Perrault's version are retained and given a humorous twist, notably the picturesque archaic formula about the *chevillette* and the *bobinette* that becomes the object of clever wordplay accessible even to children. Much of the humor derives from the anachronistic contrast between traditional elements of the tale and the modern setting, as in the wolf's unexpected replies to Little Red Riding Hood's classic questions of the formulaic dialogue. Claverie effectively retains Perrault's climactic surprise effect at the end by suddenly returning to the familiar words of the wolf's last line after a page turn. The wolf's enormous jaws extend across the gutter onto the verso page, toward a vulnerable Little Red Riding Hood, who stares at him in frozen terror. Claverie is well known for his caricatural characters, which all bear a striking family resemblance since they are modeled on the members of his own family. Another distinctive feature of his work is the self-reflexive references to himself or his work, which constitute a kind of signature. On the final spread of this picturebook, the license plate on the back of the wolf's large pizza truck, as he waves to Little Red Riding lookalikes in blue and yellow anoraks, bears the name "Claverie." Like many of his contemporary counterparts, Claverie's wolf gives up eating little girls and grannies, but rather than adopting the rather cliché vegetarian diet, this carnivore embraces the modern-day children's food of choice.

44. *Le Petit Chaperon Rouge*, by Jean Claverie. Copyright © 2009 Éditions Mijade. Used by permission of Jean Claverie and Éditions Mijade.

᷍

LITTLE RED RIDING HOOD (1994)

Once upon a time there was a large city which, by growing ever larger, had caused a forest to disappear.

Where huge trees had once thrived now stretched, for as far as the eye could see, a scrapyard of old cars without wheels or windows, carcasses of buses and trucks, forever immobile, waiting in the sun and the rain for the final crushing under the hammer of Mr. Wolf, the scrap dealer.

In fact, from the forest of old there was still a copse of trees in whose shade Mamma Gina, a woodcutter's great-great-granddaughter, was in the habit of parking her small van.

One day, Gina, the wood-fire pizza queen, thought that her daughter was now old enough to take the daily pizza to her sick grandmother all by herself. She lived at the other end of Mr. Wolf's vast field of scrap metal.

"Stay on the sidewalk. At the end of the street, you will cross very carefully, and there, you will recognize Grandmother's house." That was a long way for the little girl. But no matter, she loved her grandmother, who told her stories of the time when the whole neighborhood was a forest. Armed with this good advice, a very red pizza, and a small pot of tomato sauce that her grandmother adored, the little girl set out. She wore her red anorak. That's why at school they called her "Little Red Riding Hood" . . . in memory of an old, almost forgotten story.

"How long and boring this straight street is!" the little girl said to herself, as she walked along the wall from which piles of old cars protruded.

Thus she came close to the entrance to Mr. Wolf's domain.

"Where is she going, this cute little girl?" It so happens that it was Mr. Wolf, pretending to talk to himself.

"I'm going to my sick granny's house, to take her her pizza and her little pot of sauce," she answered bravely.

"Hmmm, I believe that your granny lives that way?" said the wolf. "You would get there faster going through my place; besides, my old trucks are harmless."

"Not a bad idea . . . ," said Little Red Riding Hood, who found the wolf quite nice. "That way I will save time and I can play awhile with the old cars."

While Little Red Riding Hood started into the midst of this rusty paradise, the wolf hurried to the grandmother's, thinking that with a little luck he would devour a grandmother for dinner, a little girl with tomato sauce for dessert, and, if he still had a little room, a pizza, for he had never tasted it.

At the door of the house, noting that the bell did not work, the wolf adopted a ridiculous little piping voice to call the grandmother: "Granny, it's your Little Red Riding Hood, who has brought you your little pizza and your little sauce." "Oh, you came all by yourself this time, I'm glad! I'm in bed, so open the door yourself. Pull the bobbin and the latch will go up!" said the grandmother, who happily spoke in a slightly old-fashioned language. Thinking no doubt that it was granny's do-it-yourself job to repair the lock, the wolf, without trying to understand, lifted the latch and rushed into the bedroom. Everything happened very quickly. The little grandmother was eaten at once, without the wolf needing to chew.

Meanwhile, the little girl, realizing she had played enough and that it was quite late, hurried to her grandmother's house, where the wolf was hiding as best he could in the bed, keeping the television as the only light, which, fortunately, was broadcasting a film noir that evening.

"Hello, Granny! It's your Little Red Riding Hood. I've brought you your pizza and some fresh sauce. I know how to open."

This suited the wolf, who had been trying desperately to remember the grandmother's phrase since he got into bed: "The latch first, then the bobbin . . . Darn, I don't remember!"

Little Red Riding Hood approached the bed in the dark and exclaimed:

"Granny, what big ears you have!"

"It's a new device to hear you better, my child."

"Granny, what big eyes you have!"

"These are my new glasses to see you better, my child."

Noticing the dentures left on the table beside the bed just when she heard a sinister grinding under the sheet, the little girl said, trembling:

"But Granny, I thought you no longer had any teeth!"

"All the better to eat you with, my child!"

And the wolf did to Little Red Riding Hood what he had done to the grandmother. He swallowed her even more easily, thanks to the tomato sauce.

The wolf took a break, and then he tasted the pizza cautiously. He chewed it carefully and, finding it to his taste, swallowed it, and then fell asleep in front of the television.

As it began to get really late at night, Mamma Gina, very worried, took down her great-great-grandfather's old axe and traveled the path that her daughter should have taken.

Arriving at the grandmother's, she knew instantly what had happened: immediately she smashed the TV with a great blow of the axe, which woke the wolf with a start.

"Now, you are going to throw up, or else . . . !" she yelled, threatening him.

The wolf, who in any case was not feeling very well, stuffed his two paws in his mouth and restored almost everything: Grandmother and Little Red Riding Hood in tomato sauce.

I leave you to imagine the joy of this reunion. But I give up drawing this rather dripping scene. Once all three had kissed each other thoroughly, Mamma Gina turned to the wolf: "You can keep the pizza, but that will be thirty francs."

The wolf disappeared forever from the neighborhood, and, it is said, he no longer eats anything but pizzas. He has even changed his job.

The Last Wolf and Little Riding Hood
(El último lobo y Caperucita)

JOSÉ LUIS GARCÍA SÁNCHEZ AND MIGUEL ÁNGEL PACHECO

Concerns about the endangered wolf in Spain led José Luis García Sánchez (1941–) and Miguel Fernández-Pacheco (aka Miguel Ángel Pacheco, 1944–) to publish the picturebook *El último lobo y Caperucita* (The Last Wolf and Little Riding Hood) in 1975. At that time the two authors were collaborating extensively, writing eighty-five books for the publisher Altea during the ten-year period from 1973 to 1983. These included several works in a series of recreations of traditional tales titled *Un millón de cuentos* (A Million Tales), which were published in 1982–1983. Pacheco, who has won numerous awards for his illustrations as well as his texts, also illustrated several of their books, including *El último lobo y Caperucita* (plate 21).

The picturebook includes a didactic afterword titled "El lobo en los cuentos y en su realidad" (The Wolf in Tales and in Reality), inspired by the research of Dr. Félix Rodríguez de la Fuente, one of the world's foremost authorities on wolves, and based on facts supplied by ADENA, the Spanish Association for the Defense of Nature. The afterword briefly presents the image of the wolf in popular folklore and children's tales—that of a dangerous animal capable of eating up Little Red Riding Hood (the Spanish text uses the reflexive form of the verb, *comerse*, which has a strong sexual connotation)— an image that has turned these beautiful animals into a powerful symbol of fear in the collective imagination. The afterword deconstructs, point by point, the social construction of the wolf as cruel, treacherous, and murderous, and reconstructs an image of opposing qualities: loving, loyal, killing only to eat.

Despite the didactic afterword, the story itself is very innovative for the 1970s, particularly in its use of speech and thought bubbles as well as frames to convey narrative levels. The authors present multiple perspectives by combining traditional omniscient narration with first-person voices that can be read before or after or simultaneously. Generally the third-person narration appears at the bottom of the page, in the white margin that sets it conspicuously apart from the first-person narration contained in the speech bubbles in the large, vividly colored pictures framed by a double keyline. On the pages where the omniscient narrator disappears, so, too, does the frame around the picture. The omniscient third-person narrative (in roman type at the bottom of the page) is often humorously brief in comparison with the first-person narration (in italics) in speech and thought bubbles, which often dominate the illustration by their size or number. In a parody of the Grimms' cautionary scene, the mother's instructions, which she gives as she knits another of the endless, itchy bonnets, are contained in a speech bubble that fills almost half of the illustration. When the storytelling wolf nostalgically "howls" his

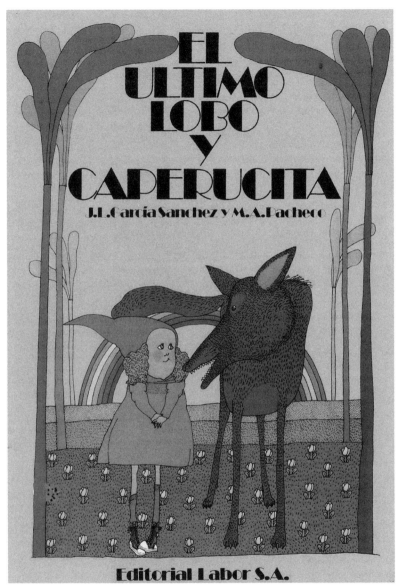

45. *El último lobo y Caperucita*, by José Luis García Sánchez and Miguel Ángel Pacheco. Text copyright © 1975 José Luis García Sánchez; illustrations copyright © 1975 Miguel Ángel Pacheco. Used by permission of José Luis García Sánchez and Miguel Ángel Pacheco.

story of the good old days to María, he takes over as sole narrator, and the huge bubble occupies two-thirds of the page. The elimination of the speech bubble as he continues his story reinforces the fact that the wolf's voice has replaced that of the third-person narrator. Another illustration juxtaposes two wordless speech bubbles, which show the very different version the storytelling hunter tells María, of his heroic exploits in the good old days when there were still lots of wolves to kill, and the version the little girl imagines, in which the terrified hunter flees a huge, grinning bear. In several instances, we see two very different Riding Hoods when the protagonist's speech and her thoughts are juxtaposed. While her speech projects the classic image of a good, obedient little girl, María's thoughts reveal a more impolite and rebellious child. In light of Pacheco's versatile and skillful use of the speech bubble, it is surprising to learn that he seldom uses it elsewhere in his work.[2]

The diverse design elements of the page layout make this a particularly eye-catching and modern-looking picturebook. The labeling of important sites on the illustrations seems to function as an ironic commentary on the disappearance of the wolves' habitat, as the "Wolf's forest" between "Little Riding Hood's town" and "Grandmother's house" is pitifully small. The manic, crazed hunter assumes the murderous role of the wolf with his indiscriminate killing. In the illustrations, the "BANG! BANG!" of the hunter's gun contrasts paradoxically with the "No Hunting" signs posted on the trees. There is lack of closure in this picturebook retelling, as the final scene shows the hunter in the police station pleading "self-defense" after his arrest, while the grandmother tries to console a Little Riding Hood who is heartbroken at the loss of her good friend the wolf (plate 22).

~&~

THE LAST WOLF AND LITTLE RIDING HOOD (1975)

Once upon a time there was a little girl called María. María Fernández Pérez, and she was neither fat nor thin, neither tall nor short, neither good nor bad . . . She was a normal little girl, like all little girls. But nobody called her by her real name.

They always called her "Little Riding Hood," although she did not mind too much. Other children were called *Fatty*, or *Freckles*, or *Acorn*. "Little Riding Hood" was not the worst name.

"Goodbye, Little Riding Hood."
"Goodbye, Little Riding Hood."
"Goodbye . . ."[3]

And they called her "Little Riding Hood" because her mother made her wear knitted bonnets that were always red and itched a lot. They sold a lot of skeins of red wool in the department store sales, and Little Riding Hood's mother was lucky enough to be one of the first to enter the store.

"Take the little jar and tell Mariano to fill it with honey and make a note of it . . . Then go to your grandmother's house, but do not dawdle in the woods, for night might fall . . . And do not play with the wolf, who has fleas . . . Tell your grandmother to return the fine needles . . . And if she needs more yarn, not to worry, that I have lots of skeins . . . And do not take off your cap, so you don't catch cold . . ."

Little Riding Hood's mother had a worse obsession than that of the red hats: she always sent her on errands, to the pharmacy, to Mariano's store, to the house of her grandma who had no telephone . . .

"Yes, Mom . . ."

"When will you buy me an anorak?"[4]

To get to her grandmother's house, Little Riding Hood had to go through the woods where a wolf lived.

The wolf was the last of a large pack. He was already old, he would be at least twelve years old, and he was not very frightening . . . Since he was not dangerous, the town mayor had prohibited hunting him; all the residents liked having a wolf in their woods.

And beyond the woods, in a cottage, lived Little Riding Hood's grandmother, who was very old and spent the day knitting, always with red wool.

One day, after shopping, Little Riding Hood set off into the woods . . .

"Goodbye, Little Riding Hood."

"Goodbye, Mr. Mariano."

"Goodbye, four eyes."[5]

And as usual when she went to see her grandma, she forgot that she could not play with the wolf.

"Hello, wolf . . ."

The wolf was fond of howling stories about when he was little to Little Riding Hood.

"When I was little many wolves lived in this wood. We lived very happily. When we were hungry, we hunted enough to eat."

There were pheasants and quails and rabbits and squirrels and foxes and bears . . . I bet you don't know what a bear looks like? But the hunter came and started killing all the animals he could with his shotgun.

BANG!

BANG!

He did not need to kill to eat, because he had sandwiches in his bag: beef with lettuce, marinated tuna, or omelet sandwiches, because men are carnivorous, herbivorous, and eggivorous . . .

BANG!

BANG!*[6]*

We wolves, as we had no bag, had to go down to the village looking for food . . . The villagers got very angry because we ate their sheep. They started killing wolves, and only I am left.

"Come on, don't be tedious, you always tell me the same thing . . . I'll race you to my grandmother's house."

Little Riding Hood and the wolf began to run, but Little Riding Hood fell behind, because she had only two legs.

The hunter was always in the woods wanting to kill the wolf.

"Hello, Little Riding Hood, you haven't met that bloody wolf . . ."

"No."

What he liked most was telling stories about when there were many wolves.

"Wolves are very dangerous for the countryside. I am going to accompany you to your grandma's house. It is not advisable that you go alone. Once I was going through this same wood when suddenly out came one or two hundred wolves ready to eat me. Well, maybe less, but I had to flee. And the next day I brought a tear gas bomb, and as they came out from between the trees, pop! pop! . . . Well, wolves and pheasants and quail, and owls, and squirrels. Imagine what luck. I took home eighty pieces."

BANG!

BANG!

"They are dangerous for the countryside . . ."

As hunters are very tedious telling their exploits,

night fell before they reached the house of Little Riding Hood's grandmother.

"I am going to say hello to your grandma."

"WATCH OUT!!"

"You have eaten her, murderer . . ."

BANG!

BANG!

"We are going to open his belly to take out your grandma."

"But what are you doing, animal . . . I had put him in the bed because he was very cold."

The hunter was taken by the police for having killed the last wolf. And since then in that town, wolves exist only in stories about Little Red Riding Hood.

"It was self-defense."

"Don't cry, I am going to tell you a story. Once upon a time there was a little girl called Snow . . ."

Waldtraut and the Wolf (Waldtraut und der Wolf)

MEIKE STOEBE AND SUSANN STOEBE

Meike Stoebe is a German children's author whose tale *Waldtraut und der Wolf* (Waldtraut and the Wolf) was published simultaneously in German and French (as *Pélagie et le loup*) by the bilingual Swiss publisher Nord-Süd in 1996. The book is illustrated by Stoebe's sister Susann Stoebe (now Stoebe-Thöne, 1964–), a German illustrator who also works as a painter, graphic designer, and sculptor. The sisters have collaborated on two picturebooks. Although their retelling of "Little Red Riding Hood" takes place in a rustic, rural setting that evokes the Alps, it presents a modern young girl wearing a red baseball cap over her long red braids. The illustrator subverts the stereotypical image of the pretty fairy-tale heroine by portraying a rather homely, gangly tomboy who lopes gracelessly through the forest. Waldtraut fearlessly muzzles the wolf in a humorous closeup that focuses on her large, masculine-looking hands clamping the wolf's jaws shut.

Stoebe's tale demystifies the fears and erroneous views that have surrounded wolves for centuries. The wolf—named Wolfgang in the German version and Jehan-le-Loup in the French version ("Jehan" is a medieval form of the French name "Jean")—is very conscious of his literary reputation as the "Big Bad Wolf," and the metafictive play adds a witty touch. The illustrator's portrayal of Wolfgang as an Afghan hound undermines his claim to ferociousness, and his despair at her lack of fear is quite humorous. In this picturebook it is the heroine herself who enlightens readers, as well as the wolf, about the true nature of wolves. The modern tale systematically deconstructs the traditional tale one point at a time. Framed illustrations on the verso page depict the myth, while the unframed illustrations on the recto show what happens in so-called real life. For example, a tiny, terrified grandmother still clutching her handbag struggles in the jaws of the wolf on one verso, while the facing illustration shows the wolf clutching a hot-water bottle to his swollen, aching stomach next to a large basin where he seems to have thrown up granny's accessories. Sitting on a stump in the forest, Waldtraut preaches her lesson on "real wolves" to Wolfgang, who sits at her feet like a pet dog, listening intently (plate 23). The final illustrations focus on their new friendship: a large closeup of their two heads side by side as they take the path to grandmother's house, and a final wordless spread that depicts the three main characters seated around a table, sharing a snack.

46. *Waldtraut und der Wolf*, by Meike Stoebe and Susann Stoebe. Copyright © 1996 Nord-Süd Verlag. Used by permission of Nord-Süd Verlag.

ↁ

Waldtraut and the Wolf (1996)

Waldtraut is seven years old. Where she lives, there are only prairies, woods, and fields. There are few cars that venture on the little bumpy road that leads to her village. For her part, the grandmother lives farther still, in the depths of the forest, and as she is sick, Waldtraut is taking her a cake and a little pot of butter, not forgetting a good bottle of red wine.

Gosh, it's dark enough to scare you in this forest, thinks Waldtraut, shivering. At the same moment she hears, from a bush, a slight crackling. Waldraut is not at all at ease.

"Grrrr . . .! I am the Big Bad Wolf and I am going to eat you!" rumbles suddenly a cavernous voice as deep as the forest.

With a giant leap, Wolfgang comes out of his hiding place and leaps on the child to eat her.

But the courageous Waldtraut meets and repels the menacing jaws of the wolf in the twinkling of an eye.

Wolfgang is dumbfounded.

"You're not afraid of me?" he asks, upset. He can't believe his eyes.

"No!" replied Waldtraut with aplomb. "Because there is no reason to be afraid of real wolves."

"But don't you know the story of poor Little Red Riding Hood and the Big Bad Wolf?" carries on Wolfgang, desperate.

"Yes," answers Waldtraut, "but in reality, that is not at all how it goes."

"Ah, right, and how does it go?" asks the wolf.

Then Waldtraut explains . . .

"It is claimed in tales that wolves eat grandmothers whole, in a single bite. But it's not true.

"A real wolf would put a hole in his stomach, and he would have a horrible stomach ache.

"In real life, the wolf is not at all greedy.

"He even eats very sensibly. He hardly even treats himself to a little hare, and even that only if he manages to catch it.

"He has the right to a little treat from time to time, no?

"It is also claimed that wolves slyly attack defenseless little children to steal everything they have.

"That is just nonsense!

"No, no, in reality, the wolf is a rather timid animal which, when it has a choice, prefers to flee.

"On the other hand, the wild wolf that is attacked confronts its enemy with as much prudence as courage in a fair fight.

"Basically, the wolf is very wise and he loves life," concludes Waltraut.

"But what am I going to do in my old age if I can't even frighten little children?" laments Wolfgang. "I don't know how to do anything else . . ."

"Don't worry. I'm going to teach you to become a wolf, the real thing," says Waldtraut, to comfort her new friend.

And, side by side, they both went joyously to visit Grandmother, who is always delighted to have visitors.

One Cake Too Many (Une galette de trop)

Gérard Moncomble

Gérard Moncomble (1951–) is a French author, illustrator, and scriptwriter. Although he initially began writing for adults, he turned to writing for children when he began having his own. A very prolific author, he has published approximately 150 books over the past thirty years. His stories are wildly inventive and almost always extremely funny. In the 1990s Moncomble published three whodunits in which great classics of the past are revisited by a detective named Romain Gallo (rendered in English as "Roman Gallo" to retain the Gallo-Roman wordplay). The three rather large-format books were illustrated, in the manner of Gustave Doré's engravings, by Sourine (1951–), the pseudonym of the French illustrator, painter, and sculptor Michel Dupuy. They appeared in the now defunct Bibliothèque Milan series, which was dedicated to publishing "what could not be published elsewhere," according to Milan's editorial statement. The company brought out unusual, outsized volumes that addressed a broad audience ranging from teens to young adults and beyond. Moncomble's Roman Gallo books were in line with this editorial mission, as the texts were not really written for children. Unfortunately, this approach was not long-lived, given the express request of booksellers, parents, and other children's book mediators of all kinds to have works that were clearly identified and recognizable.

The title *Romain Gallo contre Charles Perrault* (Roman Gallo against Charles Perrault) announces the origin of the cases the detective-narrator chronicles in the first volume, published in 1991. The following year, Moncomble published *Les douze travaux de Romain Gallo* (The Twelve Labors of Roman Gallo), a parody of the twelve tasks of the Greek hero Heracles. The pun in the third title, *Fabuleux Romain Gallo!* (Fabled Roman Gallo!), published in 1993, clearly signals that Gallo has shifted his investigations from fairy tales and mythology to fables. This time the detective's cases are strangely similar to seven famous fables by La Fontaine. When the poet accuses Gallo of plagiarism, the detective silences his illustrious predecessor by turning the tables and evoking a certain Aesop. The author intended to include a fourth volume, which would have explored the world of *Alice in Wonderland*, but unfortunately it was never written. The success of Roman Gallo's adventures led to the reissuing of two of the books in Milan Junior's Polar series of whodunits for young readers, this time with a defined age category. The smaller, pocketbook version was produced without illustrations for financial reasons, but also because, as the author explains rather tongue in cheek, the French readership of eleven- to twelve-year-olds the series targeted apparently no longer needed images.[7]

Each chapter of *Romain Gallo contre Charles Perrault* is devoted to a different Perrault tale. A small vignette decorates the title page of each tale, which is also accompanied by a large black-and-white "engraving" and a re-curring small illustration inset in the text. The first case is devoted to Little Red Riding Hood, and the vignette on the title page shows Gallo's first client, a well-dressed 1950s-era woman, knocking on his door. The large engraving depicts a veiled Mrs. Red-Ridinghood striding up a dreary-looking street, carrying a shopping basket. The cover of the 1999 pocketbook edition features this tale: a rather traditional rendering of the encounter in the woods is the subject of a large poster or photograph that hangs behind Gallo, who is portrayed as the stereotypical circa-1950s detective in trenchcoat and felt hat. (He is also endowed with variations on the idiosyncrasies and foibles that one expects of all celebrated detectives.)

The cover of the more recent 2007 edition shows the detective in the same garb, as he is confronted by five characters from his cases, two of which are Little Red Riding Hood and the wolf. The auctorial paratextual elements are written with the same witty playfulness as the text itself. Moncomble's initials, rather than those of Gallo, sign the irreverent dedication to Charles Perrault, who has allowed him to "reset the *conteur* to zero," a pun that substitutes the French word *conteur* (storyteller) for *compteur* (meter). On the same page a note informs the reader that any resemblance to "Le Petit Chaperon Rouge" and Perrault's other tales is not the least for-tuitous. The three-page foreword, however, is signed by Roman Gallo, the detective-turned-author, to refute the volume of fairy tales published by his rival, the incompetent and corrupt policeman Charles Perrault, who has taken credit for the cases Gallo had solved. The detective intends to provide readers with a true account of events and set them straight about Perrault, that "so-called author of a miserable collection of tales" which can only cause children everywhere to "snigger."[8] The first example he gives in the foreword of one of Perrault's poor victims is Leloup ("le loup" meaning "the wolf"), the vegetarian butcher imprisoned in the Little Red Riding Hood case: "Imagine being accused of eating little girls and grandmothers, when you like only soya seeds." Gallo assures his "dear reader" that such things do not just happen in novels (9).

The story is set in sinister neighborhoods characteristic of thrillers, with the exception of the idyllic fairy-tale setting of the grandmother's house in the forest. Even in the unfamiliar urban setting, however, there are incon-gruous allusions to the world of fairy tales, such as the D'Aulnoy Street ad-dress of the woodcutter (Madame d'Aulnoy was a contemporary of Perrault who also wrote fairy tales) or the name of his dog, Andersen, who conjures up images of the fiercest dog in "The Tinder Box." The familiar cast of char-acters assumes different roles and entirely different character traits. A new character is added in the role of Gallo's first client, Madame Leloup, who, although well bred and well dressed, has disquieting animal characteristics. Moncomble transposes motifs from the classic tale with playfulness and wit in his whodunit version of "Little Red Riding Hood." The eight-year-old

47. *Romain Gallo contre Charles Perrault*, by Gérard Moncomble. Illustration by Jean-François Martin. In the series Milan Poche Junior/Polar. Copyright © 2007 Éditions Milan. Used by permission of Éditions Milan.

protagonist is an accomplice to a crime, but Gallo's final reflections suggest that she is perhaps a victim of the adults who involved her, first and foremost her mother, Mrs. Red-Ridinghood. The archaic language that Perrault retains in his version of the tale becomes the target of playful parody in the detective's retelling. Like many French authors, Moncomble has particular fun with the line about the *bobinette* and the *chevillette*, which not only is worked into the suspect's statement and the detective's grand entrance but also provides a valuable clue. The antiquated terms, such as "Mère-Grand," contrast sharply with the detective's modern argot in a story that is filled with thriller clichés and humorous, outdated interjections, usually swear words.

Readers only later see the irony in Gallo's reply to little Red-Ridinghood that he is not "the bad guy" in the story, as it is not revealed until the epilogue that he spends two years in jail thanks to Perrault. It is obviously not a coincidence that the superintendent took his retirement immediately after Gallo's trial and wrote his "Mémoires," consisting of his "best investigations" (218), during the detective's imprisonment. It certainly seems like the superintendent needed him out of the way while he wrote his bestseller and established his literary reputation. Nor is it a coincidence that he runs into Perrault in the pea soup–like fog the day he is released from prison, as the former superintendent carries under his arm a package wrapped in newspaper that contains a signed copy of *Contes de ma mere l'Oye* for Gallo. When the detective finally opens the package much later, he reads it in a single go and begins that very evening to type furiously on his old typewriter. The epilogue reports Gallo's reception of Perrault's tales, ranging from initial amusement to stupefaction partway through to complete breakdown at the end. His reluctant praise for the "ingenious" titles and the author's sense of "the turn of phrase that hits home" is followed by criticism of an "outdated" style that is "sprinkled here and there with antiquated expressions." It is the content, however, that draws Gallo's wrath, as the superintendent has merely regurgitated his "feeble hypotheses" about the six cases and indulged his "wild imaginings," which are "an insult to reality." The flyleaf contains a carefully written dedication to Roman Gallo, "involuntary collaborator and cheap detective," whom the author hopes to "finally get back on the path of Justice and Truth."

In turn, Gallo writes a vitriolic dedication in the copy of the book he sends Perrault. Exactly one month after having read the "abominable tales" by the delusional Perrault, Gallo's manuscript is accepted enthusiastically by a publisher who probably hopes to set off a literary quarrel like the one in which Perrault was involved in his day (220). Although Gallo does not deny his desire for revenge, he claims the book is also intended to reestablish the facts, because the public has a right to know the truth at any cost. Moncomble's tongue-in-cheek metafictive play is particularly amusing for older readers. Perrault's book is on its way to becoming an unprecedented bestseller and has been translated in quite a few countries, reports Gallo, insisting, however, that it is just "a flash in the pan." His own book, on the other hand, has not received any attention in the literary columns of the "rags" he has been combing through (147). Moncomble's Little Red Riding Hood whodunit is a self-conscious novel that ends with the narrator-author sending his literary rival a copy of the novel readers hold in their hands.

48. "Une galette de trop," from *Romain Gallo contre Charles Perrault*, by Gérard Moncomble. Illustrations by Sourine. In the series Bibliothèque Milan. Copyright © 1991 Éditions Milan. Used by permission of Gérard Moncomble.

One Cake Too Many (1991)

I could have located my business in a chic avenue, it's true. Have air conditioning, a first-class secretary, and the bun that goes with her. Or receive my clients on a colorfast carpet, with soft lighting just right, tropical plants, and a giant aquarium. The upper-crust type.

I could have.

But I chose the ZUP.[9] It's the zone, it's urban, and even bloody peripheral. You get used to it, you know. And then I have a panoramic view of the marshaling yard. Necessarily, of the seventeenth arrondissement.

Okay, locating a detective agency on the top floor of a concrete high-rise isn't the idea of the century. Especially when the elevator is perpetually out of gas. Thus I had had to disassemble the wardrobe, the desk, and sofa bed piece by piece to successfully pull them up to the seventeenth floor by the fire escape. I had to cross off the billiard table. Too heavy.

Then there was that farcical story with my telephone, whose bell rang every time anyone used the garbage chute in the building. Hilarious.

Everything had eventually worked out, and that day, installed in my old moleskin armchair, my feet absentmindedly placed on a pile of empty files, I was able take little sips of a grapefruit cola while waiting for my first client.

My eyes were fixed on the glass door right in front of me, and I was dreamily reading the few words written in white paint:

Roman Gallo, detective

Investigations and discreet tailing

It sounded false. Too much, even. I thought that, from the other side of the door, on the landing, the visitors would read something incomprehensible, something along the lines of

ɘvɒɔɟɘb ,ollɒ⅁ nɒmoЯ

lnvɘƨɟɩǫɒɟɩonƨ ɒnb bɿɔɘɿɔƨɟ ɟɒɩlɩnǫ

but it was a little late now. Besides, a shadow loomed behind the opaque glass, and someone knocked on the door. My first case.

She entered with tiny steps, closed the door very carefully, and sat down on the edge of the chair in front of me.

A well-bred woman.

Under the black veiled hat, two eyes stared at me intensely. I took my feet off the pile of files, put my hands flat on the desk, and smiled at her with an intelligent look. That was what I could do most successfully.

"You must help me rectify a terrible miscarriage of justice."

Her odor was strong, but I had known worse.

"I am all ears, dear madam."

Classy, Gallo. All that was missing was a carnation in the buttonhole.

With a feverish hand, she took a photograph out of her purse and placed it before me.

"My husband is innocent, Mr. Gallo."

She blew her nose noisily. That perfume, for crying out loud . . .

While staring at it impassively, I took the photo, felt the weight of it, took a huge magnifying glass out of my drawer, and cast an aesthete's eye on the print. Pro, Gallo.

It was the portrait of a man, still young, with bushy eyebrows and an angular jaw. A tough guy. There was a flash in my head. Isidore Leloup! The cannibal killer! The monstrous murderer of the little Red-Ridinghood and her grandmother!

I had not followed the case at the time. Yet it had received plenty of attention. A lot of rags had a keen interest in the trial, and the verdict was spread over the first page of every daily.

That little girl and her grandmother, liquidated by this madman, and eaten piece by pie—Yuk! What a dreadful story. And it's this guy who . . .

"He is innocent, I swear!"

She was crying silently behind her handkerchief.

"But the case was tried, Madam. And your husband was sentenced to life."

She pounced and put her hand on my arm. A hand with excessively long nails.

"Reopen the investigation! I beg you!"

I disengaged myself and, dumbfounded, contemplated my torn jacket.

"Calm yourself, dear Mrs. Leloup."

I took a few steps toward the window. Her perfume was unbearable. I opened the window and took a large breath of fresh December air. Divine.

"What makes you believe he is innocent?"

She huddled in her chair. I thought she was ready to jump on me again and leaned against the windowsill, my forehead suddenly bathed in sweat.

"My husband is a vegetarian, Mr. Gallo."

I had trouble withholding a nervous laugh. That's just the way it is, I didn't yet have the stiff composure of the great elite private detectives.

"But why the hell didn't you say so at the trial?"

She lowered her head.

"My husband would never have allowed it. A butcher has a reputation to uphold."

"But that would no doubt have saved him."

"The Leloups have been butchers for five generations. You cannot understand . . ."

She was sobbing. I gently closed the window and, despite my repulsion, went to put my calm hand on her perfumed shoulder.

"Count on me, dear Madam. If he is truly innocent, I will save your husband."

She looked deeply into my eyes. I felt faint. She had seized my hand and was crushing it methodically.

"Thank you, Mr. Gallo. Thank you."

I stammered a vague "you're welcome" while taking back my five squished fingers. Hell!

She took from her crocodile bag a wad of bills that she put down on my desk.

Before I even had a chance to say that it was too much, dear Madam, that I took only three hundred francs a day plus expenses, she was already gone, trotting toward the door, leaving behind her the miasma of hell.

I was going to spend a fortune on pssss pssss to disinfect the room, guys.

But the wad contained ten bills of a hundred. Enough to buy three tons of pistachio-chocolate deodorant. Without a cone.

I spent a complete afternoon going through the archives of the local newspaper. There was plenty to keep me busy. *The Bugle of the West* had apparently been fascinated by the Red-Ridinghood case.

The investigation had been led briskly by Commissioner Charles Perrault, "a seasoned old policeman who is not taken in," said *The Bugle*.

The most shattering testimony for Leloup had been that of a woodcutter. Put on alert by Grandmother's cries, he had discovered the butcher sprawled on the grandmother's ravaged bed. It's dreadful even to say. In the blink of an eye, the woodcutter had overpowered the killer, sated by his heinous feast.

Henry Axe[10] (that was the name of the woodsman) had an excellent reputation, and his testimony was fatal to the cannibal. The jury followed the indictment of the general counsel and sentenced him to life, despite the howls of the accused calling it a conspiracy and shouting his innocence. End of the film.

I sighed. That all seemed concrete. But there must be a flaw somewhere.

With a faraway look in my eyes, I deftly uncapped one of those cans of grapefruit cola that permanently adorn the pockets of my beige raincoat. Much to the chagrin of the newspaper's archivist, who was shouting, "This isn't a bar, here, for goodness' sake, leave immediately!" And I left.

Soon installed at the wheel of my old Morgan, I began to think while sipping my favorite drink.

"I pulled the bobbin and the latch fell."

It was with this delicious, old-fashioned sentence that Axe had begun his testimony. Dixit *The Bugle of the West*.

You can't image the potential that opened up. I flung my can out the window, turned the ignition key, and drove away in my usual cloud of black smoke. With a bang. All about leaving some rubber on the asphalt and a memory for the archivist.

My first visit would be to the mother of the swallowed little Red-Ridinghood. According to the newspaper, she lived in the west of the city, in a ZUP even more peripheral than mine. I had marked down the address: 12 Mimosa

Avenue. Building C, Staircase D, Door 6, third floor. A story in itself. Fortunately I have a large notebook and small writing.

These ZUPs are real labyrinths. I got lost several times in the maze of rectangular streets crisscrossing the neighborhood, slaloming between wrecked cars and dumped trashcans. The kind of neighborhood you wouldn't wish on your worst enemy. My ZUP, in comparison, was Beverly Hills.

When I discovered Mimosa Street, it was past five o'clock in the evening, and night was starting to fall. Of course, not a hint of a mimosa.

The place was sinister. I parked near an extinguished streetlamp so as not to attract attention. Smart, Gallo. Just opposite the Staircase D, Building C. A bit of luck. No elevator, obviously.

I pressed in vain on the entrance time switch and climbed the steps of rough concrete in pitch darkness. All comfort, the ZUP.

On the third floor, there were two doors. No name. On the off chance, I rang the right. Instinct.

The door was flung open, and I had in front of me an enormous woman with eyes like grenade launchers.

"What is it, now?"

Amiable, the buxom lady. I mumbled the name of Red-Ridinghood, and the door shut with a loud "clack!" In this damn business, can't let anything surprise you. I rang pronto at the other door. Silence. Once, twice, I started again. And I even hammered, for something different.

"There's nobody there! You can see that nobody is answering!"

It was the fat lady, just behind me and annoyed, I think. I turned and flung at the fury one of those smiles that make me very popular with the ladies.

"Mrs. Red-Ridinghood no longer lives here?"

The woman softened a little.

"You're from the police?"

"No, no. Just a friend."

Liar, Gallo.

"Because we've had our fill, we have, eh, with this bloody affair!"

She wiped her hand nonstop on her apron.

"It's ages since she's been gone, the neighbor. Disappeared! Pouf! Flown! With everything she had to go through, poor thing, why would she want to stay here?"

"She didn't cope well?"

The stout matron shook her triple chins in a kind of inner laughter.

"No, but listen to you! To have daughter and mother gobbled up the same day! You've got some good ones! Didn't cope well! Ah, but it was enough to make you move, yes! Literally and figuratively, I tell you!"

Despite her corpulence, she nimbly did an about-face, disappeared a moment in the corridor, and came back and put a small, gray cloth bag under my nose.

"It's all she left, Red-Ridinghood. I cleaned when she left, necessarily, to relet. That gave me a few pennies. Well, there was only that in the cupboards. Here, I give it to you since you're family. I don't know what to do with it."

I slipped the bag in my raincoat pocket, without even taking a look.

"Good evening, my prince."

The door slammed, and I found myself in total darkness.

I groped my way down, grasping the little canvas bag in the bottom of my pocket.

I had been wrong to leave the Morgan without protection. Already it had no wheels left. As usual.

That evening, I had a long, a very long walk. That allowed me to think. Useful in my business.

D'Aulnoy Street is steep. Having little confidence in the Morgan's hand brake, I propped the front tire with a stone. (I had found four secondhand tires from a mechanic I knew. A collector. The same one who has been trying for years to buy the Morgan from me. A waste of time, it's a gift from my Dad.)

Then I strode down the street. I prefered to arrive at the butcher's on foot, in the shoes of an ordinary pedestrian. The Morgan was a bright red that didn't allow it to go unnoticed.

Axe lived in a nice villa flanked by a pretty, little, mossy, grassy garden. The gate creaked a little when I pushed it. I was certainly not expecting a welcome with marching band and cheerleaders, but neither did I expect the huge Great Dane that tumbled from a clump of boxwood, forcing me to suddenly retrace my steps. The massive mouth slammed shut on air. I shuddered at the thought that my arm could have been inside.

It was then that I saw the sign "Beware of the dog," right next to the bell. I had been a little hasty. So I rang. On the first floor, a window opened.

"Quiet, Andersen!"

The dog immediately lay down flat at the foot of the gate and continued to watch me greedily.

"What do you want?"

It was Axe. I had found his photo in the archives of *The Bugle*. A colossus. Even at a distance, in the windowframe, he was as impressive as a bulldozer on the loose.

"I wanted to ask you some questions," I shouted.

The window closed with a bang. I took a grapefruit cola from my pocket, just to moisten my tongue.

"What questions?"

The front door had half opened, and Axe was watching me with a dirty look.

"I am a detective . . ."

"Go to hell!"

Good gracious! And the door slammed like the window, with a noise that shook the street. This guy must be a big consumer of doors and windows, slamming them so viciously.

Suddenly, the Great Dane threw himself against the gate, barking furiously. I jumped back and my heart raced for a moment. Nasty creature.

People were definitely not very welcoming these days. Legs trembling, I went slowly up the street. Since the man refused to be attacked head on, I would have to be a bit clever.

I didn't find the car immediately. In fact, I had to go down the whole street to recover it. Someone must have removed the wedge, or else the stone had melted. In any case, the Morgan had crashed at the bottom against a concrete pylon. It seemed incredible that I didn't see it go by. But I am so absentminded.

The damage was not so considerable. With a new engine, two new fenders, and another radiator grill, it could still run a little while.

I telephoned my mechanic. He sniggered, I think.

Three hundred francs per day plus expenses, I had said. The expenses were more substantial, that's all.

Two nights and two days. Stuck in a wet depression against a mossy brick wall that would leave an indelible mark on my beige raincoat.

Two days and two nights of chewing ham sandwiches, drinking grapefruit colas, and tapping my feet against each other to keep warm.

Anyone who does stakeout work will tell you that it is hell, agony, torture. It is in these moments that you question the meaning of life and the dubious quality of your fur-lined boots.

Why, great gods, why had I abandoned my studies so early? Why was I doomed to the sordid and seedy? Tell me.

Not to mention that at 68 D'Aulnoy Street, nothing was happening. Damn nothing. Axe appeared to be leading the quiet life of suburban woodcutters. About six o'clock in the morning, with his axe at his side and whistling, he put his lunch on the back seat of his van and pulled away, putt, putt, fart, fart, in an incredible purple cloud. I suppose he uses lavender oil as fuel.

In my large notebook, I had marked down two lines all told, one for his departure and the other for his return. Pathetic.

But we bloodhounds are tenacious. I decided therefore to begin my third day of stakeout. In spite of the cold, the fog, and the dark indifference of my immediate vicinity.

I was finally rewarded for my infinite patience. (Thus speaks the fox lying in wait.) About eight o'clock, while the mist gradually faded, I heard the gate of no. 68 creak. A black form, light as the down of an angel, began trotting on the greasy asphalt. I let her take a small lead and, pulling my hat down over my watery eyes, I followed close behind.

A woman. Her manner was furtive, fast. The look of someone with something to hide. She was slightly stooped, and a large black scarf was wrapped around her head. On the shiny sidewalk, click, click, click, her heels made a hellishly loud clicking noise. Impossible to lose her. I saw her enter a bakery, quick as a ferret, and emerge a few seconds later with a package under her arm. She passed me without even raising her chin, and I had a whiff of fresh bread in the nostrils.

It was Sunday. The neighborhood was slow to waken. At 68, behind the kitchen window, a shadow bustled about. I was chewing my last dry crust. The delicious, fleeting smell of baking pursued me, and my stomach, fed on ham sandwiches, reproached me bitterly. But my deliverance was close.

Peacefully, I watched the fragile silhouette that was coming and going, hidden by the fogged window. I knew what she was doing. It would last an hour, at most.

I rummaged about in my raincoat pocket and brought out my box of cashews; it's the only effective thing I know for passing the time and having fresh breath.

About nine o'clock, the kitchen window opened, and the woman put something delicately on the stone ledge. From here, I could smell it. I closed my eyes and abandoned myself to the pervasive aroma.

Soon the gate squealed, and I again heard the heels clicking on the asphalt, with a heavy man's step beside them.

I slipped into the Morgan and waited for the woodcutter's van to turn at the corner of the street before following them. With my brand new engine, I could tail any TGV with peace of mind.

I spotted the van at the city's limit. It was travelling slowly, as befits Sunday drivers, dawdling at junctions, climbing the hills with the calm assurance of uneventful vehicles.

Indeed, my friends, indeed . . .

I stayed at a respectful distance, fearing that Axe should see the red Morgan in his mirror. But apparently he didn't suspect anything.

At the edge of the woods, the van entered, jolting, into a muddy trail and disappeared into the shadow of large fir trees. I parked the Morgan a little farther.

In turn, I followed the track in the forest and the two clearly visible ruts left by the woodcutter, placing my polished boots with caution and disgust in the sticky clay.

A few minutes later, I emerged in a clearing bordered with hazel trees, barely lit by the timid December sun. A true rustic picture, like those found on the post office calendar. In the middle, exactly as I expected, a small forest cottage, with its blue slate roof tiles, its tiny chimney, its apple-green shutters, and its pink bricks. A poetic note in this sad and sordid story.

The van was parked in front of the door. It looked enormous next to the small house. Four slashes of a pocketknife in the tires, and the car sank into the grass with a sigh. Sharp, Gallo.

I put the finishing touches to the work by pulling out the battery wires. Axe could always resort to fleeing on foot into the woods, if he liked Sunday walks.

Unhurriedly, I walked along the front of the house, my Colt Cobra firmly placed in the hollow of my palm. Loud voices reached me, bright laughter, and always the same scent.

From where I was, I could see four shadows around the table. The white lace curtain hid the faces, but I pinpointed Axe, because of his immense size. He was facing the door. Perfect. So it is he I would be aiming at once the door was open.

I had surprise on my side; I must act quickly.

I knocked at the door, rat, tat, and without waiting for an answer, I pulled the bobbin. The latch fell, and as fast as possible I flung my .43 gal toward the bottom of the half door.

With a bound I was inside, brandishing my Colt on an Axe who opened his eyes as round as chickpeas.

"Hello, family!" I chuckled.

I had entered at the right moment: there was one piece of cake and a touch of butter in the little clay pot.

At first pale, he very quickly became reddish and even purplish. He clenched his huge fists viciously.

"H . . . How did you guess, vulture?"

Bird names, right away! With one foot, I seized a chair and, while aiming a casual gat at them, I sat astride. It was more convenient to chat.

"Are you going to kill us, mister?" asked the little Red-Ridinghood. (You know, the one who was theoretically in the middle of Leloup's belly.)

I sniggered. She had hazel eyes and a little turned-up nose.

"In this story, little girl, I'm not the bad guy."

Axe hit the table with his large, closed fist. "Answer, pig! How did you manage to find us?"

I sighed loudly. "Chance, my good fellow. A sympathetic neighbor who gave me a troubling clue, for example." I took the gray bag out of my pocket and dumped the contents on the ground. The iron wedges rang on the tiles. "Like woodcutter's tools. Forgotten by Mrs. Mother. Admit that the conclusion was inescapable."

I indicated the cake with the barrel of the Colt.

"A scent of cake and butter, also. Like in the good old days. Who could you take a cake and a little pot of butter to, if not to a grandmother, huh?"

"It's true that it's good," said Grandmother. "My daughter has always been successful with pastry."

She munched a bit of cake and smiled at her daughter. The picture was touching. I felt bad interrupting such a pathetic family scene.

"Happy to see you in good health, Grandmother."

She picked up the crumbs she had dropped on the tablecloth and swallowed them greedily.

"Bah! Tomorrow isn't the day that they'll pull the old latch trick on me, my boy."

The little Red-Ridinghood laughed.

"Grandmother wasn't born yesterday, mister."

Touching! They were pulling the family tenderness thing. A work of art! I straightened the barrel of my Colt and looked deeply at Axe, who had his back against the wall. I needed to pick up the thread of the conversation, guys.

"At the trial, you said that you had to pull the bobbin to enter . . ."

The giant looked at me hatefully.

"For the latch to fall, you must pull the bobbin, buddy. That shocks you?"

"And why would Leloup have refastened the bobbin, hmmm?"

The woodcutter fidgeted in his chair, uncomfortable.

"Wait, I'm not well."

"You've said too much, pal. After the arrival of the child, the door should have been open from the outside. He only had to push it. Am I wrong?"

The giant had a dull and incredulous look. I think he hadn't taken everything in. I pushed my advantage.

"How much was the life insurance for Grandmother and the child?"

Axe had a silly grin.

"More than you will ever have in your life, loser."

True. I thought about my three hundred francs per day plus expenses. He wasn't wrong, the bloke. And I saw it coming.

"We'll share, if you want. Fifty-fifty."

Well, see. I must surely have the face of a corrupt cop. Must say that it was tempting, no? Enough to drink grapefruit colas to the end of my days.

"There's an innocent man in prison, Axe."

The woodcutter shrugged his shoulders.

"He wouldn't be the first."

"To start with, I didn't like him, that Leloup," said the child. "His meat smelled bad."

"And expensive, too," added Grandmother.

They were beginning to annoy me, all of them without exception. A little more, and they would be asking me to sign a petition against Leloup.

It is at this moment that the door flew open, and a cohort of cops in gabardine burst into the room, machine guns under their arms.

"Here we are. Hang in there," shouted someone.

I had never seen him before. Nor heard him. But at the guttural, pompous voice, I did not doubt for one moment that this ventripotent fellow crowned with a Tyrolean hat was the famous Commissioner Perrault, the ace of the police in the area.

"What brings you here?" I said in a calm voice.

The commissioner pushed up his hat on the back of his head with the barrel of his gun. A gesture that all cops are fond of, especially in the movies.

"An anonymous call. But I was expecting it. I have informers everywhere. The truth will always come out in the end.

Charles Perrault has his nerve. But he had a rare quality in a cop: he could change his mind.

The important thing was not that Leloup or Axe was guilty, and the little Red-Ridinghood alive or not. The important thing was that he had someone to eat. He was the cannibal.

Earlier, by calling the police station before following the woodcutter's van, I had triggered the big cat's feast.

I put away the Colt in my holster, under my armpit. A gesture that did not escape Perrault.

"It's a little late to take out your artillery, mister."

I sighed. How sweet it is to look like a fool in the eyes of a fool.

Axe left the room first, in handcuffs, hunched over like an old man. The little Red-Ridinghood brought up the rear, trotting, pleased to climb into the cops' navy blue paddywagon. I reckon she thought the flashing light was a top. Of course, when you are eight years old, life is child's play. Had she even understood what her mother and the woodcutter had gotten her mixed up in?

"You want a bit, Mr. . . . . Mr. what, anyway?"

I turned. Perrault held the last piece of cake in his hand and was sniffing it with delight.

"Gallo, commissioner, Roman Gallo, detective.

He frowned. Perhaps he had taken me for a waiter.

"So eat," I said. "It's still hot."

And I left before Perrault swallowed the final piece of Grandmother's last cake.

I can't help it. I hate guys who make noise while eating.

FIVE

The Wolf's Story

My death has always been the end of this story.

Raúl Rivero, "Versión libre 2"

The Mystery of the Disappearance of the Famous Confused Wolf (Ser ekhtifaa el zeeb el shahir bel mohtar)

Abdelwahab M. Elmessiri and Safaa Nabaa

The Egyptian author and scholar Abdelwahab M. Elmessiri (1938–2008) is a household name in the Arab world. A former professor at Cairo's Ain Shams University (he received a PhD in English and comparative literature from Rutgers University), he was considered one of the Arab world's leading experts on Jewish and Israeli affairs. He was also an activist and served as the general coordinator of the opposition organization Kefaya (Enough), a movement demanding an end to Hosni Mubarak's rule. Elmessiri authored approximately sixty books on a wide range of subjects. His writing included poetry for adults as well as books for a young audience. He began to write children's stories in the 1960s for his own daughter, influenced by theoretical concepts that view children as the catalysts of social change. Elmessiri is the author of the stories published in the Hekayat Hazal-Zaman (Tales of Our Times) series with the well-known publishing house Dar El Shorouk. This award-winning series centers on a modern Egyptian family of passionate readers who loves to hear, read, and create stories. All the books in the series are illustrated by Safaa Nabaa, who has also illustrated well-known Egyptian folktales. The series includes retellings of both "Little Red Riding Hood" and "Cinderella." In the latter, a prince named Zainab Hatem Khatoon falls in love with the heroine, as he had with the original Cinderella, but this time he must agree to wait for this modern fairy-tale heroine to finish her university studies before their marriage.

Noor and her siblings are characters in the entire series, but she also becomes a modern Riding Hood in two of the books. Elmessiri's first retelling of "Little Red Riding Hood," *Nur wa-al-dhib al-shahir bi-al-makkar* (Noor and the Not-so-Sly Wolf), relates a modern-day story in which Noor, Yaser, Nadim, and the camel Zarif defeat the wolf known as Sneaky. The picturebook won the best author prize of the Suzanne Mubarak Competition for Children's Literature in 1999. The following year, Elmessiri published a sequel titled *Ser ekhtifaa el zeeb el shahir bel mohtar* (The Mystery of the Disappearance of the Famous Confused Wolf), in which Cinderella is also a secondary character. In the new adventure, the sneaky wolf is transformed into a very puzzled and quite harmless one. References to the Muslim religion, Arabic names and music, and magic carpets set this story clearly in the Arab world. Rather than giving his Little Red Riding Hood the traditional Arabic name of Layla, meaning "night," Elmessiri bestows on her the name Noor, which means "light." It is an appropriate name for a bright, modern Riding Hood who easily outwits the wolf (plate 24). The names "Red Riding Hood" and "Green Riding Hood" appear in the text in red and green type respectively, highlighting the color play that is a crucial element of the plot (plate 25).

In Elmessiri's picturebook retelling, the simple, humorous intertextual and metafictional play is accessible to very young readers. The classic tale of "Little Red Riding Hood" is a verbal and visual *mise en abyme* that recurs on numerous pages. This wolf's obsession with the classic version of the tale in the book from which he is never separated and his refusal to accept deviations from the classic plot make it easy for the protagonist to outsmart him. The metafictional play involves a whimsical fantasy element: the clever Noor somehow knows that the wolf's rereading of the classic tale will act like a spell, causing him each time to shrink further. In the end, he is a perfect book-sized wolf. The final image of the embedded book depicts the wolf in the grandmother's bed, obviously relieved to find himself back in the familiar story where characters and events follow the time-honored plot.

49. *Ser ekhtifaa el zeeb el shahir bel mohtar*, by Abdelwahab M. Elmessiri and Safaa Nabaa. Copyright © Dar El Shorouk. Used by permission of Dar El Shorouk.

༺

The Mystery of the Disappearance
of the Famous Confused Wolf (2000)

As soon as Noor returned from school, her mother asked her to take a basket of food to her grandmother, so she took the shortcut and quickly returned after giving her the basket. At the house, she found her brothers, Yaser and Nadim, and Zarif waiting for her. And when the rooster Hasan showed up, they played and had fun, and when he crowed,[1] they went to bed with a smile on their faces.

That whole time the famous confused wolf was sitting under the tree, waiting for Noor with the red dress to pass on her way to her grandmother's house. He waited and waited and waited while flipping through his old book and looking around in confusion, saying to himself: "Why didn't the girl with the red dress show up like it said in the book? She was supposed to pass by here, right?" When night came, he felt cold and lit a fire to keep warm, but soon after he suddenly couldn't keep his eyes open, so he fell asleep, confused, upset, and sad.

A few days later, Cinderella called Noor and told her that Mrs. Zeynab Khatoun, who loves Noor very much, had left her a gift. So she asked her mom for permission to go with her brothers to Cinderella's castle; her mom agreed and gave her the weekly basket to give to her mother. When Noor and her brothers arrived at the castle on their magic carpet, they found the rooster Hasan sitting with the prince, Kamar El-zaman, listening to traditional Arabic music.

Noor went upstairs with Cinderella to her room, where she found her gift: a beautiful green dress. She was so happy, she wore it on top of her red dress. And the two girls began chatting for a while. Then Noor remembered her grandmother, so she asked Cinderella if she could borrow her bike to drop off the basket for her grandmother before returning to hang out with her.

At that time the wolf was sitting under his favorite tree, waiting for the girl in the red dress, occupied, as usual, reading his old book. For that reason, when Noor passed by him in her green dress, he did not recognize her and continued to read his story and look at the pictures with a lot of concentration.

Noor arrived at her grandmother's and gave her the food. Her grandmother thanked her and said: "You must take off your green dress and wear only the red dress so that you don't get hot." Noor thanked her grandmother for the advice and put her green dress in the basket. She kissed her grandmother and rode the bike back to her brothers at Cinderella's and Kamar El-zaman's castle.

While she was in the forest, the wolf appeared, holding his old book with a sneaky smile, and said to her: "Where are you going, Red Riding Hood?" Noor smiled and said: "I'm not going anywhere, I'm just coming back from my grandmother's house." The smile suddenly disappeared from the wolf's face, and he said: "What do you mean? I asked you: 'Where are you going, Red Riding Hood?' Exactly how it happened in the book, and you're supposed to answer: 'I'm going to my grandmother's,' not coming back from her house. I've been waiting for you for days and I never saw you going to your grandmother's."

Noor understood what was happening; she smiled and said to him: "Have you heard about the subway? Have you ever seen the "green" riding hood, Mr. Wolf? Have you ever read old fairy-tale stories?" He looked at her, wondering in confusion, and flipped through the pages of his old book. But he didn't find any sign of subway nor the "green" riding hood, so he asked her: "What are you talking about?" Noor laughed and said to him: "Keep reading your old book, but I'm going to call you the Confused Wolf because this name suits you." She left him flipping through his old book in obvious anger and mumbling to himself: "What's happening in this life? What's happening to this generation?"

Noor returned to the castle, where the king and queen were sitting with Yaser, Nadim, Cinderella, and Kamar El-zaman; also she found the rooster Hasan at the window with Zarif, who stuck his head out. She told them the story about the "green" riding hood on the way to her grandmother's and the "red" riding hood on the way back. And she told them how puzzled the wolf was and she started imitating him, saying: "What are you talking about?," and everyone laughed. Then they sat down and chatted for a while. And when the rooster crowed, the children knew that it was time to return home, so they thanked the king, the queen, Cinderella, and Kamar El-zaman, and they flew home on the magic carpet.

The wolf sat under the tree, confused and trying to make sense of his adventure with Noor. He started flipping through the story in the old book and looking carefully at the pictures. Because he was engrossed in the story and knew it by heart, he did not notice that every time he finished reading the story, he shrank a couple of centimeters. He kept reading and shrinking, reading and shrinking, reading and shrinking for a few days, until he became the size of the picture of the wolf in the book.

When the wolf looked around, he was surprised that everything looked enormous, the rocks, the flowers, the trees. He was puzzled.

After a while, Noor came by on her bike on her way to her grandmother's. The wolf saw her from far away, small like him, so he was relieved and happy, and he began preparing himself.

The closer she got to him, the bigger she looked. When she arrived next to him, he found her enormous, gigantic. Frightened, he ran and hid between her feet under the bike. He jumped very quickly into the old book and lingered in the pages, where he felt safe, because everything happens as it was meant to happen: the Red Riding Hood comes at the proper time, he dresses up easily in her clothes and arrives at her grandmother's house before her, eats the grandmother, and sleeps in her bed, etc.

Noor looked around her; she couldn't find the wolf. All she found was his book under the tree. She said: "Where is the Famous Confused Wolf? Mr. Wolf, I'm Red Riding Hood and I'm going to my grandmother's house, not coming back. Hello, I'm here!!!" The wolf did not reply. She heard a voice coming out of the story in the old book: "I have nothing to do with what is happening outside; here, in the book there is no subway nor 'green' riding hood; everything happens as it's supposed to happen, and I won't be confused. In here I'm not the Famous Confused Wolf."

Noor looked at the book, and she looked around her, but did not see anything, so she rode her bike to her grandmother's and told her what she had seen and heard in the forest. Her grandmother was surprised and kissed her. On her way back, Noor saw the old book under the tree, but she did not know that the wolf was sleeping inside it in her grandmother's bed, refusing to get out, wondering what is happening in the old fairy-tale stories.

The Wolf (Le loup)
Fourth Mission (Quatrième mission)

PIERRE GRIPARI

Pierre Gripari (1925–1990) is one of France's best-loved children's authors. His popularity there is not unlike that of Roald Dahl in Britain, although he is virtually unknown in the English-speaking world. Like Dahl, Gripari also wrote for adults; in fact, he published the vast majority of his works for that audience. Whether he wrote for adults or children, Gripari's genre of choice was the tale. He published several fairy-tale collections, of which the best known are *Contes de la rue Broca* (1967; *Tales of the Rue Broca*, 1969), which is his only book available in English translation, and *Contes de la rue Folie-Méricourt* (Tales of the Rue Folie-Méricourt, 1983). With a playfulness that does not conceal a serious critical intention, he subverts traditional tales using his own particular brand of humor and insolent wordplay. The political and religious satire and the philosophical undercurrents in his writing are not always accessible to a young audience. *Patrouille du conte* (Tale Patrol) was published for adults in 1983, but the author felt the novel had crossover potential despite its very pointed political references. Gripari rejected the proposal to turn it into a children's book, however, because he did not want to make the required excisions. He cites in particular the controversial anti-Muslim three little pigs, who viciously and greedily eat the poor sick wolf and pose a threat for other fairy-tale characters.[2] Gripari's belief that certain chapters of the novel could be read to children was proven the year of its publication, when the chapter "Le loup" was included, under the title "Le loup et la grand-mère" (The Wolf and the Grandmother), in the children's anthology *Le grand méchant Loup, j'adore* (I Adore the Big Bad Wolf, 1983).

 Patrouille du conte is a hilarious story that nonetheless constitutes a very serious commentary on the ideological revisions of traditional fairy tales, as well as on the perils of revolutionary change. The newly created Ministry of Fairy Tales and Cultural Environment in the French Republic of the real world assigns a patrol of eight boys the task of keeping law and order in the Kingdom of Fairy Tales. In a series of missions, they are given the task of cleaning up the tales and making them more humanitarian, moral, and democratic. (The political agenda includes the elimination of kings.) The modifications brought about by the patrol create total chaos, and the ministry is ultimately forced to admit its error in interfering in another world whose laws they do not understand.

 Patrouille du conte is a subversive modern fairy-tale novel that offers an excellent example of what Gianni Rodari called an "insalata di favole" (fairy-tale salad) in his ground-breaking work *Grammatica della fantasia* (*The Grammar of Fantasy*), published ten years before Gripari's novel.[3] The French

50. *Patrouille du conte*, by Pierre Gripari. Copyright © 1983 Éditions l'Âge d'Homme. Used by permission of Éditions l'Âge d'Homme.

author has great fun subverting the fairy-tale canon in a bricolage that cleverly weaves tales together with unexpected and hilarious results. The novel is not, in fact, limited to the fairy-tale genre but deals with folklore in general, as the first mission revolves around the well-known children's song "La Mère Michel" (Mother Michel). In Gripari's highly metafictional work, the diverse hypotexts are embedded in the narrative, where they play a very important role. Perrault's *Contes*, a book of fables undoubtedly penned by La Fontaine, a generic volume entitled *Chansons populaires enfantines* (Popular Children's Songs), and fairy-tale collections in English are revised and updated throughout the novel, as the patrol's actions and the resulting consequences necessitate new editions of the original works. Some texts disappear from the canon altogether, as in the case of La Fontaine's fable "Le loup et l'agneau" (The Wolf and the Lamb) and the tale of "The Little Three Pigs," while others are revised to the point of being almost unrecognizable.

The patrol is charged to begin with the most urgent cases, and the first fairy tale they tackle, in their second mission, is "Little Red Riding Hood." Two excerpts from the novel have been included in the translations that follow. Chapter 5 has been retained here in its entirety, as it is wholly devoted to revising the tale of Little Red Riding Hood. As the title "Le loup" (The Wolf) suggests, however, the plot focuses on the wolf. Little Red Riding Hood is reduced to a minor, secondary character, and the grandmother, although she plays an important role, is decidedly less sympathetic than the wolf. The patrol must await the latest edition of Perrault's *Contes* to find out if "Le Petit Chaperon Rouge" has become a moral story that can be retained or whether it has been deleted. Although the boys are opposed to eliminating fairy tales from the canon (one boy objects particularly to the elimination of this, his favorite, tale), their captain tells them that when the main story involves a murder, there is no raison d'être for the story once the crime has been eliminated, a point he illustrates with "Little Red Riding Hood": "What do we care about the grandmother, the little pot of butter, and the cake, if the wolf is no longer dangerous?"[4] The captain has obviously not heard any modern retellings about rehabilitated wolves.

The consequences of the patrol's intervention in this tale are not recounted until chapter 11, which is titled "Quatrième mission" (Fourth Mission). As this chapter also reports on the results of the "Mère Michel" mission and the progress with the ogre from "Le Petit Poucet," only the excerpt dealing with the Little Red Riding Hood mission appears in the following translation. Although they are the most important, these two excerpts are not the only passages in the novel that refer to the tale of "Little Red Riding Hood." The mission involving Little Red Riding Hood and the wolf is actually introduced in chapter 4, "Deuxième mission" (Second Mission), where the captain questions the patrol about their knowledge of that particular fairy tale. Only one member of the patrol seems to be familiar with the Grimms' version of the popular tale. The adult captain forces the young members of the patrol to reflect on the inherent morality, or rather immorality, of both classic versions, and to search for a satisfactory solution. Wolves can't be allowed to kill people, nor can people be allowed to kill wolves. They can't stop Little Red Riding Hood from going to her grandmother's when it is her mother's will and when her grandmother's health and perhaps her life depend upon it. It is the captain who provides a solution: the patrol must convince the wolf—who, fortunately, is a talking wolf—to abandon his project. This tale receives high priority because it involves a violent crime, one that involves a double murder. As the boys soon learn, wolves also have rights. The wolf points out that he has his ecological role, his niche in the food chain, an argument that the wolf in Gripari's poem "Le loup" also makes but in moral rather than ecological terms. The wolf and his family become political animals, demonstrating for their rights in the final climactic scene, which brings together all the characters in the newly created Fairy Tale Republic, including Little Red Riding Hood and her grandmother.

The political satire in *Patrouille du conte* has great appeal for adult readers in France. The patrol is given leave to resort to threats and force with the wolf if necessary. Violence and bloodshed are condoned, even morally justified, provided the ministry gives its blessing. The patrol is appalled, however, by the results of their missions. Tongue in cheek, Gripari satirizes idealistic, impractical government policies. The campaign to reform fairy tales is an unmitigated disaster, proving how dangerous it is to meddle with archetypes of the collective unconscious. The government's attempt to revise fairy-tale characters like the wolf unleashes violence and a rash of unexplained events not only in the Fairy Tale Republic but also "in the real world," where wolves attack "lone strollers" in the Morvan, the Pyrenees, and the Vosges (151–152), a witty reference to the historical events in certain regions of France which gave birth to oral versions of the tale. The patrol, which ultimately sides with the fairy-tale dissidents, is abandoned in the imaginary world and erased from history in a typical high-level government coverup. There is to be a return to the status quo, and Perrault's *Contes* is to be reprinted according to the original edition. The government is forced to officially recognize the purifying effect of evil and its pedagogical importance in fairy tales. The author of *Patrouille du conte* had undoubtedly read Bruno Bettelheim's influential book *The Uses of Enchantment*, which was published in France only a few years earlier. Paradoxically, Gripari's warning about the dangers of tampering with fairy tales is issued in one of the most subversive modern treatments of fairy tales, but his message is directed at those who would sanitize the classic stories and use them for ideological purposes to acculturate children.

◆

THE WOLF (1983)

"Hey, there! Come over here!"

"Sorry . . . Are you talking to me?"

"Yes, to you! Come over here!"

"What do you want with me?"

"Come, you are told! Who are you?"

"Well, I'm the wolf. That's obvious, I think . . ."

"You are the wolf? Very well! And . . . where are you going?"

"I am going . . . about my affairs!"

"What affairs? Where? To whose house?"

"It's none of your business!"

"Yes, it is precisely our business! We are the Tale Patrol, and we are here to play the police."

"Well, do it! Who's stopping you?"

"We are doing just that, and we are going to begin with you!"

"Me? But what do I have to do with the police?"

"You are going to see . . . Once again, where are you going?"

"I told you: to my affairs!"

"You are being hardheaded . . . Do you know what this is?"

"Hey there! Don't be bloody idiots! I hate firearms!"

"I see that you understand me . . . So, now, I repeat the question: Where are you going?"

"All right, if you take it like that . . . I'm going to Little Red Riding Hood's grandmother's house!"

"To do what, at Little Red Riding Hood's grandmother's house?"

"Well, to inform her of the arrival of her granddaughter, with a cake and a little pot of butter . . ."

"Liar! You are going to eat her!"

"Me, eat her, that old bag of bones?"

"You are going to eat her first. Then you are going to put on her night-gown, her bonnet, and her glasses, take her place in the bed, pass yourself off as her, and eat her granddaughter!"

"Why! That's a good idea, that . . . I didn't think of that!"

"You only think of that, on the contrary! There's no point denying it, we know everything!"

"You know everything? What, everything?"

"Everything that you would do if we weren't here! It's written in there!"

"Wait until I sniff . . . That means nothing to me. What is it?"

"It's a book."

"Can you eat it?"

"No."

"Then, why the hell should I give a damn?"

"You can't eat it, but it allows us to know . . ."

"Oh! what the hell, you piss me off! Yes, I'm going to eat her, the grandmother, and the granddaughter along with her, if I can! There! Are you happy? After all, I am a wolf, yes or no? I have my ecological niche!"

"What are you talking about, with your ecological niche?"

"Yeah, I am the regulator of mankind! I prevent the human species from degenerating, by getting rid of the undesirable elements, such as sick old grandmothers, rheumatic old men, retarded drunkards, disobedient little girls . . ."

"We don't want to know anything about it! We are here to prevent you from killing the grandmother and Little Red Riding Hood!"

"But in the name of what? It's intolerable! What am I going to eat, then?"

"You will eat what you want, but you will not touch a single human being. Otherwise, you are warned: with this charming instrument, we will lay you out stone dead!"

"All right, all right . . . In that case I will go eat the three little pigs . . . the lamb . . ."

"You will not eat the three little pigs either, and even less so the lamb, that poor, innocent lamb . . ."

"But, in the name of God, look at my teeth! What were they made for, my teeth? I'm a carnivore, I need my animal proteins! You don't think I'm going to graze grass?"

Silence.

"He's right, the blighter," murmurs Lieutenant Ratatam. "We must find a solution to feed him. If not, what is the good of lecturing him . . ."

Then, aloud:

"All right, we will take care of that. Take us to the grandmother's."

"Well now! You want me to go there, now!"

"Don't say anything, just take us!"

"But you promise that I will have my proteins."

"Be quiet!"

And they're off. They walk and walk, and they reach the grandmother's house. The lieutenant knocks at the door: rat, tat.

"Who's there?" shouts a hoarse voice.

"It's the Tale Patrol, Grandmother! We are here to offer you a good deal, in your interest!"

"Pull the bobbin, the latch will fall!"

"The bobbin, let's see, the bobbin . . ."

"It must be that thing that sticks out, Lieutenant."

"Maybe . . . Yes, indeed!"

The latch fell, the door opened.

"Come in, good gentlemen! Excuse me if I stay in bed, I am a little ill. At my age, you see, you have a lot of misery . . . Good heavens! But what is that? But it's the wolf you've brought me! Help, he's going to eat us all!"

"But no, Grandmother, don't worry, the wolf is not going to eat anyone! It is a perfectly reasonable wolf; we have convinced him to get along with you!"

"Me, get along with him? Is it possible?

"Yes, Grandmother, yes! There, there, lie down again and calm down! The wolf, here present, agrees to no longer eat neither you nor your granddaughter, on the only condition that you feed him, by making him his mash twice a day. Isn't that right, Mr. Wolf?"

"Oh, I don't care! Sort it out as you wish, but I must have my proteins!"

"Okay, you will have them. You hear, Grandmother? You will put meat in his mash, or, failing that, egg, cheese, milk . . . You do not mind, what do you say?"

"Why! It's just . . . I don't know! Can I trust him, that hairy villain?"

"Oh, for that you can! Because if he is wicked, he knows what we promised him!"

"And then, that mash, that's going to be expensive! I'm not rich, my good sir!"

"You prefer to be eaten, perhaps?"

"I'm not saying that, of course . . . but it will be necessary to buy bread, meat, vegetables . . . Who's going to pay me?"

"Oh, that! You'll have to manage on your own!"

"Manage on my own? But how? Think about it: meat, cheese even, the price is exorbitant!"

"It's up to you to choose! You will feed the wolf; if not, he will eat you!"

"Alas, goodness me, this poverty! At least, couldn't I have a . . . a small compensation?"

"Your compensation is that you will not be eaten alive; it's that your granddaughter will be able to go through the woods without being devoured; in addition, the wolf will guard your house against thieves. Isn't that so, Mr. Wolf?"

"I am agreeable to anything, seeing that I have my proteins . . ."

"Well, I believe that the affair is arranged. So, you are in agreement, Grandmother?"

"Alas! I must be, my poor sir . . . But life is so difficult! And so expensive, especially!"

"Good! Now we're off! Your granddaughter mustn't be far . . . There's no point her finding us here. Good-bye, Grandmother!"

"Good-bye, my good sirs . . . No, no, don't bother, leave the door open! I will replace the latch myself! Well, what a business!"

◆

FOURTH MISSION (QUATRIÈME MISSION) (1983)

"...

I tell you in confidence, it isn't official . . . I have just received the good pages of *Little Red Riding Hood*, for the new edition of Perrault's *Tales.*"

"So? It's botched, as well?"

"Botched, no, not exactly . . . Unexpected, rather! Here, I'll read you the end, you can judge for yourselves . . . Are you listening to me?"

"We're listening, my captain!"

"Well, here it is: 'So there is Little Red Riding Hood, the grandmother, and then the tamed wolf, which the old lady feeds as a guard dog. The years pass, the wolf grows old, of course . . . One day, Little Red Riding Hood arrives at her grandmother's to find her in the process of boiling water in the large cauldron.' Follows the dialogue that I am going to read to you."

"What are you doing, Grandmother?" she says.

"I am preparing the pot-au-feu, my child."

"And why are you making the pot-au-feu, Grandmother?"

"To boil the wolf, my child!"

"And why boil the wolf, Grandmother?"

"To eat it, my girl, and to make us a muff of his pelt!"

"Look, Grandmother," says the little girl, "you know very well that we don't have the right to do that. It's fascism!"

"Fascism or not," says the grandmother, "the winter is hard, famine threatens, we must hold up until spring!"

"But the wolf, Grandmother, doesn't he have the right to live too?"

"The wolf is old, my girl, he is lame and almost blind, he is no longer of much good. If we weren't there, he would already be dead. In addition, there is no more meat to make his mash . . . No, no, it's decided: he will go in the cauldron upon his return!"

On hearing these words, Little Red Riding Hood started to cry:

"Spare him for another day or two, Grandmother! Look, I'm bringing you a cake and a little pot of butter! With that, you won't die of hunger . . . Later, in a few days, you'll eat the wolf, if you don't have anything else!"

She talked so much that the old lady, in the end, relented:

"The wolf is very lucky," she said, "to have a defender like you, and as owner an old fool[5] like me! Come on! Don't cry anymore, you make me feel sad . . . Since you insist so much, I will eat the cake and the butter first, and I will kill the wolf later, when you are gone!"

"Thank you, Grandmother, you are so good!" said the little Red Riding Hood, and she flew into her arms.

But the wolf, who was at the door, had heard everything. Unlike Little Red Riding Hood, he did not have the least confidence in the grandmother's promises.

"That old carrion," he thought, "is quite capable of getting up in the night to put me on to boil! Well, I prefer to stay outside, since, moreover, I know there will be no meat in my mash today!"

So he did, and he spent the whole day in the bare wood, shivering in the wind, blinded by snow. Finally, at dusk, quite weakened, dying of cold, he lay down in a thicket. Almost immediately, the three little pigs, famished, too, arrived in the area. By dint of rooting about, digging, and sniffing, they discovered the wolf, half frozen, in his hiding place; they fell upon him, slew him, tore him apart, and ate him in no time, leaving only the bones.

MORAL

Wolves, beware of grandmothers!
Beware of little girls!
Know the right time to leave,
Before you are boiled or grilled!
But don't imagine
That the forest is without danger!
Always wandering, always voracious,
The little pigs are hunting
And dream of devouring you![6]

"There, that's all," said the captain.

"But this is appalling!"

"Appalling . . . Oh! No big words! . . . It's sad, of course . . . But, as I told you a little while ago, it is almost impossible to intervene in such a case . . . The problem of the little pigs is not simple . . . And then, they have suffered so much!"

"I understand, my captain, but we cannot let them eat everything they see . . . This would be a negation of our mission, of our actions, of all government policy! We would have no raison d'être! By what right would we go moralizing, after that . . ."

. . .

The Wolf (Le loup)

PIERRE GRIPARI

Five years after *Patrouille du conte*, Gripari published a collection of children's poems, *Marelles* (Hopscotch, 1988), which includes two poems inspired by the tale of "Little Red Riding Hood." As the title of the second poem indicates, the eponymous heroine of "Le Petit Chaperon malin" (Cunning Little Riding Hood) is a clever, modern Riding Hood who outwits the wolf by refusing to pronounce the final line of the famous dialogue, a ploy used by a number of her contemporary counterparts. The ruse depends for its success on a traditionalist wolf who, like the one in Elmessiri's retelling, feels he must adhere to the classic script. Like chapter 5 in *Patrouille du conte*, the first of the two poems is titled simply "Le loup," but this time the text is narrated in the first person by the eponymous protagonist. The short lines of rhymed verse, dripping with irony and satire, are somewhat reminiscent of Roald Dahl's *Revolting Rhymes*. Despite the light, playful tone of the monologue, there are disturbing undercurrents. The poem recounts the thoughts and actions of the wolf prior to the important scene of the encounter in the woods. Unlike the wolf in *Patrouille du conte*, this one makes no attempt to hide his true colors. In this unusual retelling, the fairy-tale heroine is seen through the eyes of the wolf, who attributes to her traits that justify his behavior. The sexual innuendos and connotations are all the more sinister because this Riding Hood is described in terms that suggest a very young child. In the philosophical reflections toward the end of the poem, the wolf exonerates himself of all blame by casting himself in the role of a moral enforcer. There are sinister, chilling overtones to this humorous poem, and there is absolutely nothing likeable about this predatory wolf.

THE WOLF (1988)

I am hairy,
Tawny and toothy,
I have green eyes.
My pointed fangs
Make me look
sinister.

The wind that whistles,
molests and slaps

The stroller,
I sniff it
And its scent
Speaks to my heart.

On the other bank
Who is it that arrives
With short steps?
Hmm! I salivate!
It's my meal
Which comes yonder!

From the end of the wood
Toward me walks
A kid
Who, I see,
Now dilly-dallies
Now trots along.

A riding hood
All red and round
Moves and quivers
With a cheeky look
On the little
Hypocrite . . .

I lick
And lick again
The end of my nose,
I hurry
To accost
This doll.

Ah! How sweet it is
To be the wolf
Of these parts,
The guardian
Of the good children
Of the wild wood!

In the Mouth of the Wolf (In bocca al lupo)

FABIAN NEGRIN

Fabian Negrin (1963–) is an Argentine-born author-illustrator who studied graphics and engraving in Mexico City and now lives in Italy. It is therefore not surprising that the images and colors of his illustrations evoke a number of cultures and landscapes. Negrin began his career in Mexico as a graphic designer and illustrator for newspapers and magazines. In 1989 he moved to Milan, where, until 1996, he continued to work for major publications such as *Corriere della Sera*, *Il Manifesto*, and *Marie Claire*, as well as a number of papers and magazines in London, including *The Independent*, *Tatler*, and *Radio Times*. In 1996 Negrin began to devote himself increasingly to illustrating books for children. He has created illustrations for many children's books in Italy and abroad. He also illustrates novels for children as well as many book covers (the Italian editions of David Almond's books, for example). Since 1995 Negrin has illustrated about one hundred books. He has been called "perhaps the best illustrator working in Italy and certainly the most inclined to get involved in and try new paths."[7] He has been selected for the Biennial of Illustration Bratislava (BIB) several times, and in 2009 he won the BIB Plaque for the books *Mille giorni e una notte* (A Thousand Days and One Night, 2008) and *L'amore t'attende* (Love Awaits You, 2009). He began to author his own picturebooks in 2001 with *Il gigante Gambipiombo* (The Giant Gambipiombo). Over the past few years, Negrin has focused largely on his own picturebook projects, but he has also continued to illustrate books written by other authors. In 2010 he won the Bologna Ragazzi Award in the nonfiction category for *The Riverbank* (2009), in which he illustrated the last paragraph of Charles Darwin's *On the Origin of Species*.

The creation of *In bocca al lupo* began in 1994, when Negrin completed the first five watercolor pictures—based on five key moments of "Little Red Riding Hood" as he remembered the tale from his childhood—for the illustrators' exhibition at the Bologna Children's Book Fair. It was the first time Negrin had done such detailed and highly finished images. After spending many years doing illustrations for newspapers and magazines, where short timelines dictated a "'quick' kind of style," he wanted to draw without the pressure of a deadline. As he puts it: "I wanted it to be the drawing, and not the watch, telling me that it was done." He chose this particular fairy tale because of the lifelong impact it had on him when he heard it "at the edge of a wood" as a five-year-old. He elaborates: "I remember well my awareness that it was fiction, and yet the absolute certainty that right there, among the trees, there must be a wolf ready to jump out and eat me. I am extremely grateful to my kindergarten teacher for having given me this very special sensation that I have been treasuring ever since. Children should never be deprived of their fair amount of fictional terror."[8] The five illustrations were selected by the jury of the Bologna Children's Book Fair for the 1995 illustrators' exhibition, where they received the UNICEF award.

In around 2000, Negrin decided to create a book in which he could use the five images, and he wrote a text that tells a very different version of the story. A recent reading of Angela Carter's *The Bloody Chamber* had left a powerful impression on the author: "I had been enchanted by the way in which her versions of the fairy tales were able to let the most ferocious and sensual aspects come out. And by the way in which, instead of betraying or narrowing down their meaning, she had been able to retrace the fairy tales back to that point, near the edge of the wood, where any five-year-old child, with both a scared and fascinated gaze, looks into the dark, waiting for the beast." Negrin rewrites the tale as "a love-story that told, from the wolf's point of view, of how the love between the animal and the little girl had been made impossible by an adverse fate." Whereas the images tell the tale in the classic manner (not at all as a love story), the text describes how things were actually quite different and could, in fact, always be interpreted in another manner. The double meaning of the title in Italian ("in bocca al lupo" has the figurative meaning of "good luck") expresses this ambiguity—this possibility that the story is a cruel, harsh, tragic one (if you read it through the images only, and if you read the title literally) or else a loving, lucky one (if you go by what the text says, and if you read the title as an idiomatic expression). Once Negrin found a publisher, the small, innovative Italian publishing house Orecchio Acerbo (Immature Ear), he needed to complete more illustrations. After the book was published in 2003, it received the Apuan Alps prize as "the best picture book of 2003" and was also selected to the international Biennial of Illustration Bratislava. *In bocca al lupo* is Negrin's best-known and longest-selling book in Italy, where it has been reprinted numerous times; it has also been translated into Spanish and French. There have also been two interesting theatrical adaptations of this book by two children's theater companies (TPO and La Piccionaia).[9]

The illustrations of *In bocca al lupo* immediately indicate that everything about this retelling of "Little Red Riding Hood" is different: characters, setting, and atmosphere (plate 26). The dense vegetation of the wolf's wood is a cross between the forests of northern Europe and the Amazonian jungle. The first illustration, which accompanies the wolf-narrator's presentation of himself, is a striking visual portrait of Adolf's head set against the strangely exotic forest. The second illustration presents Little Red Riding Hood, through Adolf's eyes, as a very vague reddish blur in the background and then again as a larger, slightly clearer figure in the mid-ground of the lush, green forest; the following spread is a closeup of the girl as she appears to Adolf when she is quite near. The latter two pictures are fragments of the cover illustration, where the movement of the red spot through the forest is highlighted as it is repeated four times with increasing clarity. The repetition of images in the

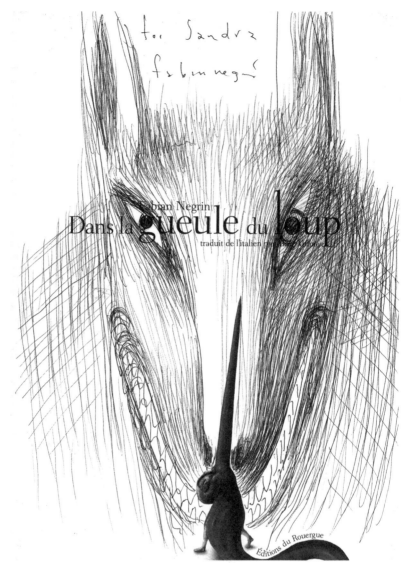

51. Original drawing by Fabian Negrin, in my copy of *Dans la gueule du loup* (the French translation of *In bocca al lupo*), by Fabian Negrin. Copyright © 2006 Éditions du Rouergue. Used by permission of Fabian Negrin.

book creates a haunting, timeless atmosphere. The two textless double-page spreads that open and close the book (following and preceding the rich red endpapers) are the two halves of an interior illustration of the key encounter scene in which the small, indistinct figure of Little Red Riding Hood sits on the ground before a large wolf disguised as part of the lush, green woods. The figure of Little Red Riding Hood standing with her back to the reader at the foot of the bed is repeated in a smaller version on the title page (plate 27).[10]

In bocca al lupo is a carefully constructed ensemble in which text, illustrations, and design work together to create a highly original, atmospheric retelling of the famous tale. Fragments of the illustrations are inserted into the text where they serve different functions, sometimes punctuating the text (as in the two leaves at the end of the last sentence on the first page or the basket at the end of the encounter scene), sometimes filling an ellipsis left in the text (as in the image of the wolf on his back, taking a siesta with his paws in the air—the rigor mortis look seems to foretell his fate—which bleeds into the left margin). The lines depicting the wolf's repeated, plaintive cry are like tears rolling down the palm-like tree, an image that has been repeated from the facing illustration, where the wolf hurls his regrets under an extraordinarily large full moon in a forest strewn with what appear to be the shreds of Little Red Riding Hood's clothing. In the bottom corner of one page of text, the small image of Little Red Riding Hood and two leaves is a foreshadowing fragment of the striking later illustration depicting a fat, mustached hunter on horseback. Little Red Riding Hood sits behind the rider, on the horse's back, and stares into the readers eyes, while a pale, winged Adolf floats on a cloud above (plate 28). The wolf's new perspective from his cloud high above the wood shifts humorously back to the ground on the final page, a closeup of the previous illustration that focuses on the rabbit in the greenery below the horse and its riders.

In bocca al lupo illustrates beautifully the extreme sensitivity for which Negrin's books are known. Expressions such as "in bocca al lupo" and "crepi il lupo" (in the throat of the wolf; also has the figurative meaning of "good luck") have their origins in age-old prejudices against the wolf which are deeply engrained in the Italian collective unconscious. Negrin subverts these images by presenting the wolf not only as an animal who merely obeys his instincts but as a sensitive being and a natural aesthete with a deep appreciation of beauty. The positive image is reflected in the animal's name, Adolf, which means "noble wolf." In this masterful retelling, lines between predator and prey become blurred. The reader is forced to question his or her beliefs and convictions. When Little Red Riding Hood ends up in the wolf's belly, it is the result of a mistake, and the wolf expresses his intense grief and remorse. For readers who may question the wolf-narrator's sincerity, the last two pages of text, which constitute a kind of epilogue, seem to corroborate his story. His ultimate destiny—becoming a wolf-angel—is proof of his innocence and lack of malevolence. Although the book is marketed for readers four years old and up, it is a charming love story for young and old alike.

❧

IN THE MOUTH OF THE WOLF (2003)

My name is Adolf, and I am a wolf.

I was born in the woods that you can see behind me.

The wood is my home. Within is everything I need to live: ducks, piglets, fawns, and other delicacies. Many say I'm wicked, but there is no malice in me. We wolves are made that way. It is in our nature to eat other animals. We can't help it.

Sometimes, though, things happen to me that do not happen to other wolves. Yesterday, for instance . . .

. . . it was hot, and I was snoozing under a tree when a slight rustle reached my very sensitive ears and made me jump. I raised my head and looked. On the edge of the wood, in the distance, a little red spot was advancing and occasionally stumbling into the bushes. Very slowly it approached, until I could see it clearly: it did not resemble any animal I knew. It was a wonderful creature dressed in red. The most beautiful thing I had ever seen.

I ran to hide.

I was so ugly. How could I talk to her without scaring her? I disguised myself as woods and asked her:

"What are you? An angel perhaps?"

"An angel? Ha, ha, ha! No, what are you talking about? I'm a little girl," she said, as she tripped one more time.

"A girl? And where are you going?"

"I am going to visit my grandmother, who lives at the other side of the woods."

"And what have you got in that basket?"

"A mirror. Yesterday my grandmother broke hers, so I'm taking her a new one. Excuse me, woods, but my grandma is waiting impatiently for me."

And with these words, she went on her way.

Little girls? I had never seen animals of that species before.

I thought that the grandmother, who couldn't go a single day without a mirror, must be even more beautiful.

"I have to see this wonder," I thought.

And I started to run to the other side of the woods by a shortcut that only I knew.

I found the little house and knocked. Rat tat. A little girl, who had to be the grandmother, opened the door. What a disappointment! I swear that I had never seen an uglier, older, wrinklier creature. In order not to have it before my eyes any longer, I ate it in one bite.

Soon after, the little girl dressed in red arrived and knocked at the door. Rat tat. In a moment I put on grandmother's clothes and slipped into the bed.

"Good morning, little girl."

"Good morning, Grandma. I brought the new mirror."

And with those words, she hung it on the wall. The reflection in the mirror, though, didn't show the grandmother, but my horrifying wolf face. The little girl wasn't scared, only surprised.

"What are you?" asked the little girl. "I've never in my life seen anyone as beautiful as you! Are you an angel perhaps?"

I was about to reply when she, approaching, tripped over the grandmother's slippers. She fell into my mouth, and before I could do anything, she disappeared in my stomach.

What despair! What remorse! I had just found my soul mate and already I had lost it. I ran out, to howl my sorrow to the moon.

I cried

and cried

and cried.

I was there, on my knees, busy cursing myself, when a strange flash shimmered in the woods. Over there! Above a tree! Was it possible? There was another little girl! This one, though, had a mustache, a large hat, and a metal stick with a hole.

"Maybe it can help me to free the little girl that's in my belly," I thought.

I quickly jumped onto the tree, but a scary lightning came out of the metal stick. On my breast appeared a little red spot that, very slowly, widened until it drenched the bush where I had fallen.

I was dead.

The little girl with the mustache reached for a knife and opened my belly. The little girl dressed in red and the grandmother came out alive.

My name is Adolf and I am a wolf, an angel-wolf.

This is my cloud. From here, I can see the whole woods, tree by tree, as I had never seen it before. Over there is the little girl in red who is going home. She raises her head and waves to me—hello hello—then disappears among the trees. I am sure that she will remember me forever. I, too, will never forget her.

Hey! What is that thing jumping over there? A rabbit? Now that I think of it, I am starving.

I'm hungry, really, wolfishly hungry.[11]

The Wolf in Love (El lobo enamorado)

José Santos Chocano

The Peruvian poet José Santos Chocano (1875–1934) is known as the "Poet of America" in tribute to the first line of his celebrated poem "Blasón" (Crest), from his perhaps most popular collection, *Alma América* (American Soul, 1906): "Yo soy el Cantor de América, autóctono y salvaje" (I am the poet of America, native and wild). Chocano led a very eventful and adventurous life, relocating to Spain early in the twentieth-century and later traveling extensively throughout Central and South America. He had prominent contacts with intellectuals, artists, and political leaders throughout the Hispanic world. After a two-year jail term following the fatal shooting of a journalist, he moved to Chile, where he lived in abject poverty; ultimately, he was stabbed to death on a streetcar. There are disagreements as to whether his assassin was a stranger, a madman, or a rival in a love affair.

Chocano's poetry, which was published for adults, first caught the attention of literary circles in Spain, but the poet gained great popularity in his day in Latin America. In 1922, prior to his fall from favor, he was recognized by the government of Peru as one of the country's most notable poets. Chocano wrote both lyric and epic poetry, experimenting with a variety of different styles, and is consequently difficult to categorize. He is considered one of the major leaders of Latin American *modernismo*, but some critics claim his work is closer to romanticism. Much of his most popular verse is essentially romantic and expresses his deep love for the landscapes and cultures of Latin America.

The poem "El lobo enamorado" (The Wolf in Love) was written while Chocano was living in Chile. It was first published in 1934 in the collection *Primicias de oro de Indias: Poemas neo-mundiales* (First Golden Fruits from the Indies: New World Poems), in the section titled "Corazón aventurero (Poemas vitales)" (Adventurous Heart [Vital Poems]). A few years later, the poem appeared in the posthumous collection *Poemas del amor doliente* (Poems of a Sorrowful Love, 1937). This collection consists of very intimate love poems written to his much younger wife prior to and immediately following their marriage in the early 1920s. In lyrical poems full of deep emotion, the poet reveals a sentimental heart that is still capable of suffering for love. Alfonso Navarro, author of the brief introduction to the collection, refers to the poet's love as "Dantesque," and calls the Margarita who inspired these poems a "new Beatrice."[12]

In a rather bashful but playful tone, the wolf portrays himself as a sad, suffering creature, a victim of love who deserves Little Red Riding Hood's sympathy. He casts himself in the role of a romantic lover throwing himself at the feet of his beloved to confess his deep sentiments. The drawing by

52. "El lobo enamorado," from *Primicias de oro de Indias: Poemas neo-mundiales*, by José Santos Chocano. Illustration by Huelén. Santiago de Chile: [n.p.], 1934.

Huelén that accompanies the poem in the original edition portrays a rather stylized wolf crouching at the feet of a sexy woman who is shown in a some-what provocative pose. This Little Red Riding Hood seems to announce the women the Chilean artist—whose real name was Juan Francisco González Ramírez (circa 1894–1976)—would draw for the magazine *Sex Appeal* a few years later. Although Little Red Riding Hood's feelings are not revealed in Chocano's poem, the fact that the wolf's tale is sorrowful suggests that his love is unrequited. The poet and the wolf-narrator merge completely in the self-reflexive stanza that expresses the latter's literary aspirations in terms of the poem we are reading. This story of Little Red Riding Hood takes on a sensuality and eroticism that is not just latent but expressed in transparent terms. The entire volume has an erotic vein that leads Navarro to claim that these poems mark "the advent of American erotic poetry" (7). It seems that it is only due to old age that the would-be seducer would be content merely to hold Little Red Riding Hood in the grandmother's bed. The old wolf lacks not sexual desire but only physical stamina. The playful tone and somewhat ambiguous ending leave readers to decide whether the wolf is sincere and has truly reformed or whether he is still the deceiver, playing on Little Red Riding Hood's tenderness and compassion.

❧

THE WOLF IN LOVE (1934)

Take pity on your wolf, Little Red Riding Hood![13]
Although I am still master of the age-old wood,
already the fangs are weak and the claws are loose:
I lack the force to devour you!

Oh! How very late I met you on my path:
if it had been at another time, what a sumptuous feast
I would have had in the enchantment of your divine body,
with a cinnamon flavor and a perfume of jasmine . . .

Tell your grandmother all the wrong that has been done to me:
ask her to take me under her protection;
and that she just let me rest in her bed
to hug you in it against my heart . . .

Little Red Riding Hood: I know that you are good.
You are good to me as no one else was . . .
The wound in my side doesn't perhaps cause you pain?
Tell me, why don't you pull the thorn from my foot?

I am in love with you, Little Riding Hood . . .
A wolf in love? Yes, a wolf. And why not?
Your mirror will have told you how pretty you are,
how good you are, I myself have already told you.

If I were a poet—I feel like one by your side—
I would write a tale of profound intention,
to tell my sorrows of a wolf in love,
who throws himself at your feet howling a song . . .

Your tale is over, then, Little Red Riding Hood . . .
This wolf is a wolf who arrives in your country
with peaceful intentions, and throws himself, trembling, at your feet . . .
This is the wolf brother of Francis of Assisi.

Little Red Riding Hood, take pity on your wolf!
Cover me with caresses and welcome me in your home:
You see that I don't kill you, nor even rob you;
Although, I would like the chance to devour you! . . .

Free Version (Versión libre)
Free Version 2 (Versión libre 2)

RAÚL RIVERO

The Cuban poet and journalist Raúl Rivero (1945–) is a former political prisoner who now lives in Spain. A supporter of the Cuban revolution initially, he
played an important role in state publications; he won national literary awards
for his collections of verse, of the kind known as "civic poetry." After a long
disenchantment with the Cuban government, he signed the historic "Carta
de los diez" (Letter of the Ten), which ten intellectuals demanding political
and economic reforms sent to Fidel Castro in 1991. The dissident journalist
founded the Cuba Press independent news agency and became internationally known for the dispatches about repression and harsh living conditions
which he managed to get out of the country. During the 2003 crackdown, he
was sentenced to twenty years in prison, although he would be released the
following year. His name and work have since vanished from the history of
Cuban revolutionary literature.

Rivero's retelling of "Little Red Riding Hood," in two parts, is a prison
love poem that was written in the spring of 2004, during the poet's incar-
ceration. The poem, which has obvious political undertones, was available on
the internet site of Acción Democrática Cubana (Cuban Democratic Action)
prior to its publication in Spain. Love was the only subject the dissident journalist and poet was allowed to write about during his imprisonment, and yet
even his love poems were censored by the police. Although he initially found
inspiration for the imposed subject difficult, the poet warmed to the project
of penning odes to "love and ex-love."[14] The poems his wife had managed to
get out of Cuba while her husband was still in prison, written in 2003–2004,
were published in the collection *Corazón sin furia* (Heart without Fury) in
Spain in 2005. The title of the collection is taken from the wolf's words in the
first part of the Little Red Riding Hood poem.

Rivero was known among Cuban readers for his precise, witty, mocking style. He had always used humor in a subversive manner in his writing,
where the irony is corrosive and the humor can be quite black. His particular
brand of absurd humor can be found in his retelling of "Little Red Riding
Hood" through the wolf's eyes. Like Chocano, Rivero presents "a wolf in love"
with Little Red Riding Hood, but, although his love is initially returned, his
story is ultimately more tragic. The first line of the poem hints at the tragic
ending that, according to this wolf, is always the end of Little Red Riding
Hood's story. (He seems unaware of Perrault's version, in which the wolf is
not the victim of a hunter.) The wolf casts himself in the role of bodyguard,
protecting Little Red Riding Hood not from other wolves but from woodcutters. This version presents both woodcutters and hunters, but their role is the

same and has clear political overtones: they cut down revolutionary wolves. The wolf's satirical self-portrait resembles those the poet composes of himself. The wolf tells a life story that becomes increasingly intimate. This poem is more graphically erotic than Chocano's, describing the lovemaking of the wolf and the girl in the grandmother's cabin. Rivero's Riding Hood returned the wolf's love, and their sexual relationship was consensual. The second part of the poem constitutes a kind of epilogue narrated by the wolf from beyond the grave. The wolf who tells his own story after his death expresses Rivero's own determination to resist his demise at the hands of Cuban authorities. No doubt wishing to ensure the posterity of his tragic story, the dead wolf composes his own elegy. He can only speculate on the events that followed, but for him his death was the end of the story. Rivero subverts the traditional image of the wolf as deceiver, giving the role of the traitor to Little Red Riding Hood. In the hands of the dissident poet, the story of Little Red Riding Hood becomes a political allegory, disguised as a tragic love story, to denounce a repressive regime.

FREE VERSION (2005)

I was a wolf once
a good wolf
personal escort of the Little Riding Hood
and proven enemy of the woodcutters.

I was a wolf a long time
and we sang
Little Red Riding Hood and I sang
Who's afraid of the Wolf, afraid of the Wolf, afraid of the Wolf
because we were harmonic, bilingual, in tune
and she played the piano.

We were wanted
we made love
in the grandmother's cabin
in the heart of the forest
with a wicker basket
on the rustic table
that gave her kisses a hint of doughnuts.

I was a wolf in love
With no wolf instinct
an elderly animal

meek and quiet
with big, sad, wet eyes
the claw nails trimmed and clean
the hair gray and shiny
the heart, red and measured, without fury.

Strolling one afternoon between the trees
the girl took off her hood
and ran to the woodcutter to denounce me
for bestiality, for love, for pleasure, for boredom
for the motives that always
provide the mysteries of the soul.

The man came with some hunters
they came to kill me
and with gun fire
they killed me.

〜

FREE VERSION 2 (2005)

I do not know what happened later in the thicket.
Perhaps Little Red Riding Hood is very happy
and one of her men kept
my big gray head
(stupid, dried, a glassy look)
on the wall
to the right of the hearth.

I was never deceived
My death has always been the end of this story.

SIX

The Wolf Within

To all the wolves of the world for lending their good name
as a tangible symbol for our darkness.

Ed Young, dedication to *Lon Po Po: A Red Riding Hood Story from China*

The wolf that you are so scared of, that you struggle against, that you flee from,
is not a wolf in the woods. It is something from your inner self, disguised as a wolf.

Paul Biegel, *Wie je droomt ben je zelf*

Green Ribbon in the Hair (Fita verde no cabelo)

João Guimarães Rosa (1908–1967) was a Brazilian author, physician, and diplomat. He is considered by many to be one of the greatest Brazilian prose writers of the twentieth century. Yet his work is little known, largely due to the fact that translating his writings is a daunting task. His most celebrated work, *Grande sertão: Veredas* (1956), translated under the title *The Devil to Pay in the Backlands* in 1963, has been compared to James Joyce's *Ulysses*. The short story "Fita verde no cabelo" (Green Ribbon in the Hair) first appeared in the literary supplement of the newspaper *O Estado de S. Paulo* in 1964. It was subsequently published, in 1970, in *Ave, palavra* (Hail, Word), a posthumous collection of poems, tales, and meditations. Thanks to the initiative of the Brazilian scholar Gloria Pondé, the story was brought out in picturebook format, with illustrations by Roger Mello (1965–), to mark the twenty-fifth anniversary of the death of this major writer, who had refused to make a distinction between child and adult audiences.

Roger Mello is an author and illustrator who works also in the fields of theater, film, and design. Considered one of the most creative and versatile of Brazil's contemporary illustrators, he was the first to be named a finalist for the prestigious Hans Christian Andersen Award in 2010, and he was also a finalist for the Bologna Ragazzi Award in 2012. Mello was an excellent choice to illustrate the story, as his artistic style, like that of the author, finds its roots in the rich blend of indigenous, European, and African influences that make up Brazilian culture. Mello experiments constantly with new techniques, changing his style to suit each new book. For Guimarães Rosa's existentialist fairy tale, he decided to use a mixed media of pencil and Ecoline, and the resulting illustrations, in shades of black and white with only touches of green, are a stark contrast with his characteristically warm, vivid colors.

The intertexuality is announced in the words "nova velha estória" (new old story), which appear in parentheses under the title of the story in the collection for adults but receive the status of a subtitle in the picturebook. The old story is transposed to the New World in both the text and the illustrations. Mello emphasizes the Brazilian environment in which the author sets his story, depicting luxuriant vegetation reminiscent of the Amazonian rainforest. However the reworking is much more complex than a mere geographical and cultural transposition. Guimarães Rosa retells the story of "Little Red Riding Hood" from an existentialist perspective, and Mello boldly chose to highlight the philosophical interpretation in his illustrations for the children's edition. The fairy tale has always been a vehicle for exploring ontological questions concerning life and death. In the Brazilian retelling, the

53. *Fita verde no cabelo*, by João Guimarães Rosa. Illustrations by Roger Mello. Text copyright © 1970 by Agnes Guimarães Rosa, Vilma Guimarães Rosa, and Nonada Cultural Ltda; illustrations copyright © 1992 by Roger Mello. Used by permission of Agnes Guimarães Rosa, Vilma Guimarães Rosa, Nonada Cultura Ltda., and Roger Mello.

world of fairy tales or "once upon a time" is equated with false consciousness and the illusory world that allows Green Ribbon to escape her metaphysical angst. The existentialist theme finds its way into the traditional motifs of the tale: the protagonist's attribute, the butterflies and flowers that she perceives differently, the path that she chooses of her own free will, and the inner wolf that symbolizes her philosophical angst. By depicting the green ribbon as a rather abstract green squiggle that is the only touch of color in the black-and-white portrait of the heroine, Mello emphasizes its imaginary nature and effectively illustrates the confusion of the real and the make-believe in the young girl's mind.

The symbolic loss of the ribbon in the woods is accompanied by a visible aging of the protagonist in the illustrations. Although Green Ribbon is referred to as a little girl in the text, Mello portrays her initially as a rather sultry, sexy adolescent, with long, loose dark hair, flirtatious eyes, a curvaceous figure, and bare feet; after the loss of the green ribbon, she appears as a more mature-looking young woman. This Riding Hood is, in fact, an existential heroine whose encounter with death, in the form of the grandmother-wolf, produces metaphysical angst, symbolized by the Wolf. (After the grandmother's death, "Wolf" is capitalized.) Mello renders the central bed scene entirely in black and white to illustrate Green Ribbon's altered perception of the physical world. Surrounded by the luxuriant vegetation that invades the bedroom, the grandmother is a dark, shadowy figure whose raised hand forms a dark wolf's-head shape, as in the game of casting animal shadows against a wall. While the narrator informs readers early in the story that the wolf has been exterminated by the woodcutters, Mello introduces several very different visual portrayals of the wolf, in both animal and human form. The most provocative blends the wolf and the woodcutter in a striking man-wolf figure. Mello's spread of the encounter of Riding Hood and the two muscular, shirtless woodcutter-wolves, which evokes the sexual connotations of the story (Green Ribbon casts a very seductive gaze their way), also skillfully illustrates Guimarães Rosa's distinctive blending of exterior reality and the inner world of the character.

Guimarães Rosa is a challenging author even for adults. The prose text of *Fita verde no cabelo* is written in a dense, evocative, and poetic language that is notoriously difficult to translate. The dizzying inventiveness, sophisticated language play, alliterations, rhythm, and repetitions of sounds and syllables are virtually impossible to capture in another language. The text can be demanding even for Portuguese readers, as the author often invents words, such as the creation of the verb *velhavam* (literally "oldering") from *velho* (old) or the adjective *encurtoso* (shorterly) to describe the path Green Ribbon rejects. In addition, he combines the Brazilian vernacular with revitalized terms from old Portuguese and words and expressions from different parts of the country, giving the language a strong local color. Guimarães Rosa's innovative, experimental use of language, which nonetheless borrows heavily from the oral tradition (even archaic orality), makes this truly a "new old story." The voice of the traditional collective narrator or storyteller, which characterizes the works of Guimarães Rosa, here tells the story of the human condition in existentialist terms. Mello succeeds in visually interpreting the complexities of the text using relatively simple means. The exchange about the grandmother's arms and hands in the ritualistic dialogue—which here confronts youth and old age—is depicted in a simple but striking illustration that contrasts the grandmother's dark, hairy, skinny forearm and clawlike hand with the smooth, white forearm and soft, delicate hand of her granddaughter as they reach longingly toward each other without touching, as if death has already separated them. Green Ribbon's initiatory journey differs from that of other Riding Hoods who come of age, because it culminates in the existentialist *prise de conscience*. Guimarães Rosa subverts the image of a passive Riding Hood by transforming her into an existentialist heroine.

After her encounter with death, her world seems to dissolve. Mello attempts to render the dissolution of Green Ribbon's once familiar and secure world in the final textless spread, which depicts the girl standing on a hill, staring at the large, empty sky, while the buildings of her village are being carried off into it. Nothing and no one can protect this Riding Hood from the wolf.

54. *Fita verde no cabelo*, by João Guimarães Rosa. Illustrations by Roger Mello. Text copyright © 1970 by Agnes Guimarães Rosa, Vilma Guimarães Rosa, and Nonada Cultural Ltda; illustrations copyright © 1992 by Roger Mello. Used by permission of Agnes Guimarães Rosa, Vilma Guimarães Rosa, Nonada Cultural Ltda., and Roger Mello.

᠊ᢒ

GREEN RIBBON IN THE HAIR (New Old Story) (1964)

There was a village somewhere, neither big nor small, with old men and old women who were getting old, men and women who were waiting, and boys and girls who were being born and growing up. Everyone had sufficient sense except one little girl, at least for the time being. One day, that little girl left there with a green ribbon imagined in her hair.

Her mother sent her, with a basket and a pot, to another village almost the same as theirs, to see her grandmother, who loved her. Green Ribbon left right away, the pretty one, everything was once upon a time. The pot contained a syrupy dessert, and the basket was empty to gather raspberries.

Then, while crossing the woods, she saw only woodcutters, who were woodcutting there; the wolf was not there, not unknown nor hairy. For the woodcutters had exterminated the wolf. Then, she said to herself: "I am going to Granny's, with basket and pot, and the green ribbon in my hair, as my mother bid me."

The village and the house awaiting her over there, after that mill that people imagine seeing, and the hours that they do not see that are not. And she, herself, decided to take this path, crazy and long, and not the other, the shorter one. She left, behind her swift wings, her shadow also running after her.

She had fun looking at the non-flying hazelnuts on the ground, uncatching those butterflies never in bouquet or in bud, and ignoring if each of the little plebeian flowers, cute princesses, and uncommon things, is in its place, as we pass by them so often. She was walking along extremely present in the moment.

She was late arriving at the home of the grandmother, who, when she rapped—knock, knock, answered:

"Who's there?"

"It's me . . ."—and Green Ribbon lowered her voice. "I'm your beautiful granddaughter, with basket and pot, with the green ribbon in my hair, as my mother bid me."

The grandmother said, with difficulty: "Pull the door's wooden latch, enter, and open. God bless you."

Green Ribbon did as told, and entered and looked.

The grandmother was in bed, hidden and alone. Her speech was stuttered and weak and hoarse, she must have caught a bad cold. She said: "Put the pot and the basket on the coffer, and come close to me, while there is still time."

But now Green Ribbon was frightened, besides being sad upon realizing that on the way she had lost the large green ribbon tied in her hair; and she was sweating, and very hungry for lunch. She asked:

"Grandma, what skinny arms you have and what trembling hands!"

"It is because I am not going to be able to hug you anymore, my grand-daughter," murmured the grandmother.

"Grandma, but your lips, oh, so blue!"

"It is because I am not going to be able to kiss you anymore, my little granddaughter . . . ," the grandmother sighed.

"Grandma, and your eyes are so deep and lifeless, in your skinny, pale face."

"It is because I am no longer seeing you, my little granddaughter . . . ," the grandmother still moaned.

Green Ribbon was more afraid, as if she was coming to her senses for the first time. She screamed: "Grandma, I'm afraid of the Wolf! . . ."

But the grandmother was no longer there, she was being too absent, except for her cold, sad, and so sudden body.

55. *Fita verde no cabelo*, by João Guimarães Rosa. Illustrations by Roger Mello. Text copyright © 1970 by Agnes Guimarães Rosa, Vilma Guimarães Rosa, and Nonada Cultural Ltda.; illustrations copyright © 1992 by Roger Mello. Used by permission of Roger Mello.

Little Yellow Hat (Chapeuzinho Amarelo)

Chico Buarque

Francisco Buarque de Hollanda (1944–), popularly known as Chico Buarque, is a Brazilian poet, writer, and musician. He is best known as a composer, singer, and guitarist whose music often contains social and political commentary. In 1998 he was voted the best Brazilian musician of the twentieth century. Throughout the military dictatorship that followed the coup of 1964, Buarque was very active in the struggle for democratization in Brazil. He went into exile in Italy in 1969, but returned to Brazil the following year. Frequent censorship of his work led him to adopt the pseudonym "Julinho da Adelaide." Buarque is essentially a novelist and playwright for adults. Three of his adult novels were awarded the Jabuti, a prestigious Brazilian literary prize comparable to the Man Booker; two of his works won the overall book of the year award in Brazil.

Chapeuzinho Amarelo, first published in 1979, is the only book Buarque has written for children, although he translated into Portuguese, under the title *Os Saltimbancos*, an Italian musical play based on the tale "The Town Musicians of Bremen."[1] Released as an album, it became one of the greatest children's classics in Brazil and was also made into a movie in 1981. Like many of Buarque's works, *Chapeuzinho Amarelo* has been adapted for the theater. His retelling of "Little Red Riding Hood" has been classified as a "book-poem." The 1979 edition was published by Berlendis, with graphic design by Donatella Berlendis; the book was reissued by Editora José Olympio in 1997 with illustrations by the world-renowned Brazilian artist, writer, cartoonist, and journalist Ziraldo (the pseudonym of Ziraldo Alves Pinto [1932–]). In 2007 it was also published in Portugal by Editora Quasi with illustrations by André Letria, who had illustrated Matilde Rosa Araújo's *O Capuchinho Cinzento* two years earlier. The work had the unusual distinction of being "highly recommended" by Brazil's National Foundation of Child and Youth Books when it was first published in 1979, and then winning the Jabuti award for illustration from the Brazilian Book Chamber (CBL) when it was reissued almost two decades later in 1998. Considered a classic of Brazilian children's literature, *Chapeuzinho Amarelo* continues to be reprinted regularly; it was in its thirty-third edition in 2013.[2]

In a playfully subversive retelling of the classic tale, Buarque effectively deals with the theme of fear. The symbolism of the color substitution is immediately accessible even to very young readers. The Portuguese word *chapeuzinho* means "little hat," so this translation has been retained rather than the "little cap" of the hypotext. Her headgear resembles a cap in Berlendis's graphic artwork, but Ziraldo depicts it as a yellow straw hat with a large brim. Despite the light, playful style, the author offers a serious message, and the

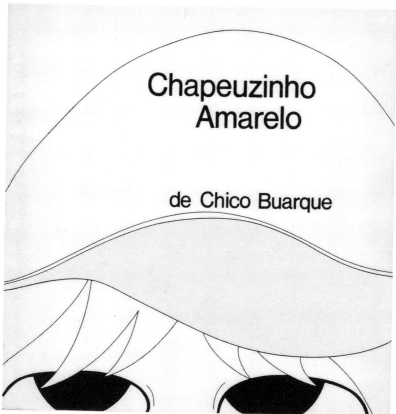

56. *Chapeuzinho Amarelo*, by Chico Buarque. Graphic design by Donatella Berlendis. Copyright © 1979 Berlendis & Vertecchia. Used by permission of Berlendis & Vertecchia.

children's tale can also be read as an allegory of the political situation in Brazil at the time. Buarque deconstructs the stereotypical images of the powerful, victimizing wolf and the powerless, victimized Little Yellow Hat. The fears of Buarque's sad, anxious protagonist prevent her from living the life of a normal child and experiencing the joys of childhood. In addition to her phobias, the prohibitions of authoritarian adults also dictate her behavior and restrict her activities. In the end, Little Yellow Hat breaks free of oppression and the resulting paralysis. When she is forced to confront her worst fear, embodied in the wolf, she suddenly overcomes all her fears and insecurities, and discovers the joy of living. Ziraldo's illustration of the face-to-face confrontation of the protagonist and the wolf portrays the curiosity and courage of a little girl who suddenly realizes that her fear was unfounded. *Chapeuzinho Amarelo* offers a lesson in overcoming fears that has appeal for all ages.

Buarque's retelling emphasizes language and the power of the word. Unfortunately, the clever wordplay is sometimes lost in the English translation. The color substitution is reinforced by further play with the word *amarelo* (yellow) in the text: *amarelada de medo* (yellowish with fear) and *amarelinha* (hopscotch, literally "little yellow"). In the original edition, Donatella Berlendis effectively used touches of yellow in the black-and-white line drawings of her simple but striking graphic layout to create a stark black-yellow contrast. Yellow also dominates Ziraldo's more colorful illustrations, but the overall tone of his visual interpretation is much cheerier. The 1979 edition has a graver tone, a reflection perhaps of the mood during that era in Brazil; the more sober graphics emphasize the sad, fearful expressions of the caricatural Little Yellow Hat with her huge, haunting, dark eyes. At one point Little Yellow Hat is reduced to synecdoche (a hat) in the enumeration of items the wolf is capable of eating.

57. *Chapeuzinho Amarelo*, by Chico Buarque. Graphic design by Donatella Berlendis. Copyright © 1979 Berlendis & Vertecchia. Used by permission of Berlendis & Vertecchia.

Often Buarque's style is rather cryptic, and sentences are deliberately written in a very condensed manner. Cryptic analogies and wordplay were two strategies used by the writer and musician to avoid censorship. The rhymes, rhythm, and repetition of syllables are a tour de force in this "poem-book." The playful, nonsensical element is particularly evident in the poetic enumerations. Fear (*medo*) and wolf (*lobo*) are often used as rhyming words, and the sound "o" echoes throughout the Portuguese text. The increasing frequency of the word *lobo* effectively expresses the little girl's obsessive fear of the wolf, just as the decreasing frequency of the word *medo* later marks the loss of her fear. Simultaneously in the illustrations, there is an increasing caricaturization of the wolf. Ziraldo portrays a ridiculous, harmless-looking animal whose colorful clothing casts him in the role of a clown. In one scene, the humiliated wolf is depicted naked to accompany Buarque's wordplay about a *lobo pelado*, which literally means a "hairless" or "naked" wolf but has the figurative sense of a wolf that has been taught a lesson. Berlendis's line drawing depicts only the wolf's back end as he disappears off to the right with his tail between his legs. The wolf, which did not exist, is an almost invisible figure in the first edition (there is one partial portrait in addition to that of his back end). The shadow the little girl casts is her own in Berlendis's drawing, but Ziraldo depicts her casting a large, black wolf shadow behind her.

Typography plays an important role in the text, especially in the first edition, where some lines were isolated in a large font on otherwise blank pages. The upper case is used initially to show Little Hat's fear of the WOLF, but later to indicate the wolf's shouting, as he tries in vain to regain his role as villain. The role reversal in this retelling is marked by significant semantic changes. Not only is the word "wolf" printed now in lower case, but the narrator also begins to omit the adjective "yellow" when he refers to the protagonist. As the wolf shouts repeatedly that he *is* a wolf, a metathesis of syllables occurs, and the WOLF (*LOBO*) is transformed into a CAKE (*BOLO*). In the first edition, where the syllables are simply repeated over and over in large font on the white space of an otherwise blank spread, the metamorphosis is marked by simply beginning the last line with "BO" rather than "LO" (in the translation, the line ends with WO). In the later edition, text and images combine to show the transformation, as the syllables appear underneath an Ensor-like drawing of repetitive black wolf heads on a white background, gradually transforming into white cakes on a black background.

Little Yellow Hat is transformed into a courageous, daring, active little girl who dominates the wolf and makes choices that defy gender stereotypes (climbing trees, stealing fruit, etc.). Even during their initial face-to-face confrontation, as depicted by Ziraldo, the somewhat ambiguous look on Little Yellow Hat's face as she stares at the wolf, whose jaws open menacingly to show sharp teeth, seems more curious than fearful. This Little Red Riding Hood conquers her fears by playing an empowering game that consists of using the letters or sounds of the word signifying her fear to make a nonsense word. The protagonist herself engages in the wordplay that characterizes Buarque's modern retelling and reminds us of the magical power of words in fairy tales. The game at the end, which constitutes a kind of brief epilogue or footnote to the story, scrambles words and encourages young readers to continue this game, much as Janosch does with the Little Red Cap game at the end of his retelling.

Little Yellow Hat (1979)

She was the Little Yellow Hat.
Yellow-bellied with fear.
She was afraid of everything,
that Little Hat.
She didn't laugh anymore.
She didn't show up at parties.
She didn't climb up
or down stairs.
She wasn't cold
but coughed.
She listened to fairy tales
and trembled.
She didn't play anything anymore,
not even hopscotch.

She was afraid of thunder.
An earthworm, for her, was a snake.
And she never sunbathed
because she was afraid of shadow.
She didn't go out so as not to get dirty.
She didn't eat soup so as not to get sopped.[3]
She didn't take a bath so as not to unstick.
She didn't speak so as not to choke.
She didn't stand for fear of falling.
So she stood still,
lying, but not asleep,
afraid of a nightmare.

She was the Little Yellow Hat.

And of all the fears that she had,
the fear more than frightful
was the fear of that WOLF.

A WOLF that was never seen,
that lived so far away,
on the other side of the sea,
inside a hole in Germany,
full of obscurity,
in such a land of mystery,
that maybe that WOLF
didn't even exist.

Even so the Little Hat
was ever more afraid
of the fear of the fear of the fear
of one day meeting a WOLF.
A WOLF that didn't exist.

And Little Yellow Hat,
from thinking so much about the WOLF,
from dreaming so much about the WOLF,
from waiting so much for the WOLF,
one day met him
who was like this:
big WOLF face,
big WOLF eyes,
big WOLF way
and mainly a big mouth
so big that it could
eat two grandmothers,
a hunter,
king, princess,
seven pots of rice
and a hat for dessert.

But the funny thing is that,
as soon as she met the WOLF,
the Little Yellow Hat
started losing that fear,
the fear of the fear of the fear
of one day meeting a WOLF.
It was disappearing, that fear
of the fear that she had of the WOLF.
There remained just a little
of the fear of that wolf.
Then the fear ended
and she remained alone with the wolf.

The wolf was upset
to see that girl
looking at his face,
but with no fear of him.
He was even ashamed,
sad, withered and ghost white.[4]
because a wolf, without the fear,
is a mockery of a wolf.
It's like a wolf without fur.
A naked wolf.

The wolf was upset.

And he shouted: I am a WOLF!
But the Little Hat, nothing.
And he shouted: I am a WOLF!
Little Hat laughed.
And he roared: I AM A WOLF!!!
Little Hat, already a bit bored,
eager to play something else.
He then shouted very loud
that WOLF name of his
some twenty-five times,
in order for the fear to come back
and for the little girl to know
with whom she was not speaking:

WO LF WO LF WO LF WO LF WO LF WO LF WO LF WO LF WO LF WO

Then,
Little Hat was fed up and said:
"Stop it! Now! Right now!
The way you are!"
And the wolf, stationary like this,
the way the wolf was
he was no longer a WO-LF
He was a CA-KE.
A cake of fluffy wolf,
trembling like a pudding,
afraid of the Little Hat.
Afraid of being eaten
whole, with candle and everything.
LO**BOLO**BO

Little Hat didn't eat
that wolf cake,
because she always preferred
one made of chocolate.
By the way, she now eats everything,
except shoe soles.
She no longer fears rain
or flees from moles.
She falls, stands, gets hurt,
goes to the beach, enters the woods,
climbs trees, steals fruit,
then plays hopscotch
with the cousin of the neighbor,
with the daughter of the news vendor,
with the niece of the godmother
and the grandson of the shoemaker.

Even when she is alone,
she makes up a game.
And transforms
into a companion
every fear that she had:
the lightning became ninglight,
the cockroach is choockrac,
the witch became chwit
and the devil is vilde.

END

Ah! Other companions of the Little Yellow Hat:

The Gondra, the Low, the Krash, the Namyboge
and all the tersmons.

In the Belly of the Wolf (En el vientre del lobo)

IZUMI YAMADA

Izumi Yamada (1973–) is a Japanese illustrator who also works as an assistant in a plastic arts workshop for the mentally disabled. She has created set designs for plays, and she produced a monologue titled *Merinda joi-no Satsuiku Nisshi* (Journal of the Massacre of Dr. Merinda). "En el vientre del lobo" (In the Belly of the Wolf) is one of the highly original Japanese retellings in the collection *Érase veintiuna veces Caperucita Roja* (Once Upon Twenty-one Times Little Red Riding Hood), published by Media Vaca in 2006. The unusual book had its origins in a workshop organized by the innovative Spanish publisher in 2003 at the Itabashi Art Museum in Tokyo. The twenty-one Japanese illustrators who participated in the workshop were given as a starting point Perrault's version of the tale; they were encouraged not to limit themselves to the classic version but to feel free to change it as they saw fit. It is rather ironic that when the pioneering publishing house started out back in 1998, the founder, Vicente Ferrer, was quite sure, according to the Media Vaca catalogue, of the type of book he did not want to produce—namely, those that had already been done "a thousand times: Little Red Riding Hood!"

Perrault's tale, which serves as a kind of preamble at the beginning of the book, is illustrated in a *ukiyo-e* style by Kaori Tsukuda. It is followed by twenty other versions that rework both text and illustrations. The book appeared in Media Vaca's "Libros para niños" (Books for Children), a series of sophisticated books that, as the back cover explicitly and emphatically states, are "NOT ONLY for children!" Although the stories were translated into Spanish for the publication, the titles are given in Japanese as well as Spanish (plate 29). The Japanese reworkings are remarkably varied in subject and tone, ranging from humorous stories to frightening stories, from adventure stories to love stories, and from ghost stories to gastronomical stories.

Although the workshop used Perrault's version of the tale as its point of departure, Izumi Yamada's retelling takes the Grimms' version as its hypotext, as the first line clearly indicates. Like many authors, she presents her story as the "true" version of the famous tale, but leaves readers to decide for themselves if indeed it is. Yamada chooses to fill a gap in the classic version of the tale, focusing on the period that Little Red Riding Hood and her grandmother spend in the wolf's dark belly. This moment is not mentioned in Perrault's version, but the Grimms' tale does refer to it in passing. Yamada's retelling emphasizes the initiatory nature of Little Red Riding Hood's sojourn in the dark hell of the wolf's belly. In keeping with the initiatory pattern, the protagonist must accomplish a series of trials and experience a ritual death in order to be reborn and return to the light. Like the oral tales that predate

58. "En el vientre del lobo," by Izumi Yamada, from *Érase veintiuna veces Caperucita Roja*. Illustrations by Izumi Yamada. Copyright © 2006 Media Vaca. Used by permission of Media Vaca.

Perrault's version, this story presents a courageous and resourceful young heroine who not only escapes unharmed without male assistance but also rescues her grandmother, as well as the monkey helper who finds his way into the tale. There are psychoanalytical overtones to Yamada's story that can perhaps be attributed to her work with the mentally disturbed. Like several of the other authors in the collection, Yamada highlights the theme of orality, which is fundamental to the tale.

The artist's illustrations for the work are all in shades of red, pink, and black. The story has a striking layout: the text appears on the verso superposed on an image in white and washed-out red. The first page of text is printed within the shape of the protagonist's pale red bonnet, while the final page of text is superposed on the ghostly image of a wolf's head in the smoke of the fire into which he disappears. In the final image, a distorted image of the wolf's head dissipates into the air above the fire in which Little Red Riding Hood has just tossed the last the dark pieces of the wolf. Yamada's Little Riding Hood overcomes her fear with fire, physically reducing the wolf to ashes.

❧

In the Belly of the Wolf (2006)

In the tale of "Little Red Riding Hood" that they have told you, a wolf ate Little Red Riding Hood and her grandmother, and later a hunter saved them.

Right, well you should know that in fact no hunter came to the rescue.

Below you can read what really happened to Little Red Riding Hood. It is a story that not everyone knows.

It takes place inside the belly of the wolf.

A little after being eaten by the wolf, Little Red Riding Hood came to and realized that she was inside the animal. The belly of the wolf was a dark forest.

At her feet she discovered a handkerchief that belonged to her grandmother. Little Red Riding Hood began to walk in search of her; the grandmother must be somewhere in that forest.

Suddenly she noticed that a warm wind was rising, and the appearance of a wolf's head startled her.

"Hello, Little Red Riding Hood," said the wolf, "welcome to the hell of my gut. Very soon you are going to meet all the trees and plants that I have eaten."

After saying this, the wolf vanished.

She found no further traces of her grandmother. Moreover, that forest seemed endless. Exhausted, Little Red Riding Hood was overcome by sleep.

In that place, poisonous flowers, which never stopped singing, abounded:

"Sleep, child, sleep. Our poison will leave you as skin and bones. Your flesh will be the wolf's blood."

Her fingertips almost became skin and bones. Luckily a little monkey shook Little Red Riding Hood to wake her up.

"Poor little monkey! The wolf has surely eaten him, too!"

Little Red Riding Hood and the monkey entered the forest and stopped opposite the entrance to a tunnel of thorns, wide open like a gigantic mouth.

They could not continue on their way without going through the tunnel. The air became eerily cool.

Determined to continue, the two took a first step. The thorns pricked them everywhere. At first the pain was so intense that they nearly fainted, but later they felt nothing.

With great difficulty, they emerged from the tunnel of thorns and came face to face with an old, ghostly-looking tree that looked down at them from above. It was the grandmother, who was turning into a tree.

They had to save her before it was too late! Little Red Riding Hood pulled with all her strength on an arm that was almost as hard as a branch. Together with the monkey, she pulled and pulled. The grandmother peeled off until she managed to become completely unstuck.

On leaving the forest, they found the wolf torn in pieces.

When they threw the pieces of the wolf in the fire, they finally felt safe. The wolf, in ashes, disappeared in the air, carried off by the wind.

Here ends the story of Little Red Riding Hood. Now it is you who has to judge whether or not it is the true one.

59. "En el vientre del lobo," by Izumi Yamada, from *Érase veintiuna veces Caperucita Roja*. Illustrations by Izumi Yamada. Copyright © 2006 Media Vaca. Used by permission of Media Vaca.

Little Red Riding Hood from the Inside
(I Kokkinoskoufitsa apo mesa)

HARA YIANNAKOPOULOU AND VASSILIS PAPATSAROUCHAS

Hara Yiannakopoulou (1972–) is a Greek author and translator. Since the late 1990s, she has published novels and picturebooks for young adults and children. Her picturebook *I apenanti monaxia* (The Opposite Loneliness, 2002), illustrated by Efi Lada, won the Greek Children's Book Circle Award. Yiannakopoulou's innovative retelling of the famous tale, "I Kokkinoskoufitsa apo mesa," is one of three illustrated stories in the collection *Mia agapi, epta chromata kai enas lykos* (One Love, Seven Colors, and One Wolf), which was published in picturebook format by the Greek publisher Metaichmio in 2007. It is a very original collective work by three highly acclaimed children's book authors and three exceptionally talented Greek illustrators. Although published as a book for children eight years old and up, the collection seems to address older children and even adults. The multilayered stories blur the borders between adult and children's literature. This is explained in part by the fact that the stories all deal with the theme of love. Argyro Pipini's opening story, illustrated by Maria Bacha, concerns a young village girl's frustrated first love for a rich young man, while the second story, written by Kostas Charalas and illustrated by Sophia Vlazaki, recounts the birth of the rainbow as a result of another unfulfilled love. The book closes with Hara Yiannakopoulou's revisioning of "Little Red Riding Hood," illustrated by the painter and illustrator Vassilis Papatsarouchas (1975–), who has become one of Greece's most prominent illustrators. In 2008 he was nominated for the prestigious Hans Christian Andersen Award for illustration.

Papatsarouchas has illustrated many books, three of which he also authored. His modern, somewhat unconventional illustrations are immediately recognizable for their blend of painterly style and childish playfulness. Papatsarouchas has returned repeatedly to the subject of Little Red Riding Hood in his work. In fact the figures of Little Red Riding Hood and the wolf have accompanied him for such a long time that the artist confesses they have become "good friends after all these years."[5] In 2004 Papatsarouchas won Greece's State Award for Illustration for his work on *Kokkinoskoufitsa* (2003), an adaptation of "Little Red Riding Hood" by Argyro Kokoreli. This Little Red Riding Hood is rendered quite distinctive by an extraordinarily long red cap and the fact that she wears her story on her dress in a very postmodern manner. More recently, Papatsarouchas illustrated *Oi 12 kokkinoskoufitses kai o kourdistos lykos* (The Twelve Little Red Riding Hoods and the Clockwork Wolf, 2007), a whimsical sequel to the classic tale by Christos Boulotis. In playful, somewhat surreal images, the illustrator evokes the fantastic world of Riding Hood duodecaplets who order a clockwork wolf and create their own forest in order to relive the adventure of their famous mother. The tale of "Little Red Riding Hood" has been a source of inspiration for paintings as well as illustrations, but each time the approach is entirely different. Papatsarouchas uses a variety of media—gouache, watercolor, colored pencils, and collage—to rework the haunting theme. In one very large painting in acrylics and charcoal, the tiny figure making her way through a wintery landscape of black, gray, and white is recognizable as Little Red Riding Hood by a very long red cap of the same style worn by the heroine of *Kokkinoskoufitsa*. Yiannakopoulou's story was inspired by a very striking painting from the same series, completed in 2007. In a stark setting on a black sphere sits a lone bed with a red mattress stabbed by a gigantic darning needle. The use of the needle motif from oral versions of the tale highlights the initiatory nature of Yiannakopoulou's modern revisioning. The book closes with this dramatic and thought-provoking painting (plate 30).

The title of Yiannakopoulou's story, like that of Izumi Yamada, focuses attention on the period after the heroine has been devoured. The Greek author, too, presents a Little Red Riding Hood who voluntarily enters the wolf's belly, but this time she sacrifices herself not for her grandmother but for the wolf. Yiannakopoulou's psychoanalytical approach to the story of Little Red Riding Hood, which is more sophisticated than Yamada's, develops the mother-daughter relationship. This thoughtful retelling focuses on the feelings of the protagonist: her fear and how she overcomes it, her anger toward her mother, and her final sense of well-being. Papatsarouchas emphasizes these feelings in the first two full-page illustrations, which depict Little Red Riding Hood fearfully peering out from behind a tree in the forest (plate 31) and later contentedly listening to her grandmother's tales (plate 32).

Like Joanna Olech, Yiannakopoulou subverts the cautionary message of the classic tale. Both Riding Hoods consciously choose to answer the wolf's question, but Olech's protagonist ignores her instincts for the sake of politeness, whereas Yiannakopoulou's heroine reasons that answering is the most sensible thing to do and ignores her mother's advice. The consequences are tragic in Olech's story, but Yiannakopoulou converts Perrault's tragic ending to a happy one, as the protagonist overcomes her fear and chooses to be devoured. Yiannakopoulou also subverts the character of the wolf, whose paternal role allows him to empathize with Little Red Riding Hood. In the painting that hangs crookedly on the wall in the second illustration, the wolf is portrayed as a rather stereotypical silent film villain wearing a bright red hood, but he no longer frightens Little Red Riding Hood, who sits comfortably just below, listening to her grandmother's story. The final scene that takes place inside the wolf's belly is humorously depicted as a comfortable living-room interior. The illustrator adds a playful postmodern element, as the red book from which the grandmother reads is undoubtedly Little Red Riding Hood's own story, a story that no longer provokes fear in the heart of the heroine.

In Yiannakopoulou's innovative retelling, the three main characters of the classic tale are happily united to become one. Papatsarouchas suggests this union with subtle details in his visual interpretation. Not only does the wolf wear a red cloak, but the grandmother seems to have a red cap under her large white cap. The inseparable nature of Little Red Riding Hood and the wolf is announced at the beginning of the story by an illustrated initial capital letter: the "H" is cleverly formed by the joining of two long red caps with teeth that resemble a wolf's jaws. Yiannakopoulou and Papatsarouchas examine the complex and equivocal relationship between Little Red Riding Hood and the wolf in a very modern, ironic, and metaphorical revisioning of the tale.

Red Riding Hood from the Inside (2007)

Little Red Riding Hood remembered well the day she was lost in the dark forest. At first, she really liked it while she was still close to the clearing. She smelled flowers, looked at bumblebees, chased rabbits, and climbed trees.

However, slowly the trees became taller and their branches thicker and their leaves denser, so much that the sun was completely hidden and it seemed to suddenly darken in the big forest. Soon, Little Red Riding Hood couldn't see the rabbits or the flowers. She couldn't hear the birds' sweet singing, but only strange screeching. And even worse, the path had disappeared. How would she find Grandma's house now?

She sat on a rock and started to shout.

But no one answered, so she started to cry ever louder, and while she was crying, all the scary noises multiplied. Legged trees were coming toward her, monsters with four hundred eyes were looking at her through the foliage, and clouds of buzzing insects were blocking the way . . . Her house was so far away and Grandma's house nowhere to be found!

Then she started thinking about her mother, who had allowed a little girl, so young, to go through the enormous forest all alone. She thought of her grandmother, sweet and pale, tucked in her quilts, sick, waiting alone for some food.

When she thought of all of this, she felt very angry and immediately stopped crying. She bravely lifted her head, picked up her basket, and started to walk, determined to find her sick grandmother.

But there was not much time left. As she was walking, a big, shiny wolf suddenly appeared before her, like the ones she once encountered in the pages of a fairy tale.

"What are you doing alone in the forest, little girl?" the wolf asked politely.

"I'm taking food to my grandmother who is sick," Little Red Riding Hood responded.

"And where does your grandmother live?"

"On the other side of the forest, but . . . ," Little Red Riding Hood hesitated for a moment. *Don't talk to strangers and especially wolves,* her mother always told her. But why not? What's the worst that could happen if she told him about Grandma's house? A big wolf like him could possibly have seen it somewhere and help her find it. So she explained everything that had happened to her.

"But aren't you scared wandering alone in the forest?"

"Umm . . . yes, I'm scared, but I'm actually more angry than scared."

"Angry?" exclaimed the wolf.

"Yes! Angry with my mother for making me go to the forest on my own and leaving my poor grandmother all alone!"

"Well that's unheard of! I would never allow my little wolves to wander alone in dangerous places!" exclaimed the outraged wolf.

Ah! How good Little Red Riding Hood felt. Finally, she had someone who understood her! So, she walked along, talking with the nice wolf, until they found themselves in a small opening on the other side of the forest. And what did they see? Through the pitch darkness, the lights of a small house appeared.

"Grandma's house!" Little Red Riding Hood shouted joyfully, and they both headed that way.

It was already dark, they'd been walking for hours, and the wolf was starting to get hungry.

Once they got inside the house, Grandma greeted them with joy. It had been a while since she'd seen a living creature, and her fever broke at once. As soon as she heard her granddaughter's story and found out about the wolf's hunger, she shared with him the food that was in the basket.

But after all, he *was* a wolf and couldn't possibly be satisfied with such a small amount of food. His stomach would not stop rumbling. Little Red Riding Hood and her grandmother, who were not ungrateful, felt sorry for the hungry wolf. So, when he opened his huge mouth, and the rumbling was ten times louder, they both dove into the deep stomach. And the rumbling finally stopped.

As for Little Red Riding Hood, she was feeling good inside the wolf's soft belly, with the comfortable sofa, the fireplace, the toys, the warmth, and Grandma's tales. And besides, the wolf was so hungry that she was certain that they would soon have company.

The darkness is outside.
The shouting is outside.
Mom is outside.
The fear is outside.
The wolf is outside.

There is only me inside, and the wolf is not hungry.
I am safe, and nobody is going to eat me.

SEVEN

Running with the Wolves

Women who are running
against the wind with the wolves

Frida Lyngstad, "Kvinnor som springer"

Little Red Pants, Bluebeard, and Wee Notes
(Petit Pantalon Rouge, Barbe-Bleue et Notules)

Pierrette Fleutiaux

Pierrette Fleutiaux (1941–) is a French novelist and short story writer who lived in New York for several years. She won the prestigious 1985 Prix Goncourt de la Nouvelle for her short story collection *Métamorphoses de la reine* (Metamorphoses of the Queen, 1984) and the Prix Femina in 1990 for her novel *Nous sommes éternels* (We Are Eternal). Her retelling of Perrault's "Little Thumbling," "La femme de l'Ogre," in the award-winning short story collection was translated under the title "The Ogre's Wife" in 1991 and subsequently published in Ellen Datlow and Terri Windling's *The Year's Best Fantasy and Horror: Fifth Annual Collection* in 1992. The author also wrote an opera libretto based on the story for the radio, as well as another about Petit Pantalon Rouge, which has not yet been set to music.

Fleutiaux has published books for children as well as adults. The collection *Métamorphoses de la reine* is also read by young adults, but Fleutiaux firmly dissuades mothers who are misled by the book's cover and want to buy it for their children.[1] It is definitely not a children's book. Fleutiaux retells Perrault's fairy tales by intensifying the violence and sexuality as well as the irony and social satire. Stereotypes are turned upside down, women's roles are developed, and narrative points of view are shifted (sometimes to secondary characters) to allow a critical reflection on social and cultural conditioning of women. The sophisticated, feminist fairy-tale collection was the result of a rereading of Perrault's tales during a difficult time in Fleutiaux's adult life. This encounter with the tales of her childhood was more enlightening than the feminist gatherings she had attended during the late 1960s and early 1970s in the United States. In the preface, the author describes the powerful impact that rereading these "children's tales" had on her when she was no longer a child. The sudden realization that, on the threshold of adulthood, she had been offered an image of "adult women [as] shrews, bad mothers, witches, cruel stepmothers" provoked an initial reaction of outrage and rejection, followed by a desire to rewrite the tales.[2] Her witty, revisionist retellings skillfully avoid the heavyhanded message of much feminist writing.

Fleutiaux parodies the classic tales in a sophisticated manner that includes a clever pastiche of the language. The author likens the rediscovery in adulthood of Perrault's seventeenth-century language, which she compares to "a period costume," to coming across the dress-up clothes of childhood play. While Fleutiaux appropriates complete lines from Perrault, her retelling is full of sophisticated and witty play with the language that corresponds to a need "to make its starched side rip with street expressions, to introduce anachronisms, to curtsey so low sometimes that the seams burst!" With masterful skill, the French author subverts the traditional tale while retaining its structures, patterns, and mythic content. The tripartite trials of the protagonist's rite of passage, the symbolism of the firebrand, the evocative prose, and the powerful images retain the haunting atmosphere of traditional tales. Like writers such as Angela Carter, Fleutiaux restores some of the explicit sexual content of the rather bawdy oral versions of the tale, while giving it a kind of modern sensual violence.

As the title suggests, "Petit Pantalon Rouge, Barbe-Bleue et Notules" is a bricolage of two fairy tales, in which Little Red Pants marries the wolf, who assumes the form of the hairy Bluebeard. The unexpected third element of the title gives humorous importance to the pseudo-scientific notes at the end of the text, which poke fun at folktale scholarship. Little Red Pants, her mother, and her grandmother are all emancipated women. Petit Pantalon Rouge (PPR, as the narrator humorously begins calling her just prior to her sexual initiation, here translated as LRP) is a fearless, unconventional heroine whose initiation, under the guidance of her mother and grandmother, prepares her to tame the wolf and to save herself, the seven other wives, and even Bluebeard. Six of Bluebeard's other wives become lesbians while in the secret cupboard. Fleutiaux's Bluebeard is portrayed in a more sympathetic light than Perrault's protagonist, turning out to be a mild-mannered, fainthearted gentleman whose polygamy is the result of a curse and a source of deep anxiety for him. Fleutiaux parodies the codes and conventions of the genre: rather than replacing Perrault's tragic conclusion with the conventional fairy-tale one, in which Little Red Pants and Bluebeard live happily ever after, the protagonist strikes off on her own in a very open ending. The metafictional play and clever intertextual allusions to other fairy tales and other genres make this witty parody a particularly sophisticated and memorable retelling.

⌘

LITTLE RED PANTS, BLUEBEARD, AND WEE NOTES (1984)

In a cottage some distance from a village lived a little girl, the liveliest ever seen. Her mother, who didn't have a husband, and her grandmama, who had had several, were crazy about her. They made her little red pants that suited her so well that henceforth everywhere she was called "Little Red Pants."

Little Red Pants grew in strength and wisdom. Her mother taught her not to be afraid of the dawn's gray paths, or the mists that trail strange phantoms at dusk, or the wind that howls hideous madnesses, or the rain that is so sad it decomposes the heart, or the storms that speak of the end of all things. She dived into whirlpools and cascades, climbed to the tops of the tallest trees, and soon, like her mother, who was a strong and solid woman, she knew how to redo the roof that time undid, plough the fields that the frost or the sun desolated, and assemble a wall so well that nothing could topple it.

As for her grandmother, she told her about the adventures she had had in the whole wide world and, with her books and her memories, taught her a thousand things which the peasant women of the village would have been very amazed to learn.

But these women, who were as prudent as they were courageous, had always taken care that Little Red Pants not find herself alone in the evening in isolated places. Many wolves actually hovered around the cottage, and when the snow fell, one or the other, more daring or more ravenous, left the edge of the woods and advanced on the path. Therefore Little Red Pants was quite surprised when one day her mother said to her:

"Little Red Pants, here is the gum-that-sticks-everything-together; go and play with the wolf."

Little Red Pants went out of the house and did as her mother had told her. When a wolf came close enough, she threw the gum between his long, pointed teeth. Believing he had caught a hand and maybe even an arm, he immediately closed his jaws, but when he wanted to open them to chew his prey, he found himself quite prevented from doing so. Little Red Pants then jumped on his back.

"Wolf, take me for a ride," she said.

Surprised, the wolf circled the house twice. And Little Red Pants found him superior to the dogs, donkeys, and piglets that she had ridden until then.

The next day, her mother called her again; then she gave her the gum-that-sticks-everything-together as well as a whip and told her:

"Little Red Pants, here is the gum and the whip; go and play with the wolf."

A second wolf having come close on the path, Little Red Pants went out and ran to him. She threw the gum into the mouth that opened, jumped on the back, and flogging the animal with her whip, made him go around the house several times. The wolf's ears, lashed by the wind, were flattened against his head, his tail flapped like a banner, his stomach grazed the ground, and Little Red Pants, hanging on to the hair, her eyes screwed up, and almost dizzy with the wild odor, stared at the landscape that bore down on her with its straight, intoxicating lines and treacherous turns. Sometimes the wolf turned its red eyes toward her, and then its fangs, glued under its chops, were bared, but Little Red Pants paid no attention.

The third day, the mother called her daughter and gave her the gum and the whip, as well as a long firebrand whose end glowed red like a live charcoal. Then she said:

"Little Red Pants, here is the gum that you know, and the whip that you know, and here is also a firebrand that you must not let go of. But don't forget, the door will be closed, and you will not be able to come home before daylight."

With a little cord whose knot she carefully checked, she attached the firebrand to her daughter's wrist, and having tenderly kissed her, she went back into the house and locked the door. Little Red Pants found herself outside and in a great hurry to go and play. But more given to observation than action this time, the wolves did not move from the edge of the woods.

"Cousin, will you go back?" one of them asked the first wolf.

This one, whose jaws had regained some play, managed to answer, though with a certain slowness:

"She is too skinny, her legs pierced my skin."

"And you?" they asked the second wolf.

But the latter, whose misadventure was more recent and who was scarcely able to lift one tooth over the other, only managed to whisper:

"U, u, u."[i] [For notes i through viii, see "Wee Notes" at the end of the tale.]

"Speak more clearly," said the others, surprised. "We don't understand you."

"My cousin is hoarse," the first wolf said hastily. "Some nasty virus that the girl gave to him."

"But what was she doing on your back then?"

"She wasn't on our backs," said the first, preferring lies to dishonor.

"But we saw her there."

"An optical illusion must have deceived you, dear cousins."

"O, i, a, i, u, i, o," added the second wolf.[ii]

"Far from guiding us, she was running behind us, because we didn't want her," continued the first.

"Wow, wow," agreed the second.[iii]

"Then how were you able to feel her legs, which were piercing your hide?"

"Cousins," said the first wolf then, pulling heroically on his jaws, "I didn't want to disappoint you. That girl was on our back, and we were counting on bringing her back to you, but she got away, that's the whole truth."

"A, o," cried the second, who almost lost a tooth with this violent effort.[iv]

Meanwhile, Little Red Pants was very bored standing in the path, and as nothing was coming, she finally decided to go farther down. Soon she was so close to the woods that one of the wolves could not resist. He arrived running sideways, like an animal with a long memory, and his mistrust was such that Little Red Pants almost had to rub her nose against his for him to finally, suddenly, open his mouth. Then she threw in the gum-that-sticks-everything-together and, jumping on his back, ordered:

"Wolf, give me a ride."

But instead of taking that trip around the house, in which the two naïve wolves, fooled by their rider, had only followed their own tracks, this wolf, more cunning than the first two and having learned by their adventure, ran off toward the forest where the other wolves, his cousins, were waiting for him.

It was already night, and the dark shadows, assembled at the edge of the woods, came and went abruptly. Little Red Pants saw them, she whipped her mount as hard as she could, and the angry wolf passed through the wall of wild animals at full gallop. But they soon joined it. Seeing the game liven up, the rider did not lose her composure. She gripped the wolf's flanks tightly between her legs, lifted the firebrand, which blazed at a prodigious height, and the cavalcade began. With one hand Little Red Pants whipped the wolf's rump, with the other she twirled the frenzied flame; the fiery eyes dashed between the trees, the wolf's fur smoked, the firebrand sputtered, finally dawn came. Under the crop, the exhausted wolf came back close to the cottage where the mother and grandmother were waiting. They washed Little Red Pants and put her to bed, where she then slept for three days and three nights.

Now, just about the same time, a man who had fine town and country houses, gold and silver dishes, chromium-plated carriages, and everything that is more pleasant to have than not to have, resolved to take a wife. But as ill luck would have it, this man had a blue beard. Since lasers and hormones were still unknown, nothing could hide his disgrace: there was no woman or girl who did not flee before him.

He asked for the hand of all the princesses in the land. As he was immensely rich, his proposal was at first viewed favorably by the kings, their fathers. But when the young ladies finally saw their suitor in flesh and blood before them, they did not fail to faint, which just as inevitably caused the marriage to vanish. And the suitor saw himself ushered out before he could even pay his compliments and win, by the art of speaking, what he did not hope to win by his face.

Bluebeard then asked to marry all the women of quality who did not yet have husbands or who had lost them by some misfortune. These women, very desirous of a husband, welcomed him with favor, but very quickly it seemed to them that chastity was preferable to the company of a man whose beard differed so greatly from that of the other men who had given them pleasure or with whom they had expected to find some.

Then Bluebeard said, "Ladies, isn't blue the color of the sky, the sea, and your beautiful velvet dress?"

"Of course," said these ladies.

"And is the color of the sky, the sea, and your velvet dress not a beautiful color?"

"It is," answered the ladies, who did not see a great trap there.

"And if some unglamorous object happened to take from the sky the celestial color that is reflected there, do you find the blue less beautiful?"

"We do not," laughed the ladies, who thought they were back in the time when, as little girls, their tutor taught them.

"And if some transparent fish passes in a clear creek, will the blue of the sea be less beautiful for being seen in its fins?"

"It will not," said the ladies.

"It will be even more beautiful," said others, whose giddy hearts were already getting excited.

"And if your beautiful velvet dress let its color fall," said Bluebeard, encouraged, "and if this blue that it displayed a short while ago for the delight of your admirers was now found on the lace of your gloves or the satin of your shoes, would this blue be less blue and less beautiful?"

"It would not, whatever do you mean!" exclaimed the ladies, who all possessed at least one pair of shoes or one pair of gloves to match the dress so admired by their suitor.

"You agree then, ladies, that the beauty of the color is independent from its support, that it is as it were a question of an ideal beauty that no material embodiment could debase?"

"No doubt," answered the ladies.

Although they did not understand any of these last words, they nevertheless saw nothing strange in them, because it reminded them of the lessons that, as young girls, they had had with their philosophy teacher, a fiery and convincing young man with whom they were always accustomed to agree.

"Therefore, ladies," said Bluebeard, "it doesn't matter where it is provided that there is blue?"

"We admit it."

"Thus, it doesn't matter if this blue that you like is found on my beard rather than in my eyes?"

"But it does matter, it does matter," cried out the ladies.

"How can that be, ladies?" said Bluebeard, confused by so much illogicality. "Didn't you say the opposite a moment ago?"

"We weren't talking about beards then," said the ladies.

"Does that mean that if the blue of my beard was in my eyes . . . ?" insisted that miserable man.

"But it isn't!" said the ladies. "It isn't."

And all Bluebeard's reasoning was unable to make them budge from that observation.

"Not to mention," added the most cruel, "that there isn't any more blue in your beard than on the storm cloud or the crow's lugubrious wing."

With this last taunt Bluebeard was obliged to admit defeat, and he had to leave, sent away by women whose minds, unable to soar to pure color, remained imprisoned in its base foundation.

Then he asked if he could marry all the servants of the palaces, castles, mansions, and hotels. But no sooner had they seen him than they laughed in his face, taking him for some theater buffoon or some carnival mask, and nothing he could say succeeded in convincing them of the seriousness of his request and of his person, since love and hilarity rarely hit it off.

Then he looked for the girls of the streets, alleys, and sidewalks, and these would willingly have accepted, but what disgusted them greatly was that he had already married several women, and no one knew what had happened to these women. Such practices reminded them too much of the condition they wanted to leave behind, and because fortune had placed them under the control of a pimp, they still preferred the one they had, because at least his beard wasn't blue.

Finally he came to the peasants, and provided that they didn't have a foot in the grave or in the cradle, he resolved to court the most ragged, the most scrofulous, and the most dirty, hoping that his riches would be a rapid and infallible remedy for these flaws. But the times were no longer such that a rich man, with the wave of a plumed hat, could win the heart of a shepherdess. Television had penetrated into the homes, and the peasant girls dreamed only of announcers with perfectly smooth cheeks and whose complexion is so peculiar that there is no word to describe it.

Because of her trips in all kinds of countries, the grandmother would probably have been the only one able to look without blanching at a man who seemed so peculiar to all the other women, but, being off again to roam the vast world, she didn't hear about this new match who was scouring the town and the countryside. As for the mother, very occupied with her daughter, and the daughter, very occupied with the wolves, they didn't hear about him either.

Now it happened that one day Little Red Pants's mother called her and said:

"Go to the village, take this cake and this little pot of butter to the inn, and ask if they have any news of your grandmother. But above all don't forget the gum, the whip, and the firebrand."

Little Red Pants looked for a wolf and, having found one, left immediately, carrying in her basket the cake and the little pot of butter, and in the large pockets of her pants, the gum, the whip, and the firebrand. She was going along the path, taking proper care to guide her wolf, when a carriage stopped and a man in it asked:

"My beauty, is this wolf taking you away?"

"No," said Little Red Pants, "I'm taking him."

"And where are you going on his dangerous equipage?"

"I'm going to the village inn to take this cake and this little pot of butter, and to ask for news of my grandmama."

"The path is long, and you're quite laden down. Climb into the carriage and I'll take you."

So Little Red Pants released her wolf, who took off immediately across the countryside, his jaws glued and his tail between his legs. Then, holding her pockets tightly against her, she sat down next to the man who had spoken to her. Then she saw his beard and said to him:

"By my mother and my grandmama, your beard is quite blue!"

"It's because I find that more amusing," said Bluebeard. "Don't you?"

"Certainly," answered Little Red Pants, and she laughed.

Soon the carriage left the road and went through the wood, breaking the tree branches and making all kinds of dislodged animals flee before it.

"By my mother and my grandmama, this carriage is quite reckless!" said Little Red Pants.

"It's because I'm repelled by beaten paths," said Bluebeard. "Aren't you?'

Little Red Pants, who bounced at each bump, laughed.

"Certainly," she answered.

Meanwhile, the landscapes succeeded one another, not one was the same, and Little Red Pants said:

"By my mother and my grandmama, I don't know this path."

"It carries us along just like at the movies," said Bluebeard, lifting the curtain of the door. "Don't you like that?"

Feeling herself indeed carried away, Little Red Pants laughed again.

"I like it," she said.

Finally they arrived on a hill on which stood a magnificent castle. The carriage stopped, they got out, and Bluebeard, who was the master of this residence, showed Little Red Pants in and led her to a room where a laid table shone with a thousand reflections.

"This inn isn't the village inn," said Little Red Pants.

"And do you prefer the village inn?" asked Bluebeard.

"By my mother and my grandmama, I prefer this one," said Little Red Pants, who did not know how to lie.

"Then let's eat," said Bluebeard, who was beginning to get very tired of this mother and this grandmama.

However, he didn't let anything show, and during the dinner, which he made last as long as he could, he did so many tricks, told so many stories, showed such astuteness and cheerfulness, that Little Red Pants finally forgot about her mother and her grandmother. Then it was absolutely necessary to clear the table, and they found themselves alone in the great room. Bluebeard, whom such a long wait preceded by so many cruel disappointments had made both very impatient and very prudent, found himself at a loss. He didn't know what to do or what to say. Noticing in his clothing something that intrigued her, Little Red Pants then let her clear voice ring out.

"Bluebeard, do show me your firebrand," she said.

"You must marry me first," he stammered, as he turned red, thinking that he had once again lost everything.

But, determined to try this other firebrand, LRP accepted immediately what was being proposed to her, and the marriage was celebrated straight away. Then it was nothing but walking in the blue paths, climbing on the high rocks, bathing in the silver rivers, picnics, poetry, and mad fits of enthusiasm which sprung up like the wind and made the landscape dance until there was nothing to do but drop to the ground and lose oneself in the large, milky sky that seemed then to descend in a parachute like a very soft feather duvet. At night, BB and LRP did not sleep, playing a thousand little tricks on each other, exchanging their firebrands, and enjoying themselves as only two people very much in love can do and that the solitude maintained in a sort of waking dream.

No one knowing what had happened to Bluebeard, and LRP continuing to forget about her cottage and her mother and grandmother, this happiness could have gone on a long time, when the beard on Bluebeard's face began to grow prodigiously.

Barely had it been cut when it began to grow again, black reflections appeared in places, and soon a bush surrounded the castle's master.

One couldn't approach him, every hair was a thorn that wounded and tore; one couldn't speak to him either, for the beard had invaded his ears, and not a sentence arrived that wasn't mutilated and rendered almost the opposite of itself. As what Bluebeard said, it was only distorted fragments that he had to shout so loudly that his voice itself was unrecognizable.

No more games, no more tricks, the firebrands themselves ignited at inopportune moments or no longer ignited; Bluebeard's disappeared completely under the brambles of his beard, and LRP even forgot the existence of hers.

That's where things were when one morning Bluebeard, whose beard now threatened to reach his upper and lower limbs and all that remained of him, sent for his wife and, with the help of gestures and groans, made her understand that he was going on a trip and that he would return only when his beard had stopped growing. He gave her the keys for the entire castle, which made a bunch almost as big as her, as well as a pass key that could get her out of a predicament if she lost one or the other of the keys. LRP immediately saw that he kept one, the last one of all, but it was so small that she didn't pay any attention. Finally Bluebeard shortened the goodbyes, climbed with great difficulty into the carriage, and left for his trip.

There was an immense relief in the castle, as his mood had changed greatly, and, since his beard had transformed into a bush of brambles and thorns, there wasn't anyone who hadn't had to suffer some cruel attack at one bend or another.

Then LRP remembered her cottage and her mother and grandmother, and had them both summoned. Unfortunately, in their joy at seeing LRP again, they didn't think to keep the secret; the rumor spread, and a lot of guests that hadn't been invited hastened to the young bride's, so impatient were they to see the ogress who had not shrunk from marrying this Bluebeard they had found so little to their liking.

They all came, the princesses, the noblewomen, the servants, the whores, and the peasants, and they were quite surprised to find, instead of an ogress, only a little village girl dressed in modest red pants and having kept the deportment of her former condition. Immediately they went all over the bedrooms, the studies, the closets, each outdoing the other with their raptures and regretting their past scrupulousness.

"If I hadn't been so stupid," each one said, "I would be mistress of all these riches, and not this Little Red Pants who doesn't know how either to dress or to behave."

The princesses then blamed the kings, their fathers, for having badly instructed them in the art of fainting, "because if you faint first, you can't judge after, so it is better to judge first and faint only after," they said. The noble-women blamed their mothers for having brought them up with the ideas of a princess when it would have been better to have those of a servant. The servants told their mistresses, the noblewomen, that they regretted the fine manners that they had been given in their homes, and that they would have been better off to imitate the whores. The whores took it out on their pimps, whose allowances would be very inferior to Bluebeard's. And the peasants realized that television had misled them as to the appearance of prince charmings. There ensued in the land such a great confusion that it still lasts today. So LRP was quite happy when everyone left and she found herself alone with her mother and grandmother.

As quite often happens in this situation, the memory returned of her marriage to Bluebeard, of their walks, their swims, and their mad fits of enthusiasm. But immediately over it spread the horrible bramble bush that had separated them, and she didn't know what to think.

She languished, the little red pants floated on her hips, and all the allure of the firebrand that had so amused her was gone.

Then one night when she couldn't sleep, she thought she heard, in the castle's sepulchral calm, a sound such as she had never heard, so faint that it was only a ghost sound, the sound of another world.

"Mother, grandmother," she said, sitting up terrified in her bed, "do you hear?"

"It is probably a cat," said the women, for whom nothing troubled their sleep.

"This noise is fainter," said LRP.

"A mouse then," said the women.

"Fainter still."

"The wing of a bat?"

"Oh, fainter, much fainter."

"A mosquito fallen from its nest?"

"Fainter than a mosquito," said LRP, but the mother and the grandmother had gone back to sleep.

Waking up shivering every night, LRP heard this sound rising like a vapor from the depths of the castle. And soon the mother and the grandmother had to yield to face facts: either their child was getting soft in the head or they were getting hard of hearing. In the goodness of their heart, they didn't hesitate, and seeking henceforth to solve the mystery, begged LRP to tell them everything that had happened in their absence. Up until then LRP had not wanted to distress them, but she could no longer hold back her heart and told them the whole story from the first day when she had entered the castle to the day when Bluebeard had left on his trip.

"Do you know what that little key he didn't give you opens?"

"No, Mother, he didn't tell me anything about it."

"Do you know all the rooms of the castle?"

"No, Grandmother, he didn't show them to me."

"This man is hiding something from you," said these women, suddenly brought back to action. "We must discover it."

The residence was vast and the job immense; there were countless keys to try; days passed, and they began to get discouraged, thinking that the little key had perhaps appeared only in a dream after all.

It was then that LRP, who was looking for her part in an isolated corner of the castle, had the idea of getting out her firebrand, which she had forgotten up until now.

After some indecisive flickering, it finally gave a light, although quite pale, and LRP noticed a small, hidden staircase, in front of which she must have passed several times. She rushed down so precipitously that she thought she would break her neck. Several corridors opened below, all plunged toward the darkness.

LRP didn't know which way to go and hesitated for a time, when suddenly it seemed to her she heard the sound that had terrified her so many nights. So faint, was it the moaning of the air, a rustle, some sick object completing its decomposition? But everything in these dark bowels of the earth was motionless; the corridors seemed empty; there was no trace of a living being, animal, bird, or insect.

The noise returned; it rose from the corridor that descended ahead, in the steepest slope. She took it. The corridor turned and turned again, like a dreamer in a nocturnal agony, like an intestine with a secret illness. Other corridors took off here and there on the sides; LRP followed the noise.

Sometimes it stopped and she also had to stop. It was during one of these forced pauses that seemed endless that LRP, feeling fear coming, decided to turn back and to go look for her mother and her grandmother. But when she turned, she understood her error and the horror of her situation. Everywhere there was nothing but corridors all the same branching into each other. A step in one or the other, and she would be lost in a labyrinth where no one would ever hear her cry out.

"Oh, Mother and Grandmother, what use are your gum and your whip, and even your firebrand to me," exclaimed LRP.

At that point the offended firebrand ceased to burn, and she found herself in complete darkness.

"Why didn't I leave little stones!"

"Or a long string."

"Or a hair!"

"Oh, why, why did I come!"

LRP, motionless and not daring either to advance or to retreat, lamented thus. A sigh answered her, a human voice that moaned and cried.

LRP started to walk again, and as she advanced, the moans became more agonizing; there were several voices that took over from one another in a hideous concert. Finally the corridor ended; LRP was in front of a little door so low and narrow, and with a lock so small, that one scarcely guessed it was there.[v] At that moment the sigh started up again, and what LRP heard made her blood run cold.

"What have you done to us, Brother!"

"What have you done to us, Husband!"

"Who are you?" she asked with a trembling voice.

"We are the wives and the brothers of Bluebeard," answered the voices.

"How many are you?" said LRP.

"We are seven," answered the wives.

"We are two," answered the brothers.

"Who are you?" asked the wives.

"I am Bluebeard's wife."

"Poor woman!" cried the voices. "Bluebeard is bringing us another prisoner."

"I am alone," said LRP, "and I come to free you."

"Do you have the key?"

"No, Bluebeard took it with him on his journey," said LRP.[vi]

Behind the door, the lamentations began again.

"He is going on a journey, his beard is becoming black; when he returns, he will kill you."

"What?" said LRP.

"When he comes back, he will kill you," said the voices.

"He loves me," said LRP.

"He will kill you," said the voices.

"Lying phantoms," said LRP, turning on her heels and walking away.

"Don't leave," cried the voices.

"What confusion, we'll never get out," the firebrand said then.[vii]

"Let's do something, because the affair is dragging," he went on. At that point he gathered all his force and began to shine more brightly, which had the effect of enlightening the darkened minds. However narrow the lock was, a little of his light nonetheless passed through. They explained.

What had happened to the brothers happened to the wives. Bluebeard, so tender at first that his strange beard was forgotten, wasn't long in transforming; a bush of brambles grew on him, blocking his ears and his mouth and tearing everything on his path. He then left on a journey, and when he came back, he was a ruthless monster who pursued his victims to this dark sojourn, where he imprisoned them with a little key. After that he regained his original form and everything began again. They were now nine in the cupboard, terribly crowded and almost dying, and if they weren't freed at once, surely those would be their last words.

Horrified, LRP promised to get them out of there. But how was she to get out herself? Finally the firebrand, who had dozed a little during this talking, began to shine properly again; the path was found again without difficulty, and soon LRP had rejoined her mother and her grandmother, who had begun to worry greatly. She told them:

"Climb up to the top of the tower to see if Bluebeard is coming. He promised he would be here today, and if you see him, signal to him to hurry."

The two women climbed to the top of the tower, and LRP went back down to the underground passage.

"Brothers and wives, are you alive?" she shouted from the end of the corridor.

"Yes," said the voices.

And immediately she ran to the bottom of the tower.

"Mother and grandmama, do you see anybody coming?"

"No," said the women.

And she ran to the underground passage.

"Are you still alive?"

"Yes," said the voices.

And she ran to the tower.

"Do you see anybody?"

"No," said the women.

And LRP ascended and descended, and the "yesses" were weaker and the "nos" more weary. In short, the firebrand was impatient to play his great role; I have to turn a long day into a few minutes. Let's say therefore that a cloud of dust appeared on the road, and with it Bluebeard's carriage returning home. "Yes," shouted the women, "barely," murmured the voices, the carriage entered, and LRP hurried. But, having passed quickly over these well-known points, I must linger on what happened then, because with the treacherous and tortuous passage of time, numerous errors have crept in, and I can't neglect to correct them now.

Bluebeard got down, but it was no longer Bluebeard, Little Red Pants's loving husband. Long, black hairs covered him from head to foot, his eyes shone like bloody, glowing coals, and as soon as he saw his wife, a ferocious howl escaped his throat, a long howl that echoed through the castle's corridors and made all those who lived there tremble with terror.

Then LRP remembered the dark forest and the path in front of her cottage; she remembered the gum and the whip that had never left her pocket, and the violent wolves that she had mounted, and her mad race at night with the savage pack, and the firebrand that blazed like a great fire. All the love that had been in her fell to the bottom of her heart like a heavy stone, her eyes puckered, her expression became sharp, and when Bluebeard rushed at her, his mouth wide open, LRP jumped to the side, nimbly took the gum-that-sticks-everything-together out of her pocket, and threw it between his shining teeth. Surprised, the wild animal clicked his jaws, which did not open again. Then LRP took out the whip and hitting mercilessly, enjoined him to give her the little key immediately. The wolf then made a horrible sound, a kind of whistling that came out from between its tightly closed fangs like the sound of a thousand imprisoned vipers. His front paws lifted off the ground, his hair stood on end, and he jumped. But he found only a wall in front of him, because his prey had once again thrown herself to the side. The castle shook right down to its foundations from the terrible shock. Rendered insensible to the whip, the monster finally charged LRP a third time, and with such fury that he would certainly have broken all her bones, if, grabbing the firebrand at last, she had not suddenly made him retreat.

Here we must stop especially and render praise to the firebrand that, rising marvelously above its modest nature, accomplished this marvel for which I undertook to tell this tale in all its truth.

This firebrand gathered all the flame that was in him and, rushing forward decisively, clung to the shortest of Bluebeard's hairs and finally succeeded, in spite of his shouts, in consuming everything in an instant.

The flame went out, and the firebrand, weary and blackened, fell into oblivion. In front of an astounded LRP was a handsome man, full of virile grace and firm gentleness. His face was smooth, and only a slight reflection indicated that his beard no doubt verged a little on blue.

"Thank you," said this man soberly, "let's go and free my brothers and these poor women if there is still time."

Everyone hurried into the underground passage and, in the scramble in front of the very low door, under the heavy vaults, they lost a little more time.

"Are you there?" implored LRP, while her husband, with trembling hands, was busy with the tiny lock.

No one answered, and they believed that all was already lost, when finally the door opened and everything was clear. None of the cupboard's inhabitants was dead yet, but, believing themselves betrayed and thinking that Bluebeard was returning to kill them, all preferred to play dead.

I skip the joy of the reunion, unable to know with certainty who embraced whom in all this confusion. Finally they found a little reason; they came up to the surface, the strongest carrying the weakest; and Bluebeard, having gathered all his brood in the castle's great room, leaned against the table and, suppressing a shiver, spoke with a firm voice.

"When I was of an age to marry," he said, "a spell was cast on me: I could not live without the love of a woman, but as soon as I had obtained it, I would have to kill the poor woman who gave it to me. This spell overwhelmed me. I swore to live in celibacy and never to cast my eyes on what was such a danger for me. Alas! I saw this woman," he said, turning toward his first wife. "It seemed to me that it would be impossible to want to harm such an exquisite creature; I believed myself saved, and I married her. But after a few months, in spite of all my efforts, my beard began to grow inordinately and with it a horrible appetite for murder. My nerves didn't cease to tremble, thoughts as black as toads came out of my mouth, and everything that fell into my ears seemed to me to be poisoned; a bramble bush separated me from others. I suffered so much that I was within an inch of throwing myself from the top of the tower or handing myself over to doctors. Instead, I decided to go away on a journey, hoping thus to forget my torture. But the thought of this woman in my castle didn't leave me; in the end I had to return, and all I could do to counter the spell was to lock up the poor woman with bread and water instead of devouring her alive as I was supposed to. And the story repeated itself thus seven times."

At that point, his voice broke, and he stopped.

"Do not condemn me on this sinister repetition," he continued, after a moment in the general silence. "After each adventure, once the woman was thrown into the prison and my body returned to itself, everything was effaced from my memory, and so I began with the same hope. What the spell had not told me was that only a woman without fear would be able to free me, and a good thing too, because if it had done so, no doubt I would never have cast my eyes on such a Little Red Pants."

Everyone was crying, and Bluebeard himself could scarcely contain his sobs. For, with his memory, returned a lot of sweet moments and a lot of bitter moments, all multiplied by seven, and already he foresaw terrible complications, rifts, and who knows, even lawsuits, and worst of all, an abandonment that ravaged his heart, which had become gentle and good again.

"Ladies, I am grateful to you for having raised your daughter without fears and without constraints, to have accustomed her to wolves from her childhood, and to have thus permitted me to escape my terrible destiny. To reward you, I offer you everything in my domains that could tempt you."

The grandmother, who was beginning to be of an age when one wishes to settle down and no doubt tired of roaming the world, said that it would please her very much to marry the youngest of Bluebeard's brothers. The mother, who had, however, always liked to change suitors, moved by one of these mysterious combinations of circumstances that sometimes direct a life, said that the other brother had stolen her heart and that she was asking for his hand this instant. Wearied by so many years of horror and madness and seeing themselves courted by women as solid as sensible, the two brothers accepted with joy.

Bluebeard then turned toward the seven wives, whom Little Red Pants had joined. They formed a kind of strange flower, these seven women who had been rendered very pale by their long stay in the cupboard, with, in their middle, the red pistil full of sap of the eighth, who had saved them and seemed, by her force, to keep them from falling like wilted petals.

Each one of these petals, as well as the pistil, had all his love, because he had loved each time with a fresh, whole heart; but if there was there the seven objects of love of the seven persons that he had been—without mentioning LRP so pink and lively that she almost took away his sight—at this moment he was only a single person, deprived of these copies of himself that would have gotten him out of the predicament, and he was certainly suffering from a strange suffering, such as no human had ever known, and that was perhaps the ultimate trick of this spell that had been cast on him. He read also, in the paleness of these wives so recently released from the darkness, all the immensity of his infamy, and the ardent, flaming spot that LRP made in the middle only deepened his horror.

There was a flower as poisonous as attractive, near which he felt his life so strongly inflated that it seemed ready to burst its dikes and to escape completely at one go, leaving him then bloodless in a desert of arid regrets.

Now once again fate thwarted his predictions. Before his astonished eyes, the pale petals, far from fading and falling, leaned one toward the other in twos, to such an extent that soon there were only three large petals, suddenly much less pale, a thin petal, and a red pistil still in the middle.

"Ladies," said Bluebeard, "so much emotion has no doubt weakened me. It seems to me that I have problems with my vision. Permit me to rest."

Obligingly, the firebrand wanted to offer itself as a bench, but no longer being as robust as in the days of its magic, it couldn't support the weight of such a handsome man and broke on one side with a dry noise. Bluebeard thought that his heart was breaking and fainted for good.

One of his ears didn't faint, however, and here is what it gathered:

"The poor man, alas!" said the weakest voice.

"Poor man, my foot," said another voice, clearly more assertive. "You are very good, my sister, to be moved to pity, and you forget very easily the ill he did to us."

"But isn't it a great pity," continued the weakest voice, "to see so much force thus spread on the floor, like mere dishwater."

"It's as it should be," said another voice, "and I don't know what's stopping me from spraying him in my own manner."

"Do you know, my sisters, that he had promised to rescue me from the cursed chains of the kitchen?"

"And me from those of diapers."

"And me from the convent."

"And me from teaching."

"Well, my sisters, all that for what?"

"To put us in the cupboard!"

"But he told you, it wasn't his fault," said the frail voice.

"You really don't understand anything, sister. Keep him for you, then, since he pleases you so much."

"But what will you tell him?"

"The truth, sister. That in the cupboard for so long, we got to know each other, and that there is no need of a man to make women happy."

At these words, Bluebeard's ear began to vibrate so loudly that it woke up the sleeper completely. He had to confront the evidence. In the confined cupboard, his seven wives, except for one, had begun to love with a tender love, and that tender love, returned to the broad daylight, remained firm and did not yield to any other attraction. The seven wives less one, joined in pairs that made only one, had become, in short, three.

The first surprise, then the first pain having passed, Bluebeard found himself again before the same dilemma as previously, no less difficult for being reduced in its elements. There remained the last of his seven wives, and Little Red Pants. His heart, too distressed, emitted only weak signals, however it seemed to him that these carried in LRP's direction. Hadn't she indeed known him in his former state as in his new state, wasn't it she who was the reason for the undoing of his bewitchment, and wouldn't she be better able to cure him again in case of a recurrence of his affliction?

At least that was what the firebrand was trying to whisper, blowing a few last wisps of smoke toward him with a great effort; and, in spite of his weakness, he strove to send just as much to LRP.

"E e o," said the weak curls, "é on a, é ou a o e é i e."[viii]

The heavier consonants fell back inside the wood, and the speech that reached LRP no longer made much sense. Smoke, smoke and ashes, never will the past come back to life again! In spite of all its good will, the firebrand could not rekindle that flame.

"Goodbye, Monsieur," said Little Red Pants. "Accept the friendship that I owe a great-uncle, uncle, ex-husband, and almost brother-in-law. Take care of your two sisters-in-law, my mother and grandmother, as well as your two brothers, your six ex-wives, and your wife."

"Madam, don't fear, you have saved me from a horrible destiny; my gratitude to you is eternal, and if some bad urges return to me, your mother and grandmother, my sisters-in-law, will immediately administer some Temesta potion that, it is said, greatly calms evil spells."

"I am leaving then, Bluebeard."

"Goodbye, Little Red Pants."

When all the other goodbyes were done, and Little Red Pants was finally positioned on the main road with her basket by way of a hobo's bundle, the seventh wife, the one who hadn't been united to one or the other of her sisters, suddenly in anguish and almost in tears, came running out of the castle and threw herself at LRP's feet.

"I'm afraid," she said.

"Don't you love him then?" said LRP.

"I love him and I don't love him," said the poor woman.

"Listen," said LRP, "I give you my gum, my whip, and my firebrand. They will be able to teach you many things."

The seventh wife stayed on her knees with a distraught look.

"You would perhaps be able to practice on dogs or cats," said LRP, looking at the wife without much hope.

"I would never dare," said that poor woman, but she took the gum, the whip, and the firebrand in memory of her benefactress.

And LRP went off. When she had walked for a time, she stopped and looked at the castle. Tears ran down her cheeks. Then she took from her basket the cake and the little pot of butter, which never dried out (that was their magic); made herself a large, lovely slice of cake and butter; and biting into it with gusto, she continued on her way.

From in front of the castle, the seventh wife, who had watched LRP go off, wanted to ask one last question.

"Where are you going then?" she shouted as loud as she could.

But who can answer such a question?

Wee Notes

i. Recent research leads us to think that the missing consonants in the speech of the wolf with the sealed jaws could be respectively: "p s r." The text would then read: "Stink, sweat, kick" and could be understood in the following manner: "She stinks, she sweats, she kicks."

Some exegetes, dissatisfied with this interpretation, of which they recognize the solid formal foundation but challenge the implied coarseness, have advanced another theory. According to this one, "u u u" should be understood as: "I saw her, I had her, I left her."

I will resume briefly the objections generally put forward against this last thesis. Why would the wolf, in a sentence visibly marked by symmetry, suddenly go to the simple past after two composite pasts? Another concerns the meaning itself. Not only did the wolf not "have" Little Red Pants, but furthermore he knows full well that all his cousins witnessed this defeat, which allows the elimination of the hypothesis of a boast.

It is also necessary to point out a curious school of thought, commonly called "the river," according to which nothing ever comes back twice. The argumentation of the adherents to this doctrine in the case that interests us is the following: It is impossible that Caesar's famous formula be repeated twice. The wolf of the tale, being a simple village wolf, could not have known the tales about the emperor. It is therefore not a question of quotation, plagiarism, or some parody with an ironic intention. Now, since it cannot be a question of a repetition due to chance either, the wolf's incomplete sentence can under no circumstances be: "I saw her, I had her, I left her."

Without wanting to enter into this quarrel, I don't think it is in vain to introduce here a simple, commonsensical remark. The vowels that escaped from the wolf's glued teeth are not "i i i," which should be the case if his intention was to quote the imperial Latin and thus to say "Veni vidi, vici." There was therefore no repetition, and the specious argumentation of "the river" collapses by itself.

For my part, I would willingly content myself with thinking that the wolf didn't want to say anything other than the three vowels mentioned, and that these, far from representing an organized sentence, were only the naturally cursory expression of a certain uncertainty due to contradictory feelings that were too evident to need naming. "U u u" would then indeed be read as "u u u." But it remains understood that, being only a storyteller and not a theorist, I submit this hypothesis here with only the most complete modesty.

May the reader forgive me this unaccustomed account, but I believed it good to give a general survey of this surprising quarrel that has caused so much ink to flow and in which so many eminent folklorists, linguists, semiologists, historians, critics, Latinists, psychoanalysts, psychologists, and stomatologists have confronted each other.

ii. "O i a i u i o": it is generally agreed that it appears to be the vowels of "optical illusion."

iii. "Oua, oua": probably "ugh! ugh!"

iv. "A o": two interpretations have been put forward: "Ah! Oh!" and "harlot." The second is the most commonly accepted.

v. It didn't escape me that, in the darkness where the firebrand had left her, LRP couldn't see this door and this lock. It is possible that this inconsistency is the fruit of an interpolation.

vi. Another inconsistency. Hadn't Bluebeard left his wife a passkey? Or should we believe that this passkey didn't open that lock? But in this case, why did the tale keep the memory of it?

vii. According to other versions, the firebrand didn't talk, and the adventure gets lost in the subterranean passages, or divides in two, sending LRP into a wolf's intestines and Bluebeard to the blade that split his. Besides all these versions are very cruel, here I trust the firebrand that, although imperfect, was at least magic.

viii. Speech of the smoke: "What a handsome man, what a good match, and at your service."

Little Red Riding Hood's
Economically Disadvantaged Grandmother
(La grand-mère économiquement défavorisée
de la Petite Chaperonne Rouge)

Pierre Léon (1926–) is a French-born author, linguist, and emeritus professor who began his career in France but has been living in Canada for many years. He has written several important books on French linguistics. In 1996 he published a volume of retellings of traditional tales bearing the perversely long title *Le mariage politiquement correct du petit Chaperon rouge et autres histoires plus ou moins politiquement correctes avec notices explicatives pour servir à la morale de notre temps* (The Politically Correct Marriage of Little Red Riding Hood and Other More or Less Politically Correct Stories with Explanatory Notes for Use in the Morality of Our Time) in the series "Contes" (Tales), put out by Éditions du Gref in Toronto. Léon humorously recasts, with tongue-in-cheek criticism of the politically correct, numerous traditional tales, including Perrault's best-known stories: "Little Red Riding Hood," "Sleeping Beauty," "Little Thumbling," "Puss in Boots," "Bluebeard," and "Cinderella."

When Léon wrote the book in the mid-1990s, the political correctness movement was well entrenched in Canadian culture, having begun in the United States and spread first to English-speaking Canada and then almost immediately into French Canadian culture as well. The French across the Atlantic were shaking their heads at the absurdities of the movement and its language, and Léon's witty parody mirrors that reaction in an exaggerated manner. The author's introduction informs readers that he discovered James Finn Garner's *Politically Correct Bedtime Stories*, which were published in 1994, just as he was submitting his manuscript. Unlike many of the politically correct retellings of classic fairy tales, Léon's witty tales have not become dated, as indicated by the reissuing of the tales in 2012 in Gref's series "Le Beau mentir "(The Beautiful Lie).

The new edition targets adult readers more directly by adding to the cover the subtitle "Contes pour adultes nostalgiques et libéres" (Tales for Nostalgic, Liberated Adults), which appeared only on the title page of the original edition, although the introduction mentions both adult and child readers.[3] The tales are accompanied by small, witty drawings, in a comics style, done in India ink by the author. Léon's collection actually contains three tales devoted to the story of Little Red Riding Hood, the longest of which is the title tale. The tale included here is the first of the three Little Red Riding Hood tales. The words that appear as an epigraph are taken from the popular French children's game "Loup y es-tu?" (Wolf, Are You There?), which is often worked into French retellings of the famous tale. In Léon's recasting, published for adults, the tale has transparent sexual overtones. For the elderly Wolf and Riding Hood's grandmother, "Loup y es-tu" evokes nostalgic memories of their youth, when their game had always ended in love-making. It is not surprising that the retelling by this well-known linguist is full of clever wordplay. The humorous variation on the archaic formula about the door—in which the Wolf copes easily on his own with the *chevillette* and the *bobinette*—highlights the couple's sudden, happy reunion. The parodic treatment of the ritualistic dialogue turns it into an exchange of compliments between two aging former lovers. The drawing that accompanies this tale portrays the grandmother and the Wolf exchanging compliments in her bed, above which a large thought bubble depicts the couple as they used to look once upon a time when they played in the woods together.

The controversial theme of euthanasia is introduced in a comical manner, as the grandmother uses the double meaning of the French expression *mignonne à croquer* (pretty enough to eat) to trick the Wolf into gobbling her up in spite of himself. Like so many of his contemporary counterparts, the old Wolf tries to justify his behavior but, in this case, by borrowing psychoanalytical theory. The first story ends with the allusion to a sequel, in which the narrator directly addresses the readers who believe they know it. Léon not only demotes Perrault's tale to the status of a sequel; he also suggests that it is not even the "true story."

In Léon's tale the Wolf and the grandmother are presented not as elderly versions of the classic characters but rather as their forebears. The tale that gives its title to the collection presents the original characters in the form of the emancipated Riding Hood and the shy Lulu, who seem to take after their grandparents closely. The granddaughter, who initiates a seductive striptease and both asks and answers the questions of the formulaic dialogue, may be slightly more "sexually liberated" than the grandmother, but the old lady seems to have been quite a flirt in her day and still welcomes the Wolf warmly into her bed. Little Red Riding Hood and Lulu, in turn, become lovers and enjoy their own sexual games. Léon's drawing for the sequel depicts Lulu, the Wolf, at the table in Riding Hood's rustic cabin as he meets her parents, and the two seem destined to marry and live happily ever after. However, the parents remain opposed to the union, despite Little Red Riding Hood's reiteration of Lulu's rather Freudian justification for his behavior (borrowed perhaps from his grandfather's story). Lulu's need to repent for his crime of having swallowed Little Red Riding Hood compromises their happiness. While on a pilgrimage to a convent in Quebec, he betrays the lovesick Riding Hood with a schoolgirl at the convent. Rather than marrying Lulu, Little Red Riding Hood makes a more politically correct marriage to a prince who seems to have stepped out of "Sleeping Beauty," complete with one-hundred-years' growth of hair, which causes her to mistake him for her wolf when she finally awakens from her long sleep.

Léon's third tale occurs chronologically prior to the sequel. It is a bricolage of the stories of Little Red Riding Hood and Father Christmas, with the
wolf, Lulu, playing the role of the latter to ensure that the eight-year-old Little
Red Riding Hood receives a doll dressed in red for Christmas. In fact, Lulu
leaves several beautiful dolls by the clogs the little girl left out in front of the
fireplace. Lulu-Father Christmas unexpectedly supplies the wolf's voice in the
game of "Loup y es-tu?" that Little Red Riding Hood is playing with her dolls,
a foreshadowing perhaps of the games to come when she will no longer be
playing with dolls.

60. *Le mariage politiquement correct du Petit Chaperon Rouge: Contes pour adultes
nostalgiques et libérés*, by Pierre Léon. Copyright © 2012 Éditions du Gref. Used by
permission of Pierre Léon and Éditions du Gref.

ॐ

LITTLE RED RIDING HOOD'S
ECONOMICALLY DISADVANTAGED GRANDMOTHER* (1996)

"Wolf are you there?"

"No."

"Do you hear?"

"Yes."

"What are you doing?"

"I'm putting on my socks!"

We were very afraid because the wolves of our childhood were bad. They ate little children. And the beast of Gévaudan has left a very sad mythology. Fortunately, since Farley Mowat, wolves are friendly. The SPPNH, LDL, and BB[4] have shown that wolves and, of course, she-wolves are our greatest friends. You can stick out your tongue or your tail at them, they take the joke well. We even know some that are sentimental and fall in love with a sheep or a ewe, a shepherd or a shepherdess. However, concerning the story you are about to read, exegetes are wondering whether the dignified end is really moral. One must accept that everyone can have weaknesses, and that with the best intentions in the world it is sometimes difficult to determine if one is always politically correct. One may also regret that this story remained only heterosexual. One can imagine the whole dimension that the introduction of a gay Wolf and a lesbian grandmother might have taken. But we wanted to stay within the historical truth here.

Little Red Riding Hood's grandmother was a non-young person, in perfect physical and mental health but tired of living. "I am as wrinkled and withered as a pippin after winter," she moaned before her mirror. "And my poor legs can no longer carry me! I'm here, alone, unable to get up from my bed. And my head is not much better than my legs . . ." In seeking to console herself, she said she had barely one quality left, that of the non-young: virtue.

"I am ugly enough to frighten even a wolf!" But she immediately added that this reflection clearly showed the alienation of the working class, ignorant that beauty is not physical but moral. So she pulled herself together and laughed. She remembered the days when she looked after her sheep in the

---

*According to archival sources (*Bulletin des commissions scolaires canadiennes*, 1992, pp. 221–228, 251, 260; and 1993, pp. 511–577 and 584–906), the grandmother was quite a feminist. That's why she feminizes the name of her granddaughter, which, incidentally, seems much more natural. In the text itself, we have left the name *Petit Chaperon Rouge*, out of respect for the authentic older texts from which we have drawn (Charles Perrault, *Contes de Ma Mère l'Oye*, 1697; see also *Archives du folklore occitan*, corpus PP-HLO 69). Unfortunately, they are not always politically correct.

mountains. She was as pretty as a spring lamb and ran faster than all her sheep and faster too than all the little shepherds, whom some call more properly *sheep technicians*. Macho, like all men, they were always trying to catch her. Oh! occasionally, she let herself get caught! And the Wolf was jealous! She scolded him sharply, informing him that she could very well put in their place all the sexists who harassed her. It was pursuits, laughter, and cries to no end. The green grass had a nice smell of clover, sainfoin, and lavender. Her hair was always full of it. How good it was to collapse from fatigue and happiness on the slopes full of sunshine and fragrances!

And each time she stood up again, he was there, in a bush! She knew it. Through the leaves, you saw only his two eyes that shone like the devil's! Red like embers. She always had a delicious shiver of fear, because it was a male, and of desire that was unobjectionable since it was biologically conditioned.

He wasn't a wolf like the others. When you had seen him once, you couldn't stop thinking about him. A beautiful black coat, fine and silky, a coquettish lock on his forehead, and little pointed ears that he moved constantly. He had a long pink tongue that he passed back and forth over his wet chops with a look that spoke volumes about his male status as outlaw of non-animal people.

Little Red Riding Hood's grandmother turned in her bed with the memory of that beautiful Wolf of her youth, which made her sigh over the good old days. What had become of him? No doubt he was as chronologically advanced as she; perhaps he had even departed this world? At last he was at peace.

But that Wolf was very much alive. It was he who had met Little Red Riding Hood and had chatted with her in the wood. When Little Red Riding Hood had told him about her grandmother, his heart skipped a beat! Not possible! She was still alive, the one he watched through the foliage of the thickets and bushes. The one who he had often accompanied through the mountain, making sure that the little sheep technicians and the big wood technicians didn't see them. It was she who made him angry by pulling his ears or his tail! Ah! What a little devil, what a little hussy she was, he said to himself, while feeling guilty about this very non-PC comment. But he couldn't stop hearing her clear laugh that the echo bounced from rock to rock in the mountains. When she knew he was in the vicinity, she would begin to sing at the top of her voice:

Let's go for a walk in the woods
While the wolf is not there!
If the wolf was there, he would eat us.
But since he's not there, he won't eat us.
"Wolf are you there?"
"No."
"Do you hear?"
"Yes."
"What are you doing?"
"I'm putting on my socks!"

He was always afraid that someone would hear them or catch them playing. He answered anyway, but not too loud: "I am putting on my socks!" When he came to "I am putting on my cap!," as it was the last piece of his clothing, she knew she had to take to her heels and run! She also knew very well that he would catch up. All the pleasure was in this evasion. When they were sated with the shared secret happiness, they stayed for long periods without thinking about anything. Just feeling the grass, the ferns, and the moss, which scratched their backs. They forgot the time and the social condition that usually worried them.

The days had passed. She must have had a worldly end, marrying a wood technician, like all the village shepherdesses. He had remained taciturn and single, retreating into the solitary refuge of the deep woods, where reigned the peace and harmony that had enabled him to develop his own sexuality, free of Freudian complexes.

And now he found her again because he had strayed while going to eat wild *friboulines*, which contained the vitamin E required in the diet of non-young people. He had understood right away, while getting Little Red Riding Hood to talk, that fate had put him back on the trail of a grandmother like no other. A grandmother he had known well, as the Bible's sheep-minding technicians put it!

In short, he pulls the bobbin, the latch falls, and our two non-young are in one another's arms, with all their memories from before the rheumatism. They had a very long time to reminisce.

"Your neck is still as soft."

"You still smell as sweet."

"You still have your beautiful black eyes."

"And you, your big blue eyes."

Then she has the right impulse and tells him that she forgives his sexist, politically incorrect remarks, on account of his lupus genes, exacerbated by isolation and lack of a sympathetic female at his side.

"Do you still love me?" she said eventually.

He was expecting the question. It's funny, he thought, in a macho reaction presumably learned from men, this need that they all have to hear us repeat that we love them.

"You don't answer, you see," she sighed.

"But of course, I love you, doesn't it show?"

"So little!"

Annoyed, he replied in an angry tone:

"I love you, I love you!"

"Prove it to me."

The Wolf sighed in turn. She always had the same demands. She insisted. Faced with his silence, she explains. Now that they had met again, she wanted more than ever to disappear from the world because she suffered a great deal from rheumatism, arthritis, and gout, despite the countless remedies with which her doctors stuffed her. He understood. He, too, did not want aggressive treatment of prostate cancer in his case, when the end drew near.

"Help me to make an end of it," she pleaded.

He turned a deaf ear, being against euthanasia in spite of everything.

"So before I go," she said, "tell me words of love as in the past."

He grunts something that sounds like reticence.

"A little word of tenderness. Just one."

Then in an outburst, she throws herself on his neck, saying:

"Love me!"

As he remains silent, she goes on talking, resigned:

"At our age, what matters is tenderness, my pet."

His hair bristles from head to tail, and his teeth, which are still very sharp, gnash wickedly.

"In former days, you found me pretty. And now?"

"Still pretty," he said, more and more annoyed.

"How pretty?"

"Enough to eat!"

And right away, he makes short work of her. To ease the remorse of this moment of temper, he told himself that he had fulfilled her wish. She wanted him to help her die quickly and with dignity. It was done. Moreover, since psychoanalysts assure it, by devouring her he had given her the proof of the ultimate and supreme love. And then, rejustifying a metaphor, that really had style!

He gets up with difficulty, saying only in a whisper—for he had remained delicate—that she had been a little tough. To give himself a good conscience, he vows never again to devour anyone else. Not even Little Red Riding Hood, who must however be much more tender.

As he leaves the poor cottage, deeply moved by what had happened, our Wolf sees his grandson! They embrace, and the grandfather Wolf tells the story of the scene you know now. In her bed, Little Red Riding Hood's grandmother was fantasizing about her youth rather than about a cake which, anyway, would have been very bad for her last teeth. He doesn't mention the pot of butter. He cries a little relating the euthanasia scene.

But he whispers to his grandson:

"If the fancy takes you, go and take my place; I know someone who is coming and who will certainly not be sorry to meet you!"

And the non-young Wolf was full of emotion, because the non-old Wolf had shiny, red eyes like the devil's, a black coat, fine and silky, a nice lock on his forehead, little delicate, pointed ears that he moved constantly, and a long pink tongue with which he licked his chops greedily. We thought that he wouldn't be displeased if someone pulled his ears, nose, or tail!

As he returned to the depths of the forest, the grandfather Wolf cried in one eye over his friend, the poor grandmother, and laughed with the other, thinking about the sequel that you think you know and that is, however, not quite the real story.

But that's another story!

(To be continued.)

Layla and Me (Laylā wa-anā)[5]

HUDA AL-NAIMI

Huda al-Naimi (1969–) is a respected Qatari writer and academic who obtained a master's degree in nuclear physics and a doctorate in medical biophysics from Cairo University. She began to write while she was living in Cairo and published her first short-story collection, *al-Mukḥula* (The Kohl Flask) there in 1997. She later published two more short-story collections, *Unthā* (A Female, 1998) and *Abāṭīl* (Gossip and Prattle, 2001), as well as a book of literary criticism in Egypt. Her latest short-story collection, *Ḥāla tushbihunā* (A Situation Like Ours), was released in Qatar in 2011. On her return to Qatar in 2000, she became director of the safety department of the Hamad Medical Corporation in Doha. In addition to her career as a scientist, Al-Naimi plays a prominent role in the Qatari arts scene. In 2012 she served as a member of the jury for the International Prize for Arabic Fiction, which is the Arabic-language equivalent of the Booker.

Al-Naimi's retelling of the classic tale appears in her collection *Abāṭīl*. The story is narrated in the first person by Luma, and it is not until the final lines of the story that readers learn she has a cousin by the name of Layla, which is the traditional name of Little Red Riding Hood in Arabic versions of the tale. Although the story initially follows the plot of the traditional tale, it has been set in the globalized technological society that was radically transforming Middle Eastern nations on the threshold of the new millennium. As in many contemporary retellings, the forest has been replaced by an urban jungle, and the distractions along the path are no longer the natural pleasures of flowers and butterflies but the delights of manmade consumer goods.

The paradoxical juxtaposition of the modern metropolis and an ancient measure of distance (the *farsakh* in Arabic, from *parasang* in Persian, is approximately comparable to the European league) situates the modern tale in the ancient storytelling tradition. Like Iram Haq's Pakistani-Norwegian Riding Hood, Luma spends her time glued to the television. The role of technology is developed in the Qatari story, as the protagonist discovers the world of the internet and video games. The wolf takes the form of a technologically savvy, bearded tramp living behind a trash bin. The name the author gives the apparently homeless wolf seems to be an ironic play on words, as Hasīb means "respected" or "of noble birth," but it also has the same root (*h s b*) as the Arabic word for computer (*haasib*) and the verb that means "to compute." As the title vaguely suggests, the story casts two characters in the role of Little Red Riding Hood. The contemporary Qatari female writer presents two young, emancipated Arabic women who choose to run with the wolf. While the name Layla means "Night," Luma means "thick, deep red lips,"[6] a suitably sensual name for this Riding Hood. The two cousins become rivals for the wolf's affections. Like

Haq's Blinder Girl, Luma rejects traditions, abandoning mother and grand-mother, to embrace the future. However, Luma chooses to follow the wolf, whereas Blinder Girl rejects that temptation in favor of total independence.

The tale may seem somewhat enigmatic and difficult to follow for West-ern readers, due to cultural differences and storytelling techniques, but it is precisely those differences that make this Arabic retelling a unique and valu-able contribution to the anthology. The author also deliberately creates ambi-guity even for the Arabic reader. She turns the stereotypical role of the mother upside down by suggesting that she sends Luma to the grandmother's to get her out of the house so she can entertain her lover, but this is only suggested by innuendo.[7] The Qatari author cleverly plays with words and the ambiguity that is easily generated in the story's original language: Semitic languages do not use letters for vowels, thus the same consonants (or roots) can form dif-ferent words with multiple meanings. Unfortunately, such wordplay cannot be retained in the translation into English.

Layla and Me (2001)

I never asked my mother to stuff my mouth with food. But that's what she did. She made me chew it down. And so I did. She didn't stop shoving down the contents of the large jar even when I was on the verge of emptying the contents of my stomach. She circled the inside of the large jar with her right index finger. Then she put her finger into her wide mouth while fixing her sharp eyes on me: "That's the way to eat."

I wanted to return to my screen and life with the Fun-TV channel, which I adore. When the phone rang in the living room, my mother picked up the receiver. Her features erupted with joy and pleasure, and that wicked look van-ished from her eyes, which were splattered with scraps of food. She smiled at the phone, breaking into a loud guffaw that made her choke. "No," she whis-pered. A moment later she went on: "Why not?" and put down the receiver. Then she attacked my screen and closed it. She handed me a twenty-euro note, asking me to go to "Uncle Kentucky Fried Chicken" to buy pieces of their car-nivorous kind of chicken with the money. After that I was to take the food to Grandma, whose home is separated from ours by two leagues of neon jungle.

When I arrived at Grandmother's, I was to tell her that it was Mother herself who had prepared the fat chickens and that she had spent the entire day preparing the delicious drumsticks of which only dear Grandmother de-served the good taste. Mother told me that I shouldn't return home before nightfall, and if I wished to comfort Grandmother in her loneliness, I might as well spend the night there, and there would be no harm in that.

I'm not in a position to decline any of my mother's requests, since she is the one who possesses the euros. Once these colored notes have reached my pocket, I'll demand that she stop issuing orders, I'll plug the mouthpiece of her phone and stop its disgusting ring-tone.

I left home and put on the Cartier sunglasses that I'd pulled out of my mother's drawer while she was engaged with the task of freshening up the colors she used on her face. The sunglasses would fall down every time I lowered my head just a little. I put them back in place and continued to walk.

"Uncle Kentucky" always wears his red tarboosh with white stripes and is ever-smiling, not only at me but at everyone who comes to buy pieces of chicken for their grandmothers, who praise the mothers for their cleverness in preparing all kinds of dishes and are confident that the fathers are well cared for. "Uncle Kentucky" dropped a bag of chicken into my hand along with three euros, which would suffice to buy a large piece of tasty chocolate. I slipped out of the crowd with the precious three euros in my hand and strolled about the neon jungle, looking for the chocolate shop. But—as far as I could tell—the shop had moved, and in its place was an internet café. I entered the café and looked at the faces of its customers. I gave the man crouching at the entrance a half euro and climbed onto one of the chairs in front of the talking screens. It asked me what I wanted. It presented pictures of a variety of chocolates in different sizes, and I chose the largest and the prettiest. It asked: "Who will pay?" I answered: "My grandmother, who lives on the edge of the neon jungle, two leagues from our city." It told me that my order would be at Grandmother's before nightfall, thanked me, and turned dark again. I left the café without saying goodbye to the man who had received the half euro. Yet I was pleased because I still owned two and a half euros of the original sum. I had obtained chocolate at Grandmother's expense and would now be able to buy a cup of pistachio ice cream.

In the heart of the jungle stands the ice-cream vending machine. It is covered with the pictures and names of the varieties available. Just drop in one euro after the other, press the red button, and the requested cup of ice cream will slide down together with a plastic spoon inside an envelope upon which is written: "When you are finished, throw me and the empty cup into the garbage bin." "I know that," I told the spoon. But it didn't hear. The one who heard was he who suddenly appeared from behind the bin, in the jungle. He was big, his belly swollen, and his beard thick. But he wasn't frightening. His eyebrows were coarse. The only visible part of his face was his narrow eyes. I wasn't intimidated. His muscles were taught, his fingers fat, and the palm of his hand full. I didn't consider him anything special. He asked my name. I searched my memory for a warning from my mother about giving my name to strangers but didn't find one. "Luma," I answered. "I'm Hasib," he said, "the friend of the children."

I raised my eyebrows. His name had touched something in the storehouse of my memory. "You're Hasib, whom my mother detests and my grandmother prays will become an extinct species!"

"No, my pretty one, extinction is not for the likes of me, and it will not cause my death. I'm a global creature, and I exist in order to quench the thirst of the children with the water from the spring of the newborn millennium. As regards those yellow papers that request my extinction, that's because I didn't turn up on the day when she was carrying food, roasted on coals, to her grandmother. Since the date palm shook and the dates fell, I've been hiding in the belly of a blue whale that ate only what I ordered him to, swallowed no other ships besides those that I directed him to, drank only rivers that I liked to swim in, and opened his mouth for only as much sun as I needed. In the belly of the whale, I became friends with a white dove and a man who carried great books and a stick that couldn't drive away a fly. My friends told me that the belly of the whale was a safe haven. But the whale had a collision, while dreaming of a beautiful woman, and broke open, and we had to leave. The dove was received in Urshalim.[8] The man threw away his heavy books and went to where people manufacture ink to wash in it, and the stick became an armrest on a throne in an ancient sanctuary headed by the three men clad in turbans. I chose to create a toy that dances, talks, and prevents mothers who talk on the phone from ordering beautiful girls like you to return home—if they don't wish to. You deserve to acquaint yourself with my toy, which dwells with me at the top of the mountain. A game made especially for you is also waiting for you. If you wish to walk with me, I'll direct you to the place and show you the secrets of this fabulous game."

I remembered our neighbor, Yusuf, and his gnawed-off ears and blood-stained shirt. Perhaps Yusuf wasn't savvy about the game, and being bit on the ears was his lot? I put my hand over my ear and then my mother's words stirred: "All kinds of people grow in the jungle. You have to choose those who fill your needs."

Hasib owns a terrific game that I don't have and that isn't to be found anywhere on the vast internet. His house seems to be far away, and I'm exhausted today. The food that I'm carrying is getting cold, and Grandmother's bedtime is near. Besides, the tasty chocolate must have arrived by now, and I have to pick it up before Grandmother begins to crave it and eats it.

I answered Hasib that I wasn't interested in toys, that my grandmother was expecting me, and that I mustn't be late. Hasib wasn't concerned. He shrugged his shoulders and said: "The loss is yours," and went back to hide behind the garbage bin. It annoyed me that he didn't try to coax me to accompany him to discover the game. I followed him to his place. I saw him undo the buttons of his shirt, and I saw his chest, which was covered with thick hair exactly like his beard. He adjusted his pillow and yawned. I asked him about Yusuf, and he replied that he'd never heard the name before and added: "Let me sleep now."

I didn't disturb Hasib with my questions. I knew that the number of games he possessed was 99, that they had different names and worked in different ways, and that Fate placed lucky people in his way only when he was awake and in high spirits, so that he would teach them his secrets. He said that this was his sleeping place when he visits the jungle. Otherwise he never leaves his heights and his games.

I approached Hasib and touched his bare chest, and a peal like the ring of the school bell ran through my body. Hasib was a school in which hands were not struck by a cane and where a sign, on which was written "I am an ass," was not fastened to the back of the one who had not done his homework. There were no thorns on Hasib's shoulders, nor were there any sharp horns on his head. His cheeks were the color of the ice cream that had melted in my hand and perhaps had the same taste. Hasib didn't pay any attention to my nearness. He drew the cover over his head. Then I heard the sound of him sleeping, which was like when my mother filled glasses with drinks and kept me from going near them. I feared that the drink would be spilled and the ice cream would melt once again, so I withdrew a bit and then a bit more.

At Grandmother's house the wine terraces where I had climbed as a child had died, the doorbell wasn't working, the window glass had been shattered, and the cat would enter through it. Grandmother fed them with food from my mother and the wives of my paternal uncles.

I went in the same way as the cat and found Grandmother in front of the chess board, playing with my grandfather, who had died before the wine terraces and no longer moved the chessmen, so she would stand in for him.

Grandmother was surrounded by bags from Hardee's, McDonalds, Arby's, and others whose names I didn't read. She said that all her daughters and daughters-in-law had brought delicious food to her that day. But their children had kept them from staying for the night. She asked me if I would agree to play with her dressed in her old wedding gown.

I didn't wait for Grandmother to begin telling the story of how she met Grandfather when the Red Sea had been dug out on the order of the Sultan to prevent the Bedouins of the Arabian Peninsula from fooling around with his pyramids so that their guard became more fearsome. Grandmother related the story of how Grandfather had left a small piece of land to all the grandchildren in the city and the nearby towns for the people to work on, digging a narrow canal that would connect his sea with the sea of the Europeans. She would laugh when she told how people died on the banks of the canal whereas he—Grandfather—lived until the day that he danced with Aïda and sang her songs as he got drunk. Then he died.

This time Grandmother was unable to stir my curiosity with her tales about the pearl that Grandfather had planted in the waterbed before he permitted the surrounding waters to flow in. The stories about the pearl oysters and those who live inside did not expel Hasib from my imagination. Hasib could grab Alaska and use it to fill the crack that my grandfather had accomplished. I could ask Hasib to do that and he wouldn't hesitate. I chose to wave goodbye to Grandmother from a distance and didn't go to kiss her cheek or let her grasp my hand to read the lines of my palm.

I jumped out through the window the same way I had entered and proceeded, one step after another, to the neon jungle, with its steel bin at its heart and with the sleeping Hasib behind it in my heart. But Hasib's cover was on the ground without a living being under it! I was afraid that he had returned to his cave without my knowing his address. I let my eyes wander around the bin and the expanse of the jungle until I heard him grumbling and my cousin Layla laughing. Her red dress was shining in the sun. Her braids were let out, and her locks were flying over Hasib's face, which was covered with his beard. They were going westward. I know how selfish Layla is. She wants to monopolize the game. I won't let her.

I ran after them.

The Wolf and Little Red Riding Hood (Ulven og Rødhette)

ANNIE RIIS

Annie Riis (1927–) is a Norwegian writer, poet, and translator. Since the beginning of her career, she has been writing for adults, adolescents, and children. She debuted as a writer at the age of forty-eight with the poetry collection *Satura* in 1975. She has since published several poetry collections, as well as novels and children's books. Beginning in the 1970s, she contributed to the renewal of Norwegian children's literature with a range of books, most of which are illustrated. In 2001 she won Norway's prestigious Brage Prize in the open class for poetry with *Himmel av stål* (Heaven of Steel). Her work is influenced by Norwegian folklore, and she often uses folklore figures to subvert conventional gender roles. Riis published a very poetic, atmospheric retelling, "Ulven og Rødhette" (The Wolf and Little Red Riding Hood), in a short-story collection titled *Kom inn i min natt! Kom inn i min drøm* (Come into My Night! Come into My Dream!, 1992). Edited by Solveig Bøhle, the collection was based on the radio program Bøhle broadcast after midnight. Although the stories were not addressed to young readers, the hour at which they aired meant that their audience was made up largely of young adults. The contributors to the collection were asked to submit a short story or fairy tale about the feelings experienced in dreams.

Riis attributes her choice of this particular tale to the fact that she had recently read the Swedish translation of Bruno Bettelheim's *The Uses of Enchantment* and had been particularly impressed by his interpretation of "Little Red Riding Hood."[9] His influence is seen, for example, in Riis's treatment of the grandmother's role. Riis borrows from both literary and oral versions of the tale, but those borrowings are always subverted in a highly original manner. Hers is certainly not the first version to turn the Grimms' hunter into Riding Hood's lover, but that is after he rescues the Wolf from the girl's belly and leaves the grandmother to her fate. In imitation of her medieval predecessors, the girl throws her red cloak on the fire, but she does so of her own accord and only after eating the Wolf. Riis's feminist perspective on the tale is filled with evocative sensory images that create a very sensual atmosphere. This is established already in the short poem, signed with the author's initials, that constitutes a kind of lyrical prelude to her poetic "dream-story." The sensual eroticism and poetic nature of the text heightens the shocking, dramatic effect of the unexpected twist at the end.

Riis's retelling is an initiatory tale written in a very intimate first person by a young girl "between childhood and puberty" who is simultaneously "frightened by and attracted to this Don Juan in the shape of a Wolf." The description of the Wolf emphasizes his sexual attractiveness. A gray landscape is colored by her red cloak and the powerful presence of the charismatic Wolf.

The erotic scene is described rather naïvely through the eyes of the young girl. Fam Ekman illustrates this moment of sexual awakening in a caricatural illustration on the title page of the tale: an anthropomorphic wolf holds the young girl from behind and licks her cheek, as she smiles and gazes rather seductively up at him out of the corner of her very big eyes. After the ritualistic dialogue, Little Red Riding Hood seems initially to submit to the Wolf, undressing of her own accord and symbolically covering them with her red cloak. Riis retells the story of Little Red Riding Hood as a tale of sexual initiation. As the author puts it, the protagonist's encounter with the Wolf has prepared her "for an adult life with the Hunter." The apparently conventional happy ending is tongue in cheek, if we believe the author's rather ambiguous statement that "we can hope [it] will last as long as the fairy tale-dream!" Riis's blend of sensuality and irony is somewhat reminiscent of the writings of Angela Carter.

61. "Ulven og Rødhette," by Annie Riis. Illustrations by Fam Ekman. Copyright © 1992 Gyldendal Norsk Forlag. Used by permission of Fam Ekman and Gyldendal Norsk Forlag.

๛

The Wolf and Little Red Riding Hood (1992)

—WHAT IS THAT

THE REDNESS IN THE GREEN

—AM I DREAMING?

AN ALARMING WIND IN THE AIR.

SOMETHING ENTICES

TO A SORT OF WARMTH

—TO A SORT OF SOFTNESS

—TO A SORT OF NEARNESS

—TO WOLF NEARNESS

A.R.

I am standing at the stem of the flat-bottomed boat, with my grandmother's ruby-colored velvet cloak hanging loosely over my shoulders, punting my way slowly through the reeds. The river is hardly visible in between the grass straws. I have to feel my way forward with the oar.

It is bright without really being bright, dark without really being dark. Everything is empty of color, the gray hues are hard to distinguish from each other. Only my cloak is shining bright red. I have pulled the hood up over my head to protect myself, not against wind and weather, as it is quiet and mild, but against all the vaguely unknown that I cannot see, and that I perhaps am punting my way slowly through.

At my feet is the basket intended for Grandmother. The wine bottle stretches its neck above the tablecloth with which my mother has covered up the warm, fresh pancakes. Sweet wine, pancakes with honey, strawberry jam, old ladies have a sweet tooth.

Big, black birds graze my head in their flight; dragonflies crisscross about me in intricate embroidery patterns; large clouds of mosquitoes dip drowsily in the humid air; frogs croak like mad in the silence of the river.

The river bends lazily, the water is milky white and almost immobile, sliding down—sliding down—sliding down.

Far out in the mist I become aware of the shadow of tall trees, like a wall above the water. The river grows deeper, broader, the reeds disappear; I can no longer touch the bottom with my oar. I squat and let the boat follow the imperceptible current.

I do not understand where I am until I discover the little landing pier. From here I will have to walk. It is still far to go to Grandma's house, through the forest. I am not scared, though. I am a big girl now, and I know how to get there. I make fast the boat, pull the cloak tight about me, grab the basket, and find the path under the enormous oak trees.

It is even darker here among the huge trunks of the trees. I hardly sense the light from the tiny lilies of the valley on either side of the footpath, but the odor makes me dizzy, and I do not know exactly who I am anymore.

I do not see him until he is standing right in front of me, where the broad and the narrow, rugged paths meet. At first I notice only two yellowish, green-ish luminous points, two peculiar eyes, staring right into mine for a fraction of a second before they yield. Then I see the big, pointed head, the resilient body, the four paws, always on the alert, and the long, wagging tail. It is the Wolf I meet.

Then I hear his voice, sweet like the honey in my basket:

"Where are you going, Little Red Riding Hood?"

"To Grandmother's," I whisper.

"And where does she live then?"

"Oh, far, far away along the rugged, narrow path."

"If I were you, I would rather take the other way; have you seen the beau-tiful lilies growing there? You are more beautiful, though, than all of them, Red Riding Hood. Come here and sit down to get some rest!"

Then he sinks down on the grass, and now I see the ground he is sitting on turning shiny green, and wonderful red, yellow, and blue flowers pop up every-where. The sunbeams fall through the foliage, and high above the blue patches of the sky sparkle between the leaves. I cannot but sit down beside the Wolf.

He puts one of his front paws into my lap. It is covered with soft fur, but I feel the strong muscles under the gold and gray hair. Never before have I met anything so wonderfully soft, so wonderfully strong. The pointed, black snout, wet and smooth, the warm breath, the red, swollen, long tongue ap-proaching my throat. My hood has fallen off my shoulders, the red cloak em-braces us in the grass.

I feel the warm tongue licking the skin of my throat, my cheeks, search-ing for my mouth. The lilies of the valley—the odor, the defenselessness.

Then suddenly he retreats a little, lifting the huge head as if scenting out a danger.

"Woodcutters," he says, in a sharp and different voice. And then I notice the terrible, pointed canine teeth, saliva running from the half-open throat, and the sharply pointed claws that he tries to hide in his paws. He shakes his shoulders, straightens himself up.

"And this grandmother of yours, where does she live, did you say? That way?" He is pointing with his snout, and I nod. In the twinkling of an eye, he has jumped between the tree trunks.

And I am left alone. However, Grandmother is certainly not afraid of Wolves, I think to myself. She has certainly met all the Wolves there are in the world, considering how long she has lived. She surely knows how to deal with them.

Then I take my cloak and the basket and struggle on all day long down the bends of the path. The twigs tear at me and the thorns clutch me, but when it gets dark, I am finally there in front of Grandmother's house, knocking at the door.

And Grandmother is shouting: "Who is it?" The voice is so peculiar.

When I enter, I see that she is in bed, being even more peculiar than her voice, so I say:

"What big ears you have, Grandmother."

"All the better to hear you with."

"What big eyes you have, Grandmother."

"All the better to see you with."

"What big hands you have, Grandmother."

"All the better to hug you with."

"What a big mouth you have, Grandmother."

"All the better to eat you with!"

Only then did I realize that Grandmother was gone, and that it was the Wolf that was lying in the bed. I undressed, lay down beside him in the bed, and covered us both with the red cloak.

However, when the big, warm, and wet tongue came near me, it took me only a second to devour his tongue, his head, and the whole big Wolf in one great gulp!

The Wolf was inside me, and I threw Grandmother's red cloak on the fire, crept back into the bed, and fell asleep, because I was so tired.

When the brave hunter came by, I was still asleep. He understood, though, that I had the Wolf inside me, took out his big, sharp knife, ripped open my stomach, and pulled out the Wolf. The Wolf crept out of me and slunk away between the bushes, his tail between his legs and with Grandmother still in his stomach.

However, Little Red Riding Hood and the hunter drank their toast in sweet wine and lived happily ever after.

Mina, I Love You
(Mina, je t'aime)

Patricia Joiret and Xavier Bruyère

Patricia Joiret is a French children's author. She offers an ambiguous and disturbing reversal of the classic Riding Hood tale in the picturebook *Mina, je t'aime* (Mina, I Love You), published for young readers in 1991. The picturebook is illustrated by the Belgian illustrator Xavier Bruyère (1965–), whose predilection for opaque techniques (pastels, gouache, and alkyds) lends itself well to this equivocal, troubling story (plate 33). It was the ambiguity of this "slightly perverse reversal" of the classic tale that initially interested the illustrator when he read the text.[10] Joiret dedicates her story of a bold, self-assured, but ultimately callous protagonist to "all the little 'Minas' who lie dormant in all the little girls of yesterday, today . . . and tomorrow I hope." In seeking to waken all the Little Riding Hoods who have been repressed for centuries by the dominant male discourse of the classic tale, Joiret gives her tale a disturbing feminist slant. The passive, innocent, victimized image of Little Red Riding Hood is counterbalanced by a heroine who, contrary to appearances, is not a victim of three would-be wolves but rather a predatory wolf-girl, thus subversively turning the story into a cautionary tale for boys.

Many motifs of oral and literary versions of the tale are retained (the path of needles, the undressing scene, even a vague reference to woodcutters), but their function and position are often radically transformed. The story is given a modern setting (certain details evoke the late 1960s or early 1970s), but it is unobtrusive and does not disrupt the timeless, fairy-tale atmosphere. Joiret also preserves the traditional tripartite structure in the three encounter scenes and the three love notes. The subtle sensuousness of the text is enhanced by the Mediterranean-like setting and the illustrations' bold, vivid colors, reminiscent of the Fauvist school. The result is a very sensual and aesthetically beautiful picturebook that renders the violent ending particularly shocking. From the initial spread of the girl standing in front of a mirror in a red shirt and underpants, the illustrator subtly develops the duality of a girl who is at once girl and wolf. Mirrors and reflections are a leitmotif throughout the illustrations. The mirror motif is taken up in the striking layout of the picturebook, in which a narrow, vertical fragment of the full-page spread on the recto is repeated, like a reflection, on the outer edge of the text on the verso. Bruyère, who favors luminous climes, also plays skillfully with light and shadow to emphasize the duality theme and heighten the mysterious atmosphere of the story. Interiors are dark, and figures are often vague shadows. Madame Wolf appears only as a partial, dark shadow in the doorway and on the floor of the kitchen. The boys' faces are never seen clearly, and Carmina's admirers are generally only three shadowy figures depicted against the light. On the final spread, the grandmother she-wolf, who is clearly visible to Carmina and the three terrified boys on the doorstep, is seen by readers as only a dark shadow behind a curtain.

The mysterious nature of this little girl is adroitly maintained throughout the story by both the author and the illustrator. The protagonist is often portrayed from the back, and in numerous illustrations her face remains a vague image reflected in a mirror or in water, or, more often, it is completely hidden. Numerous clues to Carmina's true identity are sprinkled throughout both the text and the illustrations, but it may be only on the last spread that many readers realize that the little redhead is a dangerous seductress whose name evokes the fiery gypsy Carmen from Georges Bizet's celebrated opera. (She is only "Mina" to her friends.) Bruyère's sensual portrait of a rather mature-looking Riding Hood (with red nails, red lipstick, and long, red hair flowing erotically over her shoulders)—who lounges seductively on a divan in a scene modeled after Titian's *Venus of Urbino* before she leaves for her she-wolf grandmother's with a basket laden with carnivorous treats—should, however, alert readers to her true nature.

The same can be said of the terms Joiret uses to describe the protagonist early in the story. While the wolf metaphor of the protagonist descending the stairs "à pas de loup" is lost in the English translation, another is added when she "wolfs down" (the French term is *engloutir*) her breakfast. Animal metaphors are used ironically to describe the three naïve and inept seducers who are lured to the she-wolf grandmother's by the lovely but predatory Mina, the object of their puppy love (plate 34). The ambiguity is adroitly maintained even on the final page, when readers of all ages discover the wolf identity of a little girl whose complete name, Carmina Wolf, casts her in the dual role of Little Red Riding Hood and the wolf.

❧

MINA, I LOVE YOU (1991)

Carmina had just jumped out of bed when her mom called her:

"Mina, hurry and get up, your grandmother just called, she sprained her ankle and she . . ."

The rest of the sentence is lost in the "bloub bloub" made by Carmina, who blows in the pitcher filled with cold water to freshen up. She blinks in front of the mirror, puffs out her carmine cheeks, wrinkles her nose, showing little sharp fangs, shakes her tawny mane, stretches one by one her long limbs numb with sleep, then goes down the stairs stealthily.

"Boo!" shouts Carmina, seizing her mother by the waist.

"Aaaah!" screams the latter, dropping the bottle of milk that spreads over the kitchen linoleum, to the delight of Cric and Crac, the Siamese cats.

"That's no way to behave, Mina," smiles her mother, "no time to dawdle this morning, swallow your breakfast quickly. You'll keep your grandmother company all day, and I'll come get you this evening." Carmina smiles, she adores her grandmother.

"Will you be able to take her this large basket? I'm afraid of having over-loaded it!"

"No problem, Mom," says Carmina, wolfing down her boiled egg.

"I'm off," shouts Mrs. Wolf, seizing her raincoat, her car keys, and her nurse's kit.

Carmina, once alone, weighs the basket: it's true that it's awfully heavy! She bites a nail till the blood comes, pensive . . . What to wear for a day with Gran? From the dresser drawer, she takes out her red tights and large sweatshirt of the same color that she wears as a mini-skirt. She brushes her long red hair that bounces with each movement. She is ready.

"Let's take advantage of Mom's absence to color my little bitten finger-nails bright vermilion."

Carmina blows on her nails to dry the sticky polish.

Outside, the fog is lifting, the sun is shining.

The day will be beautiful. Carmina tucks a pair of heart-shaped sun-glasses in the kangaroo pocket of her sweatshirt.

She leaves the house with the handle of the large, bulbous basket on her left arm and locks the door. A quick glance around. Nothing. So she hides the key in the large pot of geraniums. At that moment a little round pebble wrapped in a piece of paper comes rolling to her feet.

Mina, I love you. Edouard

Carmina, who read the message on the crumpled paper in a low voice, looks angrily at the rustling privet branches.

"Edouard! Come out of there, pighead!" she shouts, furious.

His face cracked in a grin and his hair tousled, Edouard springs out of the foliage. With one hand then the other, he sends resounding kisses in the direction of Carmina who, very dignified, takes her basket again and goes off with a jog-trot in the direction of the woods.

"Where are you going, pretty Mina, darling Mina? Can I carry your basket?"

"No way, get lost, go back behind your counter."

Edouard is the son of a merchant of souvenirs, candy, tobacco, and cigars, who is located in the village square. He always has his pockets bulging with sweets, which he never fails to share in spite of his father's reprimands.

Haughty, her torso straight, but her little behind dancing, Carmina takes the Poachers' Trail that will take her, after multiple meanders, to her grand-mother's cottage.

Sheepishly, Edouard watches her: a luminous, small, red dot that dazzles him and accelerates the beating of his heart.

The morning air puts color into Carmina's cheeks. The chattering of magpies accompanies her step. From time to time, on the left or the right, there is a furtive cracking sound, but nothing slows the girl's pace.

About ten o'clock, the sun is already high in the sky, and Carmina is hot. Everything rustles, everything stirs around her. She knows that she can cool off on the bank of the Nébleu, a small stream that meanders on the edge of the forest.

She deposits her heavy basket on a tuft of grass, undoes the laces of her slippers, nimbly unrolls her tights down her long legs, and soaks her little white feet in the pure water with sheer delight. At that moment a thud makes her jump. A ball of cloth has just hit the basket.

Carmina comes out of the water, seizes the handkerchief held by an elastic band around the stone, opens it, and reads:

Mina, I love you. Adrien

Summer and winter, Adrien, the pharmacist's only son, always looks superbly healthy, thanks to the "healthy-look" vitamins that he doesn't stop swallowing.

Carmina shrugs her shoulders, tucks the handkerchief-message into her pocket next to a little ball of paper, and slowly she starts slipping back into her tights. Before embarking on the crossing of the silent forest, she swallows a slice of *cramique*.[11] Then she energetically stands up and heaves, and, the basket properly secured on her arm, she continues walking.

Pressed against the bark of a birch, Adrien, simpering, follows her with his myopic gaze . . . until she is only a small, red moving spot with vague outlines.

The invigorating smell of the forest makes Carmina's nostrils quiver, and her tennis shoes crush the carpet of brown needles with a muted sound. The two noisy screeching jays briefly trouble her steady progress between the dark and hairy trunks of the fir trees.

A clearing: it's the clearing of the woodcutters. It is empty for the moment, and Carmina sits down on a large, dead tree. She stretches her long arms toward the blue sky and yawns lazily. At that moment a small rocket of pink paper terminates its graceful trajectory on her knees.

Mina, I love you. Hervé

The sentence stands out in red capital letters on the side of the rocket. Carmina stands up and turns around. A suppressed laugh directs her to the lowest branch of a large oak.

Perched astride like a knight on his fiery steed, Hervé, the pork butcher's son, smiles like a nice pork's head in his father's shop window.

Carmina purses her lips, briskly picks up her basket, then crosses the clearing with long strides.

"Wait, wait, don't leave so quickly," shouts the strange bird, who tries clumsily to climb down from his tree.

But Carmina walks faster, and at the first strike of the twelve hours marked by the village clock, her grandmother's cottage is in sight.

A little out of breath from her long walk, she hammers on the heavy dark door.

"Gran, Gran, it's me, open . . ."

"It isn't bolted, my darling, push the door, come in quickly."

Carmina pushes with all her might, and the heavy door opens, creaking plaintively.

Inside it is dark. However, the girl distinguishes the long table of the dining room and puts her basket on it.

In a corner of the room, wrapped in the lambskins, Carmina sees a form stretched out that is trying to get up.

"Don't move, Gran, look at everything that I've brought you . . ."

And proudly she enumerates: three pigs' feet, a smoked ham, two beef tongues . . .

Gran's eyes sparkle, her whiskers quiver . . .

"And three nice, fat boys for dessert!" exclaims Carmina, opening the door wide.

On the threshold and too surprised to be terrified yet, Edouard, Adrien, and Hervé see appear in the middle of the lamb furs the enormous jaws of a gray she-wolf who is licking her chops.

End

My Red Riding Hood (Mon Chaperon Rouge)

ANNE IKHLEF AND ALAIN GAUTHIER

Anne Ikhlef is a French writer, journalist, scriptwriter, and filmmaker. She has long had an interest in folk and fairy tales. In 1985 she retold the story of Little Red Riding Hood in a short film titled *La vraie histoire du Chaperon Rouge* (The True Story of Red Riding Hood), which was presented at the Cannes Film Festival. Her approach was to return to the tale's medieval sources, researching the different variants. The film was largely inspired by the ribald and grisly tale collected in Nièvre, known as "Conte de la mère-grand" (Story of Grandmother). The role of Little Red Riding Hood was played by a five-year-old actress, Justine Bayard, and the wolf was played by the actor Didier Sandre in a daring and provocative interpretation that casts the tale in the disturbing light of pedophilia. Ikhlef wanted to reintroduce the sensuality of the tale and deliberately chose Sandre for his seductive qualities. The young Bayard played her role, which included a lengthy nude scene, with both sensuality and tenderness, a depth of emotion surprising in a five-year-old.

Ikhlef's first picturebook, *Mon Chaperon Rouge* (My Red Riding Hood), which was not published until 1998, is based on the earlier film. Despite the years that had passed between the two works and the very different medium, they are hauntingly similar. The picturebook also creates an intimate atmosphere in which the ageless relationship between Riding Hood and the wolf is evoked in all its violence, sensuality, and tenderness. At the same time, the illustrations by Alain Gauthier (1931–) heighten the oneirism of the text and bring a surrealist, modern touch to the mythical content. Gauthier, an internationally renowned poster artist, turned to illustration later in his career, and his very refined work for children's books bears the mark of his poster art. Many critics feel his sophisticated illustrations appeal more to adults than to children. Published by Seuil Jeunesse for children ages six years and up, the provocative, sophisticated picturebook is often considered more suitable for adolescents and adults. In 2002 Ikhlef and Gauthier collaborated on a second picturebook, *Ma Peau d'Âne*, a similarly intimate retelling of "Donkeyskin." Their recasting of Perrault's tale about incest is targeted this time at readers nine years of age and up, although critics agree that it is more appropriate for older readers. Gauthier's large acrylic paintings need the very large format of these two picturebooks to do them justice.

Gauthier's unique surreal, abstract, oneiric style, with its sensual colors, is a perfect complement to Ikhlef's poetic, sensual retelling, which explores the profound initiatory and psychological elements of the tale. Gauthier works in a very instinctive manner, refusing to analyze his fantasies; however the author and illustrator did discuss the story, and there is a very intimate relationship between image and text. In this memorable picturebook, Ikhlef and Gauthier offer an erotic, nocturnal version of the tale that is powerful and disturbing. The poetic text is organized in "verses" of varying length, some as short as a single line, and this grouping of lines has been retained for the most part in the translation that follows. (The rhyme that occurs in some lines could not always be retained in the English translation.)

Ikhlef's evocative language includes archaic phrases and figurative expressions that increase the powerful impact of the text; for example, when Red Riding Hood puts her hand into the wolf's jaws, the words are charged with the figurative meaning of the French expression "se mettre dans la gueule du loup" (to throw oneself into the wolf's jaws). The rich, multilayered, enigmatic text constitutes a complex dialogue with folkloric and literary traditions that is reminiscent of the work of Angela Carter, who also revised the tale in both film and prose. Fragments of both literary and oral tales, as well as nursery rhymes, counting rhymes, riddles, and songs, are woven throughout the poetic tale. An excerpt from Perrault's version is written in an embedded book that takes the form of the cradle in which Red Riding Hood listens as the mother tells her the story with the ancient origins. The numerous detailed allusions to pre-literary versions (the path of needles, the cannibalistic scene, the ritualistic striptease, and the scatological ending) are borrowed from many different variants and can be fully appreciated only by cultured readers with some knowledge of the rich oral tradition. The contrast between these archaic elements of the text and Gauthier's surrealistic images, which are sprinkled with modern motifs (the wolf's business suit and his enormous, black automobile), creates an anachronism that heightens the timelessness of the tale. Symbolic, dreamlike visions emphasize the oneirism of the story, as in the enigmatic illustration of a decapitated Red Riding Hood, who seems to have been punished for her unwitting act of cannibalism.

Ikhlef and Gauthier explore the complex and ambiguous relationship between the little girl in red and the wolf, who, as the cover illustration clearly demonstrates, constitute an indissoluble couple (plate 35). Red Riding Hood is one of Gauthier's recognizable doll-like chalk figures, a sister to his Alice or his Belle. Red Riding Hood and the wolf are both complex, multifaceted characters cast in a variety of conflicting roles, effectively exploding the stereotypical images of the classic fairy-tale characters. The wolf's dark, angular shapes contrast sharply with the bright, rounded, soft shapes of the girl, but that does not prevent a complete role reversal in certain scenes. Riding Hood wears a wolf mask in one scene, casts a huge diabolical shadow in another, becomes the temptress Eve, and assumes the role of the seducer as she shrugs one shoulder out of her red dress in the ritualistic striptease while smiling seductively at the man-wolf who watches voyeuristically. She is also the young, naïve, innocent peasant girl, a victim of a sophisticated, urban wolf, and an object manipulated by the wolf (a Red Riding Hood cello played by a Picasso-like wolf). She becomes, in turn, the courageous heroine of the oral versions, saving herself by impaling the wolf, and a serene young girl who sleeps peacefully on the wolf's back. The wolf is also ever shifting. Both Ikhlef and Gauthier emphasize the theme of the man-wolf. The title page presents a striking series of images that trace the metamorphosis from wolf to man or man to wolf, depending on the direction they are read. The wolf is alternately animal, human, or a hybrid creature. The mask, which is a recurring image in all of Gauthier's work, is used with particular skill in this book to blur the borders between human and animal, Riding Hood and wolf. In his illustrations, masks are "the real faces," serving not "to hide what one is, but to show it."[12]

Like the oral versions from which Ikhlef borrows so heavily, this tale is an initiatory story. This is clearly indicated already on the dark, mysterious endpapers, which depict the tiny figure of Red Riding Hood climbing a monumental staircase between two enigmatic stone wolf-sphinxes, toward a temple of dark columns that resemble the tubular trees of Gauthier's forests. On the final page of the story, the protagonist's enigmatic, sphinx-like smile reveals that she is now in possession of some secret knowledge. Ikhlef and Gauthier portray the awakening sexual desires of the prepubescent Riding Hood. (Although she is depicted as much older than the actress in the film, she is still flat-chested.) The mixed sentiments of attraction and fear that the adolescent heroine feels with regard to sex and its metaphor, the wolf, are conveyed in both the text and the images. Certain scenes have a disturbing eroticism, in particular the striptease and the later bed scene that depicts a nude Red Riding Hood lying on top of the wolf, their eyes locked in a powerful gaze. These scenes are presented as erotic spectacles with a theatrical setting, and readers become complicit spectators, sharing the voyeuristic perspective of the wolf. The theme of sexuality is associated with mythical and religious motifs of hell and the fall from paradise. The age-old struggle between good and evil is expressed in the popular terms of children's games. The ambiguous open ending of the tale does not tell readers whether Riding Hoods who run with wolves end up in heaven or hell (plate 36).

MY RED RIDING HOOD (1998)

Are we stone?
Are we earth?
Are we wind?
Are we blood?

Turn, turn, turn moon!
"What goes around the earth?
It's the moon! It's the moon!"

A village child curled up between
two huge gray rocks
dreams of the moon which says to her:

"On the earth there is everything!
children with soft hair
but also wolf calls!"

Not far from there, a shadow from the woods—
Is it a man?
Is it an animal?
rolls about in the wind and blows
into pan pipes.

"Are we trunks
Long foliage?
Dust
Or roots of flesh?"

The child stood up and began
to climb on a silver rock.
The child lay down and caressed the worn stone.

The man wolf howls at the moon and
becomes a werewolf.

Turn, turn, turn moon!

The wind passes through the nocturnal forest
and murmurs in the brown leaves:

"What is dead
and still dances?"

The leaves whirl round and say:

"We leaves, we still dance!"

The clever wind plays in the foliage:

"What speaks without a mouth
runs without legs
strikes without hands
and passes unseen?"

Laughing, it answers:
"It is I the wind!
It is I the wind!"

And the child walking along under
the giant oaks
lifts her head and sees in the firmament
diamond rocks.
Up there, very, very high thousands
of crystals sparkle.
Down there, at the very bottom
a large bonfire burns!

"And my wooden clogs tap!

My head thinks
My eyes dance!

My head thinks
My two feet advance

My head thinks
My two arms soar

And my head thinks
I am an animal!"

Behind the closed door, the child
has left her hay-stuffed clogs,
then comes near the fire:

"It's in the blue flames
that the devil
is wide-eyed!"

Then on the hard-packed ground, she taps with
her two bare feet:

"Black eyes will go to purgatory!
Blue eyes will go to heaven!
Gray eyes will go to paradise!
Green eyes will go to hell!"

And believing she sees the devil, she repeats:
"Green eyes will go to hell!"

The mother took the child in her arms:

"It's late, come to bed!"

The child lay down against
her mother's tummy:

"Mommy, tell me a story!"

"Very quietly, very quietly
As you fall asleep, listen to the wind

A tale is more than a thousand years old
Everything you hear
Is not only for children
A tale comes from afar
From the most ancient times

And everything that is said there
Is only one of the pages
Of the great book that is life!"

"Once upon a time there was . . .
A little village girl
the prettiest that ever was seen!
Her mother doted on her and her grandmother
even more!
This good woman made her a little
red hood."

The child fell asleep and dreams:
she is Little Red Riding Hood.

"Go see how your grandmother is
I have heard that she is very sick!"
In her basket, the little girl put a
cake, a round loaf of bread, and a little pot
of butter. Then tying her red
hood, she goes out into the wind.

"To go to grandmother's,
you must go through forest and field!"

Turn, turn, turn sun!

A tiny forest
an immense blade of grass
the whole earth turned upside down
frayed clouds
and dewdrops . . .
The child picks flowers
by the thousand.

Turn, turn, turn sun!

Who is going to win?
Light or darkness?

God or devil?

"And my wooden clogs hop!
God's feet!
the devil's feet!
god's fingers!
the devil's fingers!
god! devil! god! devil!"

Little Red Riding Hood
goes into the dark woods and walks
amidst the shadows.

Suddenly at the crossroads of two paths
she sees the wolf:

"Where are you going?"

"I am taking a hot
cake to Grandmama!"
"Which path are you taking?
The path of pins or the path of
needles?"
"I prefer the path of
pins with which you can
adorn yourself rather than the path of
needles with which you must
work!"

While the little girl lingers gathering
needles with large holes for her grandmama,
the wolf takes the shorter path.

He arrives first at the grandmother's.
He kills her, puts some of her flesh in the pantry
and some of her blood in a bottle.

The sun has turned,
it has set in the cypresses
and the darkness has won.

To reassure herself the child counts
on her fingers:
"This one (the thumb) saw her
This one (the forefinger, index finger) killed her
This one (the middle finger) cooked her
This one (the ring finger) drank her blood
This one (the little finger) ate her all up,
all up, all up!"

The wolf finishes swallowing the rest of the
grandmother and slips as quickly as possible
into her bed.

Sated, he crosses his hands
on his belly and says:

"When will we be good?
Never . . . never . . . never!
When will we be devils?
Always . . . always . . . always!

The earth nourishes all
the madmen with the madwomen
the earth feeds everything
the madwomen with the madmen!"

Rat-Tat-Tat

To the child who knocks on the door
the wolf answers:
"Pull the bobbin
the latch will fall
the door will open!"
The door groans.
"How are you Grandmama?"
The wolf answers her with a disguised voice:

"No better, no better!
Are you hungry?"
"Yes, I'm hungry! Is there something
to eat?"
"Take some of the meat that is in
the pantry, and a bottle of wine on the shelf."

She pours the blood from the bottle
on the meat in a cauldron.
As she gets ready to eat
she hears:
"Fry fricassee
the blood of your big old hussy
fry fricassee
the blood of your slut of a granny!"

The birds in the cage chirp:

"Rintintin, you are eating the flesh
of your grandmama and you are drinking her blood!"

"What is that bird saying Grandmama?"

"It isn't saying anything, keep eating,
it has time to sing!"

While the child eats and drinks
and the cat under the alcove watches her closely,
the wolf repeats:
"Throw your clog at it my beauty!
Throw your clog at it!

Throw your cap at it my beauty!
Throw your cap at it!"

When she has eaten and drunk,
The wolf says to her:
"Come and lie down my little one . . .
Come and lie down close to me,
I have cold feet, you will warm me!"

"I'm coming! I'm coming!"

The wolf doesn't take his eyes off her!
"Undress, my child!"

The child removes her garments one at a time:
"Where should I put my apron?"

"Throw it in the fire, you won't be needing it anymore!"

"Where should I put my bodice?"

"Throw it in the fire, you won't be needing it anymore!"

"Where should I put my stockings?"

"Throw them in the fire, you won't be needing them anymore!"

"And my skirt?"

"Throw it! Throw it in the fire, you won't be needing it anymore!"

The child jumps onto the bed and
stares at the wolf's black
jaws. She shivers!

"What big eyes you have!"

"The better to see you with, my
child! The better to see you with!"

Then she lets herself slide onto the
dark body:

"Oh, Granny, how hairy you are!"

"It's from old age, my child!
It's from old age!"

"What big arms you have!"

"The better to embrace you with, my child!
The better to embrace you with!"

"What big legs you have!"

"The better to run with, my child!
The better to run with!"

The child sits up suddenly and
puts her hand in the wolf's jaws:

"What big teeth you have!"

"The better to eat you with!"

The child is very afraid and cries out:

"Oh, Granny, I need to go outside!"
The wolf ties a woolen string
to her foot and lets her go out. Then not seeing her
return, he asks her:

"Are you making a load?
Are you making a load?"

Without answering, she grabs a stake
that she brandishes at the wolf. With all
her might, she drives it into
his jaws! And looking him straight in the eyes
she tells him:

"Deliver yourself!
Deliver yourself!"

"Can a wolf
thus wounded
come back to life?"

Turn, turn, turn night!

She falls into the dark
gaze of the wolf:

"I'm afraid!
I'm afraid! I'm afraid!
so black! so dark so black!
I'm afraid! I'm afraid! I'm afraid! I'm afraid!
so black! so dark! I'm afraid! I'm afraid! I'm afraid!"

Turn,
turn, turn night!

Sun! Earth! Moon!
Each his counterpart!
Water! Light! Stars
Heat up the stove!

Turn, turn, turn night!
The stars are on him
On the black fleece of the wolf
the child has fallen asleep.

Can a wolf thus caressed
still be hungry
when the story has ended?

Rat-Tat-Tat
The wind knocks on the earth
Rat-Tat-Tat
It is so black and so bright
Rat-Tat-Tat
The wolf blinks his eyelids
Rat-Tat-Tat
Is there lightning?
Rat-Tat-Tat
Is there thunder?

No! No! No!
It's the devil
in hell!

The door has given way
The devil has entered
The child has looked at him

Is it hell or heaven?

And she smiles at him!

Notes

Introduction

1. Sandra L. Beckett, *Recycling Red Riding Hood* (New York: Routledge, 2002); Sandra L. Beckett, *Red Riding Hood for All Ages: A Fairy-Tale Icon in Cross-Cultural Contexts* (Detroit: Wayne State University Press, 2008).

2. Rodari's tale had appeared, under this same title, in the children's magazine *Cricket* in 1973.

3. See, for example, Francisco Vaz da Silva, "Review of *Red Riding Hood for All Ages: A Fairy-Tale Icon in Cross-Cultural Contexts*, by Sandra L. Beckett," *Folklore* 121, no. 2 (August 2010): 238–239.

4. Jack Zipes, *The Trials and Tribulations of Little Red Riding Hood: Versions of the Tale in Sociocultural Context*, 2nd ed. (New York: Routledge, 1993), xi.

5. Jane Yolen, "Happy Dens, or A Day in the Old Wolves Home," in *Dragonfield and Other Stories* (London: Futura, 1985): 186.

6. Beckett, *Recycling Red Riding Hood*, xviii.

7. Sandra L. Beckett, "Le Petit Chaperon rouge globe-trotter," in *Tricentenaire Charles Perrault: Les grands contes du XVIIe siècle et leur fortune littéraire*, ed. Jean Perrot (Paris: In Press, 1998), 365–375.

8. Jack Zipes, *Sticks and Stones: The Troublesome Success of Children's Literature from Slovenly Peter to Harry Potter* (New York: Routledge, 2001), 109.

1. Cautionary Tales for Modern Riding Hoods

1. Gabriela Mistral, *Selected Poems of Gabriela Mistral*, trans. and ed. Doris Dana (Baltimore: Johns Hopkins Press, 1971), 40.

2. Gabriela Mistral, *Selected Poems of Gabriela Mistral*, trans. Ursula K. Le Guin (Albuquerque: University of New Mexico, 2003), 55. It was not always possible to reproduce the meter, rhythm, and rhyme of the original in the poems translated in this anthology.

3. Francisco Villaespesa, *Poesias Completas*, compiled by Frederico de Mendizabal, 2 vols. (Madrid: Aguilar, S.A. de Ediciones: 1954).

4. Letter from Wim Hofman, May 26, 2000.

5. Aukje Holtrop, "'Things Never Work Out for Snow White': Wim Hofman's Fairy Tales" (interview with Wim Hofman), *Vrij Nederland* (May 17, 1997).

6. In the Netherlands, a cord was sometimes passed through the letterbox so that people could open the door by simply pulling the cord—a simple mechanism that facilitated entry for children. E-mail from Wim Hofman, October 23, 2011.

7. The Dutch expression used is "met huid en haar," literally "with skin and hair."

8. In Japan, a woman with a child is addressed in this manner.

9. Clément has a similar passion for the combination of text and music. She created the company Auteurs-en-Scène (Authors-on-Stage) to adapt some of her works into "contes-concerts" (tale-concerts), which appeal equally to adults and children.

10. Letter from Isabelle Forestier, October 5, 2003.

11. The medieval-sounding name has a transparent symbolism, as Cité des Bergeries means "Sheepfolds City," implying that its inhabitants are innocent prey for the wolf that lurks in the nearby woods.

12. E-mail from Mia Sim, June 4, 2012. Subsequent comments by the author are taken from this e-mail.

13. E-mail from Joanna Olech, April 30, 2012.

14. E-mail from Grażka Lange, May 15, 2012.

15. E-mail from Grażka Lange, May 12, 2012. Unless otherwise indicated, subsequent comments by the illustrator are taken from this e-mail.

16. E-mail from Grażka Lange, May 15, 2012.

17. The expression "za górami, za lasami," literally "beyond the mountains and the forests," is the traditional incipit of Polish folktales, comparable to "once upon a time."

18. E-mail from Manuel António Pina, February 4, 2009.

19. In Portugal newspapers often publish books separately, especially literary classics and works in the public domain; but sometimes, as in this case, they also publish contemporary works by Portuguese authors at prices that are normally lower than those of bookstores, due to their large print run. Except in the case of very popular authors, a publishing house's first edition is usually about 4,000 to 5,000 copies, whereas newspaper editions are often ten times that; unsold copies are sent to bookstores.

20. E-mail from Manuel António Pina, March 11, 2009. Subsequent comments by the author are taken from this e-mail.

21. Sara Reis da Silva, "O Capuchinho Vermelho revisitado: Leituras de História do Capuchinho Vermelho contada a crianças e nem por isso, de Manuel António Pina," in *A Criança, a língua, o imaginário e o texto literário*, Centro e Margens na Literatura para Crianças e Jovens, Actas do II Congresso Internacional (Braga: Universidade do Minho– Instituto de Estudos da Criança, 2006).

22. The other titles are "Happy Family—Mother, Red Riding Hood and Grandmother," "The Wolf," "The Wolf Chats Up Red Riding Hood," "Mother Takes Revenge," and "Mother Wears the Wolf's Pelt."

23. In Portuguese there is a pun with *menina*—(female child) and *menina dos olhos* (apple of the eye).

24. In Portuguese the title "Engineer," like that of "Doctor," does not necessarily mean that the person is an engineer (or a physician). The use of the title expresses an attitude of reverence for the social status of the person.

25. The statement was published in *Pravda* on December 5, 1935.

26. The diminutive in the Russian title could have been translated to produce the title "The Tale of Little Red Cap," but the title of the MIT Press translation has been retained.

27. Peter France, "How Poetry Is Made—Translator's Notes," in *For the Voice: Voices of Revolution—Collected Essays*, ed. Patricia Railing (Cambridge, MA: MIT Press, 2000), 42.

28. El Lissitzky, "Typographical Facts," in *Gutenberg Festschrift* [1925]; reprinted in Sophie Lissitzky-Küppers, *El Lissitzky: Life, Letters, Texts*, introduction by Herbert Read, trans. Helene Aldwinckle and Mary Whittall (London: Thames and Hudson, 1968).

29. Martha Scotford, "Notes on the Visual Translation of *For the Voice*," in *For the Voice: Voices of Revolution—Collected Essays*, vol. 2, 59.

30. Ibid., 49.

2. Contemporary Riding Hoods Come of Age

1. Interview with Fam Ekman, April 25, 2001.

2. E-mail from Fam Ekman, January 12, 2001.

3. In Norwegian the compound noun *ekspeditriseulven* increases the humor.

4. Bruno de la Salle, *Le Conteur amoureux* (Paris: Casterman, 1994).

5. Carmen Martín Gaite, *El cuento de nunca acabar* (Madrid: Trieste, 1983), 23, 158.

6. Aurelio is her grandmother's former boyfriend.

7. Greg Monroe is Mr. Woolf's employee and friend.

8. Mr. Clinton is a director who had been thrilled with the extraordinary Fellini-like characters of Sara and Miss Lunatic when they tried to get into a café where he was filming a movie.

9. Letter from Anne Bertier, July 31, 2003. Subsequent comments by the author are taken from this letter.

10. E-mail from Endre Skandfer, October 24, 2011.

11. "*Skylappjenta* av Iram Haq," *Mammadamen*, http://www.mammadamen.com/2009/11/skylappjenta-av-iram-haq.html/ (accessed 10 March 2012).

12. E-mail from Endre Skandfer, March 13, 2012.

13. Interview, Salaam Film Festival, October 14, 2010. Other quotations by the author are taken from the same interview. There is an intertextual reference to a well-known Norwegian song, "Sommerfuggel I vinterland" (Summer Bird in Winter Land).

14. The author uses the Old Norwegian expression "Ti kniver i hjertet," which means literally "with ten knives to the heart."

15. E-mail from Ioulita Iliopoulou, January 8, 2012.

16. His Greek name, Agathon, has two meanings: a good person, as well as, in modern Greek, a silly person in a nice way.

17. Sara Reis da Silva, "O Capuchinho Cinzento, de Matilde Rosa Araújo: Uma 'história de claros segredos,'" *Solta Palavra*—Boletim do CRILIJ (Centro de Recursos e Investigação sobre Literatura para a Infância e Juventude) nos. 9–10 (2006): 15.

18. In Portuguese the author uses two different forms of the diminutive to refer to the birds, *passaritos* and *passarinhos*. Many words in the text contain the diminutive ("-inho" or "-ito"), which is very common in Portuguese and has a nuance of endearment that is not rendered in English. The diminutive appears often in Manuel António Pina's text as well.

3. Playing with the Story of Red Riding Hood and the Wolf

1. There is a clever play on words in the original because the French expression "règlement de compte" contains a homonym for *conte* (tale).

2. E-mail from Zoran Pongrašić, February 27, 2012. Other comments by the author are from this e-mail.

3. E-mail from Smiljana Narančić Kovač, December 10, 2011. She kindly assisted with the introductions to the two Croatian retellings.

4. In the English translation, a new pun is created: narcosis = *narco* + sis(ter).

5. The only change Pongrašić made to the text originally published in the magazine was the substitution of the word *priča*, meaning story or tale, for *bajka*, meaning "fairy tale," so "tale" has been used in the translation.

6. This is the literal translation of a figurative Czech expression used to say that one really liked a meal. The author continues the common expression by referring to the fact that Little Red Riding Hood had braided them.

7. Jack Zipes, *Sticks and Stones: The Troublesome Success of Children's Literature from Slovenly Peter to Harry Potter* (New York: Routledge, 2001), 110.

8. Carles Cano, *T'he agafat, Caputxeta!*, illus. Gusti (Valencia: Bruño, 1995), 31. Subsequent page references to this work will appear parenthetically in the text.

9. The monkey's "Ee, Ee, Ee" (in Catalan "Hi, Hi, Hi") has not been included in the translation, although other onomatopoeia by the main characters—the elephant, the grandmother, and Little Black Riding Hood—have been retained.

10. There is a play on words in Catalan, because the words for *trunk* and *blow* are *trompa* and *trompada*, respectively.

11. The humorous play on words is lost in English. The Spanish word for vegetables is *verduras*, which shares the same root as green (*verde*), as Little Green Riding Hood demonstrates to the wolf by dividing the word into two syllables in the original ("verd-ura").

12. Anita Wincencjusz-Patyna, *Butenko venit, pinxit*, vicit, catalogue of the exhibition, Jelenia Góra, 2011.

13. The Polish version includes a pun on the words *matjas* (a kind of herring) and *majtasy*, a colloquial term referring to large-size, unattractive underwear. As Little Red Riding Hood recites off her list of victuals for Grandma, there is a slip of the tongue and she says "majtas" instead of "matjas," with a comic effect that raises some eyebrows in adult audiences. This has been rendered in English by a different slip of the tongue: "loincloth" instead of "loin chops."

14. Every Pole recognizes the intertextual allusion to the well-loved poem "Lokomotywa" (The Locomotive), by Julian Tuwim, a children's classic.

4. Rehabilitating the Wolf

1. Antoniorrobles, *Rompetacones y 100 cuentos más* (Mexico City: Oasis, 1964), 20–21. Subsequent references are to this text.

2. Letter from Miguel Ángel Pacheco, May 28, 2001.

3. The text that appears in italics in sometimes lengthy speech bubbles in the illustrations has also been included in the translation, as it is an essential element of the narrative in this picturebook, which uses the technique borrowed from comics to add internal multiple perspectives to the omniscient third-person voice.

4. While the first comment is in a speech bubble, the second is in a thought bubble.

5. This comment is in a thought bubble.

6. The layout changes on this page, where the "Bang! Bang!" appears within a frame beside the hunter, while the wolf's subjective voice replaces that of the third-person narrative underneath.

7. E-mail from Gérard Moncomble, May 10, 2012.

8. Gérard Moncomble, *Romain Gallo contre Charles Perrault*. Milan Junior Polar. (Toulouse: Milan, 2007), 9. Subsequent textual references are to this volume.

9. This is the abbreviation for "zone à urbaniser en priorité," or urban development zone.

10. In the original, his name is Henri Cognet, which refers to a *cognée* or "felling axe," used by woodcutters.

5. The Wolf's Story

1. The Arabic word *azan* means both "to crow" and "to call to prayer." It is an implicit reference to the Muslim religion (praying when the sun sets or when worshipers hear the rooster).

2. Pierre Gripari, *Pierre Gripari et ses contes pour enfants*, interviews with Jean-Luc Peyroutet (Mérignac: Girandoles, 1944), 8.

3. Gianni Rodari, *Grammatica della fantasia* (Torino: Guilio Einaudi, 1973), 64.

4. Pierre Gripari, *Patrouille du conte* (Lausanne: Éditions l'Âge d'Homme, 1983), 34. Subsequent textual references are to this volume.

5. There is undoubtedly a play on words, as the French word *bête* also means "beast" or "animal," and Gripari has inverted the traditional roles to cast the grandmother in the role of the villain.

6. It was not possible to retain the original rhyme of AB AB CC DD C.

7. Francesca Lazzarato, quoted on the Orecchio Acerbo website.

8. E-mail from Fabian Negrin, April 11, 2012. Unless otherwise indicated, subsequent comments by the author are taken from this e-mail.

9. A clip from the TPO production in Prato, directed by Edoardo Donatini, can be viewed on YouTube (www.youtube.com/watch?v=lujpDvd4jM0).

10. The illustrator drew a large, smiling wolf's head in black pen behind her on the title page of my copy, which has been reproduced in figure 51.

11. As in a number of other languages, the Italian expression for "to be very hungry" is literally "to have a wolf hunger."

12. In José Santos Chocano, *Poemas del amor doliente* (Santiago de Chile: Nascimiento, 1937), 8. Subsequent textual references are to this volume.

13. I have not attempted to retain the rhyme, which is AB AB in the original.

14. Fabiola Santiago, "Raúl Rivero: A Poet Unbowed by Cuba's Jails," *Miami Herald*, October 9, 2005.

6. The Wolf Within

1. The Italian musical, *I Musicanti*, was adapted by Sergio Bardotti and Luis Enríquez Bacalov in 1976.

2. The edition with illustrations by Ziraldo is available in Portuguese on the author's website: www.chicobuarque.com.br/livros/mestre.asp?pg=chapeuzinho_01.htm.

3. In Portuguese, the poet plays with *sopa* (soup) and *ensopar* (to sop or soak).

4. Buarque uses the expression "branco azedo," a mildly derogatory term used by black people to refer to white people (*branco*), meaning they were like sour (*azedo*) milk—colorless and tasteless.

5. E-mail from Vassilis Papatsarouchas, November 22, 2012.

7. Running with the Wolves

1. E-mail from Pierrette Fleutiaux, November 7, 2005.

2. E-mail from Pierette Fleutiaux, September 1, 2003. Unless otherwise mentioned, subsequent quotations are taken from this e-mail.

3. Pierre Léon, *Le mariage politiquement correct du Petit Chaperon Rouge: Contes pour adultes nostalgiques et libérés*, Le beau mentir no. 20 (Toronto: Éditions du Gref, 2012), 17.

4. Léon explains these acronyms at the beginning of the book. The SPPNH is the Société Protectrice des Personnes Non Humaines (Society for the Protection of Non Human Persons); the LDL is the Ligue des Droits du Loup (League of Wolves' Rights); and BB is Barbe-Bleue (Bluebeard).

5. Editor's note: the diacritics in the name "Layla" were omitted in the translation, as the name is used thus in English. Likewise, the diacritics have been omitted in the names Luma, Hasib, and Yusuf.

6. E-mail from Huda al-Naimi, June 18, 2012.

7. An e-mail from the author on May 15, 2012 confirmed this.

8. An ancient Semitic name for Jerusalem.

9. Letter from Annie Riis, March 4, 2001. Unless otherwise indicated, subsequent comments by the author are taken from this letter.

10. E-mail from Xavier Bruyère, June 11, 2001. Subsequent comments attributed to Bruyère are taken from this e-mail.

11. *Cramique* is a kind of raisin bread that is a specialty of Wallonia.

12. Letter from Alain Gauthier, July 28, 2003.

Bibliography

Primary Sources

Abayo et al. *Érase veintiuna veces Caperucita Roja*. Trans. Kiyoko Sakai and Herrín Hidalgo. Libros para niños. Valencia: Media Vaca, 2006.

Agostinelli, Enrica. *Cappuccetto Blu*. Turin: Giulio Einaudi, 1975.

Al-Naimi, Huda. "Laylā wa-anā." In *Abāṭīl*. Cairo: Al-Dar Al-Masreyah Al-Lubnanya, 2001.

Araújo, Matilde Rosa. *O Capuchinho Cinzento*. Illus. André Letria. Prior Velho: Paulinas, 2005.

Argueta, Manlio. *Caperucita en la zona roja*. La Habana: Casa de las Américas, 1977. Translated by Edward Waters Hood under the title *Little Red Riding Hood in the Red Light District*. Willimantic, CT: Curbstone Press, 1998.

Aymé, Marcel. *Les contes du chat perché*. Illus. Nathan Altman. Paris: Gallimard, 1934.

———. *The Wonderful Farm*. Illus. Maurice Sendak. Trans. Norman Denny. New York: Harper & Row, 1951.

———. *The Magic Pictures: More about the Wonderful Farm*. Trans. Norman Denny. Illus. Maurice Sendak. New York: Harper, 1954. Also published as *Return to the Wonderful Farm*. Illus. Geoffrey Fletcher. London: Bodley Head, 1954.

———. "Le loup." In *Les contes bleus du chat perché*, 8–28. Folio Junior. Paris: Gallimard, 1987.

Bertier, Anne. *Mon Loup*. Orange: Grandir, 1995.

Biegel, Paul. *Wie je droomt ben je zelf*. Illus. Carl Hollander. Haarlem: CPNB (Commissie voor de Collectieve Propaganda van het Nederlandse boek or Committee for the Collective Promotion of Dutch Books); Uitg. Mij I Holland Uitgeversmaatschappij Holland (now Uitgeverij Holland), 1977.

Boulotis, Christos. *Oi 12 kokkinoskoufitses kai o kourdistos lykos*. Illus. Vassilis Papatsarouchas. Athens: Papadopoulos, 2007.

Buarque, Chico. *Chapeuzinho Amarelo*. Illus. Donatella Berlendis. Rio de Janeiro: Berlendis & Vertecchia, 1979. Reissued, with illustrations by Ziraldo; Rio de Janeiro: Editora José Olympio, 1997.

Butenko, Bohdan. "Czerwony Kapturek (Bajka myśliwska)." In *Krulewna Sniezka*. Warsaw: Nasza Księgarnia, 2008.

Cano, Carles. *T'he agafat, Caputxeta!* Illus. Gusti. Valencia: Bruño, 1995.

——. *La Caputxeta Negra*. Illus. Paco Giménez. Picanya: Bullent, 1996.

——. "El lobo y las Caperucitas." In *El Puchero del Tesoro*. Seis con Pe. Madrid: Anaya, 2007.

Chocano, José Santos. "El lobo enamorado." In *Primicias de oro de Indias: Poemas neo-mundiales*, 297–299. Illus. Luis Meléndez and Huelén. Santiago de Chile: n.p., 1934. Reprinted in *Poemas del amor doliente*, 63–64. Santiago de Chile: Nascimiento, 1937.

Claverie, Jean. *Le Petit Chaperon Rouge*. Paris: Albin Michel Jeunesse, 1994; Namur: Mijade, 2009.

Clément, Claude. *La frontière de sable*. Paris: Syros, 1999.

——. *Un petit chaperon rouge*. Illus. Isabelle Forestier. Paris: Grasset & Fasquelle, 2000.

Dahl, Roald. "Little Red Riding Hood and the Wolf." In *Revolting Rhymes*, 30–33. Illus. Quentin Blake. New York: Knopf, 1982.

Delarue, Paul. *Le Conte populaire français; catalogue raisonné des versions de France et des pays de langue française d'outre-mer: Canada, Louisiane, ilots français des Etats-Unis, Antilles françaises, Haïti, Ile Maurice, La Réunion*. Vol. 1. Paris: Érasme, 1957.

——, ed. "The Story of Grandmother." In *The Borzoi Book of French Folk Tales*, 230–232. Trans. Austin E. Fife. Illus. Warren Chappell. New York: Knopf, 1956.

Dumas, Philippe, and Boris Moissard. "Le Petit Chaperon Bleu Marine." In *Contes à l'envers*, 15–26. Illus. Philippe Dumas. Paris: L'École des loisirs, 1977.

Ekman, Fam. *Rødhatten og Ulven*. Oslo: Cappelen, 1985.

Elmessiri, Abdelwahab M. *Ser ekhtifaa el zeeb el shahir bel mohtar*. Illus. Safaa Nabaa. Cairo: Dar El Shorouk, 2000.

Ferron, Jacques. "Le petit chaperon rouge." In *Contes*, 162–165. Montréal: HMH, 1968. Translated by Betty Bednarski under the title *Tales from the Uncertain Country*, 3–43. Toronto: Anasi, 1972. Reprinted in *Tales from the Uncertain Country and Other Stories*, 208–212. Toronto: McClelland, 2010.

Fetscher, Iring. "Rotschöpfchen und der Wolf." In *Wer hat Dornröschen wachgeküßt? Das Märchen-Verwirrbuch*. Hamburg: Classen, 1972.

Fleutiaux, Pierrette. "Petit Pantalon Rouge, Barbe-Bleue et Notules." In *Métamorphoses de la reine*, 103–138. Paris: Gallimard, 1984.

——. "The Ogre's Wife." Trans. Leigh Hafrey. *Grand Street* 37 (Spring 1991). Reprinted in *The Year's Best Fantasy and Horror: Fifth Annual Collection*, 488–505. Ed. Ellen Datlow and Terri Windling. New York: St. Martin's Press, 1992.

García Sánchez, José Luis, and Miguel Ángel Pacheco. *El último lobo y Caperucita*. Illus. Miguel Ángel Pacheco. Barcelona: Labor, 1975.

Garner, James Finn. *Politically Correct Bedtime Stories: Modern Tales for Our Life and Times*. New York: Macmillan, 1994.

Grimm, Wilhelm, and Jacob Grimm. *Complete Fairy Tales of the Brothers Grimm*. Trans. Jack Zipes. 2 vols. New York: Bantam Books, 1988.

Gripari, Pierre. *Contes de la rue Broca*. Paris: La Table ronde, 1967. Translated by Doriane Grutman under the title *Tales of the Rue Broca*. Illus. Emily Arnold McCully. Indianapolis, IN: Bobbs-Merrill, 1969.

——. *Contes de la Folie Méricourt*. Illus. Claude Lapointe. Paris: Grasset Jeunesse, 1983.

——. *Patrouille du conte*. Lausanne: Éditions l'Âge d'Homme, 1983.

———. "Le loup" and "Le petit chaperon malin." In *Marelles*, 13–14, 33–34. Illus. Chica. Paris: Grasset Jeunesse, 1996.

Guimarães Rosa, João. *Grande sertão: Veredas*. Translated by James L. Taylor and Harriet de Onis under the title *The Devil to Pay in the Backlands*. New York: Knopf, 1963.

———. "Fita verde no cabelo." In *Ave, palavra*. Rio de Janeiro: José Olympio, 1970.

———. *Fita verde no cabelo: Nova velha estória*. Illus. Roger Mello. Rio de Janeiro: Nova Fronteira, 1992.

Haq, Iram. *Skylappjenta*. Illus. Endre Skandfer. Oslo: Cappelen Damm, 2009.

Hofman, Wim. "Roodkapje." In *Van A tot Z*. Ed. Arie Rampen. Den Bosch: Malmberg, 1982. Reprinted in *De Kleine Hofman: Wim Hofmans Werk Van A–Z*, 123. Ed. Wim Hofman, Klaus Baumgärtner, and Ida Schuurman. Vlissingen: Oppenbare Bibliotheek Vlissingen, 1991.

———. *A Good Hiding and Other Stories*. Trans. Lance Salway. Woodchester: Turton & Chambers Ltd., 1991.

———. "Roodkapje." *Mikmak* 1 (October 1993): 10–11. Reprinted in *Van Aap tot Zip*. Amsterdam: Querido, 2006.

Hoogland, Cornelia. *Woods Wolf Girl*. Hamilton, ON: Wolsak and Wynn, 2011.

Ikhlef, Anne. *Mon Chaperon Rouge*. Illus. Alain Gauthier. Paris: Seuil Jeunesse, 1998.

———, director. *La vraie histoire du Chaperon Rouge*. Short film. Starring Justine Bayard and Didier Sandre, 1985.

Iliopoulou, Ioulita. *Ti zitai o Zinon?* Illus. Yannis Kottis. Athens: Ypsilon, 2005.

———. *Prassini Soufitsa*. Illus. Yannis Kottis. Athens: Ypsilon/Vivlia, 2008.

Iwasaki, Kyoko. "Akazukin-chan." In *Senso to Heiwa Kodomo Bungakukan*. Illus. Toshio Kajiyama. Vol. 12. Ed. Gennosuke Nagasaki, Imanishi Sukeyuki, and Kyoko Iwasaki. Tokyo: Nihon Tosho Centre, 1995.

Jacintho, Roque. *O Lobo Mau reencarnado*. Illus. Joel Linck. Rio de Janeiro: Federação Espírita Brasileira, 1974. Translated by Evelyn R. Morales and S. J. Haddad under the title *The Big Bad Wolf Reincarnate*. Illus. Joel Linck. Rio de Janeiro: Federação Espírita Brasileira, 1981.

Janosch [Horst Eckert]. "Das elektrische Rotkäppchen." In *Janosch erzählt Grimms Märchen und zeichnet für Kinder von heute: 50 ausgewählte Märchen*, 102–107. Weinheim: Beltz & Gelberg, 1972. Translated by Patricia Crampton under the title *Not Quite as Grimm: Told and Illustrated by Janosch for Today*. London: Abelard-Schuman, 1974.

———. *Janosch erzählt Grimms Märchen: Hans Im Glück und andere Geschichten*. Compact disc. Hamburg: EMI Music, 2007.

Joiret, Patricia. *Mina, je t'aime*. Illus. Xavier Bruyère [Xavier Van Buylaere]. Paris: L'École des loisirs, 1991.

Julien, Vivane. *Bye Bye Chaperon Rouge*. Montréal: Québec/Amérique, 1989. Translated by Frances Hanna under the title *Bye Bye Red Riding Hood*. Montréal: Montréal Press, 1990.

Lamblin, Simone, ed. *Le grand méchant Loup, j'adore*. Illus. Françoise Boudignon. Paris: Le Livre de Poche, 1983.

La Salle, Bruno de. *Le Petit Chaperon Rouge*. Illus. Laurence Batigne. Paris: Casterman, 1986.

———. *Le Conteur amoureux*. Paris: Casterman, 1994.

———. "La petite fille qui savait voler." In *La pêche de vigne et autres contes*, 55–61. Illus. Catherine Rebeyrol. Paris: L'École des loisirs, 1996.

Léon, Pierre. *Le mariage politiquement correct du petit Chaperon rouge et autres histoires plus ou moins politiquement correctes avec notices explicatives pour servir à la morale de notre temps.* Toronto: Éditions du Gref, 1996. Reissued as *Le mariage politiquement correct du Petit Chaperon Rouge: Contes pour adultes nostalgiques et libérés.* Le beau mentir no. 20. Toronto: Éditions du Gref, 2012.

Martín Gaite, Carmen. *El cuento de nunca acabar.* Madrid: Trieste, 1983.

———. *Caperucita en Manhattan.* Madrid: Siruela, 1990.

Mayakovsky, Vladimir. *Dlia golosa.* Book constructor El Lissitzky. Berlin: State Publishing House, 1923.

Mayakovsky, Vladimir, El Lissitzky, and Patricia Railing. *For the Voice.* 3 vols. Vol. 1: Facsimile of original, Mayakovsky and Lissitzky, book constructor, *Dlia golosa* (1923), ed. Railing; Vol. 2: Mayakovsky and Lissitzky, *For the Voice,* trans. Peter France (text) and Martha Scotford (visual translation); Vol. 3: Railing, ed., *For the Voice: Voices of Revolution—Collected Essays.* Cambridge, MA: MIT Press, 2000.

Mikulka, Alois. "O Červené Karkulce." In *Dvanáct usmívajících se ježibab,* 24–25. Brno: Blok, 1974.

Miloš, Damir, Radovan Devlić, and Krešimir Skozret. "Little Red Riding Hood." An excerpt from *Snježni kralj.* Zagreb: Naprijed, [1986].

Mistral, Gabriela [Lucila Godoy Alcayaga]. "Caperucita Roja." In *Vida,* 225–226. Ed. José H. Figueira. Montevideo: n.p. [1923]. Reprinted in *Ternura,* 136–137. Buenos Aires: Editorial Espasa Calpe, 1945.

———. *Selected Poems of Gabriela Mistral.* Trans. and ed. Doris Dana. Baltimore: Johns Hopkins Press, 1971.

———. *Selected Poems of Gabriela Mistral.* Trans. Ursula K. Le Guin. Albuquerque: University of New Mexico, 2003.

———. *Caperucita Roja.* Illus. Paloma Valdivia. Critical commentary by Manuel Peña Muñoz. Santiago: Editorial Amanuta, 2012.

Moncomble, Gérard. *Romain Gallo contre Charles Perrault.* Bibliothèque Milan. Toulouse: Milan, 1991. Rpt.: Milan Junior Polar. Toulouse: Milan, 1999; 2007.

Munari, Bruno. *Cappuccetto Verde.* Turin: Giulio Einaudi, 1972. Published in English under the title *Little Green Riding Hood.* Mantova: Corraini Ed., 2007.

———. *Cappuccetto Giallo.* Turin: Giulio Einaudi, 1972. Published in English under the title *Little Yellow Riding Hood.* Mantova: Corraini Ed., 2007.

———. *Cappuccetto Bianco.* Mantova: Corraini Ed., 1999. Published in English under the title *Little White Riding Hood.* Mantova: Corraini Ed., 2004.

———, and Enrica Agostinelli. *Cappuccetto rosso verde giallo blu e bianco.* 1981. Rpt: Trieste Einaudi Ragazzi, 1993.

Negrin, Fabian. *In bocca al lupo.* Rome: Orecchio Acerbo, 2003.

Olech, Joanna. *Czerwony Kapturek.* Illus. Grażka Lange. Warsaw: Jacek Santorski & Co., 2005.

Ommundsen, Åse Marie. "Eventyr på nye veier: Multimodale nyskrivninger av eventyr i skandinavisk samtidslitteratur." In *Til en evakuerad igelkott: Festskrift tilt Maria Nikolajeva/Celebrating a Displaced Hedgehog: A Festschrift for Maria Nikolajeva,* 231–242. Ed. Maria Lassen Segér and Mia Österlund. Stockholm: Makadam Förlag 2012.

Pef [Pierre Elie Ferrier]. "Le conte du Petit Chaperon Rouge." In *Contes comme la lune,* 391–393. Vol. XIV. Paris: Messidor/La Farandole, 1991.

Perrault, Charles. *Les contes de Perrault*. Illus. Gustave Doré. Paris: Pierre-Jules Hetzel, 1861.

———. *Contes de ma mère l'Oye*. Illus. Gustave Doré. Folio Junior Édition Spéciale. Paris: Gallimard, 1997.

———. *Cuentos*. Trans. Hernán Rodríguez Castelo. Quito: Edit. LIBRESA, 1997.

——— et al. *Bruno Bettelheim presenta los Cuentos de Perrault: Seguidos de los cuentos de Madame d'Aulnoy y de Madame Leprince de Beaumont*. Trans. Carmen Martín Gaite. Barcelona: Crítica, 1980.

Pina, Manuel António. *A História do Capuchinho Vermelho contada a crianças e nem por isso*. Illus. Paula Rego. Porto: Público/Fundação de Serralves, 2005. Translated into Danish by Jorge Braga under the title *Historien om den lille Rødhætte*. Copenhagen: Forlaget Orby, 2005.

Pongrašić, Zoran. "Crvenkapica na drugi način." In *Zašto (ne) volim bajke*. Illus. Ivana Guljašević. Zagreb: Knjiga u centru, 2010. First published in *Prvi izbor* 14, no. 6 (February 2006).

Riis, Annie. "Ulven og Rødhette." In *Kom inn i min natt! Kom inn i min drøm*, 25–31. Ed. Solveig Bøhle. Illus. Fam Ekman. Oslo: Gyldendal, 1992.

Rivero, Raúl. "Versión libre" and "Versión Libre 2." In *Corazón sin furia*, 47–48, 49. Logroño: AMG Editor, 2005.

Robles, Antonio [Antoniorrobles]. "Caperucita Encarnada pasó un susto . . . y luego ¡nada!" In *Rompetacones y 100 cuentos más: Relatos de 10 minutos para el colegio y la radio*. Mexico City: Secretaría de Educación Pública, 1962. Reprinted as *Rompetacones y 100 cuentos más*. Mexico City: Oasis, 1964.

Rodari, Gianni. "A sbagliare le storie." In *Favole al telefono*. Illus. Bruno Munari. Torino: Guilio Einaudi, 1962. Translated by Patrick Greagh under the title "Little Green Riding Hood." In *Telephone Tales*. Illus. Dick de Wilde. London: George G. Harrap & Co., 1965. Rpt.: *Cricket* 1, no. 1 (September 1973): 17–19.

Rodríguez Castelo, Hernán. *Caperucito Azul*. Bogota: Ediciones Paulinas, 1975.

Rusinek, Michał. *Kopciuszek*. Illus. Malgorzata Bieńkowska. Warsaw: Jacek Santorski & Co, 2006.

Sim, Mia. *Ches! Eotteohge alassji? Honjaseo gileul gadaga yugoebeomeul mulrichin bbalganmoja iyagi* (Pooh! How Did She Know? The Story of a Little Red Riding Hood Who Escaped from Her Abductors). Paju: Nurimbo, 2010.

Solotareff, Grégoire. *Le Petit Chaperon Vert*. Illus. Nadja. Paris: L'École des loisirs, 1989. Rpt.: *Mouches*. Paris: L'École des loisirs, 2000.

Stoebe, Meike. *Waldtraut und der Wolf*. Illus. Susann Stoebe. Zurich: Edition Jürgen Lassig, Nord-Süd Verlag, 1996.

———. *Pélagie et le loup*. Illus. Susann Stoebe. Trans. Michelle Nikly. Zurich: Nord-Sud, 1996.

Talko, Leszek K. *Jaś i Małgosia*. Illus. Anna Niemierko. Warsaw: Jacek Santorski & Co., 2005.

Tayara, Sana. *Laylā wa-al-dhi'b wa-l-hātif*. Illus. Talar Kizirian. Beirut: Asala, 2011.

Tuwim, Julian. "Lokomotywa." In *Lokomotywa i inne wesołe wierszyki dla dzieci*. Illus. Jan Levitt and George Him. Warsaw: Wyd. J. Przeworski, 1938.

Valenzuela, Luisa. "Si esto es la vida, yo soy Caperucita Roja." In *Simetrías*, 111–125. Buenos Aires: Editorial Sudamericana, 1993. Translated by Margaret Jull Costa under the title *Symmetries*. London: High Risk Books/Serpent's Tail, 1993.

Vendel, Edward van de. *Rood Rood Roodkapje*. Illus. Isabelle Vandenabeele. Wiels-beke: Uitgeverij De Eenhoorn, 2003.

Villaespesa, Francisco. "Caperucita." In *El Patio de los Arrayanes*, 63–64. 2d ed. Madrid: Balgañon y Moreno, Colección "Apolo," 1908. Reprinted in *Poesias Completas*. Compiled by Frederico de Mendizabal. 2 vols. Madrid: Aguilar, S.A. de Ediciones, 1954. 1:557.

———. "Caperucita." In *Poesias Completas*. Compiled by Frederico de Mendizabal. 2 vols. Madrid: Aguilar, S.A. de Ediciones, 1954. 2:1479.

Wiemer, Rudolf Otto. "Der alte Wolf." In *Neues vom Rumpelstilzchen und andere Märchen von 43 Autoren*, 73. Ed. Hans-Joachim Gelberg. Illus. Willi Glasauer. Weinheim: Beltz & Gelberg, 1976.

Yamada, Izumi. "En el vientre del lobo." In *Érase veintiuna veces Caperucita Roja*, by Abayo et al. Trans. Kiyoko Sakai and Herrín Hidalgo. Libros para niños. Valencia: Media Vaca, 2006.

Yiannakopoulou, Hara. "I Kokkinoskoufitsa apo mesa." Illus. Vassilis Papatsarouchas. In *Mia agapi, epta chromata kai enas lykos*. Athens: Metaichmio, 2007.

Yolen, Jane. "Happy Dens, or A Day in the Old Wolves Home." In *Dragonfield and Other Stories*, 184–198. London: Futura, 1985.

Secondary Sources

Agosín, Marjorie. "Introduction: Gabriela Mistral, the Restless Soul." In Gabriela Mistral, *Gabriela Mistral: A Reader*, 17–24. Trans. Maria Giacchetti. New York: White Pine Press, 1993.

Alwakeel, Saeed. "Intertextuality in Children's Literature: Elmessiri and Al-Sharuni as Examples" [in Arabic]. *Alif: Journal of Comparative Poetics* 27 (2007): 133–156.

Araújo, Matilde. "Pelo sonho é que vamos" (autobiografia). *JL Jornal de Letras, Artes e Ideias* 928 (April 26–May 9, 2006): 44.

Ariza, Manuel. "Estudio de variantes del cuento de Caperucita." In *Actas del IV Simposio Internacional de la Asociación Española de Semiotica* (Seville, December 3–5, 1990), 525–536. Madrid: Visor libros, 1992.

Bacchilega, Cristina. *Postmodern Fairy Tales: Gender and Narrative Strategies*. Philadel-phia: University of Pennsylvania Press, 1997.

Bates, Margaret. "Introduction." In *Selected Poems of Gabriela Mistral*, xv–xxvi. Trans. and ed. Doris Dana. Baltimore: Johns Hopkins University Press, 1971.

Beckett, Sandra L. "Le Petit Chaperon rouge globe-trotter." In *Tricentenaire Charles Perrault: Les grands contes du XVIIe siècle et leur fortune littéraire*, 365–375. Ed. Jean Perrot. Paris: In Press, 1998.

———. *Recycling Red Riding Hood*. New York: Routledge, 2002.

———. "Retelling *Little Red Riding Hood* in Contemporary Canadian Children's Lit-erature." In *Windows and Words: A Look at Canadian Children's Literature in English*, 61–76. Ed. Aïda Hudson and Susan-Ann Cooper. Ottawa: University of Ottawa Press, 2003.

———. *Red Riding Hood for All Ages: A Fairy-Tale Icon in Cross-Cultural Contexts*. Detroit: Wayne State University Press, 2008.

Chu, Elsa, et al. "A Tale of Three Translations." *La linguistique* 40, no. 1 (2004): 131–142.

Clément, Claude. "Entretien avec Claude Clément." Interview with Annie Vénard. *Les Cahiers pédagogiques* 462 (April 7, 2008).

Colomer, Teresa. "Eterna Caperucita: La renovación del imaginario colectivo." *Cuadernos de literatura infantil y juvenil* 87 (October 1996): 7–19.

———. "La formació i renovació de l'imaginari cultural: L'exemple de la Caputxeta Vermella." In *De la narrativa oral a la literatura per a infants: Invenció d'una tradició literària*, 55–93. Ed. Gemma Lluch. Alzira: Ediciones Bromera, 2000.

Dundes, Alan, ed. *Little Red Riding Hood: A Casebook*. Madison: University of Wisconsin Press, 1989.

Erny, Pierre. *Sur les traces du Petit Chaperon Rouge*. Paris: L'Harmattan, 2003.

Ferreira, Aline. "O grotesco é belo." Interview with Paula Rego. *Ler* 58 (Spring 2003): 56–67.

Flor Rebanel, Javier. "Caperucita Roja cumple 300 años (. . . y todavía está como una jovencita)." *Peonza (Revista de Literatura Infantil e Juvenil)* 42–43 (December 1997): 11–18.

Genardière, Claude de la. *Encore un conte: Le Petit Chaperon Rouge à l'usage des adultes*. Nancy: Presses Universitaires de Nancy, 1993.

Gomes, Sara. "Quem ainda tem medo do lobo mau?" Interview with Manuel António Pina. *Público* (March 11, 2005): 55.

Gripari, Pierre. *Pierre Gripari et ses contes pour enfants*. Interviews with Jean-Luc Peyroutet. Mérignac: Girandoles, 1994.

Haase, Donald, ed. *Fairy Tales and Feminism: New Approaches*. Detroit: Wayne State University Press, 2004.

Holtrop, Aukje. "'Things Never Work Out for Snow White': Wim Hofman's Fairy Tales." An interview with Wim Hofman. *Vrij Nederland* (May 17, 1997).

Hoogland, Cornelia. "Real 'Wolves in Those Bushes': Readers Take Dangerous Journeys with *Little Red Riding Hood*." *Canadian Children's Literature* 73 (1994): 7–21.

Lissitzky, El. "Typographical Facts." In *Gutenberg Festschrift* [1925]. Reprinted in Sophie Lissitzky-Küppers, *El Lissitzky: Life, Letters, Texts*. Introduction by Herbert Read. Trans. Helene Aldwinckle and Mary Whittall. London: Thames and Hudson, 1968.

Malarte-Feldman, Claire-Lise. "Les Couleurs du Petit Chaperon . . . " *Merveilles et contes* 1, no. 2 (December 1987): 88–96.

———. "The French Fairy-Tale Conspiracy." *The Lion and the Unicorn* 12, no. 2 (December 1988): 112–120.

———. "La Nouvelle Tyrannie des fées, ou la réécriture des contes de fées classiques." *The French Review* 63, no. 5 (April 1990): 827–837.

Maña, Teresa. "22 Caperucitas." *Cuadernos de literatura infantil y juvenil* 30 (July–August 1991): 42–49.

Martin, Serge. *Les contes à l'école: Le(s) Petit(s) Chaperon(s) Rouge(s)*. Paris: Bertrand-Lacoste, 1997.

Mieder, Wolfgang. "Survival Forms of 'Little Red Riding Hood' in Modern Society." *International Folklore Review* 2 (1982): 23–40.

———. "Grim Variations from Fairy Tales to Modern Anti-Fairy Tales." *The Germanic Review* 62, no. 2 (Spring 1987): 90–102.

Orenstein, Catherine. *Little Red Riding Hood Uncloaked: Sex, Morality, and the Evolution of a Fairy Tale*. New York: Basic Books, 1992.

Perera Santana, Ángeles. "Caperucita Roja en la LIJ contemporánea," *CLIJ* 151 (July–August 2002): 15–22.

Perrot, Jean, ed. *Tricentenaire Charles Perrault: Les grands contes du XVIIe siècle et leur fortune littéraire*. Paris: In Press, 1998.

Pondé, Gloria. "Les relectures des *Contes* de Perrault au Brésil: *Fita verde no cabelo*, de Guimarães Rosa." In *Tricentenaire Charles Perrault: Les grands contes du XVIIe siècle et leur fortune littéraire*, 331–337. Ed. Jean Perrot. Paris: In Press, 1998.

Puentes de Oyenard, Sylvia. "Una aproximación a Caperucita Roja desde Perrault a nuestros días." In *El cuento: Mensaje universal*, 71–93. Montevideo: Ediciones A.U.L.I./Asociación Uruguaya de Literatura Infantil-Juvenil, 1994.

Quentin, Sophie. "De la tradition orale aux adaptations modernes: 'Le Petit Chaperon rouge' ou le carrefour des écritures . . ." In *Écriture féminine et littérature de jeunesse*, 203–217. Ed. Jean Perrot and Véronique Hadengue. Paris: La Nacelle/Institut Charles Perrault, 1995.

Ramsay, Gail. "The Past in the Present: Aspects of Intertextuality in Modern Literature in the Gulf." In *Intertextuality in Modern Arabic Literature since 1967*, 161–186. Ed. Luc-Willy Deheuvels, Barbara Michalak-Pikulska, and Paul Starkey. Durham: Durham Modern Language Series, 2006.

Ritz, Hans. *Die Geschichte vom Rotkäppchen: Ursprünge, Analysen, Parodien eines Märchens*. Göttingen: Muriverlag, 1997.

Robles, Antonio [Antoniorrobles]. *¿Se comió el lobo a Caperucita?: Seis conferencias para mayores con temas de literatura infantil*. México City: Editorial Américana, 1942.

Rodari, Gianni. *Grammatica della fantasia*. Torino: Guilio Einaudi, 1973. Translated by Jack Zipes under the title *The Grammar of Fantasy*. New York: Teachers & Writers Collaborative, 1996.

Rodríguez Castelo, Hernán. "El cuento de la vida de Andersen." Serial in *Caperucito* 29–36 (March 1–April 26, 1984).

Santiago, Fabiola. "Raúl Rivero: A Poet Unbowed by Cuba's Jails." *Miami Herald* (October 9, 2005).

Silva, Francisco Vaz da. "Review of *Red Riding Hood for All Ages: A Fairy-Tale Icon in Cross-Cultural Contexts*, by Sandra L. Beckett." *Folklore* 121, no. 2 (August 2010): 238–239.

Silva, Sara Reis da. "O Capuchinho Vermelho revisitado: Leituras de História do Capuchinho Vermelho contada a crianças e nem por isso, de Manuel António Pina." In *A Criança, a Língua, o Imaginário e o Texto Literário*. Centro e Margens na Literatura para Crianças e Jovens. Actas do II Congresso Internacional. Braga: Universidade do Minho–Instituto de Estudos da Criança, 2006. N.p.

———. "O Capuchinho Cinzento, de Matilde Rosa Araújo: Uma 'história de claros segredos.'" *Solta Palavra*, Boletim do CRILIJ (Centro de Recursos e Investigação sobre Literatura para a Infância e Juventude) 9–10 (2006): 14–17.

———. *De Capuz, Chapelinho ou Gorro: Recriações de* O Capuchino Vermelho *na Literatura Portuguesa para a Infância*. Porto: Tropelias & Companhia, 2011.

Skjønsberg, Kari. "*Le Chaperon Rouge* en Norvège." In *Tricentenaire Charles Perrault: Les grands contes du XVIIe siècle et leur fortune littéraire*, 349–354. Ed. Jean Perrot. Paris: In Press, 1998.

"*Skylappjenta* av Iram Haq." *Mammadamen*. http://www.mammadamen.com/2009/11/skylappjenta-av-iram-haq.html/ (accessed 10 March 2012).

Verdier, Yvonne. "Grand-mères, si vous saviez . . . : Le Petit Chaperon Rouge dans la tradition orale." *Cahiers de littérature orale* 4 (1978): 17–55.

Wincencjusz-Patyna, Anita. *Butenko venit, pinxit, vicit*. Exhibition catalogue. Jelenia Góra, 2011.

Yannicopoulou, Angela. *Sti Hora ton Hromaton: To Syhrono Eikonografimeno Paidiko Biblio*. Athens: Papadopoulos, 2008.

Zipes, Jack. *Fairy Tales and the Art of Subversion: The Classical Genre for Children and the Process of Civilization*. New York: Wildman, 1983.

———. *The Trials and Tribulations of Little Red Riding Hood: Versions of the Tale in Sociocultural Context*. 2d ed. New York: Routledge, 1993.

———. *Sticks and Stones: The Troublesome Success of Children's Literature from Slovenly Peter to Harry Potter*. New York: Routledge, 2001.

———. *Relentless Progress: The Reconfiguration of Children's Literature, Fairy Tales, and Storytelling*. New York: Routledge, 2009.

Index

Text Credits

Grateful acknowledgment is made for permission to use the following copyrighted texts (in order of appearance in the anthology).

"Little Red Riding Hood," a translation by Sandra L. Beckett of "Caperucita Roja," from *Ternura*, by Gabriela Mistral (Buenos Aires: Editorial Espasa Calpe, 1945). The Franciscan Order of Chile authorizes the use of the work of Gabriela Mistral. The equivalent of the authorship rights are given to the Franciscan Order of Chile, for the children of Montegrande and Chile, according to the will of Gabriela Mistral.

"Little Red Cap," a translation by the author of "Roodkapje," from *De Kleine Hofman*, by Wim Hofman. Copyright © 1991 Wim Hofman. Used by permission of Wim Hofman.

"Little Red Cap," a translation by the author of "Roodkapje," from *Van Aap tot Zip*, by Wim Hofman. Copyright © 2006 Wim Hofman. Used by permission of Wim Hofman.

"Little Red Riding Hood," a translation by Sonomi Consul of "Akazukin-chan," by Kyoko Iwasaki, from *Senso to Heiwa Kodomo Bungakukan*, edited by Gennosuke Nagasaki, Imanishi Sukeyuki, and Kyoko Iwasaki. Copyright © 1995 Kyoko Iwasaki. Used by permission of Kyoko Iwasaki.

"A Little Red Riding Hood," a translation by Sandra L. Beckett of the text from *Un petit chaperon rouge*, by Claude Clément and Isabelle Forestier. Copyright © Éditions Grasset & Fasquelle, 2000. Used by permission of Claude Clément and Éditions Grasset & Fasquelle.

"Pooh! How Did She Know? The Story of a Little Red Riding Hood Who Escaped from Her Abductors," a translation by Sungyup Lee of the text from *Ches! Eotteohge alassji? Honjaseo gileul gadaga yugoebeomeul mulrichin bbalganmoja iyagi*, by Mia Sim. Copyright © 2010 Mia Sim. Used by permission of Mia Sim.

"Little Red Riding Cap," a translation by Katarzyna Wasylak of the text from *Czerwony Kapturek*, by Joanna Olech and Grażka Lange. Text copyright © 2005 Jacek Santorski & Co, Agencja Wydawnicza, and Joanna Olech. Used by permission of Joanna Olech.

Pacheco. Text copyright © 1975 José Luis García Sánchez. Used by permission of José Luis García Sánchez.

"Waldtraut and the Wolf," a translation by Sandra L. Beckett of the text from *Waldtraut und der Wolf*, by Meike Stoebe and Susann Stoebe. Copyright © 1996 Nord-Süd Verlag. Used by permission of Nord-Süd Verlag.

"One Cake Too Many," a translation by Sandra L. Beckett of "Une galette de trop," from *Romain Gallo contre Charles Perrault*, by Gérard Moncomble. Copyright © 2007 Éditions Milan. Used by permission of Gérard Moncomble and Éditions Milan.

"The Mystery of the Disappearance of the Famous Confused Wolf," a translation by Layal Aboukors and Emma Wakim from the text of *Ser ekhtifaa el zeeb el shahir bel mohtar*, by Abdelwahab M. Elmessiri and Safaa Nabaa. Copyright © 2000 Dar El Shorouk. Used by permission of Dar El Shorouk.

"The Wolf" and "Fourth Mission," a translation by Sandra L. Beckett of the chapters "Le loup" and "Quatrième mission," from *Patrouille du conte*, by Pierre Gripari. Copyright © 1983 Éditions L'Âge d'Homme. Used by permission of Éditions L'Âge d'Homme.

"The Wolf," a translation by Sandra L. Beckett of "Le loup," from *Marelles*, by Pierre Gripari. Copyright © 1988 Éditions De Fallois/L'Âge d'Homme. Used by permission of Éditions L'Âge d'Homme.

"In the Mouth of the Wolf," a translation by Giorgia Grilli of *In bocca al lupo*, by Fabian Negrin. Copyright © 2003 Fabian Negrin and Orecchio Acerbo. Used by permission of Fabian Negrin and Orecchio Acerbo.

"Free Version," a translation of "Versión Libre" and "Free Version 2," a translation by Sandra L. Beckett of "Versión libre 2," from *Corazón sin furia*, by Raúl Rivero. Copyright © AMG Editor. Used by permission of AMG Editor.

"Green Ribbon in the Hair," a translation by Irene Blayer and Sandra L. Beckett of "Fita verde no cabelo," from *Ave, palavra*, by João Guimarães Rosa. Copyright © 1970 Agnes Guimarães Rosa, Vilma Guimarães Rosa, and Nonada Cultural Ltda. Used by permission of Agnes Guimarães Rosa, Vilma Guimarães Rosa, and Nonada Cultural Ltda.

"Little Yellow Riding Hood," a translation by Claudia Mendes and Sandra L. Beckett of *Chapeuzinho Amarelo*, by Chico Buarque. Published in Brazil by Editora José Olympio. Copyright © Francisco Buarque de Holanda, 1979, 1997. Used by permission of Chico Buarque.

"In the Belly of the Wolf," a translation by Sandra L. Beckett of "En el vientre del lobo," by Izumi Yamada, from *Érase veintiuna veces Caperucita Roja*. Copyright © 2006 Izumi Yamada and Media Vaca. Used by permission of Media Vaca.

"Little Red Riding Hood from Within," a translation by Eugenia Psaromatis of "I Kokkinoskoufitsa apo mesa," by Hara Yiannakopoulou, illustrations by Vassilis Papatsarouchas, from *Mia agapi, epta chromata kai enas lykos*. Copyright © 2007 Metaichmio. Used by permission of Hara Yiannakopoulou and Metaichmio.

"Little Red Pants, Bluebeard, and Notules," a translation by Sandra L. Beckett of "Petit Pantalon Rouge, Barbe-Bleue et Notules," from *Métamorphoses de la reine*, by